Gemma,

For you reading

Please

The Iron Horse Club

The Iron Horse Club

Ronald L. Reman

iUniverse, Inc.
New York Lincoln Shanghai

The Iron Horse Club

Copyright © 2005 by Ronald L. Reman

All rights reserved. No part of this book may be used or reproduced by any means, graphic, electronic, or mechanical, including photocopying, recording, taping or by any information storage retrieval system without the written permission of the publisher except in the case of brief quotations embodied in critical articles and reviews.

iUniverse books may be ordered through booksellers or by contacting:

iUniverse
2021 Pine Lake Road, Suite 100
Lincoln, NE 68512
www.iuniverse.com
1-800-Authors (1-800-288-4677)

ISBN-13: 978-0-595-36173-1 (pbk)
ISBN-13: 978-0-595-67344-5 (cloth)
ISBN-13: 978-0-595-80618-8 (ebk)
ISBN-10: 0-595-36173-0 (pbk)
ISBN-10: 0-595-67344-9 (cloth)
ISBN-10: 0-595-80618-X (ebk)

Printed in the United States of America

ACKNOWLEDGEMENT

To Marcia Elbrand, for her superior editing, helpful hints and continuous support. Marcia, you made me believe the story was worth telling.

CHAPTER 1

▼

The Iron Horse Bar & Grill, located near the corner of 55th Street and Seventh Avenue in midtown Manhattan, is an obscure establishment that never made its way onto the pages of New York City's tour guides, with poorly maintained black and brown tile floors, old fashioned heavy wooden tables and chairs, and walls covered with baseball paraphernalia from the early 1900's, including a painting of Lou Gehrig just above a sign describing him as, "The Real Iron Horse." Despite its appearance, it always had a certain charm, and, as was often the case, it was packed on that balmy June evening, though nobody was paying any particular attention to the painting, and the crowd had better things to do than to focus on the four of us huddled at a table in the back. We were able to maintain a low profile, even though our attire—suits and ties—didn't quite fit in with what everyone else was wearing that night. We were thrilled to be there, because the place had a special meaning for us, as well as the date. It was Monday, June 30, 2003, which marked our twenty-fifth annual "June 30th" dinner at the Iron Horse. And we were making the most of the occasion, when one of us, Kavi Chander, was interrupted with a call.

The crowd was loud and lively, with emphasis on the word loud, and Kavi had to crouch against the wall, trying to hold his cell phone and cover both ears at the same time. About ten minutes into the conversation, he blurted, "If someone's going to jail, it won't be me." That took me by surprise, so I checked to see if he was joking, but the frown on his face indicated he was dead serious. On the other end of the line was his assistant controller, Debra Jennings, who was calling from Ukraine, where he'd sent her to get information about delays and cost overruns at their company's construction project. Although I couldn't hear much of what he said after his declaration, I did catch the word bribery a couple of times. Needless-to-say, Kavi didn't appear to be too thrilled after he hung up.

That put a little damper on things. It was supposed to be a night to appreciate how much we had accomplished, and each of us had done well, although Kavi had done the best. He was the high profile chief financial officer of American Dynamics Group, or ADG as they were known, one of the largest corporations in the world. If split up, it could create at least ten new Fortune 500 companies. Kavi was very well respected and was understood to be in the running for ADG's top spot which would likely be open within two to three years. Yet none of the success had gone to his head. He was a down-to-earth kind of guy who was as comfortable in a bar as he was in a boardroom.

Shortly after introducing his fist to the wall, Kavi sat down, picked up his beer, and almost crushed the bottle with one hand while at the same timing giving us a brief explanation of what he'd been told. He said Debra had found some evidence that ADG may have illegally bribed some Ukrainian government officials, and before I could say anything, Marc Abrams jumped right in with his usual twenty questions. He was a senior tax partner with the prestigious New York law firm of Bartman & Cross, and at times liked to pretend he was Perry Mason on speed. "Is she reporting through you or your legal counsel? Who knows about her work? Is her information reliable? Can it be controlled?" The questions continued at a blistering pace. Actually, Marc was probably the smartest of our group and knew the right questions to ask. Although he didn't look intimidating at 5 foot 8 with a slim-build, his style could quickly put you on the defensive, even though he had your best interests in mind. We always thought there was a chance he'd be killed by one of his clients.

I wasn't surprised that Marc didn't get all his answers that night. You didn't need to be Einstein to know that Kavi didn't want to say anything else about the situation. He was uncomfortable discussing it further until he had a chance to learn more and collect his thoughts, and he knew Marc would be available for help when the time was right. So instead of complete answers, he tried to dodge the questions, and it didn't take long for Marc to get the message and defer his inquiry for another day. After a few minutes, Kavi tried to make light of the situation by doing his impersonation of Marc as a prosecutor cross examining an 80-year-old grandmother, and the mood at our table quickly improved. Kavi was great at telling jokes and doing little skits, and he could get you to laugh at stories that weren't very funny. We always said he'd have made a great comedian had he not chosen to become a CPA. Somehow it helped that he was a big man—a very big man—the only 6 foot 6, 250 pound guy from India that I knew. But all that aside, he was incredibly capable and decent, and was probably my best friend.

When Kavi was through with his routine, Ken Tanner, the member of our group who had never met an attractive woman he didn't like, was once again busy checking out one of the blondes at the bar. She'd had his attention for a good portion of the evening, and she must have scrambled his brains, because he suddenly turned his head to Kavi and said, "Careful pal. You know studies have shown that companies lose between twenty and fifty percent of their stock market value within two weeks of making any scandal public. What'd your stock hit today, $65? There's a lot to lose."

I wasn't sure how Kavi would take that, but after a moment he smiled, shook his head and said, "You trying to cheer me up? What's next, statistics about CFO's getting fired?"

Ken laughed and raised his beer, responding, "You have to be a CFO to worry about that in the first place. So why are you complaining?" Despite his ill timed comment, Ken was also a very smart guy. In fact, he was a senior vice president and head of the tax department at NV Industries, a multi-billion dollar company, though it wasn't as big as ADG. If you didn't know what he did for a living, you would never have guessed. He certainly didn't look the part. He stood a shade under 6 feet tall but had muscles on his muscles. He worked out constantly, maintaining his athletic form. During his college years, he had been a baseball prodigy, and with a little luck could have made it to the majors. Still looking like a ballplayer, he had a way of attracting women, doing what he could to encourage them even though he was happily married, or at least we thought he was.

We let Ken's comment pass and got back to our burgers, fries and beer, and my thoughts turned again to what we had accomplished over the years. As for me, Carl Messina, I was the only one of us who had remained with the firm. For an Italian boy from Brooklyn, making partner in the world's largest accounting firm was a pretty decent accomplishment, and it was something about which I was very proud. But I didn't think I measured up to the others, and it also bothered me that I was the only one who wasn't married, though it wasn't from any lack of effort. Anyway, I wasn't thinking about women that night, and I suspect no women were thinking about me.

Getting together for our annual dinners was a great tradition, and we considered ourselves fortunate that it had started at the Iron Horse. Though it could never be mistaken for a four-star restaurant, the food was actually pretty good, especially after about five or six beers. What's more, we could afford the prices with our 1979 salaries of $13,300 per year, which at the time seemed like all the money in the world. As the years passed by and our paychecks grew, we sometimes talked about switching to a better place, but tradition always won out, and we stuck with the Iron Horse.

* * * *

"Carl Messina—Report to conference room 515, at our offices at 1251 Avenue of the Americas, by 9 am on Wednesday, June 13, 1979." The firm had sent the letter to my college dorm a few weeks before my May 16th graduation. Although it included instructions for my first day of work, it sounded more like a subpoena and it scared me half to death. I knew enough to graduate in a few weeks with a degree in accounting, but had no idea what to do at the firm. What scared me more was the thought that all the other new recruits would know exactly what to do.

I would be one of thirty-five people who would start that day, and another seventy would get their start later that summer. We would be that year's audit staff recruits for the New York office of Winston Knight & Co., one of the "Big Eight" accounting firms, as they were known at the time. It would later merge with one of the other Big Eight firms to become Winston Walker & Co., the largest accounting firm in the world. The plan called for three days of in-house training followed by two weeks of offsite sessions. After that we would be sacrificed to the lions. That's when we would get assigned to audits and other projects.

I'll never forget June 13 and the first time I set eyes on Kavi. He was a big guy and stood out in our group. They had arranged about fourteen tables in the form of a large rectangle in conference room 515 so everyone could see everyone else. I took some comfort that most of the others in the group looked nervous, but when I looked at Kavi, it seemed as if he had been with the firm for years. He appeared to be so comfortable, and when the group session started he was the one with the first question and it was a good one. He asked what criterion the firm used to assign staff to specific audits. The only question I had was how to get to the bathroom. I also remember seeing Ken. You couldn't miss how all the women would periodically glance his way. Even through his suit you could tell he had a great physique.

I must have been watching Kavi too closely, because he came over to me after our first break and introduced himself. He said I looked a little nervous, which wasn't an entirely brilliant observation. My response was, "So why are you so calm?"

"Relax," he said, as if I had the ability to do so at his command. "Most people here are nervous. Although a few of us spent some time as interns, and that helps. You'll feel much better in a few weeks." I remember thinking I couldn't feel much worse.

He told me a funny story about one of the other interns who was there that day, and then the training session resumed. Our chat was brief but it did help calm me down a bit.

I felt even better as the session progressed, but when we broke for lunch, I got nervous again. I thought they would bring food in, but instead we were given ninety minutes and were on our own. Fortunately, Kavi and Ken were organizing a small group and before I had to make an awkward advance Kavi came to me and asked if I'd like to come along.

There were about nine of us, and we took off for the Iron Horse which was about five blocks away from the office. It was a gorgeous day and I enjoyed the fresh air, although I didn't recall noticing the weather on my way in that morning. Marc was in our group and he introduced himself and asked if I had been an intern.

"Can't you tell it's my first day?" I asked.

"It's mine too, but I did get to speak to some people here for one of my law school projects at Penn. They let me ask a few hundred questions."

When he said he had gone to law school, I realized he did seem somewhat older than the others. But everyone seemed older to me. By skipping eighth grade and graduating from college in three years, I was probably the youngest in the group. I wouldn't be twenty until December.

At lunch, I wanted to speak with some of the women, but couldn't say much of anything except hello. Skills for dealing with the opposite sex were something I didn't have. They were always a few years older than me and that made a big difference. Compounding matters, I had to listen to Ken say all the right things. He had the looks to get women interested and the personality to keep them interested—I wasn't sure if I admired him or hated him for it.

In the afternoon we were given details about the offsite training that would start the following Monday in Carlisle, Pennsylvania. They said we would be reimbursed for our travel expenses and would get $30 if we drove our own cars. I planned on taking a bus, so I wasn't really thinking about the money, but during the break I could overhear three guys who agreed to drive together but tell the firm they'd driven separately so they would get $90 in total with only one car expense. This was their first day of work out of college and they were joining the audit staff of one of the most prestigious accounting firms in the country. Yet they were making plans to issue fraudulent expense reports so they could each make an extra $30. It made me wonder what kind of people I'd come across later in my career.

The Thursday and Friday sessions were less structured and from time to time senior staff people would join us to answer questions and provide helpful advice. They knew what we were going through and genuinely wanted to help. They said we would be surprised by how much we would learn after just two months on the job and I remember thinking how I couldn't wait to find out.

On Sunday, some of us met at the Port Authority Bus Terminal to catch a chartered bus to the training facility. Although the start of summer was a few days off, the weather was perfect and everybody seemed relaxed. I sat next to a beautiful Chinese woman by the name of Nancy Wong and we had a great conversation. Ken was on the bus and would periodically glance my way and give me an approving nod. Of course, I knew she was married. It was easy to do well with a woman when you had no chance.

As we got closer to the facility, it was clear why we were there. It was in the middle of nowhere and they had us at their mercy for two full weeks. When we arrived, we were joined by new recruits from a number of other offices, and I recall there were over one hundred of us in total. Although they would split up individual office groups in the classes, they tried to keep them together in the dorms, and, as luck would have it, Kavi and I were assigned to share a room. Needless to say, we got to know each other quickly.

That first night we were pretty tired and went right to sleep, but Monday night we couldn't stop talking. He told me what it had been like growing up in a small town in India, how there were goats everywhere and how they always got in the way when the kids played football, making sure to emphasize the correct word was football and not soccer. At the time, my international travel had consisted of a family trip to Toronto in 1968, so I had no idea what it was like to be in India. He seemed so proud discussing his hometown, even though it sounded like a slum to me.

When I asked him why he had left, Kavi broke into a big grin and replied, "I'll never forget 1969 when they said people were on the moon. My friends were talking about it after school and I thought they were nuts. But my father said it was true. So I stayed up all night staring at the moon and couldn't believe some Americans were actually there. That's when I decided I was coming here—to become an astronaut. Can you believe that?"

"The moon landing was great," I said. "But to me 1969 means the New York Mets. It's probably hard for you to understand, but I'm a die-hard Yankees fan.

Sure they're champions now, but back then it was pretty difficult rooting for them. I think the only thing worse was being a Cubs fan." As my ode to baseball continued, I realized only ten years had gone by, but 1969 seemed like ancient history.

Kavi told me how he got his big chance to get to the States, although it had nothing to do with NASA or going to the moon. He said there was a special US-India exchange program and he managed to land one of the ten slots that were available in his region. He had to compete with more than three thousand students to get in. The program allowed him to live with a family in Boston so he could finish junior and senior years of high school in the States. He was a top student and won a full academic scholarship to Boston College. And some time during his senior year in high school he'd decided he would be practical and major in accounting.

We kept talking, and I sensed I was boring him with some of my stories about what we had done as kids in Brooklyn, like the time we stole all the red Christmas lights from the houses on our block. We finally called it quits around 2:30 in the morning.

As could be expected, throughout the first week we all gravitated toward small social groups. I was pretty fortunate to have been rooming with Kavi and he was also close to Ken because they had interned for the same client five months earlier. Marc was in my class and we were also becoming friends. As the first weekend approached, about twenty-five of us made arrangements to take a bus to Baltimore on Saturday night to see the Orioles play the Tigers. Another group went to a nearby racetrack to bet on the horses. As it turned out, Kavi and Marc had an affinity for betting, and Ken and I couldn't turn away from a ball game. It was my first opportunity to watch one outside of New York, and I wasn't going to pass it up.

During the first six innings, Ken spent as much time talking to Nancy Wong as he did watching the game, even though he had been told she was married. He said later that marriage is just the first step toward a divorce. During the seventh inning stretch, I switched seats and asked him about playing ball in college. He closed his eyes and rubbed his forehead before giving me an answer. "I was always good at it. I guess it just came easy. I had my pick of schools and knew Texas had a great program. During my freshman year, we won the national championship, and I thought I had what it takes to make it to the show. As a sophomore and junior I did well, but it wasn't good enough."

Doing my best impersonation of an idiot, I asked, "You think you'll give it another shot?" It was a pretty dumb question, since he was spending his time at a training session for starting accountants.

He pointed to his face and said, "I've got a problem with my right eye and the doctors said it would hold me back. I blew a few tryouts for single A clubs my junior year, and, well—" It looked as if he wanted to say more but he stopped mid-sentence, keeping his eyes glued to the infield, even though a ball had been hit hard to left field.

A little later, he asked if I'd played any ball, and I told him how I blew the big game in seventh grade at Roy H. Mann Junior High. They stuck me in right field thinking nothing would be hit there, but a ball was hit right at me and I missed it, allowing the other team to score the tying and winning runs in the ninth inning. I admitted that I wasn't too popular for the next few days at school and that's when I decided to end my baseball career.

We didn't think that Carlisle was such a bad place. It was home to Jim Thorpe's college exploits, the Washington Redskins practiced there during the preseason, and it had a nice small town feel. But by Thursday of the second week everybody had had enough and was ready to go. Thankfully, the plan called for a half day on Friday and then we could leave, and on Monday the real work would begin.

Just before we left, the four of us agreed to meet Saturday night for dinner so we could compare notes and celebrate the start of our careers. As it turned out, that was the beginning of a great tradition of twenty-five annual dinners at the Iron Horse.

* * * *

Kavi was driving me home, and he hadn't said more than two words by the time we crossed the George Washington Bridge, not counting his screaming match with the driver of a yellow cab that had cut us off entering the West Side Highway. It wouldn't have been so bad if we had been listening to some decent music, but Kavi kept fidgeting with the radio. Finally, he turned it off and said, "Shit! Like I really need this."

I waited a moment before I asked, "You mean Ukraine?"

"It's like a can of worms, and it's the last thing I need right now."

"I didn't want to say anything," I admitted. "You seemed pissed after your call."

"You're right. It's not what I expected, and I didn't need Marc's questions. You know, once he gets going he can't stop himself." After a pause, he continued, "I'll call him in a few days. I think I'll need his help this time."

He let off some steam, and we were still talking about it when we arrived at my apartment building. Stepping out of the car, I offered whatever help I could give, knowing full well there wasn't much I could do. As he sped off, I realized I had never seen him that upset before.

CHAPTER 2

▼

Wednesday was shaping up to be a busy day for Marc. One of his clients was acquiring a major pharmaceutical company and was meeting at his firm's offices to assign the closing work. He was responsible for the tax aspects of the transaction and was an important part of the deal team.

Marc was well respected in the mergers and acquisitions arena. He focused on traditional tax planning techniques, and had shied away from the aggressive tax shelter work that had made others wealthy during the boom years of the 80's and 90's. He never approved of some of the crazy tax schemes being peddled by some of the other major firms. All things considered, Marc was a lawyer's lawyer, with a deep rooted respect for the law and a desire to never see it abused. He was the perfect tax advisor for a multi-billion dollar deal.

During the meeting, his assistant handed him a message from Kavi, 'Call ASAP re: Ukraine.' He thought the sense of urgency seemed strange since Kavi had been so reluctant to talk just two days earlier. Marc left the conference room during the first break in the action, and returned the call.

"We just hired your firm," Kavi announced. "A lot happened yesterday, and I can update you when we get a chance to meet. But I didn't want you to be surprised if you got a call from Phil Mentz."

Phil was one of Marc's partners at Bartman & Cross, with particular expertise in handling cases of corporate fraud. He had a great reputation, but for some reason the news made Marc uncomfortable. He temporarily put his concerns aside and said, "I have a few minutes now. Tell me what happened yesterday."

Kavi replied, "I informed the key players and we agreed to get Debra on the first flight back. She's arriving later today with a detailed trip report, and we've asked her to address it to our general counsel, Steve Halpern. You remember? I know you met him before. Anyway, Steve's taking control of the work, and it was his idea to get Phil involved. We're meeting tomorrow morning to get organized and I'd like you to be there. Steve wasn't sure why I wanted a tax guy to sit in, but I insisted."

While Kavi was still talking, Marc made a note on his calendar, and tapped both ends of his pencil on the desk about fifty times in less than a minute. Then Marc said, "I'm not sure I like where you're going with this. On one hand I'm glad Steve hired us but I think it can make things complicated."

"Steve can be a real asshole, but he knows what he's doing and I understand that Phil's pretty good."

"I'm not talking about Steve." After pausing to think of the best way to express his concern, Marc said, "My interest is in you, not your company. Now we've been hired to represent ADG, and that means our first loyalty is to the company and not to you. But there may come a time when your interests and theirs conflict."

"I think you're worried about nothing."

Marc had to get back to his meeting, so he asked Kavi to meet him at the Iron Horse after work for drinks.

Before rejoining his client, Marc made a quick call to Kevin Baker, one of Phil's junior associates in the firm. Marc wanted to get prepared and, more importantly, he wanted to get Kavi prepared, so he asked Kevin for a summary of the laws and other background material that could be relevant. Of course Phil was a step ahead and had already asked Kevin to do it. Marc and Phil shared similar traits. They believed in doing their homework, they placed limited reliance on their memories, so they often referred back to the original text of laws, regulations or cases and they also liked getting associates heavily involved with their work.

Later that day, Kevin delivered a draft of his write-up. Although it wasn't Marc's area of expertise, he did know something about the subject. When he took a quick glance, he noticed references to the laws he had thought would be applicable, including the most important one:

> Under the Foreign Corrupt Practices Act of 1977 (FCPA), it is illegal for a US company to pay foreign officials for the purpose of obtaining or keeping business. It is also illegal to make payments to a third party, while knowing that all or a portion of the payment will go directly or indirectly to a foreign official. US companies are expected to exercise due diligence and take pre-

cautions in developing business relationships to avoid being held liable for corrupt third-party payments.

What the materials didn't say, because it wasn't considered pertinent, was that from 1977 until early 1999, the US was one of the only countries with laws to prohibit its companies from bribing foreign officials. Most other countries viewed bribes as a necessary cost of doing business, going so far as to allow their companies to deduct them for income tax purposes. Since 1999, some countries had enacted legislation similar to the FCPA, but there were significant and notable exceptions. This one-sided playing field made it difficult for US companies to compete in many developing nations.

The draft did include descriptions of other laws that could apply, as well as a discussion of relevant criminal penalties. Marc placed two copies in his briefcase and left for the Iron Horse.

When Marc arrived, Kavi was already there and had commandeered a table in the corner. Kavi waved for Marc to join him and ordered another beer.

After placing a copy of Kevin's draft on the table, Marc pointed to it and said, "Here's your homework for tonight."

Kavi took a quick look at the memo and shook his head. "I'm glad I've got a drink." He flipped through the pages, paying special attention to the sections on criminal penalties, then placed it in his case and said he'd look at it later that evening. Then he continued, "I'm glad you'll be with us tomorrow. Phil has a great reputation, but it's you that I trust."

Marc nodded and asked, "So what else happened yesterday?"

"I think you got the gist of it. After I got home Monday night, the first thing I did was call Charles Goodman, not wanting our Chairman & CEO to find out about this from somebody else. Then Steve and I met yesterday and agreed that he should take charge of the work. Of course that was his idea, but I didn't object."

"What did he say when you suggested that I get involved?"

"I didn't exactly suggest it. You'll be involved, and that's non negotiable. Of course he said it was a waste of money and you wouldn't have anything to add." Kavi grinned, then asked, "Does that surprise you? He likes to protect his turf, but I can handle things even though he's in the lead."

"It was a smart move getting Debra back here," Marc noted. "She's too junior to handle this."

The waitress returned with the beer, and Kavi watched as she walked away. Then he looked around the room and shook his head slowly. "It's too bad Debra had to call Monday night instead of Tuesday morning. After that I wasn't able to enjoy our dinner. One way or another, I'll make sure I can't be reached next year. Can you believe it was our twenty-fifth?"

"Hard to believe, isn't it? I can remember our first one just like it was yesterday. But it also seems like it was another lifetime."

Kavi agreed and added, "This place was much busier Monday night, and loud, very loud."

Marc examined Kavi for a moment and then said, "Before I forget, there's something I need to ask you before tomorrow's meeting."

"Don't worry, I remembered to renew our directors and officers insurance."

Marc laughed, then asked, "Who's the head of the business unit that handles the Nikolaev project in Ukraine, and where is he with all this?"

"It's a French guy named Maurice Granville. He's actually quite good. He heads up our Far East merchant power group, one of our most profitable units. They're big, but you know ADG. No division makes up more than ten percent of our size."

"Ok, so he's good, but what I want to know is what does he say about Debra's work?"

"He's as surprised about this as I am. He wanted to fly in to meet with us, but I told him to hold off for now. We can tie him in by phone when he's needed."

Marc took some time to consider Kavi's response—too much time, because Kavi held out both hands and asked what Marc was thinking. Marc hesitated, then asked, "Can you trust him?"

Kavi smiled, leaned back in his chair, took a deep breath and then replied, "I hadn't thought about it. I've had no problems with him in the past, so why shouldn't I trust him?"

Marc massaged his chin and said, "If there were bribes in Ukraine, isn't it just possible he knew about them?"

"Not likely. He's been with us a number of years and his group's constructed more than twenty power plants which they operate today. All finished on time and on budget, and most of that was on his watch. Two other projects are in the works right now, plus the one at Nikolaev, and the other two are doing fine."

"Ok, but how is he politically?"

"I really hadn't thought about that either." Kavi paused for a moment and then continued, "He's done well for himself but that's because his unit's done well. There's been some talk of moving him up. He's not any competition for me if that's what you're getting at."

"I'm not talking about competition." Marc looked around at the crowd and then leaned in toward Kavi. "Assuming he had nothing to do with the problem, I'm also worried that if he doesn't play his cards right, the company might still blame him and, if they do, who knows? He may try to hurt you because you uncovered the whole mess. Just keep your eyes open and be careful."

The discussion continued for some time, with more warnings from Marc, and Kavi finally checked his watch and realized he had better leave soon, in order to get home in time for dinner. Before leaving, he said, "I know I don't need to say this, but even though I tell you that you worry too much, and you do worry too much Marc, I still appreciate your watching my back."

* * * *

You had to take two elevators to get to the conference room. The first one took you to the 38th floor executive reception area. The second one took you from there to the 50th and top floor. It was easier to get into the White House.

When you made it to the 50th floor at ADG you were in the big leagues. Only five executives had offices there—Kavi, Charles Goodman, Steve Halpern, the company's President and the head of their largest business unit.

As you walked through the dimly lit hall, you could smell money and power. The walls and furniture were made of redwood, cherry and mahogany. Dark colored Italian marble covered the floor. The boardroom was huge with fifty luxurious leather chairs, and it looked familiar to most people because it had been used in scenes for a number of popular movies. To top it off, even Kavi's two assistants had offices that would make any ADG vice president envious.

Marc made it through security and was escorted to the main conference room on the floor, where he said hello to Steve, whom he recognized, and then introduced himself to Debra Jennings. From some of the things he'd heard, he had pictured her as a short and somewhat older woman. But standing in front of him was a 5 foot 10, athletic looking, 32-year-old, auburn haired beauty. While waiting for the others, Marc listened as she told a funny story about the hotel in Nikolaev. She had no sooner finished when they were joined by Kavi and Phil.

As soon as Kavi saw Debra, he smiled and said, "What a trooper. I didn't think you'd make it back on time. You look so tired you're making me feel guilty. Rough trip coming back?"

It was clear she had yet to recover, and while rubbing her forehead, she said, "Getting back from Kiev wasn't so bad. It's great flying business class, and I got some sleep. The problem was getting to Kiev from Nikolaev. I had chartered a two-engine plane and the flight took only about ninety minutes, but before that I had to wait three hours for the guy to show up."

"Well, it's great you made it, and I really appreciate your efforts these past few weeks. By the way, how's your little boy?" Before she could answer, Kavi told the group that she had a 4 year-old at home, and that it was really tough for her to be away for more than a few days.

"Greg's doing great," she said. "Although he couldn't understand why I was away for so long. Neither could my husband, for that matter."

Kavi quipped, "If you need a note from us, just let me know." After getting a laugh out of Debra, Kavi walked over to a table stocked with different types of coffee, juices, assorted muffins, and some of the best bagels in town. He poured himself a cup of a high powered Colombian blend and joked about one of *his* trips to Kiev. Out of the corner of his eye, he could see that Steve was getting impatient, so he made his way to his seat and volunteered, "This is your ballgame, Steve. We're at your service."

At 5 foot 4 and 130 pounds, Steve might have had success as a jockey. He was definitely a marked contrast to Kavi's large frame. Steve was very sensitive about his height, and it was bad enough that a big guy like Kavi towered over him, but even Debra was a good six inches taller. That was tough for him to handle, especially in view of the secret crush he had on her, since he was sure she wouldn't go for a shorter guy, not to mention a shorter *married* guy. He pictured her going after the tall ones, and she and Kavi were actually very close—too close in Steve's view of the world. But despite his sensitivity, he was a highly skilled lawyer and one of the most senior officers at ADG, though unlike Kavi, he had no chance at the CEO position. He did an acceptable job of keeping his frustrations to himself, but it was easy to tell that he and Kavi worked together only when they had to.

Ignoring Kavi's introduction, Steve took a quick drink of water, cleared his throat, and then opened a folder and took out five copies of a memo addressed to him and stamped 'Confidential—Attorney Client Privilege.' It was the Nikolaev trip report. As he passed the copies around, he said, "I couldn't get this to you earlier. I wanted to review it first, and Debra gave it to me this morning." He proceeded to discuss the key aspects of the memo, maintaining his focus on Phil Mentz, and just about ignoring the others in the room, save for an occasional glance at Debra.

Marc tried to listen and read at the same time. According to the memo:

> ADG is leading the construction of a power plant in Nikolaev, Ukraine, an industrial city about 250 miles south of Kiev. During Soviet times, access to

the city was restricted because of its strategic importance to the defense industry. It was a major support center for the Black Sea fleet, with substantial ship building and repair facilities and raw material processing plants. The city is now open and in recent years has received a large inflow of foreign capital due to its strategic location and the expected 2004 entry of many of its western neighbors into the European Union. The local power facilities are antiquated and heavy polluters and will either need to be retrofitted with expensive new pollution control devices or removed from service. It has been estimated that approximately 1,000 megawatts of new power facilities will be needed to meet the growing local industrial power demand, taking into account the expected reduction in power supplies from the older plants. In order to meet this need, in 2001, ADG's Far East merchant power group organized a consortium to build a 660 megawatt gas-fired power facility in Nikolaev. ADG owns a 60% interest, with the remaining 40% split equally between Kenton Aluminum, an international aluminum company that's building a nearby smelter which will be a major customer for the plant, and OPIC, an export financing agency of the US government.

The memo also indicated that construction had begun in September, 2001 and was expected to last two years. Total construction costs were expected to be between $630 and $660 million. The revised estimates were a March 2004 completion date and total costs of approximately $700 million.

Marc stopped reading when Steve asked Debra to discuss her key findings, which had only been briefly summarized in the memo. She took a drink of water and pointed out the relevant section of the memo. "In order to get the required licenses, the Ukrainian government required us to spend at least ten percent of the project costs on purchases from Ukrainian firms. The original budget included an estimate of $75 million to cover this. It's all being run through one local firm, Vasylko, Kiel and Bohdanko, or VKB. They're middlemen. They reviewed our project plans and identified what they could get done through local contractors. It's not unusual. We do this in other countries."

Phil asked her if she was going to tell the group how VKB had been selected, but she said she didn't know. She took a sip of coffee, and then continued, "A few months back, it was becoming clear that the project was seriously over budget and behind schedule. We were getting estimates of cost overruns of about $50 million, which is about eight percent of the total project budget."

Kavi interrupted her, and added, "Eight percent may not seem that bad, but it's unusual for us. Our policy is to scrutinize anything over five. Also, *any* overage is unusual for the Far East merchant power group. Maybe they've been too good, but they've completed all their projects within the original budgeted range, unless there was a change in the project specification."

Debra continued, "As he said, eight percent is unusual for this business unit." She glanced quickly at some of her notes and took another sip of coffee. "We could understand if there was some problem with the project site or if the specs had changed. But there was nothing like that, so it made no sense to have a $50 million overage due to VKB. And keep in mind the original budget for them was only $75 million, and now it would be about $125 million, and that's way too big an increase to ignore without something to point to." She looked at Kavi to see if he had something to add, but he just nodded. She continued, "We were also told there were problems getting a required environmental certificate from the Ukrainian government. This made no sense because we hadn't made any changes from the original plans and they had been pre-cleared with the government. We couldn't get adequate explanations, so Kavi sent me to Nikolaev to learn more. Kavi cleared it with Maurice Granville, I cleared it with my husband, and then I left for the trip. And now I'm back and in serious need of more sleep."

"He didn't try to stop you from going?" Phil asked.

"Who?"

"Maurice."

"No, although he didn't seem as concerned about the situation as we were." Debra waited while Steve said something about Maurice being an all around great guy. Then she continued, "The first few days I spent most of my time reviewing construction cost details with the local project accountants. After that, I was given a tour of the site and had a chance to speak with the construction supervisor and some of his crew. We confirmed the problems related to VKB, but nobody could explain how the original estimates could be so far off, and I found it strange that they were surprised that I was even asking about it. I wasn't sure if people didn't know what was going on, or didn't want to know. And when I asked to be put in touch with our lead contact at VKB, they discouraged me from doing so. That's when I really got suspicious."

"Were the local people trying to dodge your questions?" Marc asked.

"It seemed like that to me. But they had to know I would keep at it until I got answers, but they were actually surprised when I didn't back off. It was as if they had expected me to know more than I did, like I was there just going through the motions."

"That seems strange," Marc noted.

"Tell me about it. But I kept it up, and finally, at dinner, one of the project guys said I should understand that dealing with VKB was just a cost of doing business. Another guy said he wouldn't question VKB, that they were well known and could get whatever they wanted. He said he'd do whatever they told him to do because of what they'd done to others. They said VKB would probably not hurt me since I was from the head office of a big American company, but they could do things to make sure the project got screwed up."

"You don't seem to mention any names in your report," Phil said. "I assume you recall the names of the people who were with you at that dinner?"

Debra hesitated, glanced over at Kavi and then turned back. "I would prefer to keep that confidential. Some of them said they were speaking off the record." Pausing for a moment, she expected to hear an objection, but when she heard none, she continued, "Others repeated the same story. VKB controls all the strings and we can't finish the project without them. If they want more money, we have to pay it. As one person talked, others became more comfortable and added their views. One said he believed VKB is controlled by ex-Soviet KGB agents who are now affiliated with Russian organized crime groups. I'm not sure we should believe that."

"Did anyone at dinner say that VKB, or its owners, provide money or property to government officials?" Phil asked.

Debra smiled, and leaned in to study Phil's face to see if he was joking. Realizing he was serious, she sat back, thought for a moment, and then responded, "No, not that I recall, but I assume if all that they said is true, then people in the government must be getting paid. How else could VKB get away with this?"

"So what happened after dinner?" Marc asked.

"I went right back to the hotel and tried to call Kavi. The phone system was upgraded last year but it was still pretty bad, and it took me hours to try to get through. I began to wonder if someone was messing with my phone on purpose, like I was acting out a movie and maybe I wouldn't make it back. Anyway, I finally got through to him about four in the morning, Ukraine time." She leaned in toward Marc and got him to smile by adding, "Sorry if I messed up your anniversary dinner, by the way."

The group took a couple of minutes to digest the report, and after a brief discussion, Phil looked at Debra and asked, "So what do *you* think was behind the cost overruns and delays?"

Once again Debra was puzzled, and she looked over to Kavi for help. Phil had a habit of asking questions the answers to which seemed obvious. But to him, nothing was obvious. After getting a nod from Kavi, she turned and replied, "I think what they're saying about VKB is true and we're being extorted. They want more money and they've got the government behind them to make sure they get paid."

With a serious look on his face, Kavi said, "I guess we needed something exciting to wake people up around here."

Marc nodded, turned to Phil and said "If the allegations prove to be true, what did Maurice Granville know and when did he know it?"

Steve was annoyed by the question and quickly jumped on Marc with his response. "I think it's premature to ask that. We don't know if any of this is true and, if it is, we certainly don't know who knew about it. We should keep in mind that Maurice has been with us for many years, and his business unit has performed extremely well. In my view, there is no reason to suspect him of anything improper." Steve didn't wait to see if Marc had anything to add. Instead, he asked Phil if he thought they needed to make any public disclosure.

Phil rubbed his chin and replied, "Just as you indicated, right now you have suspicions of impropriety but they're just suspicions. Of course they seem credible and you need to take them seriously. However, I wouldn't make any public disclosure now. I do suggest that you alert the board of directors. You don't want any of them caught by surprise. I would also tell your external auditors, so that—"

"We need to get confirmation first," Kavi interrupted. "They'll jump on something like this to cover their ass, and we'll spend more time dealing with them than we will dealing with the problem. I don't want this getting out of control."

Phil started to respond but Steve jumped in. "We have to tell them now. I think the earlier you do, the more likely they won't overreact."

Phil agreed and said, "Kavi, you're right that they'll probably want to jump on it. Especially these days, where auditors have more responsibility for catching corporate crime. But you should still tell them now. Otherwise, they'll overreact even more later, if the suspicions prove to be true." Phil put both his hands on the table, leaned back in his chair, and nodded. Then he looked at Steve and said, "I would also inform OPIC, as well as Kenton Aluminum. They're both minority owners in the project and they have a right to know. I think it would also make sense to inform the US State Department and, on balance, to tell the Department of Justice."

Kavi's body immediately tensed up. He looked down, gritted his teeth, and seemed to be talking to the floor when he said, "It just seems crazy to do all that." He looked up at Phil and explained, "ADG's gross revenues this year will exceed

$60 billion and we've got over $100 billion book value of assets. The numbers we're talking about in Ukraine are peanuts in the scheme of things."

"I understand," Phil said. "The problem is we're talking about possible criminal acts and materiality doesn't matter. The reasons for telling each of them differ, but in each case if you tell them, and the suspicions prove to be unfounded, then no harm will have been done. On the other hand, if we do have a real problem, then trust me, we'll be better off telling people early in the process."

Kavi shrugged his shoulders and said, "Maybe so, but keep in mind that ADG has very few friends in this administration. Charles Goodman's about as Democrat as you can get, and we've got two senior members of the previous administration's staff on our board. Things like that may influence some folks at the Department of Justice."

"That's a risk," Phil admitted. "But I don't think it will have an impact in this case."

"I agree with Phil," Marc said. "You've got to be concerned how this will play out when the news gets out, and at some point it will. You know what could happen to your stock if you don't manage the press. If the allegations are true, I think it will help to say you alerted the authorities and the other project owners early on. You may actually get some *good* press out of it."

Phil added, "I have other reasons for suggesting that you do this." He glanced briefly at Debra and continued, "As some were suggesting at her dinner, we're probably not dealing with the friendliest of characters here. Who knows what they might do to a lawyer or accountant asking the wrong questions?" He paused so his words could sink in, and then added, "While her dinner companions were probably right about the odds against VKB doing something to hurt one of your employees, we shouldn't take any chances. And when it comes to safety, it will help to have the US government involved with our efforts."

Steve mentioned something about his understanding of US and Ukrainian relations, and then asked Phil if he had any other suggestions.

After making his way to the window, Phil massaged the back of his neck and looked out into the distance, while the others waited for him to speak. "We need to go back there, and quickly. Maybe in a week." He turned and looked at Debra, "You and I should certainly go. I'll take one or two of my associates and we can probably use a few people from your corporate accounting or internal audit group."

"Anyone else?" Kavi asked.

"I'll have to think about it." As he walked back he said, "I'll also schedule a visit to the US Embassy in Kiev as part of the trip."

"What about the Department of Justice?" Steve asked. "Will they just sit on the information and do nothing until we report back, or will they want to send someone with you?"

"I'm sure they'll give us a few weeks to do our work."

Marc nodded and said, "Someone should speak to Maurice Granville to make sure he's in the loop. In my view, it's very important that he be involved in the process and given every opportunity to participate."

"I agree," said Phil. "I'd like to meet him in Ukraine when we're there."

Steve said he would call Maurice after the meeting to fill him in on their plan. He asked Phil to summarize his recommendations in writing, and then said, "After I speak with Maurice, I'll meet with Charles Goodman to make sure he's on board. I'm sure he'll agree with your approach and then we'll get this in gear." After hearing Kavi say he needed to be involved with the call and meeting, Steve reluctantly agreed.

Kavi stood up, thanked everyone for coming, and offered to walk Marc and Phil to the elevator. While walking back, he suddenly remembered that Friday would be July 4, and he had promised his wife Aarti to bury his cell phone and stay away from work for the long weekend. But with all he needed to do to inform people and to get the group prepared for their trip, it didn't look like he was going to keep his promise. For the time being, that was the most important consequence of the Nikolaev mess.

Chapter 3

▼

It was a beautiful day; it would have been better to be outside, instead of sitting in my office on a conference call with a client. There was a time when I had enjoyed discussing internal controls for financial reporting, but that time was long gone. Not that my client enjoyed it either. Under new rules they were required to do much more than they had done in the past and they needed my help. Although good for business, it wasn't good for my long holiday weekend. It was Thursday afternoon, July 3rd, and we had already let the administrative staff go home to get a head start on their holiday plans. As it turned out, most of the partners and other professional staff had also left.

I had also been ready to leave an hour earlier, when my client asked if I could participate in their call. Of course I was assured it would last no longer than fifteen minutes or so, but after an hour there was no end in sight. It was hard to stay focused and my mind would periodically wander as I watched the crowds on the street below. My office was on the fourth floor, so I had a good view of 50th Street and Avenue of the Americas, and there was a set of binoculars hidden in my desk drawer in case an attractive woman caught my eye. And during the summer months that happened often.

Someone on the call was droning on and on, when a Latin beauty walked out of the building across the street to talk to some women standing near the corner. She was hard to miss in the crowd, and I immediately hit the speaker button so I could listen to the call and use my binoculars at the same time, although you could see plenty with the naked eye. She had legs that would stop traffic, and beautiful long dark hair that covered about a third of her fashion model's build. With binoculars and a little imagination, you could see more than she wanted you to see, and after a few minutes of gawking, I wondered if the client would mind if I left my office, ran down to the corner, and told Ms. Venezuela that an accountant could be the answer to her prayers.

My call finally wrapped up, so I put the binoculars away and started to organize some papers on my desk when the phone rang again. Since my assistant had already left, it was up to me to answer. I gave some thought to just letting it ring but figured it might be my client again and, as the firm always says, the client comes first. It turned out to be Kavi returning my earlier call.

"Sorry I took so long getting back to you," he said. "What's up?"

"I was wondering what happened with your Ukrainian problem."

"That's why I didn't get to you sooner. We've been busy dealing with it. We have a plan and have to scramble to get it going. You know the timing of this is terrible. I'll need to work almost all weekend, and Aarti's planning to kill me." Kavi had to put the call on hold for a moment. While waiting, I looked out the window and saw that my Latin friend was no longer there. Another chance for lifelong happiness had passed me by. He got back on the line and asked, "When are you planning to leave?"

I instinctively looked at my watch although I didn't need to. "In a few minutes. Why?"

"Can you meet me for a drink? I can spare about an hour and can use a beer."

"The Iron Horse? That's twice this week, but you don't mind, do you?"

"Actually it's three times for me. I had to meet Marc there yesterday. I'll tell you why when I see you."

*   *   *   *

When I arrived, Kavi was sitting at a table near the back with three beers and a large order of French fries. I figured one of the beers was for me. He waved to get my attention and when I got to the table I asked, "These fries enough for you, or should I order more?"

"They're not that bad." He sucked-in his rather large stomach and massaged his shirt. Then, after demonstrating that he had a soft spot in his heart for Pizza, he grabbed a beer and asked, "Did you hear about the new diet? Instead of eating all protein and drinking lots of water, you eat nothing but fried foods and drink lots of beer. You don't lose any weight, but you make sure you eat and drink around people who are heavier than you."

I helped myself to a couple of fries and said, "Actually, I shouldn't be the one to talk. When I was in high school, a friend of mine and I would get together every Thursday after school and we'd go to the coffee shop on the corner and order French fries and soda. Not exactly health food, was it? You know, it doesn't sound like much, but I would look forward to it all day."

After talking about how to avoid losing weight, Kavi spent about twenty minutes telling me what had happened since Monday night, including the meeting he and Marc had had with others earlier in the day.

Having heard their strategy, I tried to analyze it from my perspective. "I guess it makes sense to tell your partners in the project, but why tell the Department of Justice? I'd want to know if the accusations were true first. I agree you should tell the auditors though."

"I wanted to ask you about that." Kavi looked around at some of the people in the crowd and then leaned in toward me. "What would you do if one of your clients came to you with something like this?"

Although Winston Walker was the largest accounting firm in the world, we didn't have ADG as an audit client. The work was done by one of the other large firms, Larson & Kirsh, or L&K as they were called. Charles Goodman was the top guy at ADG and he had a longstanding relationship with L&K. I would have loved to have landed the account, but L&K had done a good job over the years and there was no real reason for a change. In any case, since Kavi wasn't an audit client, he could more easily confide in me and that had often proven to be beneficial.

After considering his question I replied, "It's hard to tell. I'd probably start by getting everything I had about the work done on that business unit."

"Why look at the whole business unit? Why not limit it to Nikolaev?"

"You know about the problems there, and I'm sure you'll get to the bottom of it. I'd check the other projects to get ahead of the game. A problem at Nikolaev is one thing, and you can understand how the auditors could miss it, especially at a company the size of ADG. On the other hand, if there are problems at the other projects, somebody is going to blame the auditors and that's what would worry me the most."

Kavi nodded and sat back in his chair. He didn't like my answer, but I could tell that he agreed with my reasoning. He admitted, "That's what I'm afraid of. Now we'll have L&K crawling all over the place at their highest hourly rates. Of course I can't stop them because if I do, and then we find problems at other plants, you know how that would look."

"Believe me I understand. L&K will have a field day with this." As I spoke, I noticed Kavi look at his watch. "I know you need to get back soon, but tell me what you think of Phil Mentz."

"I'm sure he knows what he's doing, but some of his recommendations surprised me. But Marc's involved. He'll let me know if there's a problem with anything Phil plans to do." Kavi finished his second beer, looked at his watch again and said, "I do need to head back. How about you? Any big plans for the weekend?"

"Yeah, I have a date with a sixty-eight year-old woman."

"Your mother's great. Tell her to send some lasagna to my office tonight."

"I'll have it hand delivered." As he stood up to leave, I prepared to make an offer I knew he'd never accept. "If you need my help with any of this, just let me know."

"Thanks, but we have it covered. Tell your mom I said hello."

I stayed behind to finish my beer. There was no rush to get to Brooklyn to see my mother, and I also needed some time alone. It was disappointing to listen to Kavi talk about his problem, knowing there was nothing that I could do to help. He had done so much for me over the years, and it would have been nice to be able to return the favor with something other than my mom's food.

From time to time, he needed Marc and Ken for tax advice, and he also looked to Marc as something akin to his personal lawyer. But there was nothing Kavi ever needed from me. I was an audit partner, and that's what he had been before he left to join ADG. Whatever I knew, he knew too. And he was way ahead of me when we started back in 1979 and stayed ahead of me throughout the years. It didn't make me jealous though. He worked very hard and he deserved whatever he got.

He wasn't just technically strong. He had a way of reading people, so he knew what was important to them and how to get on their best side. I wouldn't say it was political though. I'd say it was a genuine desire to help people get where they wanted to go, and it was no accident that he was the first of us to make partner at Winston Knight. The normal track was anywhere from eleven to thirteen years. It took me thirteen years to make partner. He made it in nine.

I wasn't even sure I'd have made partner were it not for him. Not that I wasn't good enough, I was very good. It's just that I'd made a number of mistakes dealing with people along the way and he was always there to help me straighten things out. To make partner in an accounting firm, you had to be competent and have sufficient partner support, but even with that, you wouldn't make it if you made an enemy of an influential partner. Thanks to Kavi's help, I never did. And it didn't hurt that he was still a partner with the firm when they voted me in. He said a lot of great things about me during their deliberations and that may have put me over the top. And, as luck would have it, he announced he was leaving for

ADG just two weeks after the vote. I always wondered if he'd delayed the announcement in order to be there to help me.

Kavi knew I was grateful, but he often told me I was destined to be a great partner and would have made it without his help. He certainly didn't expect anything from me in return.

After finishing my beer, I thought about trying my luck with a blonde at the bar. But when I was ready to walk over and introduce myself, she got up to hug a guy who had just walked through the front door. I was relieved it had taken me so long to decide what to do, and on that note I got up to head off to Brooklyn.

*   *   *   *

My mom's building was in the middle of the block, just off Flatbush Avenue. I found a place to park on the corner, walked past three single family homes built in the 1930's and in serious need of repair, and made my way into her building and up to her third floor apartment. And no one needed to tell you which one was hers. You simply followed the aroma. I kissed her and made the mistake of asking how much food she had cooked. It turned out to be enough chicken parmesan and spaghetti to feed an army.

I was always careful to be nice when describing my mother's physical attributes. Anne Messina wasn't tall and she wasn't thin, but I thought she was a sixty-eight-year-old beauty. Her mother and father were born in Naples, Italy, and immigrated to the US before she was born. She was raised in Little Italy and lived just two blocks from where my father, Joseph, grew up. Even though they lived close to each other, they didn't meet until high school. My father was Sicilian, so her parents weren't too pleased when he and my mom started dating. A few years after they were married they moved to our old house in the Bergen Beach section of Brooklyn, and she moved to her apartment shortly after my father died in June of 2000.

"Expecting anyone else?" I asked.

"Why, you got a problem?"

"You're the only one who cooks for twenty people when you expect one person."

"Don't bust chops." She smiled, put more food than I needed on my plate, and said, "You'll take some home. You need some food in that refrigerator of yours."

"Yeah, like I need a few more pounds." I started to eat and got prepared for my mom's questions.

"So what's with Kim?"

She was referring to Kim Darcy, my soon to be ex-girlfriend. We had one of those on-again off-again relationships. The kind where I always thought it was on and she always thought it was off. We had made plans for the weekend, but she called me during the week to cancel.

"Unfortunately she needed to go to Las Vegas to meet a few of her sorority sisters. I really didn't ask her for the details, but apparently one of the sisters is named Ralph."

She shook her head in disgust. "What's with women these days? They all think they need to play games. You two were planning on watching the fireworks, right? Sounds like a real nutcase to me."

"Look, I really don't want to talk about Kim."

Without my asking, she got up to get some parmesan cheese and started putting it on my spaghetti. My mom had a funny way of getting you something before you knew you needed it. When she finished with the cheese, she sat down and looked like she wanted to say something more about Kim but thought better of it. Instead, she asked about my Monday night dinner.

"It was great and the guys asked about you. Actually, I was having drinks with Kavi just before I left to come here. He said he's working late tonight and he wants me to have some of your lasagna delivered to his office."

"See big shot, some people appreciate my food. How's he doing?"

"He's got some problems and it looks like he'll be working all weekend."

"You guys all work too hard." She made a face so there was no way I could miss her displeasure, then got up to get a small wet cloth and started cleaning the countertop. My mom liked to clean things *before* they became dirty. "People think they're big shots with their cell phones, beepers and all that other stuff. They really want that? It's a bunch of crap, like working all the time. People are crazy."

"I agree with you, but it's a balance. You need money to live a good life. Anyway, my friends make a lot of time for their families."

"You think so? Tell me, how often do they see their cousins, uncles and aunts? Families are more than a wife and kids."

"Times change. It's not like it was when you were growing up."

"When I was growing up? How about when you were growing up? We had people at the house all the time. Everybody lived close by and we made an effort to stay together. You don't remember the way it was back then."

"I remember. People are busy these days."

"People are nuts. They make themselves busy. When you were growing up, being together was a priority. Our family was who we were. Nothing was more important. Now you're lucky to get a phone call from a cousin once a year."

Of course my mother was right. I had loved it when I was a kid. There were always people stopping by, we'd visit relatives at least once a week, and the whole extended family would get together often throughout the year. I think it was my generation that changed all that. We can fly anywhere on a moment's notice, so people live all over the country, but even that's not a good excuse. We didn't see our cousins much, and they lived not more than an hour away. We just didn't make the time.

I tried getting up from the table to put my dish in the sink, but my mom grabbed it before I could move. While washing she said, "People put things off with their relatives because they think they'll have plenty of time later, but later never comes. Carl, you know life's short."

"You're right."

"That reminds me, have you been thinking about visiting Greenwood? I'd like the two of us to go."

Greenwood was the cemetery in Brooklyn where my father and my older brother Joe were buried. My brother died in 1976 from a rare form of brain cancer. In February of that year he was a great athlete. By the end of April, he was dead.

"That's a good idea. We've only been there once since dad died."

After dinner, I took a walk around the neighborhood to get some air and attempt to work off a pound or two. Flatbush Avenue always brought back great memories from when I was a kid. It didn't take much to remember movie theaters which weren't very big but always seemed big to me, and candy stores about every six blocks, and great Chinese restaurants, including one my dad took us to all the time. Of course my dad's favorite Chinese restaurant had closed up years ago. The movie theaters were gone, replaced with a video rental store or some fast food restaurant. And candy stores, at least the ones I remembered, were nowhere to be found, not in Brooklyn anyway. Nonetheless, there was enough that had survived the years, and it still looked and smelled like my childhood home.

While walking, I thought about my mom living on her own. I had asked her to move in with me, but she said she liked her independence. In a way, I was glad she had turned me down. We probably would try to kill each other if we lived under the same roof. I knew she had everything she needed within walking distance of her apartment and probably would have been uncomfortable living in

New Jersey. At least she knew there was a place for her if she needed one, plus I had a good excuse to visit Brooklyn from time to time.

All things considered, I would miss being with Kim, but I was looking forward to spending the long weekend with my mom.

CHAPTER 4

▼

It was a wet and dreary Monday, July 14, and the conditions inside the hotel in Nikolaev were not much better than the conditions outside. Although significant foreign capital was flowing into the city, little of it had made its way to the hotel and the surrounding area.

Debra Jennings was sitting on the floor of Phil Mentz's room when she said, "There's some money being spent around here, but I can't see it."

"I know what you mean," Phil said. "The ride from the airport was interesting to say the least. The buildings were old, but that wasn't the worst part. I don't think they had any architectural charm when they were first built."

The hotel was just as drab as the surrounding buildings. The guests used the rooms facing the street. The other side of the hall was in complete disrepair, with exposed cinder blocks and missing doors. The occupied rooms weren't much better, although you couldn't help but notice that the linens and draperies were fresh and clean. The hotel staff took pride in their work. It wasn't their fault that they had limited funds with which to work. There was a hotel under construction on the other side of town, but it wasn't expected to open until later in the year.

Phil and his group had arrived in Nikolaev Sunday evening and had agreed to meet first thing Monday morning. The lights weren't working in the small conference room in the hotel, so they agreed to meet in Phil's room. It wasn't large, so it was a tight fit for eight people. Phil had brought two of his associates, including Kevin Baker, and Debra Jennings was joined by two of ADG's internal auditors. Although not technically a part of Phil's team, two auditors from the L&K Singapore office were there, including Yu Cheng, who was the audit partner responsible for work on the Far East merchant power group.

Although Phil had participated in a number of separate phone conversations and the group had spoken briefly on the plane from Kiev to Nikolaev, it was their first chance to meet in a setting where they would not be overheard. He had previously arranged to get each person a copy of his write-up, which included a detailed action plan for their trip, and he wanted to review it briefly before they left to visit the project site. The action plan was twenty pages long, with detailed procedures and assigned responsibilities. Among other things, it provided for interviews with VKB personnel, as well as with the firms that VKB had brought in to do the actual work and to supply materials at the site.

Phil closed the door so they could get started. "Sorry for the tight quarters. What is it they say? It's not just a job, it's an adventure." He sat down and picked up his copy of the action plan. "We have our work cut out for us this week. There's a lot to do and very little time. Let's review this, and if you have any questions we should address them now before we get to the site. If you turn to—"

"We're not working for you," Yu Cheng said, taking advantage of his first chance to interrupt Phil. Yu didn't look that great on his good days, and on this morning he looked even worse, as if he had gotten up on the wrong side of the bed. He added, "We have our own requirements we'll need to address." One of them was to cover his firm's ass, but he neglected to mention that.

While thinking about what he should say, Phil laughed at the thought of Kavi back home saying "I told you so." It was too early in the day for any conflict, so he tried to be tactful. "I realize you're not working for me. Nonetheless, we should coordinate our efforts. The company has been very forthcoming and because of their efforts you're here today. And if you think there's more for us to do, please let me know."

"They had to tell us," Yu said, as he struggled to keep his right hand from shaking. He quickly glanced at his colleague, who looked even more nervous, and added, "We need to think about the other projects too."

Phil insisted, "At this point my only interest is Nikolaev, so let's please stick to it for the time being."

Yu's colleague, who needed a little more practice with his English language skills, gathered enough courage to make an incoherent statement, after which Yu followed-up with another self-serving declaration.

Phil was getting a little upset, but the L&K boys finally settled down, and let Phil get back to his agenda. He made his way through the details of his action plan, and after about twenty minutes, was ready for questions.

"I looked this over last night," Debra said. "I think it's very good, but how do you plan to prove the Ukrainian government was bribed?"

"We're not here to try to prove that. This isn't a James Bond movie and you're not Agent 007. We're here to do our best to get the facts. If we find evidence of wrongdoing involving the government beyond what you've been told, it will likely be handled by the authorities. If not, we will report to senior management with the expectation that the matter will be closed."

One of the ADG internal auditors said, "I see that you plan interviews with some of the Ukrainian firms and with VKB. You think they'll really tell us anything?"

The rain was coming down harder and Phil had to raise his voice to be heard. "Whatever they do, we'll be sure to get what we need. If they have nothing to hide, then they have every reason to cooperate and give us the information we'll request. If we don't get it, we'll know what that means. In regard to the subcontractors for VKB, I want to know how much they originally planned to charge and the amount of, and reasons for, any increase in those charges. I also want to get the same information separately from VKB. If the information is not consistent, we have definitive evidence of a problem. Even if it is consistent, it will still enable us to see if the cost increases make any sense, and we can also determine the true profit margin retained by VKB, and if it's unreasonably large, that could also be evidence of a problem."

Phil answered a few more questions, and by lunch time the group was ready to leave for the project site.

* * * *

It was Wednesday, and the team's work was well underway. Monday and Tuesday had both been productive days, and Phil agreed to meet Maurice Granville in Kiev in order to save him the trouble of making another trip to Nikolaev.

Maurice shook Phil's hand as if they were lifelong friends and said, "So you must be Inspector Clouseau?"

Since they were meeting in the lobby of the hotel, Phil looked around to see if anyone could overhear their conversation, before responding, "Not quite, I'm just a boring lawyer from New York."

"That's not what I hear. They tell me you catch big-time corporate criminals."

"It's not what I like to do."

Phil had expected a much taller man. Maurice didn't stand more than a shade above 5 feet. He was slightly bald, with jet black hair not typical of a man in his late forties. He spoke multiple languages and had an accent that was closer to Italian than to French. Phil was caught off guard by Maurice's cavalier attitude but thought it best to play along, at least for a while.

Maurice lit a cigarette and said, "Thanks for meeting me here. I'm sure you can appreciate I've seen enough of Nikolaev. As you can see, this hotel is a big improvement for you."

"You're right, and I was glad to make the trip. I'm staying over tonight and will return to Nikolaev tomorrow."

"So Phil, found any criminals at ADG?"

Phil wasn't sure how to respond. He'd come to Kiev expecting to meet a concerned leader of a business unit with a problem, but instead was sitting in a hotel lobby with a person who didn't seem to have a care in the world. "Maurice, as you can appreciate, we're not looking to find criminals. We're looking to gather the relevant facts."

"I understand. No criminals, just the facts."

"So Maurice, as the head of the business unit, what can you tell me about all this?"

"Phil, want a cigarette?"

"I don't smoke."

"So you're a health nut?"

"No, I just never started smoking. I can't say I really thought about it. So what are your thoughts about Nikolaev?"

"You know, Americans think they'll live forever. They work out, don't smoke and eat healthy, or at least they think they eat healthy. Maybe they do live longer, but so what? They get to live in some retirement home in Arizona and watch their kids screw up. Europeans think you live life for today." To emphasize his point, Maurice shook his fist as he added, "Embrace life while you can."

Phil thought if he asked the question a third time he might at least get one answer. "I appreciate your philosophy for living life. However, my only concern at the moment is Nikolaev. Maurice, what are your thoughts on that?"

At first Maurice didn't respond. He looked out the window as if searching for a way to word his answer. He turned, put out his cigarette, and immediately lit another one. He smiled and said, "Phil, do you know that song about a hungry guy who had to dance in order to get food?"

"I think I know what you're talking about. Why?"

"Well the guy learns he can dance, and he gets fed."

"What's that got to do with Nikolaev?"

"It has everything to do with it. You say you want the facts. I'm sure you know more about the facts than I do. What I know is if you want to be successful in a developing country, you need to do the local dance. Whatever it takes. Each place is a little different, but it always comes down to dancing with the right people. I've done it successfully at project after project. Nikolaev is our first problem."

Phil was uncomfortable with where the conversation was going, though he had no other choice than to pursue it further. "Maurice, I need you to be clear. I can't read between the lines."

"I'm saying in Ukraine you can't get anything done without the help of Vasylko, Kiel and Bohdanko. So we say fine, we'll work with them. As long as they can deliver at a competitive price, then we're ok. What they do with their money is their business as far as I'm concerned."

"And what do you think they do with their money?" Phil asked.

"I don't know but you can guess. When they told us we needed to pay more because they had trouble with some of their contractors, we originally balked. Then, some of the licenses we had were magically revoked. Is it just a coincidence? I'm not here to solve a puzzle. I'm here to get a plant built. After a while it just seemed best to pay the extra money and move on to bigger and better things. Kavi's group didn't quite see it the same way."

They continued their discussion for over an hour. Phil wasn't sure if Maurice was being entirely forthcoming but there wasn't much point to continuing the discussion any longer. Phil wanted to go to his room and prepare for their late afternoon meeting at the US Embassy with Andrew Westmoreland, the US ambassador to Ukraine. They wrapped things up and agreed to meet later in the lobby.

The hotel was not very good by Western standards, but it was a big improvement from the one in Nikolaev, and Phil was pleased with the relative upgrade. It was only Wednesday but it seemed as if he had been there much longer, and he needed a good night's sleep. The weather had finally cleared up and the thought of spending the night in Kiev sounded pretty appealing.

The phone in Phil's room was an old model and its ring could hardly be heard. It finally caught his attention and he rushed over to pick it up.

"Hello, please may I speak with Mr. Mens?"

"It's Mentz, and this is he."

"This is hotel manager. We have a clean woman for to come to your room. You want I send her up?"

This didn't make any sense and he wasn't sure if he had understood what was said. Phil had just checked in about two hours before so there was no need for his room to be cleaned. "My room's clean. Can you repeat what you said?"

"I am hotel manager. You want me send clean woman for your room tonight?"

"You mean a woman to clean the room?"

"Mr. Mens, I ask you want clean woman for your room tonight."

"No thank you." Phil hung up and immediately called the operator. "Can you connect me to your hotel manager please?"

"Hello, can I help you?"

"Yes, did you just call my room?"

"No sir. Why?"

"Is there another hotel manager or someone who would call and identify himself as the manager?"

"No, it's just me sir. Is there something wrong?"

"No. Thanks for your help." Phil hung up and thought about the call. They'd asked for him by name, or at least something that sounded like his name, so it probably wasn't a mistake. He wondered if the caller worked in the hotel. Although most of the staff spoke English, some were not as proficient as others, and he could have misunderstood what they had said. But it sounded as if someone was offering him a woman for the evening, and he had no idea who would do that or why anyone would want to. All kinds of thoughts raced through his mind, and it made him recall what Debra Jennings had said about her concerns when she was having trouble getting though to Kavi. Phil had made it a point to tell his crew this wasn't a James Bond movie. Yet here he was in the heart of Ukraine, about to meet the US ambassador, accompanied by a five-foot tall, chain-smoking Frenchman, and wondering if someone was trying to set him up.

* * * *

The US embassy was a good thirty-minute cab ride across town. About halfway there Maurice asked, "Phil, you a George Bush man?"

"I didn't vote for him, if that's what you're asking."

"So you're against the war in Iraq?"

"No. Actually I support what we're doing there."

"Why, because they might hurt you? You hit them in 1990. Don't you think they would have done something by now?"

"After September 11 we couldn't wait to find out. That's what I believe anyway."

"What does September 11 have to do with it? Iraq wasn't involved. Americans are funny. People are killed all the time and all over the world. That's not news. People die in the US and all hell breaks loose."

"Let me guess, you're against the war. What a shock that someone from France is against the war."

"Chirac had it right. There was no reason to fight." Maurice turned his head to admire a cute woman in a short skirt. She was walking along the street in the opposite direction. "Take a look at that!"

Phil ignored Maurice's latter comment. "I suppose his position had nothing to do with France's business interests in Iraq."

"The US plays that up, but it's a lot less than you know. The only reason Bush went to war was to help his father with unfinished business."

Phil was going to respond but thought he had said too much already. As the taxi pulled over it was clear which building was the US Embassy. Aside from the US flag there was incredible security. The taxi had to let them out more than a block away.

As a French citizen, it took Maurice longer than Phil to clear security, but he finally made it through. A young woman, who looked more like a man, escorted the two of them to the ambassador's office on the third floor. On the walk down the hall they couldn't help but notice the great many pictures of President Bush.

"There's your man." Maurice put his hand on Phil's shoulder as he spoke. "Did you know you can't walk more than ten feet in any US Embassy without seeing another picture of the sitting President? In France, we figure one or two pictures per building will do. Say Phil, you ever wonder what they do with all those pictures when there's a new President?" Before Phil could answer, they were greeted by the ambassador, Andrew Westmoreland, and a member of his staff, Michael Walker.

They sat down in ornate red leather chairs surrounding an antique white marble table, which was little more than five feet away from a life sized picture of President Bush. Maurice winked at Phil after they had simultaneously eyed the picture.

"Gentlemen, I want to thank you for getting my office involved with your, shall we say, dilemma." The ambassador was a tall and well built man who spoke with a formal style that was in sharp contrast with that of Maurice Granville. His deep voice and stoic look added to the formality. "Until you called, we had surprisingly little involvement with ADG's activities here in Ukraine but are pleased to be involved now. As Michael will explain, we have done some research that may be of interest to you."

Mike organized his notes on the table. "We've had suspicions about VKB for some time now. They certainly get around. They've been on the radar screen in a number of ex-Soviet republics, including Russia, Belarus and here in Ukraine. When you called, we checked again with our embassies there. We had work in process being led out of Moscow, and we decided to speed things up."

"How long have you had these suspicions?" Phil asked

Mike looked over at the ambassador, turned back to Phil and replied, "Let's just say from this office's perspective we became aware of their activities some time after you began construction work at your project."

"So what have you guys learned so far?" Maurice asked.

Mike replied, "I can't share all the details but I can tell you we have reason to believe VKB is controlled by two or more individuals who were senior members of the Soviet KGB. They have ties to various government officials and apparently have their strongest influence in Belarus and here in Ukraine."

Phil asked, "Can you tell us any names?"

"We're not at liberty to share that with you. Not right now, anyway." Mike flipped through his notes, then continued, "We also understand these individuals are making a major push for more influence in Russia. They're competing with some rival factions and they need more money to succeed. Apparently they've been pushing to get it from their affiliates such as VKB."

"That's explains why VKB has been pushing us." Maurice said.

"That's right, and it's not surprising your project has had certain licensing problems in conjunction with their requests." Mike studied the last few pages of his notes and apparently decided against sharing their contents. "Of course, there's a lot more to this, but I think I've given you the big picture."

The ambassador stood up and walked to a solid oak table laden with what looked like enough vodka to satisfy the whole embassy staff, although it was clearly his private stash. He offered the group a drink and poured himself a glass. When he finished, he said, "Gentlemen, at this time I must tell you we have been contacted by the Department of Justice."

The room became so quiet they could hear the ambassador's assistant tapping away at her computer keyboard, even though the door to his office was closed. Phil and Maurice found themselves staring at the picture of President Bush, and thinking that a glass of vodka wouldn't be so bad after all. Phil had informed the DOJ about developments before he left for the trip, so it made sense for them to get involved. But he was still startled to hear the ambassador mention that they had called.

The ambassador returned to his chair, sat down and crossed his legs. They waited for him to speak but he savored his drink and remained silent. It seemed clear he was waiting for a reaction from Maurice or Phil.

Phil broke the ice and said, "I called and informed them about our suspicions and our plans on how to address them. They thanked me for telling them early in the process and assured me that no action will be taken until we have had a chance to evaluate the results of our trip."

The ambassador smiled and said, "You have nothing to fear from the US Embassy. We are here to help." He took another drink and said, "It is safe to say that the Embassy's objectives in this matter are consistent with those of ADG. We would like to see your project completed and placed in operation as soon as possible."

Maurice sat back in his chair and looked relieved. He shook his head and said, "Sounds good to me. It's a great project and I'm sure you're aware of the strategic importance of new power sources in Nikolaev. Believe me, they need our plant. So how can you help?"

Mike replied, "We've always discouraged government corruption." He began to organize his notes and put them away as he spoke. "We want US companies to be competitive in Ukraine, and we've had some success. Your project will be on the agenda when we meet next week with Ukraine's president."

"So you'll tie up US aid unless they do the right thing for us?" Maurice asked.

"Keep in mind we can't support a specific commercial project. But we do evaluate a country's ability to create a competitive environment, free of government corruption, when we consider US aid. We'll reemphasize that point at our meeting next week. Also, there are other ways we can have some influence. All things considered, I'll bet it will be easier to address your licensing problems after our meeting next week."

The ambassador stood up and said, "Of course the Department of Justice has a different mission and we have nothing to do with that. We may provide them certain background information about Ukraine from time to time. However, you should be assured that we will not share information you volunteer about ADG. We don't want to discourage US corporations from seeking our help."

They exchanged pleasantries, then Phil and Maurice were escorted past security and out of the building. Although it was about 6 pm, it was so bright outside it seemed more like noon. Kiev is actually as far north as Quebec, and the days were very long in July.

As soon as they stepped into the taxi to head back to the hotel, Maurice asked, "You think he was trying to tell us something about the DOJ?"

"No. I think he was being sincere. He just wanted us to know they had called."

"You think the DOJ will do anything with this?"

Phil wasn't sure what to make of Maurice's interest in the DOJ, so he decided to keep his views close to the vest. "You never know. We just need to be prepared for whatever they do."

Phil thought things had gone well at the US Embassy, but that was to be expected. They do try to help US companies compete in local markets and would have no interest in embarrassing the local government with suspicions of bribery. Instead, they would prefer to keep things stable, and stability in Ukraine would be enhanced by completion of the Nikolaev power plant. On the other hand, the DOJ had a much different agenda. Phil wondered if they would think Maurice knew or should have known more about VKB. If yes, then they could follow-up aggressively. And after having met Maurice for the first time, Phil was afraid that he knew the answer and it wouldn't be good.

Later in the evening, Phil decided to try his luck with a restaurant near the hotel that specialized in local cuisine. Maurice was on his way to the airport to catch a late flight to Frankfurt, so Phil was on his own, unless he decided to find a 'clean woman for his room.' The perogis he ordered weren't healthy, but they tasted great.

Before leaving for dinner, Phil had thought about calling Kevin Baker to see how things were progressing in Nikolaev. He decided to wait until after dinner and figured Kevin would have called if anything was urgent. As Phil was eating, he suddenly realized he had turned his cell phone off during the afternoon meetings and had forgotten to turn it back on. When he did, he noticed he had missed a call from Kevin, so he immediately dialed his number. "You called? Sorry my phone was off."

"Where are you now?" Kevin asked.

"In a restaurant near the hotel."

"Maurice there with you?"

"No, he left for the airport. Why?"

"We've learned some things about him today. I feel uncomfortable discussing it over the phone."

"I plan to get back to Nikolaev before noon tomorrow. Fill me in when we meet."

Chapter 5

It was late afternoon on Monday, July 21, and Marc's mind was growing numb. He loved working on acquisitions, but the reality was that many aspects of the work were downright boring, and his client's pharmaceutical company transaction had hit a boring stage. By his count, he had proofread the acquisition agreement more than twenty times since Friday morning, and he wasn't sure if his mind was seeing what should be on the page or what was actually there. It had reached the point where any interruption would be welcome, when he was handed an urgent message from Kavi. He quickly left the conference room where he had been working, and returned the call from his office.

A few blocks away at ADG, things were anything but boring, and Kavi would have been thrilled to work on an acquisition. Instead, he was busy poring over seven years of financial reports for the Far East merchant power group when Marc returned his call. After getting back from Ukraine, Yu Cheng had wasted no time requesting L&K site visits to the fifteen largest plants in the power group, and Kavi and his staff were struggling to get the trips organized. On top of that, Phil and his team also made it back over the weekend and they had their own follow-up requirements.

Kavi threw some papers aside and grabbed the phone. "Tell me again. If Maurice was involved with bribes, it's a criminal offense and the Department of Justice gets involved, right?"

"Right, and from what we learned last week, he *is* in trouble. Phil went over this on Friday's call, so why are you asking again?"

Before replying, Kavi took a quick look at the note from his assistant. "I got a message to call a Gary Bevins from the enforcement division of the Securities and

Exchange Commission. It says it's regarding Nikolaev. So why would the SEC get involved?"

"I don't know. Let me follow up with one of my guys and get back to you"

"Just what we need, another government agency on our backs."

"Let's not get carried away," Marc said. "It may be nothing."

"Well I sure hope so. We're inundated with work as it is. Just the logistics for L&K's trips are enough to keep us busy all week. I'll see if I can talk them out of it."

"You should let them go. I think it makes sense to check out other projects to see if the problems go beyond Ukraine. And with what we're learning about Maurice, I'd brace myself for more bad news if I were you."

"You trying to cheer me up?"

"I just want you prepared for the worst. By the way, what's going on with the draft press release?"

"That's a royal pain. Everybody has an opinion and we're getting nowhere. One way or another we've got to get something out, before this leaks on its own. We just don't know what to say about Maurice. Sure everything points to him knowing what VKB was doing, but we still need to give him a fair hearing."

"Whatever you do, you'd better do it soon. If the story leaks, you'll be forced to play catch up and you don't want that. Anyway, let me check with my guys and I'll get back to you about the SEC."

A young administrative assistant was standing outside Marc's door waiting for his call to end. When it did, she handed him a draft of Phil's confidential trip report. Although Phil had discussed some of the key findings on a conference call before he left Ukraine, it was still interesting to read the actual report:

> *The evidence strongly supports a conclusion that senior Ukrainian government officials received funds indirectly from the project, through VKB......*We estimate the subcontractors will bill VKB approximately $40 million for their work. A normal commercial markup would vary anywhere from $4 to $8 million. VKB directly performed work worth an estimated $5 million. Together, these elements support total charges of between $49 to $53 million, as compared to VKB's original estimate of $75 million and their revised estimate of $125 million......The licensing problems for the project coincided with communications from VKB concerning additional fees......The US Embassy reported that the US government has reason to believe VKB and their affiliates have made improper payments to senior Ukrainian government officials......

> *There is evidence the head of the business unit, Maurice Granville, may have been aware of the payments and their benefit to the project*……Six senior members of the local project staff indicated, each in separate interviews, their understanding that Maurice Granville was aware of VKB's payments to senior Ukrainian government officials……Two persons indicated their participation in meetings with VKB, with Maurice Granville in attendance, at which time payments to specific Ukrainian government officials were discussed……Certain of these individuals expressed surprise the head office of ADG was unaware of the payments………

The team had done great work and it was accurately reflected in the report, but it wasn't good news. The situation in Ukraine was becoming reasonably clear, the law had been broken, somebody had to take the fall, and Maurice was the likely guy. But he was a successful business unit head and had been with the company for many years. There was a chance he'd cause significant damage on his way out the door.

After glancing through the draft, Marc decided to walk down the hall to the office of Craig Markowitz, a partner in the securities and capital markets group with significant experience dealing with the SEC. After giving him about fifteen minutes of background information, Marc said, "So Maurice is on the hot seat, and we expect the Department of Justice to start a criminal investigation once they get the results of Phil's trip. But this should have nothing to do with the SEC. You see any reason for them to get involved?"

"Of course. And for any number of reasons." Craig took a deep breath and leaned forward in his chair. "For one thing, ADG's finance arm continually issues publicly traded debt. If the proceeds were used at the project, then the SEC may challenge the disclosures in the most recent registration statement. I suspect it's safe to say it makes no mention of bribery as a use of funds."

"That seems like a real stretch to me. Kavi and his staff knew nothing about any bribes and they're the ones who uncovered this mess. Don't you think they'd have to have some knowledge to be held responsible?"

"You're right from their perspective, but the company would still have exposure, and it's something the SEC would handle. There is something else, and it may be a problem for your friend. I'm not an accountant, but I'm sure all the money ADG spent on the project is being shown as an asset on their books."

"Sure. ADG owns sixty percent of the project entity, so all of its assets and liabilities are included in ADG's consolidated balance sheet, and money spent on construction is shown as an asset, as construction work in progress. So what's wrong with that?"

"Well, you have money spent on illegal bribes being recorded as assets on their books. That's what's wrong with that. The assets are overstated."

"Craig, I know we're talking about tens of millions of dollars, but for ADG, that's immaterial."

"If it were up to me I'd agree with you, but these days it doesn't matter. The SEC likes to argue that a penny a share in any quarterly report can be material. Their new definition of materiality started about five years ago, and things are even tougher now."

"Materiality aside, again, Kavi had no knowledge of any illegal payments," Marc said, sounding more and more like a defense attorney arguing on behalf of his client. "I can't see any way he could be held responsible."

"I'm not saying there is a problem," Craig said. "I'm just saying this is something that would be investigated by the SEC and not by the Department of Justice. And if they pursue it, your CFO friend will be involved. I agree the dollars are relatively small and his lack of knowledge is important."

Marc smiled and said, "Sorry, I came to you for advice and now I'm shooting the messenger. What you said is helpful." He started getting up to leave, but Craig asked him to wait.

"There's another thing you need to worry about," Craig said. "I've had experience with Gary Bevins. He's a young bulldog in their enforcement division, and I don't like the idea that he's the one who called. He's got a big ego and is trying to make a name for himself."

"I would assume the SEC wouldn't give him any leeway if it relates to a company like ADG."

"Normally I would agree with you, but these days you can't be sure about their motives. The last few years they've taken a lot of heat over lax enforcement, and the recent mutual funds scandal has given them another black eye. Once again they were beaten to the punch by the New York Attorney General's office. Congress has been very critical of the SEC's enforcement staff and it's made me think they might look for some high profile cases to show they can still be effective."

"I hear you, and unfortunately what you say makes sense." Marc looked down at the floor and took a deep breath. Then he stood up to leave. "Well I had better get back to Kavi. He can't keep the SEC waiting."

"He should just return the call. If the SEC is getting involved, he has no choice but to cooperate."

* * * *

"This keeps getting better all the time." Kavi's voice couldn't hide his frustration as Marc shared the information he had learned from his colleague. "I've got bribes to government officials. I've got a business unit leader we may have to send on a permanent leave of absence. I've got auditors ready to climb over every power project. I've got the Department of Justice. Now I've got the SEC coming after me. Did I miss something?"

"We're not saying they're coming after you." Marc said. "We're just telling you what *could* happen."

"Sure, but even without the SEC, I can't get anything done. And you know I can't delegate any of this Nikolaev crap. I actually do have some *other* things to do, and my wife would like to see me every now and then."

"Try to calm down before you call Gary. He can make things worse for you, so you need to be very cooperative, and try not to overreact to anything he says."

"So I shouldn't tell him to go to hell?"

"No."

"I know, I'll say I'll get Ken to kick his ass."

"Not good."

"What if I say the Redskins suck?"

"For a minute, I was beginning to worry about you."

"I'll be ok. I'm just getting tired of dealing with this. If I could just spend a long weekend with Aarti. She's getting a little upset with me."

"Keep your fingers crossed, and maybe this will start blowing over soon."

"Don't worry about Gary. I'll treat him like he's my best friend. I'll even give him a Redskins sweatshirt."

"Now don't go off giving gifts to the SEC."

"By the way, I think we finally agreed on the press release and can get something out tonight."

"What'd you do with Maurice?" Marc asked.

"We punted. We're going to say what we know. We're over budget at one of our plants and have evidence that some of the funds were earmarked for improper payments to government officials. We've contacted the relevant authorities and will cooperate fully with their investigation. We'll say the impact on our financial statements of any necessary adjustments is expected to be immaterial. That's it. There's no reason to mention Maurice until we or the authorities decide to take some action."

"That seems like the right way to go. The last thing you want is a lawsuit from him saying he was libeled. That would be ironic, wouldn't it?"

"We'll be slow and deliberate. We'll let the DOJ do their work and let the chips fall where they may. By the way, we all think Phil did a great job. I didn't like the results, but they are what they are."

"Thanks, I'll be sure to pass that along. Let me know how things go with Gary, and whatever you do, be careful."

Chapter 6

It was Tuesday, July 22nd, and I arrived at my office around 6 pm, after having spent way too much time with a client reviewing their plans to address Sarbanes-Oxley. That's the unofficial name for a law enacted in 2002 that, among other things, forced senior financial executives to take more responsibility for their public company's financial statements. Although some people didn't like the new rules, they had to comply. And in case they didn't plan on being good sports, the new law added additional financial penalties, and significantly increased prison terms for noncompliance.

Congress enacted Sarbanes-Oxley in reaction to the financial misdeeds of a relatively small group of companies, but the new rules applied to all publicly traded firms, including those that had been playing by the rules all along. They were forced to do more work and take on significant additional costs, including increased audit fees from accounting firms like mine. That was somewhat ironic because Congress thought we should have done more to uncover the financial frauds in the first place, but instead of acting as a punishment, the new law actually rewarded us with all the new work.

The legislation created an uncertain environment because many of the new rules were unclear, and, with the penalties and increased prison terms, the consequences of getting it wrong were significant. That's one reason I was troubled when Marc told me about the SEC's interest in ADG.

There was plenty of work that I needed to get done that day, and the fact that I arrived at my office late didn't help. But after reading an account of ADG's press release I wanted to speak with Kavi to see where things stood, so I decided to call him before doing anything else.

He sounded rushed when he picked up, and asked me to hold the line. Getting back on, he asked, "What's up pal?"

"I was wondering what kind of reaction you got from your press release."

"Did you check out our stock?"

"No. I was at a client all day and just got back to the office."

"It closed at 63, down 3."

"That's not so terrible, is it?"

"It wouldn't be if the broad market was down, but it closed way up, and we're down below 63 in after-hours trading. It appears the market doesn't know what to make of this. We're just hoping it holds steady, so tomorrow will be key."

"Is there anything I can do?"

"Yeah, call some of your friends at L&K and tell them to get off my back." Kavi put me on hold again and then came back on the line. "After we issued our press release, it was leaked that they're checking other power projects, and that hasn't helped. They've been a real pain with everything they've done."

"You don't think they'll find more problems, do you?"

"I don't think so, but then again, who knows? Anyway, there's a lot more that happened yesterday and today. I now have to deal with the enforcement division of the SEC. You ever deal with a Gary Bevins?"

"No, but Marc called me, so I know about the SEC. Did you speak with the guy?"

"Yeah, this morning, and he wants to meet by the end of the week. Maybe I'll suggest Saturday. After all, I've got nothing else to do, right?"

"Any idea what he wants?"

"I couldn't tell from the call."

"Sounds like you've got your hands full. Sure wish I could help."

"Just help me get my old job back when ADG fires my ass."

"We'd take you back in a heartbeat."

"And buy some of our stock."

"You think it's a good investment?"

"Why not? But if the SEC is tapping this call, for the record, I was just joking!"

Getting off the line, I quickly checked and had thirty new emails, six new voicemails, and the inbox on my desk was full. Someone I really respected had once told me that eighty percent of email messages will be superceded by newer ones within two days, so he'd wait a few days and wind up deleting the older messages while catching up with the most recent ones. But client service people made it a habit to respond promptly, and since I was one of them, it looked as if I wouldn't be going home anytime soon.

Just then the phone rang, and I wondered if the 'wait to respond' theory applied to live calls. But I thought it could be Kim, so I had to pick up. Instead it was Ken.

"Hey Carl, did you check out ADG's stock today?"

"Your ears must be ringing. I just spoke with Kavi and he filled me in."

"Remember what I said at dinner? About how stocks get killed by scandals?"

"Did you say something about that? I thought you were just looking at women."

"Oh yeah. Remember that gal Sharon I was talking to?"

"You mean the blonde?" I asked.

"Right. She called and wants to meet me for a drink."

"You plan on asking your wife to join you?"

"She doesn't drink."

"I forgot. By the way, this is North America, so you need to behave." I was referring to Ken's philosophy, called 'the other continent rule.' He said if you and your wife were not on the same continent, then making love to another woman was not technically cheating. I think he got the idea from a former President.

"Talking about women, how are you doing with Kim? Did you dump her yet?"

"I'm using reverse psychology and it's still in process. I just keep telling her how great she is and how much I want to be with her. That's been my sure fire way of getting rid of women in the past, and it's working with her."

"Carl, you never listen. You lost when you told her how you feel. Women want what they can't have, and don't want what they can have. And if this makes no sense to you, it's because you're a guy. Call her and tell her to get lost, and I guarantee she'll call back next week wanting to get married. You'll see."

"Sounds like great advice, but did you ever think women go after you because you bench press four hundred pounds? I can't do more than one fifty."

"So you're a wimp."

"Did you call to discuss women?"

"Is there anything else?" Ken finally decided to get serious and said, "It's really something about ADG. I spoke to Marc on Friday, so I know some of the story."

"Well, it's worse now. The enforcement division of the SEC wants to get involved."

"Because of Ukraine?"

"That's right."

"Thank heaven I only deal with the IRS. It's funny, they have such a bad reputation. People think they're a bunch of bullies who can just walk in and take your property without asking, but in reality they're probably the only government agency without any hidden agenda. They do just what they say they'll do, and they follow the rules. That's their problem. They follow the rules, while companies pay high-powered folks like Marc and me to bend them."

"Don't include Marc with you. He's very conservative, and I don't think he likes some of the things you've done at NV Industries."

"It's all legal. Like that movie *The Right Stuff*. We just push the outside of the envelope. Although if we screw up, we don't crash and burn."

"From what I hear, it must be an awfully big envelope. Talk about the right stuff, I remember that airplane deal you did. Let's see if I've got this right. The plane had already been leased for most of its useful life, so you paid about $12 million to buy the residual value. Nonetheless, you got to deduct $100 million for tax purposes because that's what the original owner had paid for it."

"So what's wrong with that? Remember, the original owner was a foreign company, and we structured it perfectly, so it was legal. It's funny though, if you mess around with your tax return and deduct $100 of contributions you never made, you save about $30 and are guilty of tax fraud, a criminal offense. We did our airplane deal and saved about $30 million, and it was perfectly legal."

"Maybe one day I'll understand that."

"It makes perfect sense to me. Anyway I don't envy Kavi. Those guys in the enforcement division can be pretty rough, and these days, it's even worse."

Ken's call had put me further behind, and though I should have forced myself to get right to work, I couldn't help but think about Kim. And with thoughts of her permeating my mind, I couldn't think about anything else. Ken was right about one thing. I should have given up with her long ago. But that was easier said than done. She was beautiful—and I mean really beautiful—and that's why I had a hard time saying goodbye. In fact, that's why I had met her in the first place. I was at a client's offices, in the elevator, and just before the doors closed, she darted in, accompanied by her naturally blond hair, sparkling blue eyes, and great looking legs. It was just the two of us, and for any guy with a little self confidence, it was the perfect opportunity to strike up a conversation and see where it would lead. But I just remained silent and stared at the ceiling. Although I was alert enough to check for the name of the company on the wall when she walked out, and followed up afterwards to get their number. I called and described Kim, and was sure they'd hang up, thinking I was a weirdo, but instead they put me right through. I'll never forget the conversation. I was an adult but felt more like a 14 year-old kid.

"Hello, I don't mean to bother you and I realize this may sound a little strange. Are you wearing a navy blue skirt that comes down around your knees, with a beige top, and did you just get off the elevator about ten minutes ago?"

"What are you, a peeping Tom? What color are my shoes, and who's calling?"

"I think they're blue. Did you notice a guy in the elevator with you?'

"Yeah, some creepy fat guy. What about it?"

At that point I had nothing to lose. "Creepy? Maybe, but I don't think I'm fat. Perhaps a few pounds overweight. Well, I was that guy, and, although we only spent about a minute together, I was really impressed with the way you handled yourself. You know, you can tell a lot about people in elevators. Anyway, I was wondering if I could buy you dinner or drinks, preferably with me present."

There was silence on the line, and I was prepared for the dial tone to kick in, when she amazed me by saying, "Sure. I've met a lot of guys over the years, but I've never met anyone in an elevator."

We agreed to meet for drinks the following week. But when I walked over to the place, I kept thinking it was a crazy thing to do—knowing absolutely nothing about her, except how she handled herself in an elevator—and what if we learned in the first few minutes that it was a complete bust? Fortunately, as it turned out, we had a lot in common and had a pretty decent time.

When we first started dating, I did my best not to get too excited. After all, she was smart, interesting, and had the great looks, so I thought there was no way she would really be interested in me. And she had also been dating another guy, although I didn't know much about him or how close they really were. So I knew if I didn't watch myself, I would fall head over heels, and that would just set me up for big trouble when she decided she had had enough.

Her two brothers had wanted to meet 'the elevator guy,' so one day we all met at a bar and were playing darts for about an hour, and then she started getting affectionate really affectionate—and the more I tried to slow her down, the more she'd try to do, and then she whispered in my ear that she'd broken up with the other guy. It was more than I could handle and, after that, I couldn't stop thinking about her.

The following Saturday, the two of us had dinner and then trekked to the Real Review, a cozy jazz club in lower Manhattan where the people are packed in, up close and personal with the performers. Of course Kim looked gorgeous, smelled great, and couldn't keep her hands off of me. The music was wonderful too. It was a great time and I thought things couldn't get any better, and I was right.

The next week she started saying things that I had heard women say so many times before, and in any language meant that she wanted to back off. After a few weeks of sitting alone on Saturday nights listening to Frank Sinatra, I began to get the message.

Having wasted my time thinking about her, I cleared my head and got ready to deal with my messages and other work. It was already 8 pm, so it made sense to finally get busy.

Chapter 7

Gary Bevins insisted the first meeting be limited to himself, Kavi Chander and Steve Halpern. They agreed to meet at ADG's offices on Friday morning, July 25, and when Gary arrived he was escorted into the conference room on the 50th floor. At first blush he didn't look very imposing. He was 29 years old and looked even younger. And he stood just 5 foot 6, with an average build. But despite his appearance, he was a bulldog who could latch onto an assignment and never let go until the job was done.

Although Gary had been with the SEC for only four years, he was already known as one of the best agents in the enforcement division. He knew how to make important friends and had managed to get assigned to a number of high profile cases. The results were outstanding, and he quickly proved himself deserving of the plum assignments. He was a tireless worker who coupled savvy political skills with a keen legal mind. His undergraduate major was in political science and he'd graduated from Georgetown Law School number two in his class. Although people in the division believed he wanted a long-term career within the SEC, his real interest was politics, and every assignment had to provide some meaningful contribution to his ultimate objective, high political office.

It was no surprise the powers-that-be picked Gary for the assignment. There was no love lost between the current Republican administration and ADG. The company had a long history of support for the Democrats, and Charles Goodman and other key members of the board had done all they could to support the Democratic candidate in the last election. In fact, they were the ones who spearheaded the effort to organize a crack legal team in support of the fight over initial election results. The SEC also had other reasons to aggressively pursue the company. As others had surmised, a high profile case against a major company like ADG would go a long way toward improving the agency's battered reputation.

Wasting no time with small talk, as soon as Gary introduced himself he said, "I thought it would be helpful to meet as a small group. As I'm sure you can appreciate, this is a very serious matter and I would like to ensure we have your full cooperation before we begin our work."

Kavi wasn't sure what to make of the guy, but quickly responded. "We alerted the government as soon as we learned there might be a problem. I think that's darned good evidence of cooperation, don't you?"

"That remains to be seen, Mr. Chander."

"Call me Kavi."

Gary opened his briefcase and took out two folders. One had copies of a three-page action plan which included a list of staff and a timetable for specific work. The other had copies of a fifteen-page document labeled 'Request for Information.' He handed out a copy of each.

"As you can see, I plan to bring a full team here Monday. We have a tight schedule and—"

Before he could continue, Kavi interrupted, "This says you want everything by Monday morning."

"That's correct, Mr. Chander. As I was beginning to say, we have a rather tight schedule and will need this information when we start our work."

"You do know it's Friday. I'm sure you can understand our people are somewhat busy right now." Kavi spoke as he flipped through the fifteen pages of the Request for Information.

Gary paused to get Kavi's full attention. "Yes, but as I said, this is a very important matter."

Steve glanced over at Kavi and shrugged his shoulders. He looked back at Gary and said, "You mean our Nikolaev construction project is an important matter."

"Nikolaev is certainly a part of our work."

Kavi asked, "What do you mean a *part* of it?"

"Mr. Chander, as you can see from the document in front of you, only a portion of our work relates to Nikolaev. We need to look at the accounting for every project in your Far East merchant power group."

Steve protested, "There's no evidence whatsoever of any problem beyond Nikolaev."

"I understand you have a full team of Larson & Kirsh auditors at many other sites. Is that correct?"

"That's right. That's one of the reasons we've been so busy. We've had to scramble this week with all the logistics." Steve was talking as if he and his staff were the ones doing the work, when, in reality, it was Kavi and his people. "L&K is a couple of days into their work and so far we've heard of no additional problems. They just wanted to cover all the bases."

"That's what we have to do. Cover all the bases, so to speak." Gary paused to make some notes. He looked up and said, "You already have an accounting problem with Nikolaev. Now we want to look at other things."

Kavi couldn't believe what he was hearing. He laughed and asked, "What do you mean we already have an *accounting* problem with Nikolaev?"

"Presumably all the money spent on the project is being shown as an asset on your books, as construction work in process. That means that any project money that found its way into the hands of Ukrainian government officials is being shown as an asset. Well, that means you overstated the true construction costs and overstated the construction asset on your books and records. That money should have been reported as an expense."

"I'll make sure to change our accounting policy for bribes as soon as I leave this meeting. Maybe we should also look at our mafia payoffs. You got any ideas how to account for those?"

Steve winced at Kavi's attempt at humor. He waited to see if Gary was going to respond. When he didn't, Steve said, "Whatever you think about Nikolaev, there's no problem with our other plants."

"A few months back you didn't think you had a problem in Ukraine and now you do. We can't assume your accounting problems are limited to Nikolaev just because you think everything else is ok. We have a responsibility to look further. Among other things, this includes looking at your other power projects."

Kavi was once again puzzled. He rubbed his forehead and asked a question slowly, as if he was afraid to get the answer. "What do you mean *among other things?*"

"When we become aware of an accounting problem, we check to see if there is a pattern of irregularities, in which case we expand our work. We can't assume your problems are limited to the power group. As you can see from the document, some of the information requests have nothing to do with that group."

Kavi looked again at the Request for Information and could see it covered much more than just the power group. The meeting was not going well, and he thought things couldn't get much worse.

They continued meeting for about an hour, at which point Gary removed a third document from his briefcase. "I think this is a good time to cover this. We think you're required to inform the public about our investigation. Here's suggested wording. We think it's pretty straightforward."

Kavi and Steve were both surprised. The draft language indicated the SEC had begun an investigation into accounting irregularities at ADG as a consequence of the recent discovery of improper payments at a construction project in Nikolaev, Ukraine.

Steve wiped his brow and took a deep breath. "Gary, bribing foreign government officials is a criminal matter under the jurisdiction of the Department of Justice. You're saying it's also an accounting issue subject to the jurisdiction of the SEC. We think that's being hyper technical. Of course, if the SEC wants to review our records, you're free to do so at any time and we'll cooperate fully. But to suggest we issue a press release that makes it seem as if you found real accounting irregularities, well, I just think that's inappropriate."

"It's also very bad timing," Kavi said, speaking louder and faster than normal. "We issued our first press release about Nikolaev on Monday, when our stock was at 66. Yesterday it closed at 61. It started slightly up this morning, so we think the worst may be over. Now, if we mention an SEC investigation and accounting irregularities, our stock will take another hit. And these days it takes a long time to recover."

Once again Gary took some time to make notes before responding. In the silence, Kavi thought he could hear one of the veins in his neck getting ready to burst. It never did, and Gary finally said, "Gentleman, the SEC can't be concerned with the impact of required disclosures on your stock price. While we can't make you issue the release, we believe it is required and will consider what you do as part of our investigation." Gary began to pack his materials while he continued to speak. "Regarding the accounting issue, we're not being hyper technical. ADG is required to prepare and issue accurate financial statements. That includes a responsibility to make sure only proper amounts are recorded as assets. It was your responsibility to uncover the improper payments."

Kavi had a good hundred pound weight advantage and knew he could kick Gary's ass if he wanted to, and he could see the headlines now: 'CFO of ADG in fist fight with SEC, wins with TKO in the fourth.' It didn't seem like a career enhancing move so he decided to keep his hands to himself, but he did take a moment to imagine what it would be like to separate Gary's head from his body. He knew he had to leave Gary's body intact, and he also knew, with all things considered, ADG would be forced to issue the SEC's suggested press release. It seemed wise to avoid any confrontation, so Kavi said that he and his staff would do their best and would be prepared to facilitate the SEC's work starting on Monday.

Gary didn't express any appreciation for the promised cooperation. He just said he'd be back with his team on Monday, and stood up to leave. After he was gone, Kavi and Steve stayed behind to talk. For a brief moment they just sat together in silence, and then Kavi broke the ice.

"Tell me the truth, is it just me, or did you think about killing that guy before he got away?"

"He did seem like a little weasel, didn't he?"

"That's an insult to little weasels. Now I know why every company seems to be under investigation by the SEC. They're on a witch hunt."

"You shouldn't joke with him. He doesn't look like the type that enjoys that sort of thing." Steve was talking about Gary, but he could just as easily have been talking about himself. "I need to tell Charles about this, and he'll probably want to update the board over the weekend."

"I need to be with you when you call Charles, but let's wait. First I need to get people going on this ridiculous information request."

Kavi stood up to walk out, but Steve asked him to wait, and after a moment of hesitation, Steve added, "It's best that I handle that. It should go through the general counsel's office."

"What's the big deal? Most of this is financial information. My people are the ones who'll get it."

"Whether we like it or not, we've got the SEC investigating our financial statements and accounting, and if they find anything, it's ultimately your responsibility. With that in mind, the company should have someone other than you coordinating the work. You know, someone with no personal stake in the outcome. I realize this looks like bullshit, but how will we look if we don't at least act as if we're taking the SEC seriously and doing what we can to facilitate their work?"

Kavi wasn't sure what to make of Steve's comments, so he took a moment to think. Steve had always been difficult to deal with, but Kavi believed it was best to pick his battles. Upon reflection, the matter seemed important enough, so he decided to stand his ground and said, "You're certainly right about one thing. This *is* bullshit. And I don't think we should go out of our way to make this look like anything more than the crap that it is. It's one thing for you to handle an investigation of bribery allegations. That's purely a legal matter, and the general counsel's office should take the lead. Here, the SEC is saying we've got accounting problems and they have no evidence of anything except Nikolaev. I don't think there's a reason for you to act as if they've got something on me."

"I'm not saying they have something on you, but I still think I should handle it. It will look better, and, as you know, looks can count."

Kavi sat back down in a chair and put his feet up on the table, and mused, "I wonder what Maurice is doing right this very minute. I'll bet he's at some fancy restaurant with some beautiful young gal, eating a fine steak and drinking some expensive red wine. I had nothing to do with anything in Ukraine, and look what I'm doing now. My staff and I have killed ourselves to get Phil's team ready and then to get the L&K guys going. Now, I'm arguing with you so I can have the privilege of working all weekend with my staff, getting ready to meet with that little SEC geek. The heck with it. If you think it's best for you to take the lead, go right ahead. I'm calling Maurice to see if I can join him, wherever he is."

* * * *

"We opened at 57, down just over 4, but we're now at 58." It was early afternoon on Monday, July 28, and Kavi was in his office doing damage control. The company had gone ahead and issued the SEC's suggested press release after the close of business on Friday, and it was having the predictable effect on ADG's stock. Kavi was on the phone with Charles Goodman, who was on a business trip in Los Angeles and had called to check in. It was good that the Chief Executive relied on Kavi, but with nothing but bad news to report, he thought it might have been better if Charles had called Steve Halpern for a change.

"This is very disturbing," Charles said, his tone of voice consistent with that of any CEO whose stock was going down the tubes. "The broad market is up and our business prospects look great. Yet our stock is down about twelve percent in a week. Tell me it's not going to get any worse."

"We did what we could, but the SEC seems hell bent on getting some good publicity at our expense. Like we said Friday, we didn't have much choice but to do what the SEC suggested."

"Kavi, we need to get on top of this and turn it around fast. I've got a pretty pissed off board of directors on my hands. They can't understand how a peanut construction project could have such an effect on our stock. It's still just Nikolaev, right?"

"We think so. The L&K guys have been at the other plants since Wednesday. I spoke with them on Friday and they hadn't found anything. They worked through the weekend and Yu Cheng assured me he would call if they found any problems. Of course you never know with L&K."

"Not that we can trust him, but what's the latest word from Maurice?"

Kavi wished he knew, and said, "He's still on that trip in the middle of China. We can't reach him, and we've been trying since we spoke with you on Friday."

"I still can't understand why he took that trip. He's responsible for this mess."

"Charles, I'm sure he thinks his days are numbered. He's probably just buying time until we take action. We've been pretty good about letting the process play out, but he knows where he stands."

"Maybe we should just fire him now and let everybody know it's his fault. That's what the board wants. It's a damned shame to lose him though. He's been a top performer."

"Nothing has changed since we talked about this last week. We'll be in better shape if we wait until the DOJ does its thing. We do need to be fair with him and not act prematurely. I'd rather act a little late than too soon. The last thing we need is a lawsuit from Maurice."

"One way or another, we need to know what we'll do with him by the end of the week." Kavi had to wait while Charles took another call. While waiting, he checked his email and noticed seven new messages had just come in, but none were from Yu Cheng or anyone else at L&K. Charles got back on the line and asked, "Anything new with the SEC this morning? No more press releases I hope."

"We spent all morning getting their group set up. Bevins has five people with him."

"Five? What the hell is he planning to do?"

"That's what I want to know, but I suspect we'll find out soon enough. You know my staff had to drop what they were doing and work all weekend getting the information Bevins wanted. That's four weekends in a row, and in the summer no less." Kavi also wanted to say it took more time than otherwise necessary because his staff had to coordinate with Steve Halpern who was supposedly 'leading' the effort, but he thought better of it.

"What about you? Are you spending any time with your wife?"

"I have a wife?" Kavi paused for effect, then continued, "Actually, Aarti and my two kids met me here on Saturday afternoon and we made an evening of it in the city. I'll tell you, I'm really getting tired of this. It's one thing to kill yourself for some great transaction but it's another thing to work on this nonsense. Maybe it will end soon. The L&K guys should finish their site visits this week, but the SEC is the real wild card. We'll keep our fingers crossed."

"Are you sure the SEC won't find anything besides Nikolaev?"

"Charles, you know how it is. Accounting is no exact science. If they plan to be reasonable, we have nothing to worry about, but if they want to make trouble they can. There's always something where ten accountants will have twelve different opinions, and the SEC has been doing a lot of second guessing lately."

"You think I should get to Washington this week and meet with a few people to nip this in the bud? Even with a Republican administration, we still have some friends there."

"Let's hold off. I admit we've got bad vibrations from Gary Bevins, but maybe he's a straight shooter. We worked pretty hard getting him set up and we did issue his suggested press release. We'll give him lots of cooperation, so maybe he'll be fair. Anyway, I'll let you know if anything changes."

"Keep me posted, and if you need me to get back there, just let me know."

* * * *

Although the week had started off badly, things seemed to be settling down. It was Wednesday morning, July 30, and Kavi still hadn't heard from Yu Cheng, and from Kavi's perspective, no news from L&K was good news, or at least it wasn't bad news. Bevins and his crew were keeping everyone busy, but their work seemed to be under control. Gary even came close to complimenting Kavi for his preparation and cooperation. And, best of all, ADG's stock price was recovering. It looked as if the worst might be over, when Marc called.

"I noticed your stock was at 60."

Kavi checked his computer to see for himself. "We're almost at 61 now. Maybe people realize the SEC has no business being here. Talking about government agencies, how's Phil doing with the Department of Justice?"

"Actually, that's been going well. They really appreciated being brought in so early. If the problem is limited to Nikolaev, then ADG should come out ok. They seem to think it didn't go any higher than Maurice."

"Well it really didn't go any higher. I can tell you that. So when do they plan to bring charges against him?"

"We're not sure they will bring charges."

"What do you mean you're not sure? It's pretty clear he knew about all this."

"It depends on a number of things. If they come after Maurice, some people may ask why they aren't going after executives at some other US companies in Ukraine. And if they go after more companies, it may get in the way of US-Ukraine relations. Who really knows? This is all beyond me. In any case they may want to keep things low key. Maybe impose a fine on him and possibly fine the company as well. One thing's for sure. All bets are off if this goes beyond Ukraine."

"You know, that makes sense, but it's still funny. This is a matter for the DOJ to handle, and they're moving slowly. This has nothing to do with the SEC, and they're all over the place, telling us to issue that bullshit press release before they even started their work."

"From what you tell me, Maurice is lucky Gary Bevins isn't with the DOJ."

"I think Maurice would do ok. He seems to know how to handle government officials. And they'd also need to find him first."

"He's still in China?"

"We assume so. We haven't heard from him since last week."

"That's incredible. He can't dodge this forever."

"I'm sure if we get the 'All Clear' from L&K and the DOJ, he'll turn up soon enough."

"You know it's a shame you have to deal with this mess. The SEC has no business being there. Bevins must have a hidden agenda."

"It certainly looked that way when Steve and I met him on Friday, but now I'm not so sure. Gary may just be bad at first impressions."

"So Steve didn't like him either?"

"Nobody can like this guy. That reminds me, after Gary left, Steve acted really strange, as if I were the one being investigated. He said he needed to take the lead so we wouldn't look bad."

"I don't like the sound of that. I think he's out of line."

"He is, but I decided to just let him have his way. It's funny though. He says he's leading this, but my staff and I do all the work, and when Charles has a question, he calls me. Go figure."

"It looks to me like he's trying to protect himself, in case there are more problems."

"I'm sure you're right, but if any new problems arise, he's the last person I'd worry about."

After the call, Kavi walked across his office and sat in his favorite chair—a plush leather recliner from which he had great views of the skyline in midtown Manhattan. Every so often, he would sit and stare into the distance to relax and clear his mind. He had been pushing hard with Nikolaev and needed a break. As he watched the clouds roll by, he thought about Marc and how it was typical of him to focus on the worst that could happen. But while his concerns were sometimes painful to hear, they did push Kavi to be better prepared. Nonetheless, it was time to close his eyes. He decided that more worrying could wait.

The rest of the day went well. ADG's stock closed at 61 ½ and there was still no word from L&K. It was 5 pm and Kavi decided to head home. He hadn't left the office before 9 pm in about a month and it was as good a day as any to break the streak. Still, he first stopped by to check with Gary to make sure he and his staff had what they needed. It was all quiet on the Western front.

During his ride home, he was just beginning to forget about work when his cell phone rang.

"Kavi, I hear you've been calling. You ready to lock me up?"

"Maurice, is that you?"

"You plan on locking up someone else?"

"Are you still in China?"

"No, I'm calling from Abidjan."

"Are you serious? What're you doing in the Ivory Coast?"

"I flew here so I could call you. The country's phone system is great."

Kavi usually liked speaking with Maurice. He didn't fit the mold of a typical ADG business unit leader—boring and stiff. He could charm the toughest audience, and had a great sense of humor. But Kavi thought this wasn't a time for jokes.

"It's bad enough you went to China," Kavi said. "This is a serious matter, and you need to be available."

"What's so serious? Did I steal from some old ladies, or spit on the sidewalk?"

"Everybody's convinced you knew about VKB."

"Of course I knew about VKB, but what they did with their money was their business. So what if a few government officials might have been paid off? Who cares? It's Ukraine. What did you think might happen there? The only thing wrong with VKB is they got greedy and held a gun to our head."

"How about Laos and Indonesia? Does it happen there?"

"How are your friends at L&K doing with their all-expense-paid trips around the world?"

"We set up a conference call for tomorrow to go over their results. I haven't heard from them since last Friday. They said they'd call if they found additional problems, but who knows with those guys."

"Maybe their phones don't work. They should fly to the Ivory Coast."

"Maurice, are you really in Abidjan?"

"Why? You think I'd lie to you?"

"Maurice. One straight answer please."

"Yes, I'm here. There's a possible project I'm checking out. Could be good for the company. They're looking at building a gas-fired plant on the coast, near the border with Ghana. It would help them get the financing they need to develop their offshore gas fields. They need the power and could export some to their neighbors."

"Can I reach you there tomorrow?"

"What do they say? Don't call me, I'll call you."

"Maurice, I must be able to reach you. We're dealing with the Department of Justice. And if we keep up the cooperation, they could be lenient. You may think Ukraine is not a big deal, but it's a criminal offense. So it's in your best interest to be on your best behavior."

"I'm at the Yellow Tulip hotel and should be here through the weekend. My secretary has the number. Call in the late afternoon or later my time, and remember there's a six hour time difference. Don't try my cell. It doesn't work here, and I'll be out during the day in meetings. Tomorrow, I'm meeting with some senior government officials to discuss the project. Don't worry. I don't have much cash with me."

Kavi wasn't sure if he should just quit while ahead. Instead, he asked, "So are there any problems at the other locations?"

"I'll tell you straight. I don't think we did anything wrong. We've been right on budget at every other location and we're one of the most profitable business units within ADG. That's not easy, operating in places like the Philippines and Malaysia. You have to know the local customs to keep things running smoothly. Everything we did was proper. Go have your call tomorrow with the L&K people. From what you said, it seems as if they agree."

Although he would have preferred a simple "no," Kavi figured the response was good enough for now, so he said, "I'll get in touch with you after the call, and let's hope you're right."

Chapter 8

It was Thursday, July 31, and the work had been piling up. A couple of my key audit client's were keeping me busy, so I made sure to get to the office early for a change. In fact, I was at my desk with orange juice, coffee, a whole wheat bagel and the Wall Street Journal, by 7 am, which was something akin to the middle of the night for me. In my case, 9 am or later was a more typical, and more comfortable, arrival time. Most of my friends and colleagues knew my work habits, and rarely called me before 9, so I was surprised when Marc called shortly after I had arrived. He was getting ready for an ADG conference call and wanted to share some of his concerns with me.

"Why are you so worried?" I asked. "That Bevins guy is stretching if he makes bribery an accounting issue. And knowing Kavi, there won't be any other issues."

"The SEC can always find something," Marc said. "And once they do, they can make it seem like a big deal. I just have a bad feeling about this."

"You have a bad feeling about everything."

"I hope you're right. Kavi doesn't seem to be too worried about it. He thinks everything's coming together."

"I'll bet it is. So, you heard anything from L&K?"

"Not since Friday, but they'll be on the conference call we've got lined up for later this morning."

"If they'd found more problems, you'd probably have heard by now." I was trying to talk, eat and read at the same time, and wasn't doing a very good job of it. My coffee almost spilled onto a document that needed to be signed and I almost took a bite out of the paper.

"I agree, but I'll feel better after the call."

"Let's assume they found nothing new. What happens next?"

"Phil thinks the DOJ will wrap things up, maybe with some small fines. He's done a great job dealing with them and it seems they prefer a low key ending. Maurice Granville may survive after all."

"So why are you so worried about a good guy like Kavi?"

"It's the SEC that worries me. And you know, the good guys are the ones who get screwed."

"That won't happen to Kavi with you around. And if I need a lawyer, it's you."

"I appreciate your confidence in me."

"I'm speaking from personal experience. Remember that time at the Costa Rica airport?"

"You mean with the security guard? Yeah, you were lucky I was there."

"That was funny. I thought I'd be arrested for sure. Nobody understood a word you were saying but you scared him away."

"Sometimes a little hot air does wonders."

"Well it worked, and it felt great getting on that plane."

I heard silence on the line and it appeared Marc had been cut off, but then he said, "That was a great trip, wasn't it?"

"Sure was. We need to plan a return visit. And I'll wear a disguise."

* * * *

The Costa Rica trip came up on the spur of the moment. It was back in 1989 and Ken and Kavi were still with the firm. Ken had just made partner and Kavi had made it a year before. But I wouldn't make it for another three years. Marc had already joined Bartman & Cross back in mid 1983. We were at the Iron Horse for our annual dinner, and the more we talked about getting away the better it sounded. It took us only two days after the dinner to organize the trip, and then we were off. We flew down on a Friday night and came back the following Wednesday. All we had planned was one day of white water rafting on Sunday, and everything else was to be improvised.

During the trip, I purchased wood carvings from a local merchant who wound up thinking that I had underpaid by $30. Somehow he managed to contact airport security on the day we were scheduled to leave, and the four of us were at the visitors' lounge when a security guard the size of a bus said he needed to take me away. That's when Marc came to my rescue by making things up about a US law that made it a criminal offense for a foreign security guard to detain an American at an airport. Marc can scare people when he doesn't want to, so he had no trouble scaring the security guard who finally decided to let me go.

Actually, I had been lucky just to get to the airport in one piece. Everybody says white water rafting is safe, but they should say that after going through a couple of class five rapids at Rio Tropicales in Costa Rica. After six hours of rafting, and thirty near-death experiences, we had gone to the hotel bar to recover. It was actually outside the hotel in the back, although part of it was covered, so you could drink while it rained. The lush forest was only about twenty feet away, and monkeys and other interesting creatures entertained the people sitting at the bar—or maybe it was the other way around.

Something that looked like a miniature Tyrannosaurus Rex was checking out my foot to see if it was edible, but I remained focused on Ken and admonished him for suggesting that we match our wits with the great rapids. "You trying to get me killed before I make partner?"

"What are you complaining about?" Ken smirked as he waved for the waitress to order a round of beer. "That was a piece of cake, and none were class fives."

I checked my body parts to see if anything was missing. After finding everything intact, I leaned forward, put my arm on Ken's shoulder and said, "You don't recall a guy, bearing a strange resemblance to me, who kept flying over to your side of the raft screaming at the top of his lungs?"

"Yeah, I'm surprised you can still talk."

"Well, the volume of my screaming matched the force of the rapids. Those were definitely class fives."

Marc had been busy massaging his feet. We had to wear special rubber shoes in the raft, and his were apparently two sizes too small. He stopped rubbing, looked up at Ken and said, "You're a great athlete. But for us mere mortals it was pretty bad. You have to admit even Brad, the so-called 'fearless guide,' freaked out when we went over that one boulder."

"That was a little scary," Kavi agreed. "I think we were supposed to steer to the left of the rock but Brad was afraid we wouldn't make it. There's been so much rain lately the rapids were faster than usual. If we kept at it and screwed up, we'd have gone over backwards so he just gave up. When your guide tells you to duck down in the boat and hold on, it's probably a good time to say your prayers."

"See, I'm not the only one who was scared." While I was talking, a couple of scantily clad young gals sat down at the table next to us. Although we all took a quick look, Ken kept staring. I looked at him and warned, "Eyes on the road. You're married, and with two little kids I might add."

"This is Central America, so I'm safe." Ken was referring to his 'other continent rule.' It was ok for him to be with other women, but I never asked if the rule also applied to his wife, who was probably back at home getting busy with the milkman. As we were talking, a couple of college-aged guys walked in and joined the young girls.

Kavi pointed in their direction. "See, Carl, that's what you need to do. We're all married with kids, but you're still free. You ought to stay over and get yourself a girl."

"I can't get a girl in the United States and I've lived there all my life. What makes you think I can get one in Costa Rica in a matter of days?"

"You can get as many as you want," Ken explained, as he pointed to a beautiful older lady at the bar. "Take a look at her, $100 and she's yours."

"How can you tell?" Marc asked.

"Isn't it obvious? They're all over the place. Hey Kavi, stop drooling."

"That's sweat," Kavi noted, leaning in toward Ken. "You know, you do seem to know a lot about these hookers. Come to think of it, where were you late last night?"

"Talk to my lawyer. Marc, back me up?"

Marc put his hands on Ken's shoulder. "I normally advise my clients to take the fifth, but with you, I want to know everything."

"Come on, guys, be nice. I just made partner." Ken got the waitress to come to our table, and interrupted his flirting just long enough to ask for menus. As he watched her walk away he smiled and said, "God, women here are beautiful."

"And so is your wife," Kavi added.

I laughed and said, "I still can't believe your wives let you come down here and play when you've got babies at home." I was a free man, but Ken had a two-year-old boy and a nine-month-old girl, and Marc had a three-month-old daughter. Kavi's were older, a seven-year-old boy and an eight-year-old girl.

It took a while to get our food, because Ken wouldn't let the waitress leave the table to place our order. But she was used to the attention and liked flirting with her male customers, and was showing more than a casual interest in Ken. When she finally returned, the food wasn't half bad. We had lucked out with the hotel. Not that it was anything fancy, and it didn't cater to tourists, but it had lots of local charm.

While taking a break from his dinner, Ken put his hands on Marc's shoulders and asked, "What's the latest with becoming a partner?"

"Everything's on track for next March," Marc said. "I've been told I've got great support so I should make it easily. The senior partner said I should keep away from the other partners until they hold the vote, because I can't make things better, I can only screw up."

"It's nice to have support," I said. "Maybe I should get a law degree and join you at Bartman & Cross."

Kavi patted me on the back and said, "Don't worry, you'll make partner soon enough. The only reason it's taking so long is your age. You're too young, not even thirty."

"I just don't understand why that should be such a big deal. Maybe they don't like my work, but I'm doing the best I can."

"The firm rarely makes anyone a partner under thirty," Marc said. "It's nothing personal. It's not fair, but it's the way it is."

"That's what you get for starting when you were nineteen," Ken said. He stopped talking briefly so he could point out what appeared to be another lady for hire. "You should have taken more time in college and fooled around with the coeds."

"Maybe it would have been better if I had sat in a closet for a couple of years and started with the firm when I was older."

Kavi added, "I know it must be tough, but just hang in there. You're as good as anyone and don't ever think you're not. I can see it. In some ways, you're better than any of us."

Ken was eyeing another "woman-of-the-evening" when he said, "Speak for yourself, big guy."

"I agree. You are really good," Marc said. "You have a great attitude, you care about your clients, and you're not political."

Kavi nodded and said, "Politics is a part of it, and you sometimes make mistakes dealing with influential partners. But your honesty is also what makes you a great audit partner. You have high integrity and the firm knows it. Your time will come. Take the long term view and be patient."

Our conversation had followed a familiar pattern, and I really wasn't looking to be consoled, so I said, "Thanks for the support, but we're here to have fun so let's change the subject." Looking to Kavi, I asked, "How's everything with your flying instruction? You plan on flying the plane for our next trip?"

He was learning how to be a pilot, and it was driving his wife crazy. Aarti was scared he'd screw up and she'd be a young widow with kids, but he insisted on it. He said he'd given up his dream of becoming an astronaut when he decided to get an accounting degree, and this would be the next best thing to being in space.

"So far, so good," Kavi replied. "My instructor says I'm a natural. I need another ten hours of flight instruction and I should be ready to get my license."

"Don't expect me to fly with you," Ken exclaimed.

"Why, you scared?" Kavi asked.

"Not of you. It's those small planes you fly. I think they're dangerous."

"Well it's probably safer than white water rafting," I said.

"Oh yeah? Remember Thurman Munson?" Ken asked. He shuddered and looked down at the table. He was referring to the great catcher for the Yankees who crashed his plane and died in 1979.

"Don't remind me," I said. "Speaking of the Yankees, you think they'll ever win another World Series?"

"Not until they get rid of their owner," Ken said. "He got lucky in the seventies but that's it. I'll bet the Mets win another five series before the Yanks win again."

"So Ken, do you ever think of what might have been if you'd made it in baseball?" Marc asked.

"I really don't think about it. This is my life now, and it's not too bad, is it? I've got a great wife and two healthy kids, and I just made partner in a great firm."

"And you get to fool around whenever you travel," Kavi added.

"I can't help it if women love me."

"So you have no regrets?" Marc asked.

"Why would I have any regrets?"

We were never sure that Ken was being honest with us and with himself. He once said he had a problem with one of his eyes, but I never saw him bothered by it. He looked so strong and athletic. If I were him, I would have spent at least a couple of years in the minors. I just couldn't imagine what it must have been like to have been so close to a dream like playing Major League baseball and to stop just short of making it. I sometimes wondered if his fanatical exercise regime and his banter about other women had something to do with him having second thoughts.

Kavi ordered a round of tequila and made a toast. "To the Iron Horse Club. After ten years, it's still going strong."

"Can you believe it's been ten years?" Marc asked.

"In some ways it seems much longer," Kavi replied. He studied his beer and laughed. "Those were the good old days, weren't they?"

I nodded and said, "I look at some of the new staff people on my jobs, and can't believe I ever did that work. Ken, remember when you and I were on the audit of the YMCA?"

"How can I forget? The Village People had just come out with their song, and whenever we told people where we were working, they started singing 'YMCA.' I came close to killing people a few times."

Marc said, "I remember when Kavi made senior after just a year and a half. It seemed like such a significant promotion at the time."

"I thought that was a big deal, but I changed my mind shortly after making it," Kavi said. "Every time I was promoted, I thought the next level would be the real promotion. But now I'm a partner and I realize that in an accounting firm, only a few people get to manage. For the rest of us, we're just staff people with fancier titles, so there really isn't any true promotion."

"Sure, but we no longer have to check inventories on December 31," Ken said.

"That was actually fun," I admitted. "One year I did an inventory of a toy manufacturer in Pennsylvania. They had all this great stuff, and I didn't mind doing it on New Year's Eve."

"That's because you didn't have a date."

"Thanks, Ken. Actually I was dating Stephanie that year. Remember her?"

"Is she the one you brought to my wedding?" Kavi asked.

"That's the one."

Kavi said, "I remember you two looked like a great couple. Everyone said they thought you were married. Whatever happened?"

"You think I know? Things were going great, and then out of nowhere she said she wanted to see other people, just to be sure about me."

"When things are going really well, women get scared," Ken said. "They think they can probably do better with someone else. You need to be the first to say you want to date other people. She'll say no and you'll wind up getting married."

"Well I had no choice. She started seeing other people and that was it. I tried to get her back but it didn't work. Anyway, we've all come a long way since then. It's been ten years. Wow. You guys are all married with kids and we can afford trips to Costa Rica."

Marc sat back in his chair and sighed. "I wonder where we'll be in 1999. You think you guys will still be with the firm?"

Kavi quickly replied, "I won't last that long. I need to manage something, and the key partners are too entrenched."

"Just make sure you take me with you when you go," I urged.

"You won't need me," Kavi said. "You'll do better than all of us."

I said, mostly to myself, "From your mouth to God's ears."

* * * *

We always had a great time on our trips, and we were overdue for another one, maybe even a return trip to Costa Rica. But first Kavi would need to clear up his little mess, as I was sure he would. And my half-eaten bagel was still waiting, so I cleared my mind and got back to the early morning agenda.

Chapter 9

It was Thursday morning, July 31, and it was time for the conference call with the L&K auditors. Marc joined Kavi on the call, along with Steve Halpern, Debra Jennings, Phil Mentz and Kevin Baker. The L&K auditors included Yu Cheng and four of his colleagues. The operator said everyone was on the line, and before Kavi had a chance to speak, Steve greeted the group and asked Yu for his report.

"First, I must tell you I'm missing the most recent updates from our teams in the Philippines and Laos, but should have them tomorrow. In Thailand things look pretty good. We're basically finished there, although the Chumphon work may take another day or two. I'm told we've had excellent cooperation and have found no evidence of anything improper at the three facilities. In South Korea we're finished, and no problems were noted at either Pusan or Kunsan."

Kavi began to feel a sense of relief. He thought L&K would have notified him earlier if they'd found any problems, but in the back of his mind he knew that might not be the case. He had given some thought to calling them daily, but figured bad news would be bad news whenever he heard it. In any case, if they had found any problems, he was certain they would have discussed it at the beginning of the call. He was wrong.

"Now I'll discuss the bad news. We think you've got major problems in Indonesia, Malaysia and Kazakhstan. In Indonesia, we first spotted problems at Lake Toba, but there's also trouble at the other three plants. We think about $100 million found its way into the hands of Indonesian government officials. There's another $20 million in Malaysia, and in Kazakhstan it's about $30 million, although we're still doing work at the Leninsk facility."

"What makes you think there's a problem with those payments?" Steve asked.

"It's pretty clear. We followed the same procedures we used at Nikolaev a few weeks back." Yu was doing his best to take credit for the action plan developed by Phil Mentz, and the effort wasn't lost on his audience. "We focused on local contractors and tied payments to specific materials or services supplied. If the payments couldn't be supported, or if they exceeded the value of the materials or services, they were noted as problems."

"And why do you think the money found its way into government hands?" Debra asked.

"That's what we were told by the local project staff, as well as certain other sources. It took some time, and a little creativity, but once our teams identified the excess payments, we were able to get the information."

Steve asked, "Do you have anything else to report?" He wasn't sure he wanted to hear the answer.

Yu paused for a moment before responding. "You should also know, based upon preliminary reports, you may have the same problems in Laos and the Philippines."

When Yu finished speaking, nobody said anything and the silence was deafening. He had stunned his audience. Then, in a slow and deliberate manner, Kavi asked, "When did you first get word of any problem?" He then put his phone on mute while he called Yu an asshole.

"I think it was Saturday, at Lake Toba."

Yu and his colleagues had known about the problems for five days, but until this call they'd given no indication that anything was wrong. Kavi thought about making a big stink, but realized it would serve no purpose and would probably make things worse. Nothing he could say would change the facts. There were problems beyond Ukraine and the dollars were starting to add up. He had expected to get a clean report, after which the DOJ would wrap up their case, and he'd focus his efforts on getting rid of the SEC. But all of that was out the window. The bribery mess would not go quietly into the night, and for the first time he started questioning himself and what he had done, and what he hadn't done, with Maurice's business unit. Missing a problem at Nikolaev was one thing, especially in a company the size of ADG, but missing problems in multiple countries was something else altogether. Kavi was disturbed and not quite sure what to do next.

Steve said, "Yu, I need to update the board of directors. But I'd like to have something in writing first. Do you have anything prepared?"

"We plan on preparing full trip reports but won't have them ready until next week."

"Just summarize what you said on the call and fax it to me. I don't want to misquote you."

"Yu, this is Phil Mentz with Bartman & Cross. Your findings are very disturbing. We were under the impression you would alert us at the first sign of any problems. Otherwise we would have insisted upon having some of our people together with ADG corporate staff join you at the sites. We would have liked more time to prepare and to coordinate appropriate next steps."

"We wanted to make sure we confirmed our findings before we got back to you," Yu said. He sounded defensive and wasn't being entirely truthful, but he had anticipated the question and had given the prepared response.

"I can appreciate that and, in any case, it's too late to change." Phil asked if he could put the call on mute. Apparently he and his Bartman & Cross colleagues needed to confer. He got back on the line and said, "We do have a number of additional concerns. For one thing, you have people at fifteen plants in seven different countries. We need to ensure your findings don't leak to the press. We are also concerned about the content of your trip reports. They're not privileged communications so they could ultimately be used against the company. I realize they're your work product and we can't tell you what to do, but would appreciate if you share a draft with us, and with the company, before you finalize anything."

"I can assure you there will be no leaks. At least not from any of my people." Reluctantly he added, "We can send you the drafts, but like you said, they're a part of *our* work papers."

They continued talking for another thirty minutes or so and scheduled a follow-up conference call for the next day. The non L&K contingent also agreed to meet in the afternoon so they could discuss appropriate next steps. When the call ended, Kavi knew he needed to have a separate conversation with Marc, and before he could dial the number, Marc was calling him.

"This is serious," Marc said. "I can't believe they didn't say anything sooner."

"Not much we can do about it now. Got any great ideas?"

"No ideas, just some thoughts. You'll almost certainly need another press release, and the DOJ is going to get tough and I'm sure Gary Bevins won't ratchet down his work. We need to start thinking about protecting you."

"This really sucks, doesn't it?"

"I had a bad feeling about Maurice," Marc said. "Didn't he tell you there were no problems beyond Nikolaev?"

"He said he didn't think he did anything wrong, and I chose not to push him. You know, I'll bet he really believes that." Kavi paused. He was thinking about Maurice and how successful he had been, and what he had meant to the company's bottom line. "Well, he can't survive now. Like you said, the DOJ will go after him, and we need to make sure they stop there."

"They're not the ones that worry me. It's Gary Bevins who could cause you the most trouble. Now he's got his full fledged scandal. He can set up shop at ADG and have carte blanche to look at anything he wants, and it won't seem like an abuse of power. Remember, the financial statements are your responsibility."

"Don't remind me. I should have stayed with the firm. Right now, I wouldn't mind being an audit partner."

"I can just imagine what's going through Yu Cheng's mind right now," Marc said.

"He's covering his ass. That's why the son of a bitch didn't tell us any sooner. He figured we'd tell him to stop his work while we sent your people and mine to take control, and he's right. That's exactly what we would have done. You know I screwed up letting them go without us. I really thought they'd find nothing."

"They're just as worried about Bevins as you are. Accounting firms have so much exposure these days. I'm sure they'll write their trip reports to make it seem like you personally misled them all these years. You should assume you have no friends at L&K."

"I'm sure you're right."

Marc added, "And I would also be wary of Steve Halpern. If you think he was unreasonable before, just wait until you see him this afternoon. He'll also be running for cover and he'll become Gary's best friend."

"You know, I need a better brain."

"We've got four brains. Let's get Ken and Carl together and talk about it. The four of us can help you think this through."

An assistant interrupted the conversation. She handed Kavi a note, which prompted him to say, "Let me go. It's Maurice on the other line."

"Call me after you're done with him. Meanwhile, I'll call Carl and Ken."

Kavi hesitated before he picked up the other line. He wasn't quite sure what to say, and it wasn't clear he could trust anything Maurice had to say, although Maurice hadn't really lied about anything. He just didn't tell all that he knew.

"Your timing's great," Kavi said.

"I thought you might be done with your conference call. How are things with our good friends at L&K?"

"They said things look great in Thailand and South Korea."

"Is that right? I kind of like those countries myself. Women will do anything for you and they're really cute. Ever get a massage in Bangkok? I know this great place and they'll give you a—"

Kavi interrupted, "You also know a great place in Malaysia, Indonesia or the Philippines?"

The line was silent for a moment and then Maurice said, "Yeah, I know a few good spots. So why do you ask?"

"Why do you think?"

"I asked you first."

"Maurice, I've been a big supporter of yours all these years. I can't believe what they're telling me. You really let us down."

"Is your phone bugged?" Maurice asked.

"Why? You plan on finally telling the truth?"

"When did I ever lie to you?"

"You think hiding the truth isn't as bad as lying? You sound like the ex-President."

"What's the line from that movie? You can't handle the truth."

"Go ahead and try me."

"I want to know what L&K told you first."

"You know what they said. When you boil it all down, it looks like we paid a whole bunch of money to foreign officials all over the globe. Isn't that what you thought they'd say?"

Once again the line was silent. It took Maurice some time to absorb the implications of what was being said. Apparently it was not what he had expected. When he responded, he sounded more serious than he did before. "That's too bad. We had a good thing going. I was hoping those bozos would give us a clean bill of health."

"Are you kidding me? In today's environment an accounting firm is going to jump all over this, and that's what they did. Forget them. I can't believe you knew about this and let it happen. So tell me, is what they said true?" When Kavi didn't get a response he asked again.

"You know it is. Look Kavi, I did what I thought was right. Like I said, you guys at corporate couldn't handle the truth. Anyway, I never lied about anything. I just kept you out of the gory details that were necessary to get things done."

"What gory details? You mean bribes."

"Call it what you want. I'm talking about an expense that's necessary to do business in some of these countries."

"None of our other business units bribe government officials. They're successful all over the world."

"They may operate around the world but they don't face the same issues we face. They don't need a whole host of government licenses to build a plant. They don't need to get a contract to sell a significant amount of the power to the national or local government to prove that the plant can be financially viable. They don't need to negotiate with some local tribal chief so you can get his blessing to build a facility on some ancient burial ground, and they don't need to take care of some other locals to make sure they don't accidentally blow up your gas storage facilities or something like that. I'm telling you, it's not like selling a television set."

"Go tell that to the Department of Justice," Kavi said. "Not that any of this matters anyway, but as I recall we did have success building power plants before you came on board. I'm sure we could have succeeded in your group without your extra-curricular activities."

"Is that right? You forget how this business unit got started and how it really did before I got here. ADG's energy equipment division built turbines and other equipment for power plant construction, but didn't take ownership in the facilities. It just built and sold the equipment. It thought there'd be a big market in the Far East because of the growth of their economies and their lack of power. But the demand didn't materialize because western investors didn't want the risks associated with building power plants in the countries we're talking about. So ADG decided to sponsor a few facilities, and I think that was a great idea. The company was large enough that it could take those risks."

"That's right, and as I recall we were successful before you got here."

"Sure, the company had success with the first plant, but then hit a brick wall. The first facility was built in Japan, at Hamamatsu. It worked like a charm, but ADG was getting nowhere with other projects in Indonesia, the Philippines and Malaysia. It couldn't get the required licenses, or it couldn't get contracts to sell the power, or something else, but in every case it couldn't begin construction. ADG was about to give up when they brought me in to give it one more shot. I knew why ADG succeeded in Japan but not elsewhere. In Japan the government is clean. No corruption whatsoever. Sure, they're tough negotiators, but you know where you stand, and once you've got a license it's as good as gold. Their courts work and they respect contractual rights. ADG thought it could easily duplicate that success because it was financially strong and had all the technical expertise. Sure it would have been a smart move for any country to let us in, so we could help solve their power needs. Problem is, most of the government folks in these countries could give a rat's ass about their country's needs. They care about themselves. You can criticize it all you want, but you either deal with them or you don't build power plants there. It's that simple, and I don't care how big or how good you are."

"So you came in and saved the day. I guess we should be grateful. Never mind we've got two government agencies and an outside audit firm about to kick our butts."

"That's the problem with the United States. You have your strange sense of morality. How do you think you get things done inside your own country? You think you don't bribe government officials in the US? You sure do. You're just more creative about it. Like a publishing company that gets some great legislation and the Senator who was responsible leaves office and magically gets a $5 million advance for his book. How about some of those multimillion dollar speaking fees for former Presidents? People heard them speak for free for four or eight years. You think they're really paying to hear them again? I could understand if they got that money to keep their mouths shut for a decade or two. In France we don't hide any of this."

"Maurice, you don't work for a French company. You chose to work with a US multinational and you were responsible for obeying all relevant laws."

"I was responsible for building a successful business, and that's what I did. Think of it. We've got more than twenty plants operating in ten countries, including some fun places like Kazakhstan and Laos. That's quite an accomplishment. If we did this with a French company, we wouldn't have to keep everything quiet. We could take care of government officials out in the open. Call a spade a spade."

"So maybe you should work for a French company."

"I still can."

"What's that supposed to mean?"

"ADG's not the only company interested in doing business in the Ivory Coast."

"So you're really there on a job interview?"

"I didn't say that. I just plan on keeping my options open. I can build a plant here for ADG or I can build it for someone else. There's a large French company interested and I can get a piece of the equity if I go with them."

"The Department of Justice may have some different plans for you."

"You think I care about them? Last time I checked, I was a French citizen."

"Did you ever hear of extradition treaties? I think they can get to you."

"Oh you think so? A country doesn't just hand you over to the US, especially if what you're accused of doing isn't against that country's own law. When you think about it, I'm really beyond the DOJ's reach. I've got nothing to worry about. And I'm in great shape financially I might add. As you know, the bonuses the last few years have been huge, and I just sold all my ADG stock. I'll be fine."

"So you created the problems and now you're bailing out?"

"ADG's been great to me, but I've done my part for God and country. If all this gets settled that's great, but if not then I'm gone. I'll help you and the company any way I can, but you won't catch me behind bars. That's never going to happen."

"So how long you plan on sticking around?"

"If I leave, you'll be one of the first to know."

Chapter 10

For a midday Saturday, there was unusually heavy traffic heading into the city on the George Washington Bridge. Although I was running late, I remained patient and made my way across and into Manhattan as fast as possible. When I finally arrived at the Iron Horse it was 1 pm and Marc and Ken were already there, but Kavi had yet to make it in. Presumably he had also been delayed at the bridge. Marc wanted the four of us to get together and Saturday, August 2nd, was the most appropriate day. When he called on Thursday, he told me about the latest developments at ADG, including the verbal report from L&K, and I was more than willing to take time from my summer weekend to meet. Walking over to the table I could hear Ken say "53."

"About time you got here," Ken said.

I pulled up a chair and asked, "What's 53?"

"That's where ADG's stock closed yesterday."

"You're kidding. It was 60 when I last looked."

"That was Thursday and what a difference a day makes." Ken took a quarter from his pocket and twirled it in the middle of the table. While concentrating on the spinning coin he said, "It opened yesterday at 51 and came back a little before the close."

"The news leaked," Marc said, as he motioned for the waitress to bring another beer. "There was a report late Thursday by Reuters and they knew about most of L&K's findings. We don't know how they got it, but they got it. A number of other wire services picked it up Friday morning and I'm sure it will be front page news on Monday."

"That's terrible, but I assume the company had to make it public anyway, right?"

Marc said, "Sure, but it's much better to have the information come from the company. They can give it the right spin, so to speak, and can give people a greater sense of comfort that there won't be more surprises."

"That makes sense." I got my beer and guzzled about half of it before putting the bottle down. "You know, this thing has a life of its own. How's Kavi doing?"

Ken looked at me with a face that confirmed I had just asked a dumb question. "Let's see now, he's the CFO of a very public company, and he just learned he'll be front page news, very bad news that is. How would you be doing?"

"That's why I wanted us to get together," Marc said. He looked over at the door, presumably to see if Kavi had arrived. He turned toward us and said, "I'm worried about him. I know he's incredibly capable, but I'm not sure he's ready for what's coming. He'll be thinking about how to protect ADG and not himself, while everyone else will be running for cover. And knowing him, he'll blame himself even before others do." Marc stopped talking when he saw Kavi walking in.

"Speaking of the devil," Ken said.

When Kavi arrived at the table he took a rather long look at us, laughed and sat down. "You'd think somebody died around here. You're supposed to cheer me up."

"We're here to help," I said.

"Good, you can pay for the beer." Kavi called the waitress over and ordered two bottles of beer for each of us, even though we were still working on our first ones. "We'll keep 'em coming. I'm not sure what to do on Monday, but right now I'm drinking heavily."

Marc shook his head and said, "If that helps."

"It can't hurt." Kavi was momentarily distracted by something at the next table, but then he turned to me and said, "If you really want to help, get your Sicilian friends to fly to the Ivory Coast and take care of some business. Maurice Granville is there. We're getting hit by one big shit storm and he's at some hotel sipping margaritas. While you're at it, there are a few L&K auditors who could use a broken leg or two."

"Have you heard anything from L&K since we last spoke?" Marc asked.

Kavi eyed Marc, and, instead of immediately responding, took some time to savor his beer. When he finished drinking he said, "Remember they told us we might have similar problems in Laos and the Philippines? Well, you can now add another $100 million to the list."

"That's unbelievable," Marc said.

"You had problems at every location?" Ken asked.

"Just about," Kavi responded. "Out of eleven countries we've got problems in at least six. We don't know about China or Turkey, but at this point I wouldn't be surprised if there are problems there too." He looked down at the table and laughingly said, "At least we're clean in Thailand, South Korea and Japan, but don't ask me why."

"How much money are you talking about in total?" I asked.

"It looks like it's more than $300 million."

"You mean $300 million in bribes?" Ken asked.

"Don't say bribes, say unsupported payments. Do you know $300 million is less than one percent of our total assets?"

"It doesn't matter," Marc said. "It's a lot of money and you've got problems at so many locations. It's like a cancer that spread."

Ken said, "So what are you saying Marc? Size doesn't count?"

Marc looked somewhat annoyed and quickly responded, "Come on, now's not the time."

"We could use a little humor," Kavi said. He put his beer down and put both hands on the table and leaned in. "Seriously guys, thanks for coming here today. I think it will be helpful to discuss this with three people I really trust."

"Sure thing big guy. How can we help?" Ken asked.

Just then the waitress came by and we took time to order lunch. When she left, Kavi said, "Maybe I'm too close to the situation, so I can't see straight. It might help me to hear your points of view."

"And I have a few thoughts for you to consider," Marc said. "I wanted Ken and Carl here when we discussed it. I think they can be more helpful than you know."

Kavi laughed and said, "Marc has some things for me to consider. What a shock."

Marc motioned for the group to lean in toward him so others at the Iron Horse couldn't overhear, although there wasn't much chance of that. "Let's look at where we are and how this is likely to play out. ADG's employees have committed criminal acts to the tune of hundreds of millions of dollars and they did it in a number of foreign locations. This is too big for the Department of Justice to sweep under the rug, so they're likely to make a big stink about it."

"That's Maurice Granville's problem, right?" I asked.

"You're right," Marc said. "But I don't think they can get to him, and, if they can't, they may go after some other senior company officials including Kavi."

"Come on Marc," Ken said. "He didn't know anything about it. So how can they come after him?"

"Who knows? I just think it's possible. But I'm really worried about the SEC. This guy Bevins has worried me from the start. Look at what he was saying when the problem was limited to Ukraine. God knows what he'll say now. And he may do more, just so he's not upstaged by the DOJ. Keep in mind there's a lot of great press he can get out of this, and now there's a lot more meat to the story."

Kavi called to the waitress, "Two more beers please."

"You still have a full one," I said.

"I know. So Marc, when do you get to the helpful part? There *is* a helpful part, right?"

"Just let me finish. You should expect to see the other senior officers at ADG running for cover. And we should assume they'd gladly sacrifice Kavi to save themselves. I think they—"

Kavi interrupted, "Wait a minute. I know you mean well, but don't you think you're going a little too far?" Kavi looked away, shook his head and laughed. Then he turned back and said, "This whole situation is a mess and I need to handle it correctly, but not because I'm worried about being sacrificed. No matter how bad this looks, I had nothing to do with it. My job is to make sure we handle the situation so I can protect ADG from further damage."

Marc was beginning to get frustrated, although he wasn't surprised by what he was hearing. He took a deep breath to calm himself and said, "You're worried about ADG, but I'm worried about you. I understand you had nothing to do with any bribes, but I'd believe anything you said. The DOJ may not be so trusting, and I doubt Bevins will take what you say at face value. Also, who knows what others might do to drag you into this thing. Someone has to take the fall. Maybe I am going overboard, but I'd rather be safe than sorry and that means a strategy that gives you the best personal protection."

Kavi gave in and said, "So what are your other thoughts?"

"First, you should think about protecting your assets."

"Get rid of his wife's charge cards," Ken said.

Kavi ignored Ken's comment. He leaned in toward Marc and asked, "What are you getting at?"

"This is important," Marc said. "Some time early next week you'll be named in a number of lawsuits by all those bloodsucking trial lawyers claiming they're representing stockholders who have lost billions of dollars over the past few weeks."

"That's to be expected, but they won't win anything in court. Sure, we might settle with them to avoid the hassle, but it won't matter. In any case, I'm indemnified by ADG for any loss."

"That's all probably right, but the operative word is 'probably.' Who knows what your board of directors might do to get the SEC and DOJ off their back? They could conclude you knew about the bribes or were negligent in not finding them as the senior finance officer in the company. Keep in mind, their indemnification doesn't cover criminal acts or gross negligence on your part."

At first I had thought Marc was going off the deep end, but then I realized he was making some sense, so I chimed in. "Marc's right. No matter what happens, you should protect your assets, just in case."

Nodding, Ken added, "Don't forget you've got L&K in the mix. They'll be sued as well, and don't think they'll be quoted in the papers saying it's their fault. You'll never hear them say they simply messed up when they audited that business unit. They'll use the standard accounting firm playbook. They'll be quoted around the world saying their audit was the greatest thing since sliced bread and they were the victims here. They'll put the blame where they always do, with management, and that means you. They won't use your name, but they won't have to, and it will all come back to you."

When Ken finished speaking, nobody else spoke. There was nothing more to say until Kavi considered the advice and decided what to do. After all, it was his problem. While waiting, I wondered if people at any of the other tables noticed that the four of us were sitting silently. It must have been a rather strange sight. The waitress stopped by with a puzzled look on her face and was asked by Marc to come back later.

Kavi finally broke the silence. "What's today, August 2nd? So it's been about a month since our anniversary dinner. I can't believe this has all happened since then. Ken, I remember that night you said something about the stock of a company with a scandal. What was that?"

"I was referring to an article I had read. It talked about studies done on what happens to stock prices of companies when they make a scandal public. They found that within two weeks those companies lose between twenty and fifty percent of their market value. I didn't know you were paying attention."

"So let's see how we've done. It's been public about two weeks if you count our Nikolaev press release. We were at 66 at the time and now we're at 53. That's about a twenty percent drop. I guess your study was spot on. Did it say what happens to CFO's and their assets? Never mind. I don't want to know."

"I just hope your stock stays where it is. Twenty percent is a lot better than fifty percent," Ken said.

Kavi picked up his beer and studied the bottle, as if he were studying something valuable. "You know, it just seems strange to worry about protecting my assets when I didn't do anything wrong. But maybe you're right. Anyway, it certainly can't hurt to plan for the worst. Ok, so tell me more."

Marc looked relieved. "Well, as I said, I think asset protection is the first step. We've got some good people at Bartman & Cross, but I don't want our firm involved. Among other things, I think it may be a conflict of interest because we represent ADG. I have someone in mind by the name of Victoria Richards. I think she goes by Vicki. She's got a special practice and asset protection is all she does, and from what I hear she's really good."

"So when should I meet with her?" Kavi asked.

"That's just it. You don't, not at first anyway. That's where I think Ken can be helpful. Ken, you willing to meet with her?"

Before Ken could respond Kavi interrupted, "I don't understand. Why shouldn't I meet with her?"

"First, I think it's best nobody sees you talking to an asset protection lawyer. I realize this may be a stretch, but you have to assume it's possible that some reporter will be interested in having you tailed or maybe somebody else will see you with her. Also, I understand she's great but I'd like one of us to check her out and see first hand. She should keep everything confidential but I'd like to make sure we can trust her before she knows that you're the client. I think Ken should see her first."

I was surprised Marc didn't even mention me. Ken wasn't a lawyer, and his expertise as a tax professional didn't provide any great insight into the practice of asset protection. So I asked Marc why he didn't consider me.

"I was just thinking of protecting you, Carl. You're an audit partner at the largest accounting firm in the world. I don't think it would look good if it ever became public that you were helping Kavi protect his assets from creditors. The press might like a story like that. Ken doesn't have that exposure."

"Let me worry about that. Not that you can't handle this on your own, Ken. Of course you can. But I'd still like to go with you when you meet her."

Kavi had a big grin on his face. I think he appreciated seeing his friends step up to help.

"It's really not necessary," Ken said. "One of us can handle this."

"Let's just go together," I insisted.

"Ok, if it's that important to you."

Marc looked at me and seemed ready to try and change my mind but instead he nodded and sat back in his chair. Then he said, "Fine, it may be better to get two opinions of her anyway. Now that that's settled, I'll get you guys some materials so you can get prepared. I'd like you to do your homework before meeting with her."

I said to Ken, "We can meet at my mom's place and kill three birds with one stone. I owe her a visit, you wanted some of her lasagna, and we can get prepared."

"Kavi, you need to pull together all your personal financial information," Marc said. "I've got some questionnaires and forms you can use to get it all organized. They won't really need it for the first meeting with Vicki, but they'll need it soon enough."

"Just get me the forms and promise you won't laugh when you see how little I'm worth."

Ken smirked. "I'm sure you've done ok. I know you made out like a bandit on your ADG stock options. I assume you've cashed some in over the years."

"Actually, most of my options are still unexercised. I'm not really worried though. Despite what the market thinks, we're a solid company and our long-term prospects look great, this stupid bribery fiasco notwithstanding. By the end of the year we'll be over $70 a share."

"Let's hope so," Marc said. "But Victoria will probably suggest you exercise at least some of the options, and sell the stock. I'm sure it's easier to deal with cash than stock or options. Anyway, time is not on our side, so you guys need to meet her soon. Try to set something up for early this week, and let me know what you think. Just assume it was your own money you were trying to protect."

Ken looked over his shoulders and smiled. "Now that you mention it, maybe I should do something for myself. You never know when someone might come after you."

"You mean someone or some woman?" Kavi asked. "I'm surprised that hasn't already happened."

"Never give them your real name or address. That's what I always say. That was the problem in Fatal Attraction. Glenn Close knew how to find Michael Douglas." After Ken was done, he shivered, apparently at the thought of getting caught by a woman like Glenn Close's character in that movie.

We gave Ken more grief about his exploits, and were embarrassed when he started telling the waitress about the virtues of extramarital sex. He believed it was good for the long-term health of any marriage. He told her it was one thing to be faithful to a woman when your life expectancy is forty-five, like it was at the turn of the century, but it was quite another thing when you could live to be eighty.

When she walked away, Marc got us back on track. "Another thing you need to do is pull together everything you've got about Maurice Granville, and I mean everything. I want to know who hired him, who promoted him, who he reported to, who decided his bonuses, and so on and so forth. I want you prepared to demonstrate that you could not have known about this before and you had nothing to do with his advancement at ADG."

"I thought he was good, but he wasn't my guy."

"Besides that, I want you to check all the public statements you and others have made about his business unit over the past few years. Check out press releases, articles in local papers, any statements in your annual report and other SEC filings."

"And watch Gary Bevins like a hawk," I warned.

Marc nodded his agreement. "Absolutely."

"He thinks this is an accounting issue," Kavi said.

Ken was looking over at a young couple standing in the corner. Without turning he said, "That's ridiculous. You're not a mind reader. How can you account for a bribe you don't know about?"

While listening to Ken, I remembered an article that was right on point. "You know I had forgotten, but that's one of the things they did with Enron. They had some South American operation involved with bribes and the SEC said they didn't account for the payments correctly."

Marc looked concerned and asked, "Do you recall how much was involved?"

"Sorry, but no."

"Well having a precedent like that isn't good, whatever the amounts." Marc hesitated for a moment to think. Then he turned to Kavi and asked, "Aside from this, are you sure you're clean with your accounting?"

"With all those certifications I signed, we had better be clean."

Kavi was referring to one of the requirements under the new law, which forced CFO's to sign a certification taking responsibility for the accuracy of financial information in their company's reports to the public. It made it hard for CFO's to plead ignorance if there really were problems.

Marc sat back and seemed temporarily satisfied. "You need to make sure Gary doesn't get his hands on any other issues. Although we can't be certain, I think you'll be ok if the improper payments are all he's got, notwithstanding any Enron precedent."

Ken slammed the table and knocked over my beer. He was very strong and, had he wanted to, he probably could have split the table in two. I could see people at the next table look over. "Ok, so this all makes sense, but why just play defense? Let's make you look good. After all, weren't you the one who uncovered this? You sent your staff over there. You're the one who didn't accept the answers you got. Maybe you can use this to help you get the top slot."

Kavi chuckled and said, "You know, Carl, I don't need your Sicilian friends. I should just send Ken out to take care of some people. I like the way you think Ken, but somehow I don't see anything positive coming out of this. After all, it wasn't just Nikolaev. I think it would be reasonable for someone to ask why I didn't find it sooner. I'll be glad to just break even in all of this."

"Maybe so, but I prefer to be aggressive."

"You're aggressive? That's an understatement. If you had asked me a month ago which one of the four of us could have a problem with the law, I'd have said you Ken. With all your creative tax transactions, it's a wonder you're not in jail. How long have you been with NV?"

"In three weeks it'll be eight years. Time flies when you're having fun."

Kavi scratched his head and grinned. "Haven't you had any trouble with the IRS? I assume they've audited some of the years since you joined the company. They must have questioned some of the things you've done."

"They just finished their audit of 1999 and 2000. We owe about $3 million and that's peanuts. We've got about $110 million recorded as liability reserves on our books in case they found something. And, if you think that's good, when they finished 1996 through 1998 a couple of years ago, we actually got a small refund. We had about $130 million of tax reserves recorded that we never needed to pay. I remember we had to disclose it when we took that into income and announced our quarterly earnings. We had to be really delicate. We didn't want the IRS to read in the papers that we reversed a tax liability of $130 million just after they finished an audit that said we were owed a refund."

"You're amazing." Kavi slapped Ken on the back, almost as hard as Ken had hit the table. "Marc, are you sure our pal here has been acting in accordance with the law?"

"From what I know, he's close to the edge, but I don't think he's ever crossed it."

Ken said, "I love when you guys talk about me as if I'm not sitting right next to you."

Marc did his best to push Ken away. Then, he turned his attention to Kavi, and said, "You know I don't like what he does."

"Everything we do has at least the minimum required support," Ken noted.

Marc laughed and said, "You've got it right when you say minimum. How about those Russian bonds you acquired for $10 million? You sold them after a month for $9 million. Even though you only lost $1 million, you got to deduct $61 million for tax purposes, just because the original Russian owners had paid $60 million more than you did."

"You know how that was structured."

"I understand, and it probably worked under a technical reading of the law, but there was no purpose for the transaction other than to save taxes. If Congress knew what you'd done, they would have changed the law. It's not ethical."

"What happens when the shoe's on the other foot? I remember there was a woman whose husband was killed by an explosion at work. She sued his employer and got a verdict for $10 million. Her lawyer had a contingency fee and he got $4 million of it. She only received $6 million, but the IRS had no problem saying she should pay tax on the full $10 million under a literal reading of the law. When it helps the IRS, they don't mind being technical, and ignoring the economic reality. You get them to change their ways and I'll change mine."

"Ken, I don't think you'll ever change," I said.

Marc nodded. "That's for sure. You know, Ken, maybe you were right. You *should* talk to Victoria Richards about protecting your assets."

"When Marc starts making jokes, it's time to leave," Ken said.

"What makes you think I was joking?"

Despite a few more barbs, the conversation did get back to our main topic and after about twenty more minutes we were done. We summarized what had been agreed and were ready to leave. Our get-together may have been somewhat difficult for Kavi, but it did result in more than a few helpful ideas. And, aside from anything that was said, it reinforced our willingness to help. As it turned out, I didn't have any plans for that evening, having finally accepted that things were over with Kim. But when we left the Iron Horse and went our separate ways, I was actually looking forward to spending Saturday night on my own.

Chapter 11

▼

Ken agreed to get together for dinner at my mother's apartment so we could spend some time preparing for our meeting with Victoria Richards and share some great Italian cooking. It was Tuesday, August 5. I had some things to discuss with my mom, and I left work early so we could have about an hour alone before Ken made it to her place. As usual, she gave me grief about the lack of a good woman in my life and couldn't understand why I didn't want her help. Fortunately, we were discussing something else when Ken arrived.

When my mother greeted him at the door, she reached up, grabbed his face with both hands and held it like she was holding a giant egg. Taking full advantage of the moment, she asked, "Hey handsome, want to run away with a nice Italian lady?"

"If I did, you'd be the one." Ken kissed my mom on the cheek, and then headed toward the kitchen to see what was cooking. My mother didn't move. She just turned her head to watch him as he walked in.

"Ma, stop staring. He's married."

"Who cares? When a hunk walks into my apartment, I'll stare."

Ken ignored our banter and yelled from the kitchen, "Carl, if I were you, I'd be here every day. This smells so good. So Anne, when do we eat?"

"It's almost ready," she said. "Make yourself comfortable in the living room with my unmarried son who doesn't need my help."

Ken sat down next to me and asked in a low voice, "Are you sure you're Italian? She sounds more like she's Jewish."

"I'm beginning to wonder myself."

While my mother worked in the kitchen, Ken and I took some time to prepare for Victoria Richards, whom we planned to meet the following day. In typical Marc Abrams fashion, he had faxed an eight-page document to each of us, with background information about asset protection and a list of thirty questions we should ask when we first met with her. He made it seem as if we didn't know what to ask, but to be fair, that wasn't far from the truth. And, I had to admit, the background materials were very helpful, especially for someone who had never worked with the area before. As we discussed the subject, Ken became more and more convinced he should do something for himself, and, as a partner in an accounting firm, I gave some thought to how it might also help me. We were about half-way through when my mother walked over and handed each of us a glass of red wine.

Ken asked, "Is this what you served the last time I was here?"

"That's right. I remembered you liked it, so I got two bottles. You take one home with you."

"If you insist."

My mother poured herself a glass, sat down next to Ken, and announced, "Dinner's almost ready." Then, getting herself comfortable, a wide grin commandeered her face as she looked at us and asked, "Am I interrupting anything?"

Acting as translator, I added, "That's her way of saying she wants to know what we're talking about."

"Ok, big shot, what *are* you talking about?"

Ken looked at me as if he wanted my approval, and then responded, "Marc wants the two of us to meet a lawyer to see if she can help Kavi."

"She? Is she married?" my mother asked.

"Ma, drink your wine."

While looking—and smirking—at me, she asked Ken, "How can this lawyer help Kavi?"

"With all that's going on, he'll probably be named in a few lawsuits. It's unlikely he'll lose any money, but just to be safe, there are things he can do to protect his assets from those lawsuits and others who might come after him. I don't know the details of how it's done, but she does."

"Am I crazy?" my mother asked, not really wanting an answer. "He works hard and gets trouble? I don't understand anything anymore. Let them go after that French guy you told me about. Let them get *his* assets."

Ken took a sip of wine and put the glass down, making sure to use a coaster. "I agree with you, Anne. It is crazy, but it's the way things are today. There are bloodsuckers everywhere and Kavi's got a lot of blood to give. It's tough for good people like him."

She shook her head and said, "Well I don't know about things today, but in the past, we believed if someone's a crook you go after the crook, not some other guy."

"Ma, don't you need to check the lasagna?" I asked. "I'm sure it's done."

"My son thinks I'm nosy." She leaned in closer to Ken and asked, "You think I'm nosy?" Laughing, she understood when Ken smiled and didn't reply.

The lasagna *was* ready, so Ken and I made our way to the kitchen, and were treated like two starving immigrants from some third world country. Ken didn't mind. As usual, the food was better than anything you could get in an Italian restaurant. Throughout the meal, we talked about a whole host of low-key subjects, like politics, war and religion. My mother wasn't bashful and it didn't take much to get her opinion, and she had an opinion about everything. Ken was a real trooper and he sat quietly when my mother and I went at it. To an outsider, we were arguing, but to Italians from Brooklyn, we were just having a discussion. I also found it interesting to watch Ken interact with my mom. He was so polite, courteous and attentive. Not that he was ill mannered in other social settings, but he usually had a certain 'edge' that was missing on this particular evening. He was so smooth and my mother ate it up. When we finished dinner, she ordered Ken and me into the living room and started her cleaning routine and, despite our offers, refused any help from us.

Upon seeing me head for the bathroom, my mother stopped what she was doing, walked into the living room to sit across from Ken, and asked, "Is Kavi in trouble?"

"I'm sure he'll be fine. We just think he should hope for the best and prepare for the worst."

"Tell him I said hello. You do that, ok?"

"I will."

In a low voice, she said, "Carl says he's doing fine. What do you think?"

"Why, are you worried about something?" Ken asked.

"He says he wants to meet a woman, but I don't know. Nothing lasts. Like Kim. She seemed nice and they got along. What do women want these days?"

"Well I'm no expert," Ken said. "But don't worry about Carl. He'll be fine. He's a great catch, and one of these days some smart woman is going to snap him up. He's so honest, and he'd do anything for a friend. I think some women take advantage of that."

"He's a good egg."

"As an aside, Marc didn't ask the two of us to meet with the lawyer. He just wanted me to go, but Carl insisted on coming along so he could help in some way."

"I think he sees a lot of his big brother in Kavi. You know, my older son died before you met Carl. The two were very close. When we found out that Joe had cancer, it was too late. The doctors said there was nothing they could do. He wasn't like you, but he was very strong, and we couldn't believe he could really be sick. You see, with Joe…"

"What about Joe?" I asked, having returned to the living room without making much noise.

My mother didn't turn her head. She stood up, walked back to the kitchen, and, without looking at me, declared, "And he thinks I'm the one that's nosy."

I asked Ken, "Joe Senior or Junior?"

"Junior."

"How'd my brother come up?"

"We were just talking about Kavi. Your mother said you think of him like a big brother."

"My mother didn't go to college, but thinks she's a psychologist. Believe me, she doesn't know what she's talking about, although that never stops her from talking."

"You never say much about your brother. If you'd rather not talk about him, I can understand."

"There's not much to say. I had an older brother, and he died of a rare form of brain cancer before I started college." It took a moment but I found my copy of Marc's materials. "We probably should finish going over this."

It wasn't as if I intentionally avoided the subject. I just didn't think anyone would be interested in hearing about my brother. He died of cancer and that was it. I didn't think there was very much to say. People wouldn't care. Why should they care? Why would anyone care about some guy who still thought about his older brother every day, even though he'd been dead for nearly thirty years? I just wanted to call him on the phone and ask him to stay over at my place for the weekend so we could talk. Of course I knew he was dead, but part of me thought he was on some long trip and just hadn't returned yet. There was so much I wanted to tell him, and I knew he'd give me good advice. He'd really watch my back. When I was a kid, it was like he was my own private army. I'd get picked on by some older bully and the next thing you know that kid would come to school with a black eye, and it just happened to be the size of my brother's fist. Not that we didn't fight. We fought all the time. It was just that nobody could hit me except my brother. He was a lot stronger than me, but I was never afraid of him. You can be really brave when you fight with your brother. He could be a real pain too. We slept in the same room when I was young, and he would tell me to do stupid things, like when my parents had company over at the house and we were supposed to be asleep, he told me to throw our toy trains at the door. I was a little kid, so what did I know? He said our dad would be happy with me because he would know that my arm was strong. Like a real jerk, I went ahead and threw the trains, and, guess what? Our dad wasn't happy at all. He took off his belt and started hitting me on the legs while my brother was laughing under the covers. Well, I got the last laugh, because my father heard my brother laughing and started belting him as well. Pretty soon my father didn't care what had happened. He'd just hear a noise and would come into our room and start killing us both. My brother was tough, but my father was worse. You know, my brother would win at everything. Baseball, football, stoopball, checkers, anything we did. He loved me, but he'd never let me win. I'd get so frustrated playing anything with him, and then…"

"Hello, Earth to Carl. Come in, please."

"Sorry, Ken. Let's finish this before my mother comes back and asks you for a date."

She actually left us alone and we were able to finish our preparation. It looked as if Kavi was in good hands, and the two of us were ready for a very productive meeting with Ms. Richards. My mother noticed that we were finished and offered, "An after dinner drink?"

"Nothing for me, but thanks anyway," Ken replied. "I'll be driving, you know." He stood up, stretched, glanced at his watch and added, "Actually, I do need to get going."

Ken was ready for a quick exit, but there was a ritual you had to go through before being allowed to leave my mom's place. And you had to start the routine about thirty minutes ahead of time. The first phase began with my mom asking Ken, "How about some coffee before you go? It won't take that long to brew and you probably need it before your trip."

"No, I think I'll be ok." He looked over at me and smiled. If he thought I could help, he was mistaken.

After a few more phases, my mom got ready for the finale by saying, "Let me get some food for your wife and kids."

Ken, being less familiar with the routine, and still clinging to the mistaken belief that he had some influence over the process, put his hands on his chest to signify that he was full. "You don't need to do that. I'm stuffed, and my wife and daughter eat like birds."

"So for your two boys. I'm sure they eat."

Finally, recognizing the futility of doing otherwise, he gracefully accepted the food and was granted permission to leave.

"Ma, you gave him enough to last two weeks."

"Don't bust my chops. They'll eat it." She sat down next to me, put a pillow under my head, and asked, "You're not driving back?"

"No, I probably should stay over. I brought my stuff in the car just in case."

"Great. You want something special for breakfast?"

"Can we not talk about food right now? I'm a little stuffed."

"But you didn't eat anything."

"Say, ma, do you still think about Joe Junior?"

"Of course. You never forget your son. Why?"

"I was just surprised you mentioned him to Ken. So what do you think about?"

"He's just in the back of my mind. I think about him more, now that your father's gone. It seems like it was just yesterday that your dad was here."

"It doesn't seem like it's been three years. I was really worried about you when he died, but I have to admit you've handled it really well. The two of you were so close I wasn't sure how you would handle being alone."

"I'll tell you the truth. It wasn't easy living with your father. You know his temper. He could fight about anything. Now I have more freedom. I loved him and I miss him, but being alone isn't so bad after all those years."

"He had a temper, that's for sure. Remember the time the neighbor's kid threw a baseball through the window of our car? I was sure glad it wasn't me."

"Yeah, your father could be a real nut, but he was honest and decent. You know the type of people he had to deal with to become a crane operator in New York City. Believe me, he had opportunities to make big money doing things you wouldn't want to know about, but he refused. That wasn't for him, and he certainly didn't want any of that for the two of you. It was so important for him to see you both go to college and make something honest of yourselves. At least you got the chance to do that. You know he was so proud of you, especially when you became a partner."

We both sat quietly for a while and listened to the noise from outside. Even though it was late, you could still hear the occasional car horn, people walking by and talking too loud, city buses stopping at the corner, cats fighting, or other 'sounds of the city.' I found it to be quite soothing—perhaps you have to be from

Brooklyn to understand. Our 'quiet' time gave me a chance to reflect on what my mom had said. I knew all about my father's work. It's no big secret that there were all kinds of unsavory characters involved in the New York City construction industry. My father did what he had to do to support his family, but he refused to be involved with anything illegal. It was a great balancing act, where he was able to make friends with certain influential people in his union, but without going too far. I remember how he used to tell me and my brother how important it was to get an education so we could succeed without having to deal with those kinds of people. My brother and I used to joke about it, but as we got older we understood. And when my brother died, there was no question I was going to go to college. I wanted it for myself, but even if I didn't, there was no way I would disappoint my dad.

"I miss them both," I said.

"They're together right now, and they know we're thinking about them."

"You really believe that?"

"Sure I do, and when I go, I'll keep an eye on you. That won't be very long now."

"Don't say that. You're only sixty-eight. You've got many years ahead of you."

"Whenever it's my time, I'll be ready."

"Not for a long time, ma, not for a long time."

Chapter 12

When Kavi left for work on Monday morning he was in reasonably good spirits. The Saturday lunch meeting at the Iron Horse had certainly helped, and he had spent most of the day Sunday getting organized and ready to move forward. The bribery scandal was in full swing, but he believed he had an appropriate plan of action that, given sufficient time, would reverse the negative momentum that had permeated his work environment since the day he'd sent Debra Jennings to Ukraine. What's more, he realized he hadn't been sufficiently skeptical of Maurice Granville, but would never make that mistake again. Although he didn't think there was much more damage that Maurice could actually do.

Despite his good spirits, when Kavi arrived at the office and took one look at the Wall Street Journal, he wondered if he should just turn around and head back home. It was hard to miss the paragraph in the "What's News" section on the front page. "ADG affiliates may have unlawfully paid nearly $500 million to government officials in at least five countries, according to a special review performed by Larson & Kirsh." The actual article took up a good portion of the first page and two thirds of page four. The Journal's version made the situation seem far worse than what had been portrayed in ADG's press release a few weeks back, but in reality, things *were* far worse, and the story was reasonably accurate. Although Kavi had been told to expect the article, it was still painful to see it in print.

Unfortunately, things continued to go badly as the week progressed. He spent a good part of Monday and Tuesday dodging reporters' probing questions and sticking with the company's party line. According to ADG, it had brought the situation to the attention of the authorities as soon as the first problems were noted, and the payments had not been authorized and were not in accordance with the company's policies and procedures. They violated ADG's high ethical standards and would not be tolerated. All of that was true, of course, but it hardly mattered to the press. They naturally assumed there was more to the story, and considering all the other corporate scandals that were in the news, they couldn't be blamed.

To add insult to injury, despite his efforts, Kavi couldn't even get his hands on a copy of the L&K draft report until Tuesday morning, and he wasn't pleased. For one thing, as the CFO of the company, he could not understand how the press could get their hands on the information days before he received the draft. Of course, L&K had no idea how their information had leaked. But, far worse, Kavi was extremely disturbed with the substance of the report. The first half discussed L&K's procedures and what they had uncovered through their work. Other than the fact that they took credit for Phil Mentz's action plan, it wasn't much more than a written version of the information they had previously provided over the phone. However, the second half discussed their prior audits of the business unit and described in some detail how ADG management's efforts kept L&K from performing the level of work necessary to uncover the problems. "Management," for this purpose, included Kavi.

To top it all off, by Wednesday morning, which was August 6, ADG's stock had hit $47, down $6 for the week. Although the payments in question aggregated less than $500 million, the scandal had nonetheless wiped out more than $17 billion of ADG's market capitalization in less than a month. Needless to say, Charles Goodman and the full board of directors were not very pleased. The matter was entering a new phase, and Kavi had to quickly turn the tide. As he focused on damage control strategies late Wednesday, he became frustrated when Gary Bevins showed up at his office, along with an assistant.

"There's a Mr. Bevins here to see you. Should I send him in?" Kavi laughed at his assistant's mistaken belief that he actually had a choice in the matter.

"Sure, send him in. I've got nothing else to do."

"Mr. Chander, we have some questions about the L&K draft report." Gary, acting as if it were his office, motioned his assistant to sit down in one of the two chairs facing Kavi's desk, while Gary sat down in the other chair. Kavi was actually hoping they'd walk to the other end of the office and jump out the window.

"Please, by all means, have a seat," Kavi said. Normally he viewed himself as working from a position of advantage when he met someone in his office while sitting at his desk. But on this day he didn't feel very powerful and imagined a huge picture of Uncle Sam hanging over the heads of his visitors.

"I just need a moment," Gary said.

Kavi watched as Gary put his copy of the L&K draft report in front of him on the desk. From the look of it, you'd think he'd had it for years. There were handwritten notes and highlighted sections all over the document which left no doubt he had performed a thorough review. Kavi said, "Your copy looks a little worn. You need a new one?"

"No, we've got plenty of clean copies. It makes for some interesting reading, wouldn't you say?"

"I'm glad you enjoyed it. So you have some questions?"

"Yes. Can you tell us about your relationship with Maurice Granville?"

"That's a question about the L&K report?"

"It's all related, I assure you."

"He was the head of the business unit. My relationship with him was no different than my relationship with other business unit leaders."

"Were you very good friends?"

"I wouldn't say that. He was a nice guy, but we didn't socialize, if that's what you're getting at. I didn't see that much of him. As you can appreciate, he didn't come here that often."

"He said you were very close friends."

After hesitating, Kavi asked, "You spoke to Maurice? How'd you manage that?"

"Mr. Halpern was kind enough to tell us how to reach him. For someone in his position, Granville was actually quite cooperative."

Kavi couldn't help but think that he too would be quite cooperative, if he were a French citizen, beyond the reach of US authorities, lying on a beach in the Ivory Coast with a great job offer from some French firm. "I think you know we've all been very cooperative. Wouldn't you say?" Gary didn't reply so Kavi continued, "You must have enjoyed speaking with Maurice. He's quite a character."

Again Gary didn't reply. Instead, he opened a folder and removed what looked like a confidential document from ADG's internal audit department. "We've been reviewing the annual plans for your internal audit group for the past five years, and would like to ask you about them."

Although Kavi wanted to ask Gary how he had gotten his hands on the confidential documents, he thought better of it, not wanting to appear to be hiding anything, especially when he actually had nothing to hide. Nonetheless, he was disturbed by the thought that someone, presumably Steve Halpern, had supplied the reports without even mentioning that to him. As the company's CFO, he should have been better informed, and he made a mental note to take the matter up with Steve after the meeting.

The internal audit group consisted of fifty professionals, whose main responsibility was to periodically visit different business locations to review the adequacy of internal controls and to test for compliance with the firm's policies and procedures. A primary benefit of this work was assurance that financial information being reported by these units was accurate and complete. Although a fifty-person department was one of the largest internal audit groups of any US corporation, they still needed to prioritize their work because the company was so large.

Prior to the end of October each year, they would prepare an audit plan outlining their work for the upcoming year. Some work was scheduled at random, but the bulk of the work was planned based upon an assessment of relative risks and relative dollar significance. As part of that assessment, a numeric and a letter value were assigned to each location. A lower numeric value corresponded with a higher assessment of risk. For example, 1 was assigned to a location with high risk. An A was a location with maximum financial significance, whereas an F was assigned to a location on the other end of the spectrum. A location rated A1 might be audited every year, whereas an F3 might only be audited every five to ten years. The assignment of letter values was relatively straightforward. It was based upon the financial amounts reported for the particular location, including the book value of its assets. The risk assessment was much more subjective and much more sensitive. Although most internal audit documents and reports were prepared 'for internal ADG use only' and were to be kept confidential, the annual risk assessment was included in a separate report with a more limited distribution.

In many companies, the head of internal audit reports to both the general counsel and the audit committee of the board of directors. That was currently the case for ADG. However, a few years back, the head of internal audit had reported only to Kavi, and he had the responsibility of approving each year's internal audit plan and the related annual risk assessment.

"I understand internal audit reported to you, through 2001," Gary said. "Is that correct?"

"That's right."

"And, through that year, the annual plans for the department had to be approved by you?"

"Correct."

"And you had significant influence over the determination of the audit plan?"

"Yes and no. I made sure the plan was consistent with the assessment of risk and the dollars involved at each location. I also made sure the evaluation of risk was appropriate. I don't know if you would call that significant influence." Kavi noticed that Gary's colleague was taking notes while Kavi spoke, so he asked, "You want me to proofread that when you're done?"

"I'm sure you can understand that we must document everything," Gary said. "We have a great many constituencies and we don't like being second guessed."

"Welcome to the club, pal. Remember that as you continue with your work. So, can I offer you coffee or anything?"

"No. We're fine."

"Well, I'm getting some." One of the perks of being on the 50th floor was having your own industrial sized coffee machine right outside your office. Kavi walked out and got himself a cup. He needed the caffeine and it gave him some time to think. He could understand questions about Maurice Granville. Gary would probably ask about Granville's relationships with any of the company's key officers. That's one of the things Kavi was pulling together for Marc. Others were much closer to Maurice, but Kavi didn't want to volunteer that information just yet. What he didn't understand were the questions about internal audit. Returning to his chair, he said, "I've got my own coffee supply right outside and it's quite good. It's brewed three times a day in Colombia and flown up to New York in private jets."

Without any hint of laughter, Gary continued, "Regarding the audit plan, you reviewed the report with the risk assessment of each location?"

"Of course I did. That's a big part of how we schedule audits. We want to focus on the higher risk areas."

"Did you typically make changes to the risk assessment as part of your review?"

"I wouldn't say "typically," but I did make changes from time to time. Otherwise, I wouldn't have been doing my job." Kavi wanted to ask Gary what he was getting at, but was sure he'd come to the punch line soon enough.

"It seems as if there was very little audit coverage of Maurice's group."

"It was one of our smallest units and there was no reason to have a high risk assessment."

"That's not what it says here. I'm looking at a draft report for 1998 and it says that a number 1 rating for risk should be assigned in connection with twelve plants in his group. That's your firm's rating for highest risk. It indicates the business unit was growing significantly, so they did an in-depth reevaluation, and concluded that the countries involved, and the nature of certain facilities and the contractual arrangements, made a number 1 rating appropriate in some cases. This was a big change. But the final report retained the prior years' 3 rating for every facility. And I was told that you were the one responsible for that."

Kavi couldn't remember the details, but it was certainly possible that he had been responsible, though he would not have acted without adequate support and consultation with others. But the company's policy was to destroy any draft reports and only maintain copies of the final versions, so Gary should not have been able to get his hands on the draft. In any case, it was now clear where the questions were leading and he didn't like it at all. He had tried to remain calm but was getting tired of the twenty questions routine. "You said you had some questions about the L&K report and all you've been asking about is Maurice Granville and the internal audit reports. What do you want to know about L&K?"

The order of Gary's questions was no accident. He had prepared for the meeting the way a football coach prepares for Sunday's game. He wanted Kavi off balance so he could learn more throughout the process. His associate was not just keeping a record of Kavi's answers, he was recording Kavi's body language so they knew how he reacted to each question. If he appeared uncomfortable, if he made any nervous gestures, if he did anything out of the ordinary, it would be duly noted. Throughout most of the session Kavi had done well. He had remained calm and seemed comfortable with the questions. But time was not on his side.

"Mr. Chander, among other things, L&K asserts that management encouraged them to do less work on the Far East merchant power group than would otherwise have been warranted. As the senior financial officer that includes you. We're looking for any evidence the internal audit work was also skewed in this fashion and, if so, why it was so skewed. Now we do have specific questions about L&K's report. Shall we cover them now or shall I continue with our questions on the internal audit reports?"

Kavi didn't reply. He stood up, walked to the window and took a long sip of coffee. The hot liquid had a calming effect, and it made him more comfortable taking his time before speaking. While giving the appearance that he was looking out into the distance, he was actually watching Gary in the reflection in the window to get some insight, but there was none to be had. Kavi had to admit that Gary was one smooth cookie, and a smart too—his line of questioning was well thought-out. Kavi knew the company had done absolutely nothing to limit L&K's audit of the power group. L&K was just trying to make that case because they were afraid of litigation against them for missing the whole mess. One major accounting firm had already gone under and some people thought another would be gone within a few years, so L&K had a good reason to be concerned. Although their assertions were baseless, it was nonetheless perfectly appropriate for Gary to use them to his advantage. Facing such an impressive questioner, Kavi decided it was time to shake things up. He turned and said, "So you think I told our internal audit group to lower the risk associated with Maurice's plants because he was my best friend, and I didn't want them to catch the bribes which I must have known about. And you think L&K had great audit work planned for his unit and I jumped in to make sure they never did that work. Right?"

"I didn't say that, Mr. Chander, did I?"

"My name is Kavi. Why do you keep calling me Mr.? You want me to call you Mr. Bevins?"

"Actually, I would prefer it if you did."

"What else would you prefer, Mr. Bevins?"

"It would be great if you allow me to continue with my questions while you provide complete and truthful answers."

"Ok by me." While walking back to his chair, Kavi figured, all things considered, it would be best to answer Gary's questions and then regroup with Marc as soon as possible. So he asked, "Do you have any questions about the L&K report that actually relate to the L&K report?"

"They make references to changes in their audit plan based upon representations from management as to the propriety of the financial reporting for Maurice's group."

"Like I said, they're making it seem as if they wanted to do a lot more work than they actually did. Let's keep in mind they *did* audit that group. Ok? Yu Cheng and his crew made trips to every location. Not every year, but I'll bet they hit each plant at least once every three years. And they didn't catch anything. So tell me, you think it would have made any difference if they did more work? Sure, they're experts now. They know what to look for because they were taught by Phil Mentz at Bartman & Cross. He's the one who showed them a great audit plan for Nikolaev and they copied it when they visited the other sites."

"So you're denying you ever influenced the level of their audit work in the Far East?"

"That's an unfair question. Of course we review their audit plans and if they asked me what I thought about Maurice's group, up until this past month I would have said it was a first class operation. Not because I was his best buddy, but because I really did think they were first class, based upon their financial performance. It was up to L&K to decide what to do, and if they reduced the level of their work that would have been their decision to do so. The key here is they *did* audit the plants and they didn't find anything."

"So you think they should have found something?"

"I'm not saying that either. *We* didn't find anything, so why would I second guess them? We all missed it, Gary. I mean, Mr. Bevins. The only difference is that I'm not trying to cover my butt and they are."

"How about their assertions that key facts were misrepresented by management?"

"You'll have to ask what they mean by management. If they mean local plant personnel, then it seems they're probably right. Keep in mind, we knew nothing about this here in New York. I'm the one that sent my staff over to Ukraine and that's how we uncovered this whole mess. And if I hadn't done that, you wouldn't be here with an opportunity to enjoy my fine coffee."

"So why didn't you do that earlier?"

"I didn't see any reason to. They were on budget for every other project. Think of it. You do a feasibility study, you prepare a financial plan, you get board approval and you're ready to go. Then they get the plant built, on time, on budget. Everything works. They produce the electricity they were supposed to produce. They sell it for the price they were supposed to get. Everything works at every one of their plants. You think you would call that high risk? You think you would send someone to investigate?"

"It doesn't matter what I would do."

"Oh yes it does, Mr. Bevins. You said you don't like being second guessed. Call it what you want, but that's what you're doing now. Isn't it important what a reasonable person would have done in the circumstances? Aren't you a reasonable person?"

"For some matters, that is a relevant consideration."

"When is it *not* relevant?"

"I think it would be prudent to stick with our questions. May we get back to your internal audit reports?"

Kavi let Gary continue with his questions, and tried doing a better job of keeping his emotions in check, while providing answers that were short and to the point. This continued for about another hour, and when it was over, Kavi thought he had done reasonably well, basically because he felt comfortable telling the truth. He wondered what Gary was thinking and took for granted that he was about to find out.

Chapter 13

Ken and I each had a very busy day lined up, so we had agreed to limit our meeting with Victoria Richards to no longer than two hours. It was Wednesday, August 6, and the two of us met at a coffee shop on the corner of 57th Street and Park Avenue, so we could get our morning quota of caffeine and walk from there. Her building was actually two blocks north on 59th Street, and it didn't take an expert on real estate to know it was in the heart of a high rent district, not that any real estate in Manhattan was cheap. Her building wasn't very big, and it was easy to miss unless you were looking for it and were paying attention. We found it and made our way past security and up to the fifth floor. The security guards thought we were ok because we wore suits and we each had a driver's license with our pictures on it. Evidently terrorists can't get their hands on those licenses and they're not allowed to wear suits.

Vicky greeted us at the door to her office suite, and while escorting us to the conference room, explained how she shared the place with two other firms because it helped her maintain the high class address. One firm was a private equity group and the other was a boutique investment advisor that ran hedge funds focused on commodities. I didn't know it at the time, but they were run by women, although I should have guessed from the paintings and all the furnishings. It wasn't typical of an office suite and seemed more like an upscale residential apartment, which was consistent with its size, about 3,000 square feet.

There was a small rectangular table in the middle of the conference room. She sat down on one side and motioned for us to sit across from her. While looking at Ken, she said, "You didn't tell me very much when we spoke."

"I didn't want to provide any information over the phone. Anyway, we'd like to learn more about you. Just tell us about yourself and your practice."

When women first meet Ken, oftentimes you can detect some reaction, like a quick smile or a gleam in their eye, which tells you they find him attractive. But I didn't detect any such reaction from Vicki. Maintaining a poker face, she asked about his background.

"I'm the senior vice president and head of the tax department at NV Industries."

"And you Carl?" she asked.

"I'm a partner at Winston Walker."

She nodded and brushed something from her eyelash, and I noticed she wasn't wearing a wedding ring. She asked, "Do either of you have any particular experience with asset protection?"

"I'm married, so the answer is definitely no," Ken joked.

Vicki didn't laugh but she didn't seem bothered either. She turned to me for my response.

I replied, "We have a primer that was prepared by the fellow who put us in touch with you, but I think it's best you assume we know almost nothing about the subject." Just then I noticed her perfume. It had a very pleasant fragrance, not overpowering, but hard to ignore.

"That's very helpful," she said. "I'll start with an overview of asset protection planning. It involves implementation of certain techniques to increase the likelihood that one can keep his or her assets away from future potential creditors. I think a few things are worth noting here. We are talking about a number of different techniques, each with its own advantages and disadvantages. A good part of my work is the review of different options to determine which is best suited for a client's specific circumstance."

Although I was paying attention to what she was saying, I was also wondering if I found her to be attractive. I could see she was in great shape and she certainly looked good. She was about 5 foot 6, and her weight was proportionate to her height. Her hair was dark, about shoulder length, and her eyes were dark too, but they had a sparkle that lit up her face. She certainly dressed well, and not like a woman who wore clothes that made her look like a man. She was very professional, yet feminine. And if I didn't know any better, I'd have guessed she was still in her twenties, but Marc had said she had more than ten years of experience, so I knew that couldn't be right.

Vicki continued, "It's also important to note that, aside from certain rare circumstances, we can never provide certainty. We can improve a client's overall asset protection posture, but we can't make it bulletproof. Also, in general, the techniques will only work with respect to potential *future* creditors."

And she had nice legs. When her assistant interrupted to give her a message, I managed to move my head just enough to catch a glimpse of them under the table.

"This is not an exercise to remove assets from current creditors," she added. "Let's say party A has a definitive obligation to pay $10 million to party B. In that case, there's not much I can do for party A. Of course, in many cases it's unclear if we are talking about current creditors, and there are a great many shades of grey. This is hard to discuss in the abstract, and every case is different, but in all cases, it's beneficial to plan for other potential future exposures. Are you following this?"

I said, "It makes sense to me."

"Perhaps you can tell us something about the techniques," Ken suggested.

"I can," she said. "But before I do that, perhaps it would be better if I told you something about my clients. I understand someone at Bartman & Cross referred you here."

It took me a moment to unfold my copy of Marc's primer and list of questions. Pointing to it, I said, "That's right. It was Marc Abrams, and he prepared these materials for us. He's a tax partner at Bartman & Cross, and one of his colleagues recommended you."

"He must have told you I have a number of very satisfied high net worth clients. I can't share their names with you, but I suspect you would be familiar with many of them. Their net worth exceeds $10 billion in the aggregate."

She had full lips. I hadn't noticed that before since I'd been more focused on her eyes, and her lipstick had an understated quality.

"Most of my clients are US citizens, but three are British and two are Canadians. I think it's safe to say they are all quite satisfied."

"What else do you practice?" I asked.

"Asset protection is all I do. I've been doing it for over ten years now. When I was first exposed to the area in law school there was something about it that appealed to me. But when I graduated in 1992, it seemed the major firms frowned upon it, as if the work was beneath them. Oh, they had people who would do it but it certainly wasn't a way to become partner, so I decided to start my own firm. In my view there was nothing wrong helping wealthy people preserve their wealth. Starting my own firm was risky, but I thought if I could do it well, it could be quite lucrative."

"So is it?" Ken asked.

"Let's just say I can't complain. Now, can you tell me something about the potential client?"

Ken looked to me and hesitated. Turning back to her, he said, "Think in terms of a top corporate officer. That's about all we should tell you today."

"A chief financial officer?"

"That's a possibility," Ken replied.

"Quite frankly, I'm surprised I don't see more CFO clients. With all the new legislation aimed at financial reporting, they have much more exposure than they've had in the past. And I don't think they're ready for the problems they may face in the next few years."

"You read about the few CFO's who are crooks, and that makes everyone look bad," I noted. "But in reality, most are very decent people."

"I understand, but you never know what might happen. And the time to do asset planning is *before* you have a problem. If I were a CFO, I'd do something to protect myself right now."

"So you don't have many of them as clients?" Ken asked.

"Right now I have two. One has been a client for years and the other engaged me late last year. The techniques are still the same. It doesn't matter whether you are a billionaire investor or a CFO."

"So does what you do really work?" I asked.

"Well, the goal is to protect assets and my clients have all been successful doing that. However, as I said before, none of this is foolproof."

She was wearing black high heeled shoes that looked expensive, and the heels were just the right height. Although I was no expert on women's apparel, I got the impression she put a lot of thought into everything she wore.

She continued, "I'll give you a simple example of one of the most common techniques. The idea is to contribute some of the client's assets to a trust, with the client retaining little or no control over their disposition subsequent to the contribution. If there's too much control, a court can compel the client to satisfy creditors with the trust's assets. Of course, my clients want things done in accordance with their wishes, but in most situations they can easily identify trusted individuals who are sufficiently independent to act as the trustees."

"So they have their cake but can eat it too," Ken said.

"That's right. However, the only sure way to win is to truly give up all control. Otherwise, there will be some level of exposure."

Using Marc's list of questions as a guide, I asked, "Are these domestic or foreign trusts?"

"Both can work. There has been a push among some of the states to enact legislation and attract this kind of business, but I prefer a foreign trust. As you learn more about the area, I think you'll agree."

"Do you like any particular jurisdiction?" I asked, continuing down Marc's list.

"In my view, the Cook Islands is best, although I've done work in most of the favored locations. The Cayman Islands, Liechtenstein, the Isle of Man, the Bahamas, the Channel Islands, I can go on and on."

Marc's list indicated his firm liked the Cook Islands. "So why are they your favorite?"

"Do you know much about them?"

I was about to say no when Ken jumped in, "We have a couple of Cook Islands subsidiaries. I know they're an independent country and a member of the British Commonwealth." For a moment, I had forgotten that he was there with me.

"That's right," she said. "It's actually made up of fifteen islands located in the South Pacific. And if you flew on a straight line from Los Angeles to Auckland, New Zealand, you'd be over the Islands about two thirds of the way into your trip. They speak English there."

"Is it their tie to Britain that makes them appealing?" I asked.

"That's just a part of it. In the mid-1980's they enacted very comprehensive asset protection trust legislation. And I think it's the best in the world. Without getting into all the details, let's just say it works. It provides an incredible amount of flexibility when drafting the trust, and their statute of limitations is very short."

She was gently massaging her neck with her left hand—with beautiful looking fingernails, I might add—and for some reason it had a very soothing effect. Despite my close examination, I had yet to find any flaw in her appearance.

"Let's say a client sets up a trust in the United Kingdom. The UK has a number of provisions that could allow the client to get access to the funds under certain circumstances. That may sound like it's a good thing, but it's not. As I said before, a US court could put my client in jail and keep him or her there until the client took steps to direct the use of the trusts assets in accordance with the court's directive. That's not going to happen with a Cook Islands trust. Of course he or she will draft the trust such that the assets can only be used to benefit certain persons, like themselves or other family members, and the trustees will be comprised of 'independent friends,' as I like to call them."

Ken and I continued to fire away with our questions—or should I say Marc's questions—and she had all the answers. I had to admit, for a pretty dry subject, she had a way of making it sound interesting. As it turned out, despite my being somewhat distracted, I did learn a lot. I had read through Marc's materials a few times and compared notes with Ken, but most of it didn't sink in until she explained it. I came away convinced of her expertise.

I folded up Marc's preparatory materials, looked at Ken and asked, "Any more questions for Vicki?"

"Not about asset protection." Ken loosened his tie and smiled. He put his elbows on the table, braced his chin with both hands and leaned in toward Vicki. "So tell us more about yourself. What do you do for fun?"

"It may surprise you, but I enjoy my work. I find it very rewarding."

"What about outside of work?" Ken asked. "Looking at you, I'll bet you work out a lot."

"I didn't know you were looking. I've been seen at a gym now and then."

"Maybe we can meet and work out together?"

"Actually, I have a rather strict routine, and I prefer to work out on my own. I'm sure you can appreciate that."

Sometimes you couldn't tell if Ken was flirting or being sincere, especially when it came to working out. He took a special interest in people who exercised regularly and was a very social presence at his gym. He had once said you should work out with someone if you really want to learn about them, because it helps to break down barriers. Since we were done with our questioning, I said, "Well, I have a very tough question for you, Ms. Richards. Can you direct me to the men's room?"

She smiled and said, "Go out of the office and make a right. You'll see it on your left just before the elevator." It really wasn't much of a smile, maybe a half smile. But it was something, and it was more than anything Ken had gotten from her. I think you could say that I was beginning to like Vicki, and, yes, there was an attraction and it was growing stronger by the minute.

When I came back, the two of them were standing just inside the door to the office suite. Vicki held out her hand and said, "Thanks for coming here today. I hope to hear from you and your mysterious client." She turned to Ken and shook his hand as well. It may not have had any meaning, but she was only looking at me when she said she hoped to hear from us.

Just before we left, I looked down at the receptionist's desk and noticed some magazines in the incoming mail, including a copy of Scientific American, addressed to Victoria Richards. It wasn't something I expected to see in a lawyer's office and I also subscribed. So I gave some thought to telling her, but instead just said goodbye and walked out with Ken down the hall. As soon as the elevator doors closed, I asked, "Are you meeting her this weekend for drinks?"

"Are you kidding?" he said. "I probably couldn't get her to walk me to the elevator."

"I tried to give you two a few moments alone. You seemed interested. So you didn't get anywhere with her?"

"She was cute, but has the personality of a dead fish."

"I'll bet she likes keeping her social life and professional life separate."

Ken commented, "Assuming she has a social life."

"So you think she's good as a lawyer?"

"She knew what she was talking about, that's for sure. I'd certainly hire her. So what do you think?"

"I thought she was very good. We should call Marc and tell him she's a go. So when would you like to meet with her again?"

"We don't need two people to follow-up," Ken said decisively. "You really want to do it, so why don't you just take it from here? If you need any help preparing for your meetings, let me know, but I'm sure you can handle it. Agreed?"

"You sure you don't mind?"

"Why should I mind? I think it was good that the two of us met with her today, so we could compare notes. But now it's yours."

Ken and I continued walking along Park Avenue. When we got to the corner of 51st Street, we agreed on a time to call Marc, and then we split up, with me heading west toward Avenue of the Americas. My afternoon was pretty busy, so I had to get to the office and back to work. All things considered, I really couldn't spare the two hours to meet with Vicki, but I was glad I'd made the time, not just for Kavi's sake, but for mine too.

Upon arriving at my building, I should have gone right in, but instead I stopped for a moment to enjoy the sunshine and to watch the people milling around on the street. There were always interesting things to see, like street vendors who sold foods I'd never be caught dead eating, for fear of food poisoning, or something worse. Actually, I wanted to take a moment to think about Victoria Richards. There was just something about her that really attracted me, and I couldn't put my finger on it. She had to be in her mid-thirties, since she'd graduated from law school in 1992, but she looked much younger. On the other hand, she seemed more mature than me—and more successful—and more confident. I just sensed strength within her that I wanted to explore. The more I thought about her, the more I looked forward to our next meeting.

Chapter 14

It was Friday, August 8th, and a bad week was coming to a close. Kavi was getting annoyed with the developments, so he decided to head down to the 44th floor to take a break. That's where ADG's corporate accounting department was located, although the group was so big they also had half of 43, with the other half made up of temporary offices and conference rooms for outsiders like the L&K auditors, and, since late July, the SEC. And that didn't include the accounting departments for each business unit, which in most cases were far larger than the one for corporate. Some of those business unit people were located in the building, but others were housed in different locations around the country and around the world.

Kavi liked to get away from his executive floor every now and then. It was just too quiet. Once in a while, he needed to hear phones ringing, people typing away at their computer keyboards and people in the middle of conversations that sounded urgent, although most never were. He could simply head down one floor to 49 and visit the corporate controller, but that wasn't much noisier than 50. All things considered, Kavi preferred the 44th floor.

Debra Jennings had an office on 44, and she seemed right at home in the middle of its frenzied activity. There always seemed to be someone like her in the controller's department of large corporations. Someone who did all the heavy lifting, the 'extra' work when financial reports were due or some large transaction was in process. Her problem was that she was good, and would never complain that she had too much work or was understaffed. Although she had only been with ADG for eight years, she knew more than most 25-year company veterans. She was only 32, but had a level of competence that was well beyond her years.

Most of all, she was incredibly dedicated. Even though she had a four-year-old boy at home, that didn't stop her from working late nights and weekends, and traveling to exotic places like Nikolaev, Ukraine. She kept her office well stocked with crayons, paper and small toys to keep her son occupied when she brought him along to work on a holiday or a Saturday afternoon. Most people who worked as hard as she did were driven by ambition, but she was ambivalent about further advancement. On the one hand, she loved her work and was thrilled to interact with the various ADG businesses, but she also wanted to have another child and that would require more time at home. Her husband also had mixed feelings about her career. He loved the money. ADG paid well and she earned more than he did. Yet, like many young fathers, he wanted her to spend more time at home. She was reaching a crossroads most men never face, with her family on one side and her career on the other, but if she remained in her current position, she could possibly continue to handle both.

It wasn't unusual for Kavi to head straight into Debra's office before anyone noticed he was on the floor. She was one of the few people at her level who was not intimidated by him in any way. Not that he was intimidating, but most of his staff found it hard to ignore that he had the position he had.

"Ok, show me the latest," Kavi directed.

Debra swiveled her chair around, took three of her boy's recent drawings from the credenza, turned again and handed them to Kavi. She marveled, "He's definitely an impressionist. Can you tell? I think he gets it from my husband who's never clear about anything."

There were two chairs facing Debra's desk and both were covered with files. In fact, there were files all over her office, on her desk, on the credenza and on the floor. The only exception was a table in the corner which had a bunch of crayons and toys reserved for her boy. Kavi cleared the chair that was closest to the door and sat down. He quipped, "You know those funny things out in the hall? They're called filing cabinets, for to file."

Debra shot back, "All this stuff's active. You get the SEC and L&K off my back and I'll clean up my office."

"That sounds fair enough." Kavi studied the pictures. "Your boy's only four? He looks talented to me and I can see he's improving."

"Thanks. I thought it was just me. Every mother looks at her kid's art work and thinks it's the best. You need someone objective like you. Or, are you just being nice?"

"No, this looks really good. I'll bet he's getting too much practice here in the office. You've been working too much."

Debra carefully placed each of the pictures back in its assigned spot. She turned to Kavi, blew the hair away from her face and said, "I thought summers were supposed to be slow. It's been a bit challenging this year."

"I know. Look, it's Friday and I don't want you here this weekend. I don't care what work is open, leave it for Monday. Tell the staff."

She gave him a military style salute, and then leaned over to one corner of her desk to find some papers buried under a bunch of files. While handing them to Kavi she reluctantly said, "We just got a bunch of new information requests from Gary Bevins. I was about to distribute copies. Here's yours."

It was a five-page request for information, the eighth such request received since Gary and his staff had set up shop at ADG. Kavi started to flip through the document but stopped halfway. While holding it in his lap he turned toward the window and remained silent.

Being young and energetic, Debra wasn't very tired, even though she'd been working hard. From her perspective it was only an information-gathering exercise. She wasn't worried about how the investigation might impact her because she had no reason to worry. Looking at Kavi, she could see it was getting to him, and sympathetically asked, "Did you expect this stuff to slow down?"

"No." Kavi stood up and closed the door and then sat down again. "Have you seen the papers lately? They're starting to write a lot about me."

"I try to ignore the articles about ADG. They never seem to get their facts straight."

"Well they've been pretty accurate lately. They've got some good sources. One way or another, they know what we know when we know it. Actually, in many cases before we know it."

"You think Maurice is behind the leaks?"

"No. There wouldn't be any reason for him to do that, and he's also cut himself off. He didn't know about the L&K report until I told him about it. There are just too many people involved. Once that happens it's not that hard for the press to find a confidential source."

"You think it's someone from corporate?"

"Why? You've been talking to reporters lately?"

"Forget that I asked."

"At this point the press doesn't need anything meaty. I'm not sure people read the full articles anyway. They can just mention our name and repeat the story, and people think it's new news." Kavi started to look at some of the files on her desk and laughed. "I needed a break so I came down here to get away from all this. That was a dumb idea. You're right smack in the middle of it."

"It sure looks that way doesn't it?" Debra hesitated for a moment and then asked, "So how is Charles taking this?"

"It's best we not discuss him." Kavi wanted to keep Charles, and the full board of directors, out of his mind for at least the remainder of the afternoon. With each passing day, Charles and the board were becoming more distressed and more willing to express their displeasure, with Kavi on the receiving end. What's worse, he believed their views were justified. But he was being hard enough on himself and didn't need their help.

"That bad?" she asked.

"That bad."

"Someone should tell him how hard we're working with this stuff."

"I did," Kavi said. "Debra, you're a real trooper. I know what you've been doing and I appreciate it."

"Thanks. Now if I can get my husband to appreciate me, I'd be in great shape."

"He was lucky to have met you, believe me." There was a picture of Debra and her husband on the corner of the desk. Although he had seen it before, Kavi picked it up and studied it carefully. "You look beautiful in this picture."

She acted coy and asked, "But I don't look beautiful now?"

"Debra, you know what I think about your looks."

"I'll bet you say that to all your assistant controllers."

"You know the answer to that."

Her expression became more serious and she asked, "So how do you think this will affect you?"

Kavi put the picture back and thought for a moment. "Who knows? This is one of those things where everybody looks bad and I probably *should* look bad. This should have been uncovered long ago."

They spent some time talking about that, with Kavi being hard on himself and Debra being supportive. She didn't say anything new but it was still comforting to hear. He confided that he had started the week thinking he could get his arms around the problem, but so far he'd failed. He likened it to quicksand where extra effort digs you deeper into a hole. As the discussion continued, he realized it wasn't a very productive exercise from the company's perspective, but he needed to get some things off his chest. He looked at his watch and then started flipping through Gary's latest information request and asked, "Is this more of the same, or is there something here I should worry about?"

"I'm not sure. Take a look at the last page. They want information about the acquisition of Gerard Engineering back in 1996. What does that have to do with anything?"

He looked at the last page, and sure enough there were questions about Gerard. A company the size of ADG acquires a great many companies each year. So Kavi had no idea why they'd seek information about a transaction that had occurred seven years earlier. While rubbing the back of his neck he asked, "Is there anything here about other acquisitions?"

"No, that's it," she said. "I remember when we bought Gerard. I'd been here about a year at the time. Is there anything unusual about it?"

"Not that I can think of. They made machine tools for the automotive industry and cutting and welding tools to service the construction industry. It's now a part of our engineering systems group." Kavi thought for a moment, and the only thing that came to mind was that he had led the acquisition effort, although he had also led the effort on more recent transactions. "Let's be on the safe side. Show me everything you pull together on this before you give it to anybody else."

"Ok. So I guess you weren't serious about us not working the weekend? I really don't mind and there's a lot to do."

"I certainly *was* serious. I don't want to see anyone but janitors on this floor over the weekend. Go get a babysitter and spend some time with your husband." As Kavi was speaking, Debra's assistant knocked on the door. She said Kavi's assistant was looking for him.

"Take your own advice," Debra said. "I'm sure Aarti would like to see more of you."

Kavi made it back to his office and was told that Maurice Granville was returning his call and was waiting on hold. Before picking up the line, Kavi closed his door and took a moment to organize his thoughts. He had called the Yellow Tulip hotel and left a message because he wanted to know what Maurice had told the SEC. But their last conversation hadn't gone well and Kavi wasn't sure if he could expect any cooperation. And he had to be skeptical of anything Maurice had to say.

"Sorry I couldn't call back sooner," Maurice said. "I was out of action for a few days on a side trip to Ghana. It was an opportunity I couldn't pass up."

"What's going on there, another job interview?"

"Kavi, I'm beginning to think you don't love me anymore. Actually, I was there following up on the potential Ivory Coast project. The Ghanaians need power and may be one of the project's big customers. I was able to get a meeting with some of their senior government officials."

"It's great to see you looking after the company's interests. So I see you've been busy."

"You could say that. So what did you want to know?"

"I understand you made some time to speak with the SEC."

"Yeah, I spoke with a Gary Bevins. What a weirdo. I'll tell you, he's one shady character."

With all that had happened, it was comical to hear Maurice call someone a shady character, although in the context of Gary the description fit.

Maurice continued, "Steve Halpern set up the call, and I assumed you knew about it. Come to think of it, why would Steve do that and not tell you?" Maurice waited for a response but didn't get one. He continued, "I thought it was strange that he wanted me to speak with the SEC but I did what he told me to do."

"And what did you tell Gary? He was grilling me the other day and he made it sound like you and I are the best of friends."

"You mean we're not?" Maurice joked.

"Just tell me what you said on the call."

"It was a rather brief conversation and all I did was answer his questions. When he asked if you and I were friends, I said yes, and I thought we were. What's the harm in saying that?"

"And I assume you told him I didn't know anything about the improper payments, right?"

"He never asked about what you knew," Maurice said. "I'm telling you, he kept firing away with questions and I barely had a chance to respond. He didn't let me add anything either. It was all very 'controlled,' if you know what I mean."

Kavi put the call on hold to take a message from his assistant. Steve Halpern had asked that they meet in Steve's office as soon as possible. The pause gave Kavi the opportunity to consider whether it made any sense to continue the conversation with Maurice.

"Say Kavi, you're not mad at me, are you?" Maurice asked.

"This may not be the opportune time to discuss how I feel about you."

"How about Charles Goodman? What does he think? I'm surprised I haven't heard from him lately."

"You don't want to know, and keep in mind you've taken a big dent out of his net worth. He owns a lot of ADG stock and, unlike you, hasn't sold much."

"I also built up his net worth. I didn't hear anyone complain when we reported great results all these years."

"There's no point arguing about this," Kavi said. "You did what you did and we can't change it now. So tell me, when will you be going your merry way?"

"Have I been fired? I must have missed the memo."

"Let's not play games. It shouldn't hurt you to tell me your plans."

"It won't help you either. I already said you'll be the first to know. Look, I need to go."

"You need to rest up for more meetings with government officials?"

There was silence and after a few moments it appeared as if Maurice might have hung up the phone, but then he spoke. "Just listen to me and let me finish. You think I'm the bad guy. Think whatever you want, but keep in mind I did what I thought was right and in the company's best interests. However you judge my actions, you should know I never intended to hurt anyone and certainly not you. Sure, I'm looking to protect myself now, and I'll be successful, but you don't see me hiding that fact. Can you say the same thing about others, like Steve Halpern? Maybe you think you can't trust me, but you can. I'll do whatever I can to help you and the company, as long as it doesn't hurt me."

* * * *

Of the five executive offices on the 50th floor, Steve's was the smallest. Although it was a very spacious and well appointed corner office, he nonetheless took notice of its relative size. Kavi never cared about such things and never really focused on the fact he had one third more space. He made his way to Steve's 'smaller' office, knocked on the door and walked in to find him on the phone, pointing for Kavi to sit in one of the two burgundy leather chairs facing his desk. And, except for a two-page fax, the desk was devoid of any paper, in contrast to the one in Kavi's office which was always a mess.

"So you were speaking with Maurice," Steve said. "Anything new I should know about?"

"He says he was in Ghana doing some work on that possible Ivory Coast project."

"You believe that?"

"At this point I don't know what to believe. So why am I here?"

"Brace yourself," Steve said, while passing a document across his desk. "Check out this fax. The Indonesian Power Authority thinks they no longer have any obligation to buy power from our four Indonesian projects."

Kavi took a deep breath, quickly scanned the fax, and then tried to make a meal out of his lower lip. He stopped before drawing blood, collected his thoughts, and asked, "What's their rationale?"

"They'll say we bribed people to get our contracts, so they were never valid."

"Their people were corrupt, and because of that they can just walk away?"

"That's about the size of it, although, remember, there's a different government in place today than the one that was there when our projects were built."

"But they're just as corrupt."

Steve hesitated a moment and then said, "You know what this would mean to those projects."

"We'd lose most of our investment."

Kavi looked out the window a moment and thought about the magnitude of what he had just heard. ADG built the plants in Indonesia expecting big growth in the country's industry and a corresponding increase in the county's demand for power. Even though the growth and power demand never materialized, ADG had protected itself through the contracts with the Indonesian Power Authority, which obligated the Authority to purchase eighty percent of each project's output at a set price. Were it not for such contracts, the projects would likely fail. It was similar to arrangements the business unit had in other countries.

"It's not the best timing for something like this," Steve said.

"You don't think they have a chance of succeeding with this, do you?"

"The contracts specify that they're governed by British law and I'm sure they're valid, but this is Indonesia we're talking about, so who really knows? There's always the risk they won't respect the judgment of a foreign court based on British law."

Kavi leaned forward and rubbed his face with both hands. He added, "In most cases if they tried a stunt like this it would hurt them more than it would help. They'd kiss away any foreign investment as companies wouldn't take a chance of investing there. But with the scandal, maybe they can defend what they're doing."

"Remember India and the Enron project? It wasn't the same issue but the local government was able to get out of some significant power contracts and the project was doomed."

"So what's the next step?"

"It's up to them to make the first move. To date, they're still current on their power payments. We're getting outside counsel geared up so we'll be ready to go."

"How can I help?"

Steve studied Kavi and didn't immediately respond. After a moment of uncomfortable silence, he reached for a jar of jelly beans on his desk, took two for himself and offered some to Kavi. Then, slowly and hesitatingly, he said, "I'm not sure there is anything you can do. I'll be leading this effort and I'll let you know when you can help."

Kavi returned serve with his own moment of silence, after which he said, "It seems you've been leading a lot of efforts lately."

Steve immediately shot back, "Just what do you mean by that?"

"You know what I mean. Thanks for telling me about Indonesia, I'm sure you thought you had to tell me. But you're keeping me in the dark about too many things. I didn't even know you put Bevins in touch with Maurice. I had to hear it from Bevins himself. And he's getting copies of confidential documents he should never get, or at least I should know before he gets them."

"The Granville thing was unfortunate and I can assure you it wasn't intentional. And the documents, well, I used my best judgment. It's been really tough around here. I'm sorry, but I don't have the bribery scandal playbook to guide me and I'm doing my best as general counsel to help protect this company."

"And as the CFO I also have a responsibility to protect it and I can't do my job if you keep me in the dark." Kavi paused to calm himself and to let his words sink in. Speaking more slowly, he warned, "I don't pick a fight unless I have to. But you're pushing me too far. We haven't been best buddies, but we've always managed to work together and we need to continue to do that now."

Steve sat back in his chair and looked out the window. He knew he'd lose any fight with Kavi, so he turned back and said, "Maybe you're right."

"Of course I am. We need to be very careful, and not just with Indonesia. At some point it will become public, and, once it does, we'll have fun watching what some other governments will do. They may follow Indonesia's lead. I'm telling you, we need to work together."

Steve wavered and was becoming noticeably uncomfortable. Without much intensity he said, "There is something else I should tell you." He leaned forward and rubbed his forehead with both hands. While looking down at his desk to avoid any eye contact he said, "The Department of Justice will be sending some people here to work with Gary. We're still in the dark about their plans."

The information didn't seem like a major revelation. Confused by Steve's skittishness, Kavi asked, "Wouldn't you expect the SEC and DOJ to share information?"

"They could be doing that."

"So, you think it could be something else?"

"It could be."

"What do you think it is?"

"I'm not sure."

"Come on, Steve, what are you not telling me?"

"It's really premature for me to say. Just keep in mind the DOJ would handle the government's case against anyone accused of bribing a foreign official. That's a federal criminal matter so it's under their jurisdiction. They don't need the SEC's help. This would cover any attempt to go after Maurice and anyone else who was involved."

"I know that, so why do you look nervous?"

"The DOJ doesn't need the SEC to pursue federal criminal matters. On the other hand, the SEC has only civil enforcement authority. If they want to pursue a criminal matter they have to work closely with the DOJ who will then pursue the case, with the SEC's help."

Kavi sat back in his chair and looked away as he took it all in. Then he turned back to Steve and said, "And I'll bet the SEC wouldn't target Maurice."

"That's probably right."

"But they'd have a target."

"You would think so."

"Probably not the company's general counsel."

"Probably not."

Steve's assistant walked in and handed him a message. Kavi waited for her to leave before he spoke. "So tell me, when did you know about this?"

"I found out two days ago," Steve admitted. "In all honesty, I don't know anything other than the fact the DOJ is coming here. It really is premature to talk about their motives. I'm probably worrying you for no good reason."

Kavi wasn't comforted but didn't want to pursue it further. Not with Steve, anyway. He looked at his watch and said, "I'm afraid to ask. Is there anything else I should know?"

"I think that just about covers it."

"Well, I think we've covered enough."

Chapter 15

The rain was pelting my office window and I could barely see the building across the street, which wasn't a favorable development since I had to meet Vicki Richards at her office later that afternoon. She was about a mile away, and it would normally have been a pleasant walk, but with less-than-perfect conditions outside it was shaping up to be a miserable trip. A taxi could save the day, but they were hard to find in bad weather, and the subway could only get me about two-thirds of the way there. All things considered, I was resigned to the likelihood of getting a little wet.

It was early afternoon, Thursday, August 14. I had just finished speaking with Marc, who said he called to provide the latest scoop about ADG, but I think he really wanted to make sure I was prepared for my late afternoon meeting. Were it not for Marc's concern about potential conflicts of interest, he'd have probably handled the work himself. He also tried one last time to convince me to let Ken follow up, but I was undeterred, due to a desire to help my friend but also a new found interest in working with Ms. Richards. And truth be told, I wasn't really sure which motive was more important. He backed off, but as he badgered me with questions in his effort to get me prepared, I wondered if I'd made a mistake and should have let Ken do it after all. Marc's input was helpful but it was also hard to take, and at some point he had to accept the fact that Vicki was the expert, not me.

Aside from the meeting prep, we did discuss the latest developments. The papers had the story about the Indonesian government and its power authority's contracts with ADG. It wasn't the first big story they reported about the saga and it certainly wouldn't be the last. The whole episode had caught on with the financial press and they were acting like a bunch of sharks, smelling blood, getting excited and teaming up to pounce on their victim. With ADG, it had become a feeding frenzy to see who could get the latest strip of flesh, and none of us were happy with the reporting though we had to admit they did a masterful job getting access to information. Marc was worried the saga had entered a new phase, one where the press would feel compelled to report something about it every day, even if there was nothing new to say. And the continued reporting itself could make the situation seem worse than it was, and it was already bad enough—it didn't need any help.

We also talked about Kavi and how he'd been acting throughout the week. Marc said he seemed irritable as well as indecisive, and it was getting worse by the day. Under normal circumstances I'd have never believed him, but when I spoke with Kavi on Tuesday, I had noticed something too. He was usually very calm, and was one of the most decisive people I knew. He studied options carefully but when all the information was available he'd make a decision and that was it. There was no second guessing himself, even if he'd made what would later prove to be a mistake. But his altered demeanor hadn't concerned me. I'd thought it was perfectly reasonable to be annoyed and confused by the developments and, frankly, was impressed he had kept his composure as long as he had. But Marc was concerned, and it was beginning to concern me too.

The conversation also turned to the Department of Justice, which had sent some people to join Gary Bevins at ADG's offices on Tuesday. Marc said he didn't know anything about their agenda, but was concerned nonetheless. He thought it likely meant the SEC was giving serious consideration to making a criminal case, either against the company's executives, the company, or both. And Kavi could definitely be involved. Marc couldn't see how the government could deploy so many people in a very public company and be willing to come up empty handed. Although he was the attorney, I didn't share his anxiety as far as Kavi was concerned. I believed at worst he had made some errors in judgment, although I really didn't think that he had. But in no way could I see him implicated in any criminal case. It made absolutely no sense to me.

After the conversation, it took awhile to clear my head and get back to my agenda for the day. I didn't plan on returning to the office so I needed to get to a breaking point with my own work and get ready to leave for the meeting. The rain was showing no signs of letting up, so I grabbed my stuff and got ready to get soaked.

* * * *

Just getting to the building from the subway station was enough to get me drenched. The wind was so strong my umbrella acted more like a high performance parasail than a protector from the rain, and at one point it was so bad I really didn't need the elevator to get to the fifth floor. When I arrived at the office, the receptionist buzzed to unlock the door and giggled when she saw me. Then Vicki walked over and immediately put her hand over her mouth to keep from laughing. It must have been too much for her to watch me struggling with my raincoat and umbrella. I apologized for dripping all over the carpet, and getting some of the other coats wet. But she told me not to worry and calmly escorted me into her office.

While heading there, it was hard not to notice the way she walked. At our first meeting, when we made our way to the conference room, Ken was between her and me, and I had been in the men's room when she walked him back to the reception area, so I hadn't seen her walk for any distance before. But this time I had a good view—actually, a great view—she was directly in front of me and I did my best to make sure the receptionist and Vicki's assistant couldn't see me looking. She walked like a member of a royal family, smooth and poised, with great posture, yet her gait didn't make her look like a snob.

It wasn't a big office, about 10 by 13 feet, but it was cozy, and had a nice view. She asked me to have a seat, pointing to one of two chairs at a small circular table in the corner. It was right next to the window, which took up most of the wall and overlooked Park Avenue. It was still raining hard, so you could see people scurrying along the street, and I actually took some pleasure seeing that their umbrellas didn't work any better than mine. Looking around the office I was struck by how clean she kept everything. On the other hand, my office was usually a complete mess, and people were afraid to meet me there for fear of getting lost under some files. But her office was neat and organized, and you would never guess she was an attorney from the way it was furnished. It looked like it belonged to the editor of the National Geographic Society. There was an African wood carving on the side of one wall, a small Middle Eastern carpet on a credenza, an expensive looking Russian doll on a book shelf, and assorted other eclectic foreign objects.

After removing a file from the credenza, she pulled her chair closer to mine—giving me a sudden thrill—and sat down. And when she crossed her legs, I noticed she had another pair of great shoes, and I never notice a woman's shoes.

"I'm sorry your associate couldn't make it," she said.

She was probably just being polite, but it bothered me that she had referred to Ken. I shrugged my shoulders and said, "We just decided one of us could handle this."

"So tell me, who's my new client?"

"You're required to keep this confidential, right?"

"Of course. I can't help my clients without knowing a great deal about their affairs, and it's to be kept in strict confidence."

"We're talking about Kavi Chander. He's the CFO of American Dynamics Group."

She rubbed her brow and said, "That makes sense, although it would have been nice to have met him three months ago."

"Why?"

"I've been reading quite a bit about ADG in the papers lately. Bribery, accounting issues, voided contracts."

"We're too late?"

"No. It's just that the best planning is done well before any problems arise. I'd say his are in the incubation stage."

She paused to make some notes. Turning away, I looked out the window and inhaled her perfume, while doing my best to make sure she didn't notice. It had a very pleasant fragrance. Actually, it was too pleasant. It made me think of her as a woman and not as an asset protection attorney. It was an important meeting and I needed to concentrate, so I tried to clear my head.

She finished with her notes and said, "Don't worry. I'm sure we can come up with something that helps."

"Great. But first let me tell you, regardless of what you may have read, he's one of the finest individuals you could ever meet."

"You don't need to say that. I'm required to represent my clients to the best of my abilities."

"Sure, but I still want you to know he's one of the good guys. I'm sure all your clients say something like that, but in his case it's true. This stuff in the papers, it was all caused by a French guy who's the head of a business unit, and Kavi had nothing to do with it."

Vicki smiled and sat back in her chair. "You two are close friends?"

"We are. And that's why I'm here."

"Asset protection is important for good people too, so let's get started." She reached over for two bottles of water that were on her desk, offered me one and said, "Tell me about Kavi and his family."

"He's forty-six years old."

"That's young for the CFO of a company like ADG," she noted.

"And he got the job when he was thirty-five," I added. "That's how good he is. And he's got a great shot at the CEO position in a few years, assuming the scandal doesn't screw it up." I wasn't a big water drinker, but decided to open my bottle, partly out of thirst and partly out of a desire to follow her lead.

"Kavi's an interesting name. Where's he from?"

"India. He came here when he was in high school."

"He's a US citizen now?"

"That's right."

"And he keeps in touch with relatives in India?"

"I think so. Both of his parents are dead, but he goes back every two or three years. I'm not sure about Aarti's folks."

"She's also Indian?"

"That's right. But he met her in the States, when they were students at Boston College."

"And kids?"

"They have a daughter, Sanji, who just turned twenty-two and a son, Kris, who is about to turn twenty-one. Sanji just graduated from college and Kris starts his last year next month." Vicki's assistant interrupted and asked her if she would step out for a moment. While looking around, it struck me that there were no pictures of any people on display.

She walked back in and sat down. "Sorry. You were saying?"

"So he has to pay for one more year of college education and that's it. Although there may be some graduate school at some point."

"Has he put any money aside for his kids?"

"It's very little, but he plans to help them out financially until they can support themselves." I took out the materials Kavi had prepared for the meeting, placed them on the table in front of her, and took advantage of the opportunity to move my chair even closer, so we could both view the materials at the same time. "This is a summary of his financial accounts and there's more detail behind it." I waited a moment as Vicki studied the summary page. It showed Kavi had a net worth of just under $4.5 million using values as of the end of July.

> New Jersey home, estimated value $700,000, with a mortgage liability due in the amount of $100,000. Interest in ADG retirement account, total value of $650,000. ADG stock options, option spread value of approximately $3 million, which is $1.8 million after taxes. ADG stock, valued at $800,000. Cash and other investments, $600,000. Total net worth, $4,450,000.

I watched for any reaction but there was none. For 99 percent of the world's population, $4.5 million is an incredible amount of money, but for someone who had been the CFO of a company like ADG for more than 11 years it was next to nothing, although his net worth had been much higher before the scandal. A good portion of it was tied up in ADG stock and stock options and their value had been hit hard by the recent events. Nonetheless, all things considered, it was a relatively small amount. I felt compelled to say, "I'll bet your typical clients are worth much more than this?"

"I'm not sure there is a typical client, but you're right, I usually deal with many tens of millions, if not hundreds of millions of dollars. I think asset protection takes on greater importance when you're dealing with smaller sums like this." She continued to review the summary and said, "I would have thought he'd be worth more. Does he have any unusually large expenses?"

"He gives money to charity, and I mean a lot of money. There's one in particular, called the Sisters of Jain. His wife is one of their top officers. In fact, the Chanders were one of four families that founded its Northern New Jersey branch. It's also in New York, DC, Boston, Chicago and I think one other city. You might say it's like a small YMCA for Indians. He's also had his kids' education to pay the last four years, so that hasn't helped."

"Does Jain refer to the Jain religion?"

"That's right. I understand it's reasonably large in India."

"How long have they been involved with the charity?"

"His wife was a member since before they met in college. She's the one who introduced Kavi to it, and as his career progressed, he became more and more involved. When he joined ADG, the Chanders bought some land and gave it to the Sisters to start the North Jersey Branch."

"That's where they live?"

"They're in Mahwah, and they've been there for years. It's funny, but I remember when he bought the house in the early eighties. I think he paid about $300,000 and we thought it was all the money in the world. We were sure he'd go bankrupt from the $240,000 mortgage. Now he can afford a much better house but he doesn't see any reason to move, and he drives a ten year old car. Can you believe that?"

"It's not your typical profile for a CFO, is it?"

"Not these days. It's like I said. He's a great guy, and he's unpretentious. If you met him on a Saturday afternoon, you'd never know what he did for a living. Although you'd know he was smart."

Vicki started going through the back-up materials and asked some tough questions, some of which I couldn't answer. We put together a list of additional information I needed to obtain from Kavi, although we agreed there was only so much she could do without meeting him first. After about another hour of discussion we were through. All things considered, it had turned out to be a very productive session, even though I was distracted at times. She was very disciplined and thorough in the way she pursued her work.

Since we were finished with our meeting, I stopped fighting the urge to turn my attention to her. Looking around her office, I commented, "You must really love to travel."

She smiled and said, "It's my passion, but this is nothing. You should see what I have at my apartment."

Instead of saying, "I'd love to, let's go," which was the first thing that came to mind, it seemed more appropriate to say, "Actually, I love to travel too and I've managed to get to every continent. Most through work, but some of it was personal."

I had hoped she'd say something more about the subject and we'd segue to other topics, but she didn't. Instead, she stood up, so I stood up too. While placing her notes in a folder on her desk, she said, "This was productive. I was a little worried you wouldn't know enough about your friend, but you did your homework. If you can just get the remaining information to me as soon as possible, I can get this work going. I suggest you fax it over as soon as you can and please don't use email. I never use it to communicate confidential information."

"Your office isn't that far from mine and I can always use the exercise. Assuming we have better weather, I can just bring it over myself."

"That's really not necessary," she said. "I think a fax is best."

We walked toward the reception area and I took my time getting my raincoat and umbrella, which had yet to dry off. The pressure was building up. I just had to ask her to dinner, but was thinking it would probably be a stupid thing to do. First of all, she would likely say no. She had already brushed aside Ken's advances, assuming that's what they were, and that was certainly not a bullish sign for me. Second, we would be working closely with each other and it would be very awkward if she said no. Third, there would be plenty of time to ask her out after we finished doing our thing for Kavi.

When I was ready to go, she was about to shake my hand and say goodbye. By that time, my brain had concluded it would be best to wait for anything social, but my mouth wouldn't listen, so it declared its independence by blurting,

"Vicki, there's one more thing I need to ask you." I didn't want the receptionist to overhear our conversation, so I added, "Can we step out into the hall?"

Vicki looked surprised but she followed me out and closed the door to the office suite behind her. With a quizzical look she asked, "Yes?"

After quickly checking the hall to make sure no one was close by, I tried my best not to look nervous and said, "I hope this question doesn't make you feel uncomfortable, and if it does, I apologize in advance. Just take this as a compliment. I know these days you need to be very careful and…"

She interrupted, "Do you always take this long to ask a girl out for a date?"

Her response startled me. Before fully recovering I said, "I was wondering if you would join me for dinner tonight."

The bad news was immediate as she shook her head and said, "That's not going to work."

"I understand." Although my lungs had sprung a leak and the air was escaping at an alarming rate, I maintained my composure and very quietly said, "Please take it as a compliment."

She smiled and said, "No, you don't understand. I'd like to have dinner with you. It's just that tonight won't work. I'll be here very late, and, in any case, I would prefer a weekend. I have plans for this weekend, but how about a week from Saturday?"

My respiratory system suddenly kicked back in gear. I tried to be nonchalant and do my best Don Knotts imitation so she couldn't tell that a week from Saturday sounded "absolutely fantastic" to me. Keeping calm, I said, "That should work. Is there any particular food you like?"

She leaned in close to me—and I mean really close—and whispered, "Are you a trusting person?"

"I think I am."

Backing off quickly, she authoritatively said, "Good, let me think about it and I'll make the reservations." She took hold of the door and before opening it said, "Let's meet at the restaurant, and I'll call you before then with the details."

It was still raining hard when I walked outside and onto the street, but it didn't matter. It seemed as if I'd be walking above the clouds for a while.

Chapter 16

When you're the CFO of a large public company, you like control and you don't like surprises, and Kavi's world had been practically perfect on those two counts, but not anymore. Not with the scandal and the government's investigation living a life of their own and providing a continuous string of unexpected events. To make matters worse, even things Kavi could anticipate unfolded in ways that kept him off balance. It was Wednesday, August 20, and the day's first shocker was the resignation of Maurice Granville. Not the resignation itself, but its timing and the way it was done.

The day started off well, with an 8 am meeting to discuss strategic plans for the entertainment division. It was Kavi's favorite business unit, and the possible acquisition of one of the largest movie studios was on the agenda. The two hour meeting was a welcome respite from the summer's turmoil, and he wished it wouldn't end. But at 11 am he was back at it with a conference call. The participants included Granville, as well as Steve Halpern, Phil Mentz, Gary Bevins, Gary's assistant and six people with the Department of Justice. The call lasted about two hours, but a good portion of the first hour was wasted with certain procedural requirements put forth by the DOJ. The second hour was more substantive, with Maurice fielding most of the government group's questions and Steve and Kavi responding when they could. Maurice appeared to speak truthfully and, fortunately, or unfortunately, he did confirm the essence of L&K's findings. But for some reason the government wanted a second call, with only Maurice on the line. And although the others objected, there wasn't much they could do. Steve and Kavi instructed Maurice to call back as soon as the second call ended, but he never did. Instead, without any warning or explanation whatsoever, he faxed his resignation to Charles Goodman with a copy to Steve.

After getting word of the fax, Kavi called Marc and the two did their best to make sense of it all. Kavi said he got the impression there were only a few government people on the second call, which Marc took as a bad sign. They agreed that Kavi needed to reach Maurice to get some answers.

Kavi was getting frustrated with things he didn't know, not the least of which was the DOJ's reasoning for their coordination with the SEC. They had yet to clarify their intentions, other than to say they were assisting the SEC in its effort to perform a thorough investigation. He likened it to living in California, knowing you were overdue for an earthquake, with the waiting and uncertainty proving far worse than the event itself. When he finished speaking with Marc, he briefly entertained the idea of heading down a few floors to see Gary to get some answers, but knew it would be a terrible idea, and the answers would be coming soon enough. He tried to clear his head to work on other matters and was successful until Debra Jennings came rushing into his office.

Breathing hard and looking disheveled, she took a moment to catch her breath. Before fully recovering she said, "Gary was just in my office and I came up here as soon as he left. Remember he was asking all those questions about the acquisition of Gerard Engineering. Now I know why."

"I don't know if I want to hear this. You know you look a little winded. Want some water or coffee?"

"No. I'm ok."

"You don't look ok. Want some orange juice? Maybe some Brandy?"

"Would you stop?"

"Guess not. So what about Gerard?"

"Bevins was asking about the way we accounted for its litigation reserves at the time we made the acquisition. I think he wants to say we overstated its liabilities."

"And what did you tell him?"

"Nothing, so we need to get back to him. I assume you're familiar with what he's talking about."

"Close the door, ok? And sit down, you're making me nervous."

As soon as she mentioned litigation, Gary's interest in the acquisition became clear. And it was so obvious that Kavi was surprised he hadn't made the connection sooner. When ADG acquired Gerard in 1996, it purchased all the assets and assumed all the liabilities, including liabilities that were contingent upon the outcome of certain litigation. Gerard had once operated a boiler manufacturing business that it sold in the late 1960's. Two of its boilers exploded, one in 1988 and one in 1991, killing six people, and the families had sued Gerard for damages. If the explosions were a direct result of manufacturing defects, then the company would be held liable, notwithstanding the fact that it no longer owned the business and hadn't sold boilers for almost thirty years. On the other hand, if the explosions were caused by poor maintenance, then the company would owe nothing.

At the time of the 1996 acquisition, Gerard estimated there were one hundred such boilers still in operation and pegged its exposure at $300 million. Shortly after making the acquisition, ADG increased the recorded liability to $600 million. If it hadn't done that and Gerard ultimately paid out more than $300 million, the excess would have reduced ADG's reported earnings. The higher liability protected ADG from an accounting standpoint. But it didn't mean that the company would actually pay $600 million. At a later date, if the amount proved to be unnecessary, ADG could simply reduce the liability and report higher earnings at that time. Kavi was responsible for the Gerard acquisition and the accounting treatment, including all aspects of the litigation reserve.

Debra sat patiently, allowing her breathing to return to normal, while Kavi remained deep in thought. Finally, she asked, "Were they overstated?"

Kavi squinted and asked, "What?"

"The liability reserves," she said. "Were they overstated?"

"You could say that," he replied. "As I recall, we pegged the number at $600 million and we paid about $75 million so far. Until we know all the boilers are out of commission, we can't be sure, but I think we've paid all we're going to pay. You can get the exact numbers from the Engineering Systems Group controller."

"So we have a $525 million liability remaining on the books that we won't pay. They can't make a big deal out of that. That's less than one percent of our net worth."

Kavi grinned as he listened. "You were always a wiz with a calculator. One of the many things I love about you." He looked at his watch and then down at the floor. Without looking up he said, "Actually, it's only about $275 million now."

She quickly asked, "What happened to the balance?" From the look on Kavi's face she wondered if she should have said yes to the brandy.

"We settled some litigation in 2000 and paid about $250 million. We charged it against the Gerard boiler liability reserve, even though it had nothing to do with Gerard, and nothing to do with boilers." Taking hold of his coffee mug, he stood up and walked over to the window. With his eyes fixed on some point far out in the distance, he slowly savored his coffee and acted as if Debra wasn't in the room. Finally, without turning his head, he said, "This was all before your time as assistant controller, and I know what you must be thinking. By doing what we did, it made it look like we earned $250 million more than we really did. We should have recorded the $250 million as an expense, and reduced our reported earnings. That's what we would do today."

"I know."

"And litigation reserves are always tough to address. It's not an exact science."

"I agree."

"It's only been three years but the standards for proper financial accounting are much stricter in today's environment, and it's not fair to judge what we did back then under today's standards."

"I understand."

"But someone may do that, and they can say it's material."

"Why?"

"If I remember correctly, we made that $250 million settlement in the third quarter of 2000. Not that it matters. It would have been material to any quarter's results."

Debra was right when she said the overstated liability was immaterial to ADG's balance sheet. When you have $100 billion in assets, it doesn't really matter if the liability should be $525 million, $275 million or zero. On the other hand, when you report quarterly earnings of $900 million that just beat Wall Street's consensus forecast of $875 million, it does matter that your earnings would have been $650 million had the legal settlement been accounted for correctly.

"I still think it's no big deal," she said.

"Is that why you rushed up here as soon as Gary left your office?"

She shot back, "Keep in mind I didn't know the amounts involved."

"Fair enough." While continuing to look out the window, in a melancholy tone that didn't quite match the words, he said, "So tell me Debra, you think Gary Bevins can fly? I'd like to find out but these windows don't open."

"You want me to poison his water?"

He said, "No," while letting out a quick laugh. "With the luck I'm having they'd pin it on me."

Debra watched as he walked back to his desk. "You know, you don't have to explain yourself to me. We're a huge company and you make judgments about how to account for things all the time. I'm not here to second guess anything."

"You want a job with the enforcement division of the SEC?"

"It doesn't pay well," she replied. "So what should I do about Gary's questions?"

"Answer them honestly. We're not going to hide anything. Get all the details for him but let me see it first."

"Do you want to see it before I show it to Steve?"

Kavi thought for a moment and then said, "No. Give it to him the same time. I don't want you getting caught between him and me. Not now anyway."

"So what do you think the SEC is planning to do?"

He shrugged his shoulders and said, "That's the million dollar question, isn't it?"

Debra nodded and got up to leave. Upon reaching the door, she turned back to Kavi and said, "You know how I feel about you."

"You're one of the great ones, Debra."

"I don't care what happens, my opinion of you will never change, and Gary is way off base if he says there's anything wrong with what you did."

Kavi smiled and focused his gaze on her long enough to get her to blush, which was usually hard to do. Looking like he wanted to say more, he sighed and simply said, "Thanks." After watching her leave, his thoughts turned back to the $250 million legal settlement. Although he could still argue it wasn't material, it was still wrong, and unlike the bribery scandal, he was the one responsible. Still, in the scheme of things, it was nothing compared to bribery.

The rest of the day provided even more bad news. The company got word that the Malaysian government was following Indonesia's lead and planned on challenging the validity of the company's contract to sell power. In and of itself, it wasn't that big a deal. The company had only one plant in Malaysia and the contract wasn't as favorable as any of the four contracts in Indonesia. But it was still troubling because it raised the risk that other countries would make similar claims.

It didn't seem as if the day could get much worse, but shortly after 4 pm the power went out, and Kavi wondered if the local utility also wanted to get out of a contract with ADG. One of his assistants turned on a portable radio that had probably cost less than $20. It wasn't much, but at that moment it was more valuable than all the expensive communications equipment in the building. It soon became clear the outage had hit fifteen eastern states and parts of Canada, and would likely last for some time. And the way things were going, Kavi decided not to stick around. After making sure the Human Resources department was taking charge of the situation with employees, he left to head home. But he had forgotten that the parking garage used elevators to move the cars from floor to floor, and, unfortunately, they didn't have any back-up power. He thought of calling Aarti to pick him up, but the reports indicated the George Washington

Bridge had been closed. So he decided to walk the ten miles to the bridge and have Aarti pick him up after he crossed over to the New Jersey side.

It was actually pleasant outside, and the people milling around on the streets were surprisingly in a party mood. That helped lift his spirits somewhat as he made his way west, finally crossing under the West Side Highway to get on the walking-jogging path that ran in between the highway and the Hudson River. Heading north, he couldn't help but notice the different types of trees, and the texture of the water flowing in the river. And there were people jogging and rollerblading on the path, as well as commuters from New Jersey in the same predicament as his. Other than the commuters, he had seen it all before—the highway was the route he took to and from work everyday—but he'd never really noticed. Most days, he'd leave the office late and would get to the highway after dark, and the times that it was still daylight, or in the mornings, he just didn't pay much attention. You could say his body was there but his mind was someplace else. But this day was different, and being on foot forced him to view his surroundings from a different perspective.

He wasn't in the best of shape, and it didn't help that he was wearing a suit and walking in shoes. While sitting down on a bench to rest, he watched as three young boys sat on the bank with their feet in the river, and it took him back to the times he had done that as a boy in India. Things were much simpler back then, when he had nothing compared to what he had now, but was still happy. He had the time to do all sorts of things, like playing football, or fishing for hours with his friends. But he didn't have the free time to do those things anymore. Sure, he made room for flying. Being a licensed pilot was his passion, and he was teaching his son to fly, but he hadn't even done much of that lately. As he considered the bribery scandal and the ongoing demands of his senior position, he wondered if his career was really worth the effort. And, as he stood up to resume his walk, he remembered there were other things that were fun besides work.

After five hours of walking, or twice his original estimate, he made it to the other side of the bridge where Aarti was waiting at the pre-agreed location. He hugged her as if he hadn't seen her in years, and when she pulled away he thought he couldn't have walked another inch.

Just as they were pulling up in their driveway his cell phone rang, and he was startled to hear Maurice Granville on the line. Kavi was very tired, but knew he had better take the call.

"Where've you been?" Maurice asked. "I've been trying to reach you but couldn't get through."

"We've had a power outage and everyone's using their cell phones. Say, you're up pretty early. What time is it there?"

"It's 5 am, and I haven't been to bed yet."

"That figures. I'll bet you've got a lot going on. You know I thought you'd never return my call." Aarti asked if it was Maurice, and Kavi nodded his head.

"I'm not returning your call and don't tell anyone we had this little conversation."

"Why not?"

"Look, there's only so much I can say. I just want you to know you need to watch your back."

"From whom?"

"No specifics. Just be prepared and don't trust anybody."

Kavi was both physically and mentally exhausted and wasn't in the mood for working with clues. "I assume you're referring to the second call you had with the government today?"

"I can't answer that."

"Can you at least tell me who was on the call?" Kavi heard silence on the line then said, "Maurice, it can't hurt to tell me that."

"It was one guy from the Department of Justice and one guy from the SEC."

"Just the three of you?"

"That's right, and I faxed my resignation to Charles right after the call."

"So why the timing? You said nothing about a resignation when we spoke with you this morning."

"You knew once L&K made their report that I had to leave. I was just waiting for the right time. Let's just say that once I got off that call it made sense not to wait any longer. Sorry, but I need to go now."

"Wait. You tried hard to reach me, and then this is *all* you can say?"

"I think I've said enough. If you can't make sense of what I'm telling you, then that's your problem."

"I guess everything's becoming my problem. So, tell me, you taking a job with that French company to work in the Ivory Coast?"

"That's right. You can read about it in some of the trade journals in a week or so. I'll be spending the next few years in Africa, but don't try to reach me. My calls will be screened and I won't be speaking with any ADG people. I think you can understand that."

"So there really is nothing more you will tell me?"

"Kavi, I need to go, and don't try to call me back. As of today, my old phone numbers no longer work. Also, if you try to reach me at the project site or at the hotel, I won't take your calls. And if you try to visit me, I won't meet with you and you'll have wasted a trip. Although we won't talk again, I really do wish you the best of luck."

Aarti could tell from the expression on Kavi's face that the call had him worried. She put her arms around him and said everything will be ok. But after all that had happened during the day, he wasn't so sure.

Chapter 17

It was Friday, August 22nd, and Marc was getting things organized so he could leave his office. It was humid outside, but was otherwise shaping up to be a pleasant evening and, fortunately, the power had been restored throughout most of the city. His pharmaceutical company acquisition had cleared the final regulatory hurdles earlier in the week and was ready to close. Bartman & Cross had done an excellent job and the client was thrilled with the effort. Although the deal had yet to close, the client's general counsel had reserved a room at a New York steakhouse and invited all the lawyers working on the deal to join her for dinner. Although Marc was pleased with the status of the transaction, he had spoken to Kavi earlier in the day, and was disturbed by the most recent events, particularly Maurice's call earlier in the week. And he was thinking about that when Phil Mentz stopped by his office.

Phil closed the door behind him, walked toward a large credenza adjacent to Marc's desk, and picked up a "tombstone" commemorating a public debt offering for a mining company. It had a miniature copy of the offering document enclosed in plastic, along with one ounce bars of silver, copper and aluminum. While examining it, Phil said, "I guess you'll get another one soon. I hear your acquisition was cleared."

"It was. We're having sort of a pre-closing dinner tonight, and I was about to leave." Marc studied Phil and asked, "Is that why you closed the door? So we can discuss my client's acquisition?"

"Can we have an off-the-record chat about ADG?"

"Sure. What's on your mind?"

Phil turned and leaned against the credenza. After taking his time to respond, he said, "I know you and Kavi Chander are very close. Up until a few week's ago I didn't think that would pose a problem, but I'm sure you're not surprised by my saying that things have changed." He took a breath, and then continued. "It's probably best that we no longer involve you with this work."

"I don't agree," Marc quickly replied. "Is this what Steve Halpern wants?"

"It is, and I think we should follow his instructions."

"Kavi may have a different view. I can ask him to—"

"Don't! Believe me, this is better."

Marc sat back in his chair, and while rubbing the side of his neck, said, "Ok. I'm listening."

Phil continued, "I trust your judgment and I know what you think about Kavi. I'm convinced he knew nothing about the bribery. After all, why would he have sent Debra Jennings to Ukraine if he already knew about it? It would make no sense."

Marc could see where the conversation was leading so he jumped ahead. "And you think the government will try to say that Kavi *knew* about the bribery? Is that why Steve has been distancing himself?"

"I'm guessing here, but I think the government may do just that. And Steve, well, I can't tell you what's motivating him." Phil paused. He looked away and said, "Remember this conversation is off the record and it's the last time I'll discuss ADG matters with you. But if I were representing Kavi, I'd tell him to seek counsel."

"He hasn't been accused of anything."

"I know, but it's probably best that he gets prepared, just in case."

"And why would you say that?" Marc asked.

Speaking as if he were being forced to reply and was betraying a best friend, he finally said, "I shouldn't tell you this, but Gary Bevins and one of the guys from the Department of Justice have had a number of conversations with Charles Goodman. Steve and I were involved with some but were excluded from others. You know the way the government usually works these cases. They try to get agreements with lower level employees, give them immunity or some other good deal, in exchange for the employees' cooperation in going after people who are higher up in the organization. They keep working their way up until they have a good enough case to go after the senior officers." He stopped and took a breath. "But the government hasn't done that here. From what I know, they haven't spoken with Kavi's staff about any deals, and they certainly haven't spoken to him."

Marc thought for a moment and leaned forward in his chair. "But we know they've spoken with Maurice, and now you're saying they've spoken with Charles. So you think they're trying to go from the top down. Cut some deals and then come after Kavi." Marc was beginning to see some meaning to Maurice's call. Perhaps he had a guilty conscience or perhaps he genuinely wanted to warn Kavi about what could happen.

"Not that I can say for sure, but I think it's possible. The government knows it would be tough to get at Maurice, so maybe they're willing to make a deal, and maybe he doesn't want to keep looking over his shoulder when he travels, or maybe he would like to visit the States now and then, so a deal looks good to him. You know I think he's one shady character. He struck me as strange when I met him, and now we know what he's capable of doing. But I don't know anything about Charles, not from the few times we've met, so I don't know what he'd do, and I don't know what the government might want from him. Maybe I'm just reading too much into it."

"So why are you telling me all this?"

"Because I think you should do what you can to help your friend. That's why I think we should follow Steve's directive. You can act more freely this way."

"Maybe our firm should stop representing ADG?"

"That wouldn't do any good. We couldn't represent Kavi anyway, and we can't stop the government folks from doing whatever they plan to do. And nothing's happened yet, so I don't see how we would have any basis for ending the relationship. Keep in mind I could be way off base here. I'm just reading between the lines."

Smiling, Marc asked, "Don't you tell people not to do that?"

"That's correct. I'm not good at taking my own advice."

"I'm glad. You know you're not such a bad guy after all."

"So you're not upset about being taken off this work?"

"No, I agree with your judgment. I can do more for Kavi this way."

"You understand I didn't hear you say that."

"Hear me say what?"

Phil nodded and stood up. On his way out he said, "It will be interesting to see how this all plays out."

"Kavi didn't do anything wrong. He'll be ok. We have a darned good system of justice in this country, right?"

"Right. But it's best not to have an eight hundred pound gorilla coming after you."

Once Phil left, Marc took some time to think about the conversation, recognizing how hard it must have been for Phil to provide the heads-up, knowing that the firm's client was ADG. In different circumstances, he wouldn't have been concerned with Kavi's welfare and, in any case, it was just a one-time deal. It was clear that Phil wouldn't speak with Marc about ADG matters again.

With all that was going on, the last thing Marc wanted to do was eat steak and celebrate. Although he couldn't cancel on his client, he could arrive at the restaurant fashionably late, so he called Kavi and agreed to meet him on the corner of Lexington Avenue and 55th Street, which was on the way to the steakhouse. But as luck would have it, on the way out he ran into the Bartman & Cross managing partner and couldn't politely get free, so he arrived at the rendezvous point about fifteen minutes late. When he got there he saw Kavi checking his watch.

"So where's your dinner?" Kavi asked. His tie was loosened and he wasn't wearing the jacket to his suit.

"We're meeting at Stewart & Wilkens," Marc said. "I'm already late but I wanted to see you first."

"I think you should go ahead and enjoy your dinner. It's good to see one of us is getting something done." Kavi pointed straight ahead to an area on 55th Street, so they could be away from the crowd. While walking toward that spot, he said, "I've been thinking. You shouldn't worry so much about me. This whole mess is my problem, not yours."

Confused, Marc stared at Kavi to get some nonverbal clues. "I don't understand. You don't want my help?"

"Don't get me wrong. I really appreciate everything you've done, but this just keeps getting bigger, and I'm starting to feel guilty about taking up so much of your time. Don't worry about me. It'll work out in the end."

"Don't worry about you?" Marc looked up at the sky, smiled and then looked back at Kavi. "You and the guys always said I worried about things even when there was nothing to worry about. Now there *is* something to worry about, and you think I can stay out of it?" Marc paused, then said, "Thanks for being concerned about me but don't be ridiculous. And by the way, I've been billing for most of my time. Remember, ADG is our client."

"But you shouldn't have to do more."

"Sorry, but you're stuck with me, and you've got Ken and Carl. Don't go asking Carl not to help. He thinks he owes everything to you."

An old lady walked by, struggling with her five dogs. While watching her, Kavi said, "I can't get rid of you, can I?"

"You always were a quick study."

Kavi nodded, and then he stepped on a still smoldering cigarette butt and said, "Maybe I should take up smoking?"

Marc laughed and asked, "Where did that come from?"

"I need to do something new."

"Pick something like jogging."

"I'm too big to jog."

Marc checked his watch and realized he couldn't stay much longer. "I'll need to go soon, but I have some things we need to discuss."

"Why am I not surprised?"

Marc looked up and down the street to see if they could be overheard. He leaned in closer to Kavi. "Tell me, have there been any developments since we spoke yesterday morning?"

"Nothing much, unless you call a request by L&K to write off half the value of our Far East merchant power group as a big development."

Startled, Marc quickly said, "You can't be serious?"

A limousine pulled up, stopped right in front of them and let out four of the city's 'beautiful people.' Kavi waited until the entourage disappeared into a nearby restaurant before responding. "I'd like to say that I'm joking, but I'm not. While our friend Yu Cheng was in New York, he convinced the lead L&K partner that there's a serious chance many of the power group's contracts will be voided. I guess he thinks he's a lawyer now. He thinks Indonesia has a good claim, and now that Malaysia has jumped on the band wagon he thinks other countries will follow their lead."

"Half the value of the total group? How much is that?"

"We're talking about a write down of more than $2 billion, and maybe even a lot more than that."

"Does Gary Bevins know about this?" Marc asked.

"I didn't tell him. Although the way Steve's been supplying information, I'll bet he does. It doesn't matter though. Everybody will know when we disclose the write-down."

"You mean you might actually do it?"

"If this happened four years ago, I'd have told Yu Cheng to go to hell, and then I'd have given him a head start. These days, you can't afford a battle with your auditors. It'll become public, and no matter who's right the company will look bad."

"They're wrong about this. Those are good contracts. And even if there were a problem, you don't know enough at this time to make that kind of a write off."

"I don't disagree, but it doesn't matter."

They remained silent for a moment and then Marc said, "There's something else I need to ask you. When was the last time you spoke to Charles Goodman?"

"This afternoon. Why?"

Marc thought about how best to phrase his query. "Do you think he's been supportive of you?"

Surprised by Marc's question, Kavi gave him a funny look and said, "I'm not sure what you're getting at. Up until early July he thought I was the greatest thing since sliced bread. I'm sure he still thinks that, but he's pissed about what's happened. We all are."

"Do you think he believes you were responsible? Let me rephrase that. Does he think this should have been caught sooner?"

"Marc, even I think we should have caught this sooner. He hasn't said it, but I'm sure that's what he thinks too. But he understands that Maurice worked hard to keep the bribery under wraps."

Marc thought that his friendship with Kavi was more important than his obligation to keep his conversation with Phil off the record, so he decided he would err on the side of saying too much rather than too little. "Do you trust Charles?"

"Sure. He's never given me a reason not to."

"Has he had any conversations directly with the government?"

Kavi hesitated, then asked, "Why? You think he did?"

"Just assume it's a possibility."

"If he did, you'd think Steve would have known about it, and he never said a word to me. But the way Steve's been acting, that doesn't mean anything. I never really liked him, but I always thought I could trust him. Not anymore." Kavi wiped his forehead and took some time to think. "So let's assume Charles met with the government."

"And what would that mean to you?"

"I'm not sure. Who knows what the government's looking to do. It could be nothing. Or maybe……no, I just don't know. Is this why you wanted to meet?"

"That's right. Maurice knew what he was talking about when he advised you to get prepared and watch your back. That obviously came from something the government told him, and you can only imagine what they may be discussing with Charles."

"So what do you suggest?"

"It may not hurt for you to get your own counsel."

"Counsel?" Kavi shot back, "It would look pretty silly doing that before I was accused of anything, wouldn't it?"

"You don't need to tell anyone. I'll get a few names for you and you can consider them in confidence. This way you can be ready, just in case."

"Just in case?"

Marc looked at his watch. "I really need to go. Think about it, ok?"

Kavi walked away thinking that an innocent person shouldn't need to hire counsel. It seemed like such a radical step, and he hoped Marc's fears would prove to be unfounded.

Chapter 18

The big day had finally arrived. It was Saturday, August 23rd, the day that Vicki and I were getting together for dinner. There'd been decent weather all week, albeit on the humid side, but the day was shaping up to be perfect and I took it as a sign of good things to come. It was noon, and we were planning to meet at the restaurant at 8 pm, so I had some time to relax. I was feeling so good that I actually started to feel somewhat guilty. It didn't seem right to be in such good spirits when my best friend was facing trouble, but I just couldn't help myself.

My apartment complex was built on the top of the Palisades Cliffs, way above sea level, overlooking the Hudson River. And I was twelve floors up, on the northeast corner of the building, so I had great views of the Manhattan skyline. We were directly across from the 79th Street boat basin, and on weekend afternoons in summer, I'd get something to eat and just sit outside on my thirty foot terrace and enjoy the view. That's what I was doing at the time.

Looking across at Manhattan, I was trying to spot buildings that were near the place where Vicki and I would meet. She'd made reservations at LePrince, a fancy French restaurant on the Upper East Side, and though I didn't know much about it, I was sure it would be expensive. That was fine with me—it was money I had—it was a woman that I lacked. I tried not to think about her so much. After all, she had only agreed to join me for dinner and, for all I knew, she was just being friendly. But try as I might, I just couldn't get her out of my mind.

I watched as a replica of an old fashioned sailing ship passed slowly by, and I tried to imagine what it must have been like a few hundred years earlier when the original ships passed by, and what their crews would have thought if they had the chance to see the Manhattan skyline of my day. Some of the ships were real beauties, and I oftentimes felt guilty that I didn't know more about them, and would tell myself to buy a book or two about ships, but I never did.

My mind turned back to Kavi's situation. With all the corporate scandals and new legislation, everyone was on edge, including the government authorities, and it was a good time to be an audit partner, but in some ways a bad time to be the CFO of a major company like ADG. That was pretty ironic, since we'd always thought Kavi had one of the best jobs in the country. When he started there, each of us was envious in our own way. He was only thirty-five, which was incredibly young for the position, and it had taken guts for him to get the job in the first place. ADG had hired one of the premier executive search firms, Stephenson & Hales, or S&H as they were known, to fill the position. We'd heard that there were hundreds of candidates who expressed interest, and someone mentioned Kavi to S&H, but they didn't follow up. The top search firms have a certain way of handling their assignments. If they're filling a CFO position, they want someone who is a CFO, pure and simple. Most people would have given up, but not Kavi. He showed up unannounced at S&H's head office, and asked to see the chairman of the firm. Since Kavi was a partner in Winston Knight, the chairman agreed to meet, presumably just to be polite. But after about an hour of discussion, S&H knew they'd found their man, and two months later, Kavi resigned from the firm in order to make the move. I started thinking about our anniversary dinner that year at the Iron Horse. It was June 30, 1992, the day I officially became a partner in the firm, although I'd been cleared for admission months earlier. Kavi had been with ADG for only six weeks at the time.

* * * *

Ken was drinking a little too much. He pretended to give Kavi a dirty look, and said, "Don't think I'll genuflect just because you're some big shot corporate executive."

Kavi was somewhat drunk himself. Taking longer than usual to reply, he finally said, "No, you should bow down because I'm better than you."

"You took so long and that's all you can think of? You sure you didn't have sex with some high powered broad at S&H to get your job?"

"We don't have to worry about being mistaken for intelligent businessmen, do we?" Marc asked rhetorically. He'd been sitting between Kavi and Ken, and he moved his chair away from the table so he wouldn't be associated with them.

I took a spoon and clanged it against a glass to get their attention. It was a busy night at the Iron Horse, and it was hard to be heard. "Hey, how many people sitting at this table made partner today?"

Kavi and Ken looked at me and, as if planned, said in unison, "It took you long enough."

Ignoring their comment, I tried to take a major league bite of my burger. Then, as Ken started eyeing a young woman at the bar, I wiped my hand off and reached over to cover his eyes. It seemed the appropriate time for him to start acting like the responsible father of three little kids that he'd become, instead of acting like a Playboy. To make my point, I simply said, "You've got kids."

Ken pushed my hand away, "That's all the more reason for me to look. They want a happy father, right? And this makes me happy." Ken looked back at the bar and started motioning for the girl to come join us.

Marc cringed. "Don't do that. Someone might recognize you."

"That's ok. I'll say I called her over to be with you."

"Nobody will believe that," Kavi added.

It was apparent she had no intention of joining us. I turned to Ken and said, "See, she's not interested in you."

Ken picked up his beer and raised it, as if making a toast to the woman at the bar. She smiled and raised her glass in response. Ken said, "See, she's interested. It's just too crowded at this table."

"I guess we're cramping your style," Marc said, nursing his beer.

"I'll just pursue her later." Ken looked over at me and pointed his finger at my head. "We always said you'd make partner. See, you didn't believe us."

Marc said, "That's right. We should be focusing on Carl. Seriously guys, let's have a toast." Marc picked up his beer, and Kavi and Ken followed his lead. "Here's to a new partner, an honest guy, and what's more important, a loyal and trusted friend."

The toast was great, but then they stood up and starting singing 'For he's a jolly good fellow' at the top of their lungs. It was really embarrassing. Mind you, it wouldn't have been so bad if one of them could actually carry a tune. By the time they were through, most people in the bar had turned to stare, and we must have looked like a strange group—an oversized Indian guy, a WASP with the body of Hercules, a Jewish lawyer and a paisan from Brooklyn. At least I wasn't pretending to be Frank Sinatra.

"So how does it feel, now that you've really joined the firm?" Marc asked.

After taking a deep breath, I admitted, "It's a relief. Sooner or later it had to happen." Kavi had already made partner in 1988 and Ken got the nod a year later. It generally took longer at a law firm like Bartman & Cross, so it made sense that Marc didn't make it until early in 1990. Some people said I was delayed until 1992 because of my age. I'd just turned 32 the prior December, and that was a good age to make partner, but I thought I would have made it earlier.

Kavi put his right hand around the back of my neck. While shaking a little too hard he said, "This is my guy and he made it." He let go, and I moved my toes to make sure there was no permanent paralysis. He sat back, smiled, and said, "I'll bet your parents are really proud."

"That's the best part," I said. "To be safe, I never discussed making partner with my folks, so I wouldn't get their hopes up and then disappoint them. They knew what it would mean, but they didn't know I really had a chance at it. My dad's ecstatic, and I understand he's told everybody at the construction site downtown where he's working." I had to stop for a moment to maintain my composure and keep from getting too emotional. "Just my graduation from college was a big deal for him. Remember, I was the first in the family to do it. Now he can't believe I'm a partner and you should have seen his face when I told him."

The four of us sat silent for a moment, with each of us savoring something good. I thought about my accomplishment, and what it meant to my father. Although operating a crane paid well, he wanted something better for his sons. He'd always pushed my older brother and me to stay away from trouble, get a good education, and make something positive of ourselves. He never graduated from high school, and yet he'd bring home magazines on all kinds of subjects like nature and science. My brother and I would read certain articles and talk at dinner about what we had learned. We'd argue about how the dinosaurs became extinct, what infinity really was, or the true nature of the Crab Nebula. As we got older, we realized dad didn't know anything about the subjects we discussed. But he knew there was a whole world beyond New York City construction, and he wanted his sons to be a part of it. He loved listening to us, and my brother and I knew it. We loved him, and we wanted to make him happy, but we also read the articles because we enjoyed them. My father was thrilled that we embraced learning, and looked forward to having two college-educated sons. Unfortunately, Joe Junior died before he had a chance to graduate, and in a way that added more meaning when I got my degree. And making partner was like icing on the cake. Although I wanted it for me, in many ways I did it for my dad.

As I looked around the table, I thought it was shaping up to be one of the best anniversary dinners we'd ever had. Ken ordered another round for everyone except me, since I was planning on driving home and taking Kavi with me.

When the beers arrived, Ken offered a toast to Kavi for landing such a great job. I raised a glass of zero-proof water and joined in. When we were done, I said, "Guys, let's not sing. We'd get kicked out, and they'd never let us back in."

Marc asked Kavi, "So how did it feel to leave Winston Knight?"

"It's been six weeks, but it really hasn't hit me yet. I've been so busy getting organized. Winston Knight is all I've known for thirteen years, so it'll take some time to get adjusted." He looked over at Ken and me. "Now that I'm gone, make sure you guys don't screw it up."

"They told me you were one of my big supporters," I said.

Kavi pointed his bottle toward me and some of the beer sloshed out onto the floor. "I spoke up for you, but you made it on your own."

Marc nodded and said, "You'll be a great partner, Carl, believe me. You've got what it takes."

"You were born to be an audit partner," Ken said. "Although I don't know how you do it. I hated auditing. Being a tax partner is so much more rewarding. You get to save clients money instead of checking their books."

A waitress dropped a glass while serving the next table. It shattered, and a few shards landed near our table. While watching her clean up I said to Ken, "I could never imagine you as an audit partner. I'd say you were born to be a tax guy."

Kavi leaned toward me and said, "Ken's right. Auditing was ok for awhile, but after four years as a partner, I was ready to leave. And I was very fortunate to have had this opportunity. But you'll stay for the long haul."

Having just made partner, I really hadn't thought about how long I might remain with the firm, but the guys were probably right. It was an important job, I enjoyed it and I did it well. Accounting firms played an important role in the capital markets, and I took my responsibilities seriously. Analytical skills were my strength, so I could easily identify weaknesses in audit procedures and typically did so when assigned to a new audit engagement. The improved plans sometimes meant more work and, for the clients, additional cost. And it didn't take a genius to know that wasn't the best route to getting promoted. Because of that, there'd been times when my chances of making partner looked grim. But having made it, I'd need to really screw up to get kicked out of the firm, so it gave me the freedom to be the auditor I thought I should be.

I watched as Kavi struggled to look sober as he made his way back from the men's room. "You're lucky I'm driving," I told him. "You'd have never made it home alive."

"Are you kidding?" Ken said. "With his luck, he'd make it home without a scratch." Ken had also been drinking heavily, but he could handle it well, and was staying in the city that night just to be safe.

Kavi sat down and asked, "Was I not walking straight? Funny, but I don't feel drunk."

"That's a dumb thing to say," Ken said. "If you're drunk, you won't know you're drunk, will you?"

Marc jumped in saying, "How would *you* know? You're drunk."

"Can we talk about something else?" I asked. "Kavi, are you nervous about your new job?"

"Why should I be nervous? Just because it's one of the biggest companies in the world?"

"Yes, because it's big and it's complicated and very high profile. I'd be scared to death."

Kavi rubbed the side of his neck and took a moment to clear his head. "It doesn't matter how big the numbers are. The issues are the same whether the dollars are in the millions or tens of millions. True, we have more businesses than most companies, but that just means it'll take a little longer than usual to learn about them. There's really nothing to be worried about. In fact, I'm really excited."

"So what do you do first?"

"Right now, I'm reading everything I can get my hands on about each business, but I've got to get out and visit the plants and meet the people. It'll take some time, but by this time next year I'll know what I need to know."

"It is a great job, isn't it?" Marc asked.

"Absolutely. As far as I'm concerned, it's better than anything I ever expected. Think of it—operations around the world—a major television network—over 100,000 employees. How could any job be better than this?" Kavi stopped, looked down at the table and smiled. He looked up at us and said, "Can you believe a poor kid from India can come to the United States and wind up the CFO of one of the biggest corporations in the world?"

Ken interrupted, "Let me know when he starts singing 'America the Beautiful' so I can go to the bathroom and throw up."

"Just keep drinking and shut up." Marc was talking to Ken, but was looking at Kavi when he spoke. "That really *is* something, isn't it? Don't take this the wrong way, but I never think of you as being Indian."

"That's funny, I never think of you as being Jewish."

"Marc's Jewish? I'm out-a-here." Ken stood up, and then sat down laughing.

Marc ignored Ken. "You know what I mean. I know you're from India, but I don't really think about it. It's something for you to be where you are now, and I think it's great." Marc looked over at me and Ken. "We all do."

I raised my glass to indicate my agreement and said, "It's clear you know exactly what to do. You always did. I think I'll go out and buy some ADG stock because they hired the right guy."

Ken took time away from being an asshole and chimed in, "I agree. All joking aside, it's Winston Knight's loss and ADG's gain. They couldn't find a better person to be their CFO."

Kavi nodded and smiled. "I think it was better when you were calling me a drunk."

There was some loud singing coming from the bar. Evidently other people had something to celebrate as well. Turning back to our table, I said, "It's been a good year so far, wouldn't you say?"

Marc sat back in his chair. "I'd say it's been a good thirteen years. Good jobs, families, kids. So Carl, you need to get married one of these days."

"Did my mother pay you to say that?"

Before I could continue, Ken jumped in. "Don't let some woman trap you into getting married. Believe me, when you think about it, you'll realize you've got it made. You're single, and a partner in a major accounting firm, so don't be surprised when women start going crazy over you. Take advantage and live it up." Ken paused and then continued, "I'd be very disappointed if you got married any time soon."

"Don't worry," I said. "There doesn't seem to be much chance of that. Hey, look. Your friend's getting away." The gal at the bar waved to Ken and started to leave. He got up and met her at the door. We watched as she wrote something on a piece of paper and stuffed it in his shirt pocket. When he got back to the table, we just stared and he grinned and stared back.

Finally, Ken broke the silence. "I'm not going to call. What were you all thinking? I just wanted to know that I could get her number." Actually we sort of believed him. Being a busy tax professional, and with three little kids at home, it would be very difficult to cheat, even if he wanted to. Trying to change the subject, Ken said, "Did you guys decide about Vegas? You can count me in." Marc wanted the four of us to take a few days off in October and head to Las Vegas to bet on the baseball playoffs and the football games.

"I already told Marc I'd like to go," I said. "I'm sure if I can get a girlfriend by October, she won't mind."

Kavi said, "Sounds like fun to me. Assuming nothing comes up with ADG at the last minute. Marc, you'll plan everything?"

"Just leave the details to me." If you had just met Marc, you'd never have guessed how he loved gambling, especially on sporting events. Actually, he was quite successful at it, keeping detailed records of how individual teams performed on the road, at home, after a loss, after a win, against the point spread, and so on and so forth. He played the percentages, and it often paid off. He was in heaven in Vegas betting on the sports book. I planned on doing whatever he did. If I tried to bet on my own, I'd lose.

Kavi made the mistake of asking if we should take the wives and kids, and Ken shot the idea down in a heartbeat. Over the years, we'd taken a number of trips together, and we never took family along. We told ourselves it was only once or twice a year, and the guys needed some time away from their families. Plus, I'd feel funny if I was the only one who came alone. When we were away on the trips, we were no longer four businessmen, just four guys, and having others along would take away some of the fun.

* * * *

Having left my apartment early to make sure to avoid traffic, it was only 7 pm when I parked my car in the city. I figured it wouldn't look good to be late for our first date, assuming that's what it was. I assumed it was a date, but Vicki may have had other ideas. The parking garage was only a short walk from the restaurant, so there was plenty of time to kill. It was a beautiful evening and the sun hadn't set, so I decided to take a walk to Times Square. By my estimate, I could make it there and back easily and arrive at the restaurant right on time.

It was nice to walk slower than other people for a change, and really appreciate what midtown Manhattan had to offer. Having worked in the city for years, you'd have thought I'd be bored by the scenery, but that wasn't so. On weekdays, my typical routine was to rush from one place to another, while oblivious to my surroundings. On weekends, if I didn't have a date, I'd stay in New Jersey or see my mom in Brooklyn. It was bad enough being alone, so I didn't need to see happy couples walking the streets. Of course, midtown on a Saturday night was full of single people, but when you're alone, you don't see them, or you think they're on their way to meet someone else. It was great to think that I was on my way to meet someone. In less than an hour, Vicki and I would be together.

* * * *

Walking into the restaurant, my eyes focused on a woman near the end of the bar who stood out in the crowd. She looked great with her red silk turtleneck top that accentuated her dark features and matched the color of her shoes, blending perfectly with her mid-length beige skirt. And the way she was sitting, you could tell she had beautiful legs and wanted the world to know. Trying not to stare, I looked over when she waved and realized it was Vicki. While walking toward her, I took a couple of deep breaths and kept reminding myself to keep cool.

She stood up to greet me and it just seemed natural to kiss her cheek. Smiling, all she said was, "You look nice." But that was all it took, and my ability to protect myself was gone.

"You look pretty good yourself. I'm no fashion expert, but that really is a great outfit you're wearing. I think it looks perfect on you."

"Thanks. That's very sweet."

"Have you been waiting long?"

"Not too long. It was such a nice night, it seemed like a good idea to get here early and have a drink. I find it interesting to watch people."

It seemed best not to tell her I'd been walking the streets of Manhattan when we could have been together at the bar. "Is your apartment close by?"

"It's just a few blocks away. I love the Upper East Side, especially during the summer when it's less crowded. Maybe we can take a walk after dinner?"

Our table was ready and we were escorted into the main room. As we entered, there was no mistaking the place for the Iron Horse. The window treatments must have cost a small fortune. The paintings on the walls were either originals or excellent copies. And if someone had said the décor echoed the grand ballroom at Versailles, I wouldn't have been surprised. I also loved the way the room was dimly lit. Although there were crystal chandeliers, they must have been turned down low, and each table was lit by candlelight. It was the kind of place a man would take a woman on a wedding anniversary—assuming they were happily married—and seemed a bit much for a first date.

At her office, I had tried not to get caught staring, but this was different. It was clear the night would cost me a small fortune, so it seemed I had a right to look. She walked as if she belonged, and out of the corner of my eye I could tell that other men were watching her too, and though it may sound strange, that made me feel great. They could look all they wanted to, but she was *my* date, at least for the evening.

I tried to pull out the chair for her, but our tuxedo-clad host beat me to it. As she sat down, I said, "This may seem like a funny thing to say, but I like the way you walk."

Looking amused, she said, "I'll bet you say that to all the girls."

"Actually, I don't recall ever saying that before."

We settled in, and since I knew nothing about the subject, she took the lead and ordered a bottle of some fancy French Bordeaux. Of course, the waiter went through his routine of letting us check the wine. It always amused me, and I often wondered if anybody really knew what they were doing, or if they just went through the motions so they wouldn't look stupid. I certainly didn't know what to do, and even if I thought the wine tasted lousy I wouldn't feel comfortable telling the guy to take it back to the kitchen and toss it. And I wondered if they really did toss it, or if they had some way of putting the cork back in the bottle and not telling anyone. As I watched Vicki smell the cork and roll the wine around in her mouth, it was clear she either knew what she was doing or she knew how to act like she did. As the evening progressed, it became evident she had the relevant expertise, because it was the best wine I'd ever tasted, and as I would later learn, also the most expensive.

While we savored our first glass I asked, "So where did you learn all that?"

"I took a course in college." She stopped for a moment and smiled. "I know what you're thinking, but I'm serious. It covered wines and cheeses and was just as real as any of my other electives, like philosophy or astronomy."

"You took astronomy?"

"Why, does that surprise you?"

"You don't look like the astronomy type."

"And what, pray tell, does the astronomy type look like?"

I was digging a hole for myself and needed to get out. "Did you see the movie "The Right Stuff"? It's full of astronomy types."

She let me off the hook and moved on. "My undergraduate major was in English, which is good if you plan on going on to law school but bad if you plan on staying awake in class. That wasn't a problem with my electives and it certainly wasn't a problem with astronomy."

"I know what you mean. Some people think electives are a waste of time and money but not me. Think about it. After you graduate, you don't have the time to take classes outside your main field, or maybe we just don't make the time. College is our last chance to be exposed to learning just for the sake of learning. You can take classes for the fun of it, not because it will add to your credentials or help in your career."

"That's rather deep for an accountant. Wouldn't you say?"

Of course she was messing with me. I could tell from the look in her eyes and the tone of her voice. "You think accountants are one dimensional? The last time I checked there weren't many lawyers winning the Nobel prize for science."

"I'll grant you that. We shouldn't judge a person by his or her profession." She smiled, took a drink and put her empty glass on the table. We maintained eye contact and, without her saying a word, I filled her glass with more wine. For someone who was very independent, she had a way of making me want to do things for her. She nodded and asked, "So is there a moon walker in you trying to get out?"

"Actually, astronomy is one of my favorite subjects. My father got me started when I was a kid." I explained what he did for a living and how he exposed me to magazines on all sorts of subjects, and how I learned almost as much from them as I did in school.

"What a great way to expose kids to learning, and it sure worked with you," she said. "He must be very proud."

"Actually, he died about three years ago."

"Oh, I'm sorry. Were you close?"

"We were." Our appetizers arrived, and we watched as they were placed in front of us. It was good timing. I really didn't want to talk about my father. When the waiter left the table I tried to get the subject back to astronomy. "So what's your take on string theory?"

She had taken a bite of her appetizer and almost choked upon hearing the question. After recovering with a quick sip of water, she asked, "Is that what you typically talk about on a first date?"

The wine had begun to take effect. I was feeling more comfortable, so I savored it like I really was a wine connoisseur. It gave me time to appreciate the moment. She had just confirmed she thought it was a date. Perhaps it had to be, but it sure was great to hear her use the word. While studying my glass, I said, "You can tell a great deal about a person by asking about string theory. Don't you think?"

"Perhaps, but I think it tells you more about the person asking the question."

"You've not given me an answer."

"So you want to know about string theory?" As she sat back in her chair it seemed like she didn't know anything about the subject and was stalling for time. But then she suddenly leaned forward and started sounding like Carl Sagan. "You know it's really misleading for people to continue to refer to it as string theory. That was a fine description when the theory was first postulated. At that time physicists were becoming convinced that the smallest particles were nothing more than individual strings. Today, people use it to describe so much more, like infinite and parallel universes."

The tables were pretty close together, and an older woman nearby was giving us a weird look. Maybe she was disappointed that they weren't discussing infinite and parallel universes at *her* table. Ignoring granny, I was surprised and impressed with Vicki, and it seemed the opportune time to show her that I knew a little something about the subject—although the operative word was "little"—so I said, "And don't forget about infinite dimensions."

She looked surprised and asked, "Has anyone proposed infinite dimensions? I thought there were only ten?"

"If they can't find evidence of a fourth dimension, how can they say there are only ten?"

Before responding, she asked me to taste her appetizer. Although I hadn't heard of it before and it looked a little scary, it actually tasted great. I was almost done with it when she said, "I think you're mistaken. Actually they *have* found evidence of other dimensions. Look at gravity and magnetism. You would expect them to be of similar strength but that's not how they appear to us. Did you ever see those machines at the junk yard that pick up cars before they're crushed? They use magnets. You can see that magnetism is a very strong force. Now look at gravity." She took a clean fork and dropped it on the floor. Now the woman at the other table was thoroughly intrigued.

"I could ask the waiter for an apple if you'd like."

"Just pay attention. You think of gravity as if it's such a strong force, but look how easy it is for me to circumvent it." She reached down and picked up the fork. I got a great view of her legs and wanted to ask her for a repeat demonstration. "You see how easy it was for me to do that?"

"Vicki, I know you work out, but how hard can it be to lift a fork?"

She got up from the table and stood in front of me. "How much do you think I weigh?"

Nobody ever accused me of being an expert on women, but one thing every man knows is the eleventh commandment that Moses kept hidden from females, 'Thou shall not guess a woman's weight in her presence.' "You know I wouldn't be a gentleman if I answered that question."

"Ok, just say one hundred and twenty five. Now keep your eyes on me." She didn't need to tell me to do that. I watched her as she jumped up and down twice. "You see how easy it was for me to lift my weight. Gravity is not a very strong force. At least it doesn't appear to be. You see, some scientists believe it is just as strong a force as magnetism, but we don't see its full potential because part of the force is lost to another dimension." She spoke about the subject with such authority, you'd never guess she was a lawyer.

"And if that's right, it would be direct evidence of another dimension."

"You see, your father's efforts weren't lost on you."

"So let us assume there are more than three dimensions. Why would they be limited to just ten?"

"That's a very good question. I'm not sure I can give you a good answer, but I'll try. There are certain things that are constants. For example, everything falls at the same rate of acceleration. Sound and light travel at a certain speed. Well, some scientists believe there can only be ten dimensions—there's only so much room. Now, do you want to hear something really spooky?"

"You're not going to turn into some creature like that guy in *The Twilight Zone* movie, are you?"

"I said hear, not see." A young man was filling our water glasses and was so fascinated he wanted to stay and listen to what Vicki had to say, but she waited for him to leave before continuing. Leaning in toward me, as if she was about to share a well-kept secret and didn't want anyone else to hear, she asked, "Have you heard of the Kabbalah?"

"I've heard of it, but I can't tell you much about it."

"Different people describe it different ways and I won't bore you with my interpretation. I think most scholars would agree the various documents that people refer to as the Kabbalah were written no later than 200 AD and encapsulated thoughts and ideas that originated as early as 4000 years BC."

"Ok, it's old, but how is it spooky?"

"It speaks of a universe that exists in ten dimensions."

I had to think about that for a moment. "Maybe that's not such a coincidence. Maybe the physicists to whom you refer are avid readers of the Kabbalah and that's why they're now saying there are only ten dimensions. And they know we can't prove that they're wrong."

She sat back in her chair and looked out at other tables. She turned back to me. "Carl, how many physicists do you think I'm talking about? I'm sure they're not all avid readers of the Kabbalah."

"So let's assume there's something to it. What does it mean?"

"It may mean there really are ten dimensions."

"And if that's true?"

"Think of it. There could be life in another dimension, one that's next to us at this very moment. Isn't that amazing? Can you imagine what that form of life is like and what it's doing right now?"

Before I could say something stupid our waiter brought us our main dishes. I had considered telling her there were probably two "tenth dimension' creatures sitting right next to us. We were living parallel lives and one of the creatures was really attracted to the other one, and it was wondering whether the feeling was mutual. Instead, I watched as our meal was presented, took a deep breath, and tried to remember some of Ken's advice about women.

We tried each other's food and it was wonderful. And, unlike in most fancy restaurants, the portions weren't small. They must have had people like my mom working in the back. It was great wine, great food and great conversation. Sometimes you worry you won't have enough to talk about, but we just kept on going. Science, religion, politics—we covered it all. We were both avid readers and we talked about our favorite books. She told me she'd graduated college when she was twenty. I said I was nineteen when I got my degree. She told me she worked out five days a week with a personal trainer. I told her I went to work five days a week and once dated a personal trainer. She started telling me about virtual reality, and how it would impact our society. I could tell the lady at the next table was still eavesdropping on our conversation because she looked embarrassed when I said pornography would make the technology a commercial success. It was so easy talking to Vicki, I decided it was time to get a little personal.

"May I ask you a personal question?"

She quipped, "No, I don't intend to have sex with a virtual reality machine."

"Seriously, there's something I would like to ask."

"There's no guarantee I'll give you an answer."

"I was just wondering if you've ever dated any of your clients before." She stiffened and I could see my question had made her uncomfortable.

"Why would you ask that?"

I was beginning to realize it was a stupid question, and I wasn't really sure why I'd asked. My response was less than brilliant. "I'm just curious."

She took a moment to think before responding, "No, I never have."

"None of your clients ever asked you out?"

While looking around the room and scratching the back of her neck, she replied, "I didn't say that." For the first time all evening she was beginning to look a bit nervous. And she was speaking softly, in contrast to the way her voice had boomed when speaking about string theory. I had to lean in to hear, when she said, "Actually all of my clients have asked me out at one time or another."

I wondered if I'd heard her correctly or whether she was joking, but she looked serious. I realized my question wasn't so dumb after all, and I just had to learn more. "How many clients have you had?"

"I'd have to say it's around fifty."

"And every one of them asked you out?"

"Yes, at one time or another." She paused for a moment. "Three of my clients are new, and they haven't asked me. Not yet anyway."

I had to take some time to think. "Don't you have any women as clients, or kids, or married men?"

"I have three women as clients and I wasn't considering them. My male clients are all adults and most are married."

I tried chugging a glass of water to clear my head, but it didn't help. "They're married and they ask you out?"

"Does that really surprise you?"

Actually it did surprise me. I knew how Ken would flirt, but most of the married guys I knew were faithful to their wives, or at least they said they were. I looked around the room and wondered how many of the men there had cheated before. Looking back at Vicki I said, "I just can't imagine doing that."

"From my experience you're in the minority."

From her body language it became clear she wanted me to change the subject, but I couldn't help myself. Trying to hide a smile, I asked, "But how can every one of them ask you out?" I felt relieved when I saw her smile too.

"What's wrong? You don't find me attractive?"

"I find you very attractive. That's why I asked you to dinner when I did. It would have been better to have waited until we finished working together, but I just couldn't wait. So how can they all do it?"

She looked down at the table, sighed and then looked back at me. "Carl, I don't know. It's not as if I'm trying to get them to do it. It's funny though, the more I say no, the harder they try to get me to say yes."

"You sound like the female version of Ken. And how exactly do they try to get you to say yes?"

"Most think they can buy me. I've received a lot of expensive gifts over the years."

"You don't accept them though—"

"Why wouldn't I? We're talking about some very rich men. If they want to give me something, I'll take it. They're not getting anything in return." Her answer surprised me. Not that I knew her, but it didn't seem like something she would do. She squinted and said, "So you would do something different? Have you ever received an expensive gift from a woman?"

"No, and not from a guy either."

She laughed and said, "So you really don't know what you'd do. For me, what's important is being honest. As long as I tell them I'm not available, it's ok if they ask me out or give gifts. I don't mind."

"And you never go out with them?"

"I would never date a client."

I waited while our dishes were being cleared. We ordered dessert, and when the waiter left I said, "But you said yes to me."

"You're not a client."

"I was hoping you'd say I'm more attractive than your clients."

"You are attractive." She said it like she meant it. But maybe she was just being polite. She continued, "And you're unlike any of my clients."

"I guess I should take that as a compliment."

"Actually, I don't date much at all."

That was great news. Except for her new clients and the three women, all of her clients had asked her out and she'd said no, and she didn't date much with other men either. But she'd said yes to me. Things were looking up, and it felt like I was on a roll. "So I should really feel honored that you agreed to join me for dinner?"

"I wouldn't say that." She rubbed her forehead, and appeared to be searching for the right thing to say. It seemed I had pushed my luck too far and wasn't on such a roll after all. "Carl, I sensed something about you when we met, and I did want to learn more. You seem strangely innocent, and sweet. That's why I said yes, and I've had a great time tonight, so I'm glad I did."

"I hear a 'but' coming."

"It's important that you not misread my intentions. I'm not interested in an intimate relationship with a man."

My heart sank and it took me a moment to recover. I had fallen for women and gotten hurt a great many times, but the process of twisting my insides into a pretzel usually spanned more than one date. Confused, I asked, "Is it just bad timing?"

"No. I'm thirty-four years old. If I ever had an interest in finding a man, now would be as good a time as any to do it."

All kinds of thoughts raced through my mind. "I hope I'm not getting too personal here, but is it a relationship you're not looking for, or just a relationship with a man?"

I wondered if I had hit the nail on the head. But just then the waiter brought us our desserts and Vicki looked relieved, insisting that we try them before continuing the discussion. She was force feeding me some of hers, and keeping her fork in my mouth for what seemed like an eternity, when she finally pulled it out and asked, "So you think I'm a lesbian?"

"I have nothing against them, but if you are, I'll be one disappointed guy."

"Why? Isn't it every man's fantasy to date a lesbian?" By the look in her eyes I could tell she was starting to enjoy the conversation again.

"That's funny. I thought it was every woman's fantasy."

"Do men really think that?"

"I'll go table to table and find out."

She smiled and turned to look across the room. Suddenly she stopped, and appeared to be admiring a beautiful woman whose husband or date must have been in the men's room. Finally she turned to me, and said, "I find some women attractive, but no, I'm not a lesbian. Feel better?"

Actually I didn't, because the dinner had gone so well, and now she was telling me that for some reason she wasn't available. I started berating myself for spoiling the evening with my stupid questions. Not that she would have been any more available if I hadn't asked, but at least I'd have had more time to think I had a chance. "So you're just not interested in any relationship?"

"Not really, and I thought you felt the same way. Maybe that's another reason why I said yes to you."

"Why would you think that?"

"You're in your early forties. I just assumed that if you had wanted to get married you would have done it by now."

"Why does everybody say that? You know life is short, so I'm looking for something great, not just any relationship. It's very hard to find the right person, and when I think I have, something always seems to happen."

"That's a fair point. I never really thought about it." She looked down at the table and played with what remained of her dessert. Then she advised, "You can't wait forever."

"It's not like I'm trying to take my time. Believe me, if the right girl would ever say yes, I'll say yes." I was trying to hold back, but she kept staring at me with those eyes that seemed to compel me to talk. It was like some involuntary response when I heard my self speaking. "I'm glad I'm free, so when I meet a vibrant woman like you I can ask you to dinner and not feel guilty. And I don't mind saying that you're an incredible woman. Do you know how excited I was to see you? I was counting the days."

I wasn't sure how she would react, but when I was done she appeared to be disappointed. She looked down at the table, rubbed her chin, looked back at me and said, "Then maybe this dinner was a mistake. I don't want you to think of me that way."

I sat back in my chair and looked around the room. It was such a romantic setting and I was there with an intelligent, articulate and beautiful woman, and we were both single. If an artist had captured the moment, people would think there was nothing wrong with the picture, but they'd miss the fact that the air had just been let out of my lungs. "So Ms. Richards, what is it you *do* want?"

"Well, Mr. Messina, a friend would be nice. You seem like someone who could be a good friend."

Maybe I was lying to myself, but I took that as a sign there was still hope. In any case, it was clear I wouldn't change her perspective in one evening. I raised my glass and she raised hers to meet mine. "So you'd like to be friends. Let's drink to a budding friendship."

"I'd like that very much."

"And one never knows where that friendship may lead."

She warned, "I wouldn't get your hopes up if I were you."

After paying the check, I figured there was plenty of time before filing my petition for bankruptcy. The wine was great, but $300 a bottle? The dinner cost even more than that, though I had to admit it was well worth it. She had picked the place and she had great taste. It was one of the few times I'd gone to a five star restaurant that had earned every star.

Outside, we walked slowly together, enjoying the fresh air. And, contrary to popular belief, there was fresh air to be had in midtown Manhattan, especially on a beautiful summer evening. We didn't say much but it felt comfortable to remain silent, not like a typical first date where you think it's necessary to talk. Things were going well, as we eyed other people walking, and stopped now and then to look through shop windows. And then she reached out and took hold of my hand......................I was thrilled, but thoroughly confused. Maybe I was a romantic who read too much into the little things, but walking hand-in-hand seemed inconsistent with the notion of just being friends.

"It's a beautiful night out isn't it?" she asked.

"Sure is."

Maybe she wasn't available, but we were together, and for the time being that was good enough for me. When we reached the main entrance to her apartment I didn't expect to be invited up, and she didn't surprise me. I was a real gentleman, but thought a kiss was not out of line, so I made my move. She had beautiful full lips, and when we'd first met it was hard not to imagine what it would be like to press mine against hers, and, assuming she didn't punch me in the stomach, I was about to find out. She went along with the program and the kiss was good—too good—and it made me want more. But I knew it was time to leave. It seemed foolish to say anything so I kept quiet and took a few steps back, while keeping my eyes on hers. She just stood there looking right back at me and didn't move an inch. I wondered if she wanted me to stay a little longer, but I finally turned around and walked away.

Chapter 19

It was Wednesday afternoon, August 27th, and Kavi was at his desk trying to inject coffee into his body and answer Marc's questions at the same time. Just a few minutes earlier, Kavi was handed a note requesting him to join Steve Halpern in Charles Goodman's office in thirty minutes, to meet with some government personnel. If the situation had been different, Kavi would have called Steve to learn more, but in this case his instincts told him that calling Marc would be the better move.

"I don't like it," Marc said. "Why would they give you such short notice?"

"To tell you the truth, I'm relieved. This should give us a good indication of where this is headed."

"You shouldn't meet with them until you hire an attorney. Have you looked at the list I sent you?"

The envelope with the list to which Marc referred was sitting unopened on Kavi's desk. He was sure each of the recommended attorneys could provide first class representation, but was troubled by the thought of actually hiring one. To him, that would be an admission that all was not well. "It seems premature to hire counsel, and I can act quickly if and when the time comes. And you don't know what they intend to do at this meeting. For all I know, we'll be talking about Maurice Granville."

"Speaking of Granville, you're not following his advice."

"You said you didn't trust him, and now you're saying I should listen to him?"

"I'm sure he was being sincere when he said you shouldn't trust other people," Marc said.

"Let's just see what happens and go from there."

"Fine, but make sure you don't answer their questions or provide additional information if they make any accusation against you. You just sit quietly and listen to what they have to say."

Kavi studied his coffee carefully. For some reason the caffeine wasn't having the desired effect. "I didn't do anything wrong and see no reason to act guilty. What's the harm with simply telling them the truth?"

Marc screamed into the phone, "Damn it! Listen to me!" He had never lost his temper like that and it startled Kavi, who moved the phone away from his ear. In a calmer voice, Marc continued, "I'm sorry, but you have to listen, for your own good. You are an incredibly capable individual. You were so good that you never needed to play politics or protect your back. But now I think your years of success doing things your way is actually becoming a weakness. You think because it has worked for you in the past it should work now. Well you're wrong. This is a situation you never faced before and it isn't a scene from a Frank Capra movie where good triumphs over evil. There are some bad people in the world who do bad things and you're probably dealing with some of them right now. I know this is a poor analogy, but you know how Carl loves to use scenes from "The Godfather" to make a point? You're not a wartime consigliere, but you'd better become one soon. You are in a war, and you should stop thinking things will work out just because you didn't do anything wrong, and stop thinking that everybody has honorable intentions."

It took a moment for him to respond but finally Kavi said, "Ok. I get the point."

"I'm sorry I yelled. But I want things to work out for you. In some ways it feels like it's happening to me."

"It's not happening to you, so relax. I'm the one who should be nervous. Anyway, your message has come through loud and clear, like a slap in the face. And what you say makes sense." Kavi looked at his watch and realized he'd better get off the call. There was plenty to do, and he didn't have much time.

* * * *

If you didn't know otherwise, you'd never guess it was an office, and Charles Goodman liked it that way. It was the size of a five bedroom apartment. In one corner, he had an antique desk that cost more than most homes. In another corner was a marble table surrounded by ten plush leather chairs. And you had to take two small steps down to get to the middle section, with three comfortable couches placed in a triangular arrangement, surrounded by all sorts of eclectic furnishings.

When Kavi walked in, the others were already there. Steve was sitting on one couch with Charles. On another sat Gary Bevins and an individual who would later be identified as Dennis Smith, a prosecutor with the Department of Justice. Charles motioned for Kavi to sit down on the third couch. He did so, and tried to get comfortable, but didn't like the feeling of being the center of attention. He watched the others and reminded himself that he shouldn't be the first one to speak.

It looked as if Gary was about to say something, but Charles spoke first. With his eyes on Kavi, he said, "Over the years you have made a great contribution to this company and to its people. The board has been extremely pleased with your performance and with you as an individual. I for one am very proud to have worked with you." Charles looked down at the floor for a moment and it was clear he wasn't through with his mini-speech. He looked up and said, "I'd like to think that people are generally well intentioned. It's difficult working at a public company like ADG. We make choices every day, and sometimes we don't make the right choices. I'll go to my grave thinking highly of you. I believe you were always guided by your view of what was in the best interest of this company."

Those were nice words but they weren't very comforting. In fact, they had the opposite effect. It looked as if Charles had more to say but he suddenly tensed up, as if it was becoming too difficult for him to speak. He remained silent and turned away. When it became clear he was through, Gary started to speak but was once again beaten to the punch. This time by Steve, who reached over and put his hand on Gary's shoulder to stop him from talking. It looked as if Steve had gotten too comfortable with someone he'd called a little weasel only a few weeks earlier.

"This is an informal meeting," Steve said. "We're here to express some views and explore options. We want you to feel comfortable."

"Great," Kavi said. "You want me to feel comfortable. My boss thinks highly of me. What's next? These gentlemen giving me the Medal of Honor?"

Steve looked disturbed but continued undeterred. "There have been a number of developments since we last spoke and this is the best arena to discuss them with you. It's all for your benefit."

As the patronizing speech continued, Kavi set his eyes on a nearby glass credenza where a collection of antique pistols was displayed. He figured if they really wanted him to be comfortable they would just sit quietly while he loaded one of the guns and used their heads for target practice.

Finally Gary was allowed to speak. He looked like one of those clowns who was stuck in a metal box and was ready to spring out. "It's true this is an informal meeting. It's an opportunity for us to discuss possible charges against you. It's also an opportunity for you to provide information that may influence how we proceed. Now we—"

"Wait a minute," Kavi interrupted. "This is the first I've heard about possible charges against me. If that's what this is about, why didn't you advise me to bring a lawyer?"

"Mr. Chander, by all means you should hire an attorney," Gary said. He was speaking in a tone that made him seem bored with it all. "In fact, after this meeting we prefer that you immediately do so. However, there is no need for your counsel to be here at this time. You should rest assured we won't ask you to commit to anything at this meeting."

"This is an extraordinary situation," Charles said, as he leaned forward toward Kavi. "It must be terribly uncomfortable for you. I know it is for me. But please listen to what these gentlemen have to say. It's very important for the company and for you that you *do* listen. Whether we like it or not, these gentlemen are not going away."

Kavi remembered what Marc had said. No matter what they ask, say nothing. He'd said this was a war, and he was right. The first real battle was about to begin. He realized he should just sit quietly and listen. It would be beneficial to get information but provide none. "Ok, go ahead and tell me whatever it is you want me to know."

"I think it's important that you listen to all of this before you respond," Gary said. "You need to know the weight of evidence against you." He took out some notes and started reading almost word for word. It was strange how he just kept talking and talking and didn't seem to take any time to breathe. He said there were significant accounting irregularities, including overstatement of assets of the Far East merchant power group, and misuse of litigation reserves. He mentioned clear evidence of a cover up, including Kavi's efforts to change the internal audit report risk assessments and efforts to reduce the scope of the L&K audit work. He said investors had lost billions of dollars as a result of the irregularities.

As Kavi listened, he grew more and more tense. Although he had been warned and had had his suspicions, up until this point he'd still clung to the belief that things were not as bad as they had seemed. Now he was learning otherwise and the emotions he had suppressed for weeks were making their way to the surface. He felt like a volcano getting ready to explode, though he tried not to let the others notice.

Gary spoke for fifteen minutes straight, and it seemed more like an hour. He finished reading, put his notes down and asked Kavi if he had anything to say.

"I don't know what you expect from me," Kavi said.

"This is your opportunity to address these charges."

"You want me to address them? Do you know how to spell bullshit? Put that in your notes." Kavi looked over to the other couch for help but Steve and Charles remained silent.

Dennis Smith reached into a folder and pulled out a four page document. As he handed it to Gary he whispered, "Maybe it's time for this."

Even though he had drafted the document, Gary flipped through the pages as if he were seeing it for the first time. He looked up at Kavi and said in a rather condescending tone, "If you do not wish to provide substantive information in your defense, we should move ahead. We have a proposal for you to consider that may enable us to close this matter. We suggest you give it serious consideration. It's all summarized in this plea offer sheet." Gary stood up, walked over to hand Kavi the document, and while walking back, said, "Once again, we don't expect you to commit to anything at this meeting. You should hire an attorney to review the offer with you."

It took a moment for the words to sink in as Kavi read the summary on the first page. It said they wanted him to plead guilty to committing securities fraud, resign from ADG and agree never to take a position as an officer or director of a publicly traded company again. In exchange, it said they'd ensure that any jail term would not exceed ten years and any fine would not exceed $250,000. It was time for the eruption.

Kavi, unable to control himself any longer, jumped up and rushed over to the couch where Gary and Dennis were sitting. Naturally, they covered their faces to protect themselves from punches they thought were coming, but instead of fighting, Kavi stood above them and started screaming at the top of his lungs. "What kind of morons are you? You come in here and we bust our butts to get you what you need. We worked weekends, late nights, gave you everything you wanted. Then you have the nerve to come in here and accuse me of securities fraud and talk about up to ten years in jail? Why, because of bribes I didn't know about? Hey, idiots, how the hell do you think you got here in the first place? It's because I sent Debra Jennings to Nikolaev. Why the hell would I do that if I knew about the bribes all along?" Gary and Dennis were not big guys and they were getting more and more nervous. It wasn't clear if they were listening as Kavi continued to scream.

While shielding his face, Gary said, "Please, sit down Mr. Chander, and remember we represent the United States of America."

"My name is Kavi, you idiot." He was disgusted, and leered at Gary with the eyes of someone who did intend to fight, yelling, "The men and women risking their lives in Iraq represent the United States of America. Not morons like the two of you. You sit here and pull off this shit and try to hide behind the government. It just makes me sick. Why don't you try working for a living? You couldn't be the CFO of a company if you tried." He took a quick breath and glanced at Steve and Charles who looked shocked by the tirade. It was clear they wanted him to sit down but they didn't have the courage to say anything. He looked back down at his cowering targets, shook his head, smirked, and then turned to head back to his couch.

"Perhaps he was protecting himself," Gary said in a low voice, while not looking at anyone in particular.

Not sure what he'd heard, Kavi said, "I didn't catch that, Mr. Moron. What are you talking about?"

"You probably knew this whole thing would unravel because the cost overruns in Ukraine were too big to hide." Gary stopped to take a noticeable deep breath. Before the episode he'd been able to speak for fifteen minutes without anyone seeing him breathe. He continued to look away from Kavi and said, "You probably sent Debra to make it look like you really didn't know."

Kavi shook his head and looked over at Charles. "What a moron! He's saying I should go to jail for ten years because I provided my input on the internal audit group's risk assessment and because we may not have accounted for the $250 million litigation settlement correctly. You know this whole thing is absurd. We should stop cooperating right now and start taking the offensive."

"These charges are not absurd," Gary insisted, as he struggled to get the courage to look Kavi in the eye. "You are completely underestimating the weight of evidence against you. For example, I have a statement here from Maurice Granville confirming that you were aware of all illegal payments." He handed the statement to Steve to be passed along.

It didn't say very much, just that Kavi knew about all of the payments in question, including the specifics of the intended government recipients. It was signed by Maurice Granville and dated the same day he resigned from the company. After taking a moment to think, Kavi looked at Gary and asked, "How did you get this? Did Maurice cut some sort of deal?" They didn't respond, so Kavi continued, "I'm sure I have the right to know. Was there a deal?"

Dennis leaned forward and spoke to Kavi for the first time. "The Department of Justice has entered into a plea agreement with Mr. Granville. I'm afraid that's all I can say. The terms of the agreement are to remain confidential."

It took some time, but Kavi was beginning to get the picture. He turned to Charles and asked, "Can't you see what's happening here? I'm being framed. You know Maurice is lying. He signed this to get whatever deal they gave him. That's why we received his resignation just after he got off his call with these guys. You know, Maurice really does deserve a lot of credit. He knows how to handle himself in tough environments. That's what he always said, and he was right." Kavi sat back in the couch and shook his head, as everything began to make sense. "We all knew he was going to leave. We were wondering why he didn't just go ahead and do it. But he must have thought he still had some leverage, so he held out until the last minute, and, sure enough, he was right. You really have to admire him. Now the government can take some credit for saying they made him leave, when he was planning to leave all along."

After a moment's hesitation, Gary responded, "The evidence we have is overwhelming. Mr. Granville's statement is just the tip of the iceberg."

Upon hearing that, Kavi remembered he'd been warned that Charles may have had a number of meetings with the government, and now those meetings seemed more suspicious. Although he wasn't sure he wanted the answer, he looked at Charles and asked, "*You* didn't cut any deals with the government, did you?" He could tell from the body language that the answer was yes.

Charles' hands were actually shaking, and he was blinking his eyes way too much. He looked at Steve and sighed, and then turned back to Kavi and said, "This is bigger than either one of us. Our stock's now at $39 a share. That's down from $66 when this whole thing started. That's tens of billions of dollars in lost market value. We just can't let this mess continue. We need to put a stop to it, and if some people need to be sacrificed, so be it. Yes, I did enter into an agreement with the government. I have agreed to pay a $1 million fine and to resign from the company as of the end of the year. And I've also agreed not to serve as an officer or director of any publicly traded company, and to assist the government in its investigation. You should also know that ADG has agreed to pay a $25 million fine to settle the matter from the company's perspective." He stopped and looked over at Dennis and Gary. "Believe me, this had to be done. The long-term interests of the company had to come first."

Although the picture was becoming clear, Charles's revelation was like a hard punch in the stomach. It froze Kavi and he needed some time to recover. When he regained his composure he asked, "So there's no jail time for you?"

"Of course not, why would there be jail time? I didn't know about any of this."

"Neither did I, and you know that." Kavi hesitated, rubbed his brow, and then continued, "So you agreed to assist the government. What exactly does that mean? And what have you told them about me?"

"Believe me, I only told them the truth."

"And what is the truth?"

Charles was becoming exasperated. He asked, "Do we have to do this?"

"I thought this meeting was for my benefit. And I want to know what you told them."

Charles looked over at the others and then back at Kavi. It was clear he didn't want to continue. He finally admitted, "I told them you kept us in the dark. You always told us how well things were going with Maurice's power group. We didn't hear you talk about any problems."

"That's because we didn't know of any problems, Charles. It was Maurice who kept everyone in the dark, including me." Kavi was about to say more when he noticed out of the corner of his eye that Gary was busy taking notes, so he sat back and tried to keep his mouth shut. Nothing he could say would help matters, but it could certainly hurt.

"I made a sacrifice for the company," Charles said. "It's time for you to do the same thing."

"You call this deal the same thing?" Kavi laughed, even though he didn't think it was very funny. He caught another glimpse of the antique guns and wondered who he should shoot first. "You were planning to leave in two years, so it's no big deal to speed things up a bit. You agree not to be an officer or director of another public company. Big deal. You had no plans to be an officer and you often discouraged me from sitting on another company's board, and you said you were quitting your other three board posts as soon as you retired." Kavi stopped for a moment and leaned back in the couch. He looked away and then turned back to Charles. "So you agreed to pay a fine. You know $1 million is nothing for you. You're worth over $100 million, and I'll bet they'll let you deduct your fine for tax purposes. A $25 million fine for the company is chicken feed. And you get no jail time. Isn't that great? And I know Maurice didn't get any."

"And how would you know that?" Dennis asked.

"Because you had no realistic way of getting to him," Kavi said. "From what he told me, I know he wouldn't accept going to jail."

"So you spoke with him about it?" While Dennis asked the question, Gary was busy taking more notes.

Kavi decided he had said enough. Marc was right. It was time to get a lawyer. "When I walk out of this office I'm still the CFO, right? You're not suspending me, are you?"

"You're still the CFO," Charles replied. "And under the deal you're being offered by the government you can remain the CFO through the end of October."

"You get to the end of the year, and I get to the end of October," Kavi said. "How nice!"

Charles leaned forward toward Kavi, and said, "I want this to be voluntary. Go get yourself a lawyer and take the time to study your options carefully. I trust you'll conclude it's best to settle with the government, as I did."

"Don't take too much time," Gary warned. "We need your response by the end of the day next Tuesday."

Charles shot back, "For God's sake, he doesn't even have an attorney!" He was still leaning toward Kavi and looking down at the floor when he spoke, although he was talking to Gary. Then Charles sat back, turned to look at Gary and asked, "Can't you give him more time? What's so special about next Tuesday anyway? How do you expect him to make a deal by then?"

"I'm sure Mr. Chander can find a lawyer by the end of the day. Undoubtedly he has one or two persons already in mind." Gary spoke while putting his notes away. "We look forward to your response."

Actually, Gary didn't think there was enough time and he didn't care, because the government had no intention of entering into any plea agreement with Kavi. They were giving him an offer he couldn't accept. The government was just going through the motions so they could say they had alerted him to the charges and had given him every chance to cooperate, and had also given him an opportunity to settle, although it wasn't much of an opportunity. A victory in a very public trial against a top executive at ADG would do wonders for Gary's career. With the government's resources at his disposal and the evidence in hand, he really thought he could win the case. He was so convincing that the DOJ had already assigned some of its best people, who were at that very moment busy in their hotel suite two blocks away preparing to file the charges. The trial would be much more rewarding than any plea agreement. Although the DOJ would take the lead in the courtroom, with the media, Gary would be front and center. For him, it was the case of a lifetime, to be milked for all it was worth, and that included getting mileage from pre-trial publicity over the long Labor Day weekend. The timetable was already in place. The following Wednesday was earmarked for a trip to the federal court house, so Kavi could be handcuffed and hauled in front of the US magistrate by Friday.

Gary and Dennis stood up and walked out of the office without offering to shake anyone's hand. Kavi sat in the couch and stared at the others who just stared back. He was waiting for someone to walk in with a camera and say it was some sort of joke, but nobody did.

Charles broke the silence. "I'm sorry they're not giving you more time. If it helps, they rushed me with my deal too."

"I don't need any time at all," Kavi said. "Ten years in jail. How could I accept that?"

Steve had been quiet during most of the meeting, but now he spoke. "They didn't say ten years. They said no more than ten years."

"I don't care if it's six weeks. I'm not going to jail," Kavi said. "And how about you Steve? What deal did they offer you?"

"Why would I need any deal? I'm not guilty of anything, and I've been cooperating with the government since this whole thing began."

"That makes two of us, Mr. I'm-innocent-and-you're-not. Although it doesn't seem to be doing me much good. So Charles, you've known me all these years. You're not planning to back me up?"

Charles didn't reply. Instead, he stood up, walked over to a cherry cabinet, and took out a bottle of gin. His hands were still shaking, and he struggled to prepare his drink. But after chugging everything in his glass, he appeared to calm considerably. He poured himself another, took a deep breath and then turned to Kavi and said, "I'll tell the truth, but keep in mind my agreement to assist the government, and I'll do that to the best of my abilities. I've given you my reasons. I can't let my feelings for you come ahead of my responsibilities to this company and its shareholders."

Kavi asked, "And you're one of the biggest shareholders, aren't you, Charles?"

Charles almost choked on his second drink. "What's that supposed to mean?" They all knew exactly what it meant. Charles was worth just over $100 million. However, with his large position in ADG stock and stock options, he'd been worth almost twice that amount when the scandal was first made public. He was looking forward to a comfortable retirement, and didn't want the bulk of his remaining net worth eviscerated.

Kavi sat back in the couch and didn't respond. Realizing it wasn't a productive line of conversation, he tried to collect his thoughts and determine what he could possibly learn that could help in any way. "So I am the CFO?"

"Until we tell you otherwise," Charles said.

Steve leaned forward and looked at Charles, as if seeking permission to speak. "We talked about this with the board, and everyone agreed you should remain in your position, at least for the near term. Nobody thought a suspension would be appropriate."

"You discussed this with the board?" Kavi asked. "When was that?"

Steve shrugged his shoulders and asked, "What would you do if you were in our shoes? Keep this from them?"

"You don't want to know what I'd do. I'm too honorable to do what you're doing, or maybe I'm too stupid."

"Kavi, go get your attorney," Charles said, while pouring himself another drink. "If you need some good names I can get them for you. Get someone who can negotiate the best deal possible. I'm sure the government has a lot of room to negotiate. But you know what Gary said. You need to act fast."

*   *   *   *

As soon as he got back to his office Kavi closed the door and called Marc. He was half expecting to hear 'I told you so' thirty times or more, but that wasn't Marc's style. Kavi took more than twenty minutes to cover all the gory details, and when he was through, Marc asked if he could have some time to think, and said he'd call back soon.

Kavi was mentally exhausted, so he walked over to the couch to lie down. It had been in his office for years, but he couldn't recall ever lying on it before. His assistant knocked on the door, walked in and was startled to see him in that position. She handed him seven messages from people who had called while he was in his meeting, and asked if he needed some aspirin. When he said no, she walked out and closed the door behind her. He had no energy, and could feel the messages slip through his fingers and fall to the floor, and wondered if he would ever work up the desire to pick them up and return the calls.

From his vantage point he could see directly into the building across the way, on the south side of the street. His windows came down close to the floor, so he could lie on the couch and still have a good view. There was a meeting in progress in a conference room, two people were talking in an office, and a woman was at her computer keyboard in another. He was thinking that they were all going about their business, their job, their routine, and they probably weren't thinking about it at all. They might actually have been bored with work and complained about it to their spouses and friends. But Kavi looked at them with envy because he knew what they probably didn't know, what it was like to have your world put at risk. He appreciated what he'd had, and would give anything to turn back the clock. But those days were gone. He wasn't sure what would happen, but knew his life had permanently changed and his days at ADG were probably numbered. While deep in thought he was startled when his assistant buzzed him and said that Marc was back on the line.

"The government must not want an agreement," Marc said. "That's the only explanation. They must be planning to file charges against you next Wednesday."

"I guess I should open your envelope and start looking at your list of attorneys."

"You haven't opened it yet? You don't have time to interview people. Just take my advice. Under the circumstances, the best one is Henry Jackson. You must have heard of him."

"Of course, but I wouldn't have expected you to put him on your list. Didn't he just represent a guy accused of killing his partner?"

"That's right," Marc said. "And he won the case. I listed people with different skills and personalities. You could say he was the most colorful of the group."

"You don't think he's *too* flamboyant? Wasn't he all over the news? That's how I heard of him. And does he know anything about securities law?"

"He's great in court and in front of a camera, and he wins cases. He's also nothing like you and me, and with what we know now, that's a good thing. We need someone who can bring skills to the table that you and I don't have. And don't worry about securities law. I know an expert who works with a small firm. His name is Gil Robeson. He can supplement your team with Henry in the lead."

"I like it."

"That Gary Bevins is a schmuck, please pardon my French. Let's go after the guy. It may be time to make some noise."

"You're right," Kavi said. "Maybe it is time to play some offense."

"And Henry Jackson should be a great quarterback."

Kavi became more energetic as the discussion continued. He felt like blood was returning to his veins, as if he had taken a drug and it was beginning to have an effect. After about fifteen minutes of further discussion, he sounded more like his old self. He exclaimed, "These charges are bullshit and we should be able to win this thing in a rout. Let's ram it down the government's throat. I normally like to keep things quiet and close to the vest, but all bets are off. This company was about to throw me to the wolves. Now it's payback time."

"You know what I'm thinking?"

"I'd better get myself a gun?"

"Not quite," Marc said. "If I'm not mistaken, you're beginning to sound like a wartime consigliere."

"So I *should* buy a gun," Kavi joked. "How do you like that, and I'm not even a lawyer. You know, I was in a real funk. It's amazing how you cheered me up."

"That's funny. I usually have the opposite effect on you."

"Not today. You've helped me think more clearly, and now I'm full of energy. Maybe I should go downstairs and kick Gary's ass."

"Don't get too excited. These are serious charges you face."

"I know, but I'm facing them whether I like it or not. I might as well put up a strong fight. I worked too hard to get here and no little twerp like Gary is going to take it all away."

"I'll call Henry and Gil, and see if we can all meet for dinner tomorrow to get the ball rolling," Marc said. "I'll also call Carl and Ken. We'll want their help when the time comes."

As soon as Kavi hung up the phone, for some strange reason he decided to do pushups. It was as if he was getting ready for the first round of a heavyweight fight. He wondered what his assistant would say if she walked back in at that very moment. One minute he was on the couch with no energy, and the next minute he was doing pushups. She'd probably think he'd lost his mind. The phone messages were still scattered on the floor, and it was hard for him to imagine they had seemed too heavy to hold with one hand. But now he was feeling strong. When he finished the pushups, he placed the messages on his desk and decided to return each call. He was still the CFO and that's what a CFO would do.

Chapter 20

Henry Jackson was the first African-American to play hockey at the University of Minnesota, and though it had been years since he graduated, he was in such great shape you'd think he could still play. He stood 6 foot 3 and weighed 220 pounds of pure muscle. After earning his undergraduate degree in criminology, he'd spent some time as a cop in Detroit, but grew tired of seeing his hard work go to waste and criminals being set free because of legal technicalities. He took the law boards and ranked in the 97th percentile, and was accepted at the University of Chicago law school and graduated near the top of his class. His original objective was to become an ace prosecutor, so it was somewhat ironic that right after graduation he joined a prestigious New York law firm known for their representation of white collar criminals. He did well and was a crackerjack attorney. But his style was too flamboyant and his ego too big for the firm, so they weren't disappointed when he resigned to start his own practice. As luck would have it, one of his first cases made him famous. The defendant was a Long Island socialite who'd been indicted for the murder of her rich diet doctor husband, and most people who had read about the case were convinced of her guilt. But Henry persuaded the jury and won the case. And that very public victory was followed by others. He had an uncanny ability to connect with people, whether they were jurors or other members of the general public. His words had substance and his style had flair. His delivery would vary from deep and strong to soft and smooth, depending upon the need, and his speaking skills were so good he was approached by the Democratic Party to run for a vacant US House of Representatives seat. He declined the opportunity, preferring instead to represent clients in very public cases—and to make more money—and to keep his private life private. Every now and then he lost a case, but that was to be expected with the type of clients he attracted.

It was Thursday evening, August 28, and Marc and Kavi were joined by Henry in one of his conference rooms after having just been introduced. When Marc had called the day before to discuss Kavi's predicament, Henry was intrigued and quickly agreed to take the case, inviting the two of them to his office for the Thursday working dinner to get started. The securities lawyer who would supplement their team, Gil Robeson, was busy with two large public debt offerings, and wouldn't be available until the following week.

"Let me assure you, he's innocent," Marc proclaimed.

Looking amused, Henry asked, "You're not a defense attorney, are you?"

"No, I'm a tax lawyer."

"And the two of you are friends?" Henry asked.

Marc quickly responded, "Best of friends."

Henry smiled and said, "I never ask a client if he or she is innocent. If they tell me they're innocent, it's self serving and meaningless. If they say they're guilty, then my ability to represent them is compromised." He turned to Kavi and said, "It's nothing personal, you understand."

"I know what you mean," Kavi said. "But it's hard to discuss this without saying I'm innocent. You need to know what part of the government's case is fabricated."

"We'll get to that," Henry said. Just then, his assistant walked in and asked for their food orders. It would be gourmet Chinese food from a restaurant down the block. Henry waited for her to leave before getting back to the discussion. "I'm glad you've asked someone like Gil to get involved. I haven't had a securities law case in some time, and we need an expert. You couldn't mistake me for a securities lawyer, that's for sure."

"Will that be a problem?" Kavi asked.

"Not with this Gil on our team. I'm sure he can tell us whatever we need to know." Henry stood up, walked to the window and surveyed the view.

"You've won most of your cases, is that correct?" Marc asked.

"I've lost my share. I've just been fortunate enough to have won my most public battles."

"I know you don't want me to say this, but I *am* innocent." Kavi said. "This is a case you'll win."

Henry continued gazing into the distance. Without turning he asked, "Are you an attorney, Kavi?"

"No, I'm a CPA."

"Did they teach you criminal law when you got your accounting degree?"

"No, but I don't need to be an expert in criminal law to know that I'm innocent. Once I go over the details with you, I'm sure you'll agree. This will probably be one of the easiest cases you ever had."

"You're a smart guy, right?"

Kavi was caught off guard by the question and wasn't sure what Henry was getting at. After hesitating, Kavi said, "I was dumb enough to get into this mess. But yes, I'm smart. Why do you ask?"

"If you sat on the jury for this case, you'd be able to sift through the facts and conclude you're innocent, right?"

"That's what I'm trying to tell you."

"Are others as smart as you?"

"I've worked with some very smart people. Take Marc for instance. In my mind, he's much smarter than me."

"Perhaps, and I'm sure you're not misstating things when you say you work with some very smart people. I suspect most people with whom you work are very smart."

"So what are you getting at?" Kavi asked.

"You ever serve on a jury?"

"No. I was called for jury duty three times, but was never picked for a trial."

"That's strange, isn't it? A smart guy like you was never picked for a jury. Do you remember anything about the other people on jury duty with you?"

Kavi thought for a moment, then said, "Sure, I remember."

"Were most of those people as smart as you?" When Henry didn't get a quick response he pounced, as if he were cross examining a witness. "Come on Kavi, you said you'd tell me the truth. Were they as smart as you?"

"I'm sure in certain cases the answer is no."

"I'd say you're being modest, and in *most* cases the answer would be no," Henry said. "Remember learning about juries in elementary school?"

"No, I grew up in India."

Henry turned from the window and walked back, but he didn't sit down. Instead, he continued walking slowly, counterclockwise, around the table. While walking he said, "Let me tell you what you'd have learned had you been here. Our kids are taught about our system, where you're not judged by some potentially corrupt government agency, but by a jury of your peers. They learn that ordinary people, like a mail room clerk, a school teacher or a fireman, are collectively entrusted to seek out the truth. It's a beautiful thing. They have no axe to grind, no political goals to be served, no interest in the outcome of the case. Why, they never even know the defendant when they first see him or her in the courtroom. It's just like the movie "Twelve Angry Men," although it should have been titled "Twelve Angry *White* Men," but that's another thing. The twelve men have their differences, but they have what it takes to collectively seek out the truth. It's our system in action."

"But our system does work," Marc added.

"Sure it does, for a tax guy. You get your own tax court, with specialists who know what the hell they're doing. Let me tell you something about juries for criminal cases. The plain truth is that some of the people sitting with Kavi were so stupid they couldn't spell pig if you spotted them the 'p' and the 'g'. You know what else? Many of those very same people are the ones who got picked for the jury, while smart people like Kavi got to go back to work. Jury of his peers? That's a joke. Believe me, any jury he gets will look nothing like his peers."

"I recognize there are risks when you deal with the public, but you make it seem like such a bad system," Kavi said. "From my perspective, it's the best in the world."

"The best in the world? That may not be saying much." Henry stopped pacing and sat down. He took a deep breath and said, "I'm sorry guys. Some of the people sitting on the jury will be decent, smart and hard-working people, but a mail room clerk may know how to sort the mail, a teacher may know how to interpret Shakespearean English and a fireman may know how to save lives, but none of them has any special skill that enables them to seek out the truth, especially in a complicated case like one that involves securities law."

Kavi interjected, "If a lawyer does his job, the jury should be able to do theirs."

"Is that right?" Henry asked. "Remember when Oxford Oil wanted to buy Penncorp? The two companies had a handshake deal, but then Arcotex came along and made a higher offer, so Oxford sued Arcotex. The lawyers defending Arcotex did a first class job, and under the law, it was relatively clear Oxford had no case, but the jury nonetheless awarded them a $17 billion award. Think of it, $17 *billion*. I'll never forget when they interviewed the foreman of the jury who said, "I just didn't think what Arcotex did was fair." Who the hell cared what he thought was fair? They were supposed to decide the case based upon the law."

"But my case is different," Kavi said.

"Your case is no different than any other." Henry pointed his finger toward the window and continued, "There are twelve people out there who will decide your fate. It just doesn't matter whether you are innocent or guilty, or whether the government's case is fabricated. What matters is what those twelve people will think. You know, the fireman, the school teacher, the mail room clerk, and a few of those people who have trouble spelling three-letter words. Your life will be in their collective hands. Does that make you feel comfortable? And another thing, assuming they do have a functional brain, you had better hope they're paying attention when we make our key arguments—that they're not half asleep—or thinking about sex." Henry paused for his words to sink in. "You think I'm kidding? I'm dead serious."

Marc looked concerned and didn't say anything in response. Kavi took that as a bad sign. He was also concerned, and had found Henry's dissertation unsettling. He rubbed the back of his neck and then said, "We picked you because we thought you'd know how to fight a case like this. Were we mistaken?"

"Why do you think you made a mistake? Because I'm telling you what you don't want to hear?"

Marc said, "We don't like the way you make it seem like a crap shoot."

"To a certain extent, that's what it is." Henry leaned forward in his chair. "Gentlemen, obviously I can handle this case. Your odds of winning will be as high as possible with me at the helm, but there's no such thing as a sure winner."

"So what do you suggest we do?" Marc asked.

"For starters, I need to talk to the lead prosecutor and this Gary Bevins character. I'd like to see how much this deal of theirs can be improved."

"There's no way I'm making any deal," Kavi said.

Henry sighed and looked down at his lap. He looked up again and said, "Forget for the moment whether you will or will not take any deal. We need to know the best they'll offer for two reasons. First, I take the view that I'm obligated to seek out the best deal and communicate it to you for your consideration. It's easy for you to reject an offer now, but when you finally appreciate the hazards of going to court, and if the deal's significantly improved, you may reconsider. Second, even if we reject it, our discussions will give us a sense of how strong they think their case really is."

"Perhaps, but you may also send them a signal that we think our case is weak," Kavi said.

"At this point, it's likely the government doesn't care what we think."

"I recognize there's not much time, but what about Gil Robeson?" Marc asked. "How can we evaluate a deal without him?"

Before Henry could respond, Kavi interrupted. "Irrespective of what he said, there's no deal they could offer that I'll accept, short of their dropping the case. So I won't need Gil's help to decide."

Henry said, "In any case, there isn't much time. I should really call them tomorrow morning." When no one objected, he began making some notes to himself.

Kavi waited for Henry to finish writing, and then asked, "Do you have some ideas about publicity?"

"What do you mean?" Henry asked.

"Isn't that a big part of your strategy, making your case to the public?"

Henry rubbed his eyes and was about to respond when his assistant walked in with their dinner. He looked relieved and helped her organize the food. When she left, he sat back in his chair and said, "I don't want to spoil your appetite, but I must ask. Do you have any idea what will likely happen next Friday?"

Kavi responded, "We're assuming that's when the government will get its grand jury indictment."

"You're right. That's probably the day the indictment will be unsealed by the court. You know what else will happen? That's the day you'll be marched into court in handcuffs through hordes of media personnel screaming to get a few words and a good picture." Henry leaned forward and said, "You want publicity, you're going to get it."

"I don't understand," Kavi said. "This isn't like some of the other major corporate scandals."

"It is to the government, and it sure is to the media." Henry picked up his chopsticks as if they would help him make the point, and he aimed them toward Kavi. "You think the media cares about the facts? They care that a top executive of one of the largest companies in the world is being marched into court in handcuffs. That's a big story, and it's just like all the others. And if you think it's "innocent until proven guilty," go take a poll of most Americans the day after the big event. You won't choose to run for public office, I'll tell you that. And you think this is different to the government? Gary Bevins will be screaming at the top of his lungs about corporate crimes and how the SEC is teaming up with the Department of Justice to do its part to clean up society from the likes of corporate criminals like Kavi Chander."

Kavi just looked down and stared at his food. His appetite was long gone. He had thought he'd be energized by meeting someone like Henry Jackson, but the meeting was having the opposite effect. He was feeling more and more drained. Finally, he turned to Henry and said, "I hear you telling me about all the problems I'm going to face. How about some solutions? Do you have anything constructive to say?"

Before Henry could respond, Marc jumped in, saying, "That's not really fair. I know this sounds terrible, but we shouldn't shoot the messenger."

Without any hesitation Kavi yelled back, "That may be easy for you to say, but it's *my* life that's on the line, not yours." As soon as he finished, he wished he could take it all back. Marc was obviously hurt by the comment. Kavi covered his eyes with both hands and said, "I'm sorry. Here you are killing yourself for me, and I'm snapping at you."

"Don't worry," Marc said. "You're right. It is your problem, not mine. This is really bothering me, but I can just imagine what it must be doing to you."

Henry reached over and put his hand on Kavi's shoulder. "This may sound cruel, but this is exactly what I wanted to have happen this evening. You came in here with a view that you're innocent and we should win in a cakewalk because good triumphs over evil. You now think your life is on the line, and all sorts of unfair things will happen to you, over which you have little or no control. Unfortunately, the latter is much closer to reality."

"And there's nothing you can do about it?" Kavi asked.

"I didn't say that." Henry leaned back in his chair and rolled up his shirt sleeves. "You asked for some solutions or something constructive. Believe me, I'm a very capable individual, and there'll be a great many things for you to consider, but it's premature to discuss anything until I've had a chance to prepare. First, I need to meet with the government and discuss the plea offer, and I need to study the materials you've given me. After that, I'll put together an outline of possible case strategies we can discuss, perhaps over the weekend, and I'll throw myself at your case with everything I've got. I'll be loud when I need to be, flamboyant when I need to be, and quiet when I need to be. You'll be well represented."

"I'm sure that's right," Marc said.

Maintaining eye contact with Kavi, Henry warned, "But you should never forget, and it won't be repeated after tonight: No matter what we do, no matter how confident I may sound, if we lose this case, I get to move on to my next one, but you wind up in jail."

Chapter 21

I was inundated with paperwork and could barely see the desk in front of my face. It was late afternoon on Friday, August 29th. I'd spent so much time during the week working on an asset protection plan for Kavi that I'd fallen far behind with my own work. Actually, I really didn't need to do as much as I'd done, but I wanted to spend the time with Vicki, even though we had to keep our focus on business. After our Saturday night dinner it was a little awkward for me, but she was such a professional, you'd never know from the way she handled herself that we'd been together on a date.

Now I was back in my office trying to catch up, although I kept getting distracted by one thing or another. A few times during the day the cause had been Gina Milano, an incredibly attractive 24 year-old who'd been assigned to one of my audits. Knowing I was single, the supervisor on the job must have thought he'd score some points by having Gina be the one who'd interface with me on some of the planning work. Besides having curves in all the right places, she had a great personality and it did seem as if she was flirting, but I knew how things worked regarding single male partners in the firm. If you dated someone on your staff, you'd better be prepared to marry her or kill her. Otherwise, you stood a good chance of getting hit with a sexual harassment suit. So I'd decided long ago that any woman who worked for the firm was off limits. Of course, that didn't stop me from thinking about Gina for fifteen minutes every time she walked out of my office. Needless to say, I wasn't getting enough work done.

At least the asset protection plan was beginning to take shape, but it was far from perfect. Vicki recommended the use of a special trust in the Cook Islands, and said it could work if Kavi and Aarti acted quickly. But there were a couple of significant drawbacks. For one thing, Vicki wanted their kids to be the only beneficiaries. It had something to do with the timing of possible claims against Kavi. Apparently, if they'd acted before the end of June, they themselves could have been the primary beneficiaries. But with all that had happened since then, Vicki said it would be best if they stuck with their kids. Although Kavi and Aarti had every intention of putting some money aside for the kids, they certainly weren't planning to give them everything. To partially address the problem, Vicki did suggest the use of a second trust in a different jurisdiction, like the Cayman Islands. In the latter case, Kavi and Aarti could be the beneficiaries, but Vicki was concerned that it could be successfully challenged, so she suggested putting as much as possible in the Cook Islands' trust. There also was a second problem. For some technical reasons, Vicki wanted the funding to consist solely of cash. And to do so, Kavi would need to exercise a good portion of his ADG stock options, and also sell most of his stock. At the last reported price of $39 a share, those moves weren't very desirable.

Aside from Gina Milano, phone calls were becoming a major distraction. I was actually being productive for a change when Ken called, and I had to stop what I was doing and take time to explain Vicki's recommendations. Of course he jumped on the problems and tried to second guess everything she'd said, but I knew from talking to her that she'd come up with the best solution. He finally accepted that but started going on and on about how we needed to do more to help. I agreed but couldn't help checking my watch every ten minutes as he continued with his sermon. Marc was keeping the two of us up-to-date so we both knew about the meeting with Henry Jackson and how he'd made Kavi very depressed. And Ken was getting frustrated with everything and was letting off some steam. He said Marc's way of thinking was limited, that he was too conventional and always played well within the rules. Ken went on to say he was much more creative and needed to get himself more involved. He talked as if there was some silver bullet hidden in a drawer that could make everything better, and he'd be the one to find it.

Ken said his oldest son was participating in a major soccer tournament all weekend, and he'd take advantage of the time watching the games to think about Kavi's situation and identify some good ideas. To most people that would sound crazy, but I knew how creative he was and how he sometimes did his best work around his kids. There had been one time his company was trying to sell a division and they'd had some decent offers, but the taxes associated with any sale were so high they couldn't agree to a deal. He'd been working ungodly hours trying to find a solution, with no success. At the time, his daughter Carol was on her fifth grade softball team and they weren't very good, but they were fun to watch and had a big game coming up against a rival school. Although Ken was busy, he made sure to leave work early so he could join his wife Jennie and their two sons to watch Carol's game. Despite his overtures to other women, he always said his family was his highest priority, and he tried to instill that value in his kids. Whenever one of them had a big game or event, he made sure the whole family got there to show their support. Although he was concentrating on the game, in the fifth inning, the solution to his tax problem became clear. In a flash, he thought of a way to transfer the division's assets to a foreign affiliate, move some other assets around, and then sell the stock of the foreign affiliate to the third party. He never told me why, but he said it significantly reduced the tax on the sale. And I'd heard of countless other times when something like that had happened. He said nothing made him more relaxed than spending time with his kids, and it amazed him how he could be with them and suddenly have solutions pop into his head, when he didn't even realize he'd been thinking about any problems.

After reminding Ken that we weren't facing any tax issues, he guaranteed me that he'd nonetheless come up with something good for Kavi to consider. Then, when I tried getting off the phone, he asked me about Vicki and our next date. I was leery of telling him anything because his advice was always the same and I wasn't in the mood. Not that I had ever adopted what he'd said before, but I was certain anything he suggested wouldn't work with Vicki. As it turned out, Ken was supportive for a change and wished me luck. I told him that Vicki was joining me for dinner later that evening, but that I'd actually asked to get together on Saturday and she had other plans. Ken agreed with my assessment that she probably thought another Saturday night date would appear inconsistent with the concept of 'just being friends.'

It was past 4 pm when I finally got him off the phone. Vicki was going to meet me at 6, and there was a good ten hours of work left on my desk that had to get done before Monday. Although I planned on working during the weekend, it was still important to get more done, but my concentration was completely gone, so I gave up. It seemed best to sit back in the chair and let her monopolize my thoughts.

* * * *

The margarita was beginning to take effect when Vicki arrived at the restaurant, wearing an ocean blue cotton shirt, with the top and bottom buttons undone, not quite making it to the top of her jeans. The way she was dressed, you could have mistaken her for a college coed. Maybe it was my drink, or maybe it was my imagination, but she seemed more beautiful than before.

She didn't see me, so I called out, "Hey lady, I can't find my date. Want to join me for a drink until she gets here?"

When she made it to the table she noticed my drink and teased, "You started without me? That's not very nice, is it?" She pretended to be pouting but all I noticed were her beautiful lips. When I stood up to kiss them she offered me her cheek instead.

I brushed aside my disappointment and said, "Work was getting unproductive and the thought of a margarita sounded pretty good." While I was talking, the waitress noticed me waving and came over to our table.

"Maybe I need to stay sober," Vicki said. "I'm not sure you can be trusted." She smiled and told the waitress a margarita would be fine. No salt of course. When her drink arrived we toasted Mexican restaurants. I had passed the place countless times but never thought to walk in. It was Vicki's idea to meet there. She said it was perfect for a casual Friday night dinner.

My jacket was on the chair and I'd already loosened my tie. She looked comfortable so I asked, "You didn't go to work dressed like that?"

"No, I went back to the apartment and changed." She reached across the table to pull off my tie and asked, "So why were you unproductive?"

Without thinking, I shot back, "It's your fault. I was thinking about you." Worried that I might have made her uncomfortable, I quickly continued, "Actually, it's really Kavi and the saga at ADG." For some reason I thought it best not to mention anything about Gina Milano.

"Anything I haven't read in the papers?"

"It's his lawyer. You ever hear of a Henry Jackson?"

"Of course. He's a great criminal defense lawyer and I'll bet he's expensive. We'd better hope there's money left over for the asset protection trusts."

"Kavi and Marc met him yesterday evening for dinner and it didn't go very well."

"I don't understand. They didn't think he was good?"

"It's not that. You can't tell after just one meeting anyway. It sounds as if Henry made prospects seem rather bleak."

"I'm sure it's not that bad, but he probably wanted to lower everyone's expectations," she suggested. "Can you imagine how Kavi must feel? Even if there's an eighty percent chance of winning. That means there's a twenty percent chance he'll wind up in jail." She shivered and looked away.

"That's one way to look at it. He's innocent, so I just can't imagine him going to jail." After saying that, I drank more of my margarita, but it tasted lousy. The conversation must have done something to my taste buds. Putting my glass aside, I said, "It's great sitting here sharing a drink with you, but thinking about Kavi really gets me down."

"So don't think about him. There's nothing you can do about it tonight." She reached over and put her hand on my cheek, and it was more potent than alcohol. I closed my eyes and had no trouble relaxing. But when I put my hand on hers she quickly pulled hers back. Ignoring the episode, she continued, "But we do need to discuss my proposals with Kavi and Aarti as soon as possible. I'm getting the trusts set up, but they'll need to take some action. Can we all meet early next week?"

"I'll see what we can do. In any case, I've already discussed some of it with Kavi and he understands." I sat back and, wanting to change the subject, asked, "Any interesting trips on your horizon?"

She smiled and said, "Of course. I'm always planning something. I've got a trip to Turkey coming up for next month."

"Never been there myself. Where in particular?"

You could see the gleam in her eyes when she replied, "Istanbul, Ankara, Kayseri and, if I can fit it in, Malatya."

"How long you going for, two weeks?"

"Five days."

"How can you fit all that in with only five days? Is everything close together?"

"Actually the cities I mentioned are spread out across the country. As it works out, I can only spend five days, and I'd like to see as much as possible. It's the way I do things. I'll pick a country and when I go the first time I'll see everything I can. Then I try to get back within a year and spend focused time in the major cities."

"But how do you plan to get around?"

"Trains are usually great. You can really get a feel for a place. But the trains aren't the best in Turkey, and I don't have enough time in any case, so I'm making arrangements for a chartered plane and guide. Maybe early next year I'll spend a week in Istanbul. From what I've read, it's a fascinating place, and I'm sure a week won't be enough." She was so animated discussing her plans. You'd think she'd never been on an overseas trip before.

"How often do you get out of the country?"

"Probably five or six times a year, not including any business trips."

"Not including business trips? That's incredible. I push myself to make one or two personal trips a year. But five or six, that's really something. At least I can say I've been to every continent."

"I'd like to make it to every *country*," she said. "As you can tell I have a passion for travel. There's a whole world out there, and I aim to see it all before I'm through."

I wasn't sure if I should ask my next question but was getting a little bold. I leaned in toward her and asked, "Maybe we can plan a trip together?"

She shook her head and laughed one of those quick laughs, as if I'd suggested something ridiculous. She said, "I'm afraid not."

"I understand. You don't know me well enough."

"That's true, but that's not the main problem." She leaned in closer and said, "I'm sure you can't keep up with me."

"I'm not that much older than you."

She sat back and took longer than usual with her drink. "It's much more difficult than you think. I make the most of my time, so I'm always on the move, with maybe four or five hours sleep a night, and sometimes even less." She looked away and said, "Anyway, I've always traveled alone. And it would be hard to imagine traveling with another person."

"Not just any person, but me." I was only half joking when I raised the idea of traveling together. I knew we had just met, but the thought of being away with her was very appealing. And though a more patient person would have thought differently, I loved to travel and I was interested in her—and I wasn't very patient. She continued looking away, and I wondered what she was thinking. Then my big mouth took over. "I wasn't going to say this but—"

She turned to look at me when I hesitated. "What's on your mind?" she asked.

"You. For some reason Victoria Richards keeps popping into my head. Why is that?"

Our menus came and we ordered dinner. She acted as if she'd forgotten the question, but I reminded her.

"Maybe you're just bored," she said. "Have you tried a hobby like coin or stamp collecting?"

"You might be surprised to learn that I am both a numismatist and a philatelist. That's coin and stamp collector to you."

"I know that. If I ever invite you to my place, you can study my collections. Got any 1909 S VDB pennies?" She was referring to one of the rarest Lincoln pennies. The S stood for the San Francisco Mint and VDB were the initials of the designer.

"So, you're a collector. Then you should know that coins and stamps are no substitute for someone like you."

"What am I going to do with you?" She shook her head, leaned back in her chair and smiled. "I must say you are very sweet. Girls must go crazy over you."

"Actually, it's more like I drive them crazy. Seriously though, I can't stop thinking about you. Have you been thinking about me?"

She sighed and said, "You should take it as a compliment that I'd like us to be friends. I don't have any male friends, not good ones."

"Why is that?"

"I really don't know. I'm sure part of it is that I've never been attracted to men." When she talked about traveling to Turkey she was animated and energetic, but she seemed lethargic when the discussion turned to her feelings about the opposite sex.

"Don't you find that strange?"

"I never really thought about it. I've been out of law school for only eleven years, and all my energies have gone into building my practice. There really hasn't been much time for a relationship."

"Have you ever thought about getting counseling?" Not being a big believer in it, I surprised myself with the question. In fact, some people had suggested it to me after my brother died, but I never felt comfortable pursuing it. I thought it was ok for other people but not for me.

"That's a strange thing to ask me. Do you think I'm unstable? Just because I'm a thirty-four year-old woman who doesn't think I need a relationship?"

"Did you hear me say you were unstable? No. I just think it might be helpful for you to learn more about yourself. You know. What makes you tick?"

"I'm not interested."

"Well I am, and I aim to find out. You'll let me, won't you? You'll let me learn more about you?"

Our food came, and we watched as it was being set on the table. It took only a few minutes but it seemed much longer, and when the waitress finished she told me to be careful because my plate was hot, so I immediately touched it, and burned the tip of my finger. I always thought they should have known that by just telling someone to be careful, that person's first reaction would be to touch the plate for confirmation that it was, indeed, hot. Perhaps holding the customer's hands while giving the warning would be a better approach.

After a few minutes of rubbing my finger with butter, the pain finally began to subside. I tried to get the conversation back on track. "So you'll let me explore your inner self?"

She tried to eat her fajita, but wasn't doing a very good job. "You won't let me eat, will you?" When she saw me nodding, she continued, "So you really want to learn more about me?"

"I do."

"Are you prepared for the consequences?" she asked.

"I am."

"Are you sure?"

"Absolutely." I had no idea what she was getting at, but there was no way I was going to say no.

"We'll see what we can do."

We spent the next thirty minutes or so eating quietly and making inconsequential small talk. I wasn't sure what we had agreed to do, but I wasn't going to push my luck and ask for any clarification. Not that night, anyway. Whatever it was, it was something. I did ask again about Saturday night and she repeated that she had other plans. But I felt certain she was just using that as an excuse to keep me at bay. Maybe she was right and we would just be friends, but I planned on taking our relationship as far as it could go.

Chapter 22

It was Thursday evening, September 4, and Kavi and Marc were back in Henry Jackson's conference room along with Gil Robeson, who was finally able to join them. It was raining heavily outside, and the gloomy weather matched the mood of everyone in the room. As expected, the government had filed charges against Kavi the day before, and it didn't make for a very happy occasion. Henry had spent most of the week working on the case, and had met a number of times with Gary Bevins and Dennis Smith, who, earlier that day, had provided Henry with a courtesy copy of the 76-page Indictment. He'd already read through it three times, making sure to highlight key sections to facilitate the others' review, and his assistant had made copies which were piled up in tall stacks on the conference room table, along with a three-page executive summary that Henry had prepared. Before distributing any documents, he gave a brief report on his plea discussions, which didn't include any good news, although that wasn't much of a surprise. As it turned out, the best the government would offer was assurance that a jail term wouldn't exceed eight years and, needless to say, that was a non-starter for Kavi. After some further discussion, Henry asked everyone to take their copy of each document, and then walked over to the window to watch the rain while the others read.

Although Kavi thought he knew what to expect, he was surprised when he looked at the upper left hand corner of the Indictment. UNITED STATES OF AMERICA v. KAVI N. CHANDER. It was as if the whole country was against him. He put the document aside and read through the summary. Its first paragraph said it all.

> There are a number of charges, but the primary one, and the most serious, is the government's claim of securities fraud. In particular, it is asserted that (1) the consolidated financial statements of ADG were materially misstated over several years, (2) such misstatements had a direct and material impact on the price of ADG stock and its other securities, resulting in losses to certain investors aggregating well in excess of $10 billion and (3) the company's CFO, Kavi N. Chander, was aware of the misstatements as of the time they occurred.

The summary continued with an overview of the other claims and charges. Kavi then flipped through the 76 pages of the actual Indictment, paying attention to the highlighted sections. A few in particular caught his eye.

> 23. On or about the dates set forth below, each such date constituting a separate count of this Indictment, within the Southern District of New York and elsewhere, defendant KAVI N. CHANDER did willfully and unlawfully use and employ deceptive and manipulative devices and contrivances and directly and indirectly engage in acts, practices and courses of conduct which would and did operate as a fraud and deceit upon members of the investing public, in connection with the purchases of ADG securities registered pursuant to Section 12 of the Securities Exchange Act of 1934.

> 65. Specifically, the assets of the Far East Merchant Power Group, or FEMP, as reflected on the consolidated balance sheet of ADG for the periods set forth above, were overstated (by amounts ranging from $2 billion to $4 billion), such overstatement was due in part to deficiencies in respect of key contracts for the sale of electricity to foreign authorities, such contracts were often obtained through fraud and deceit, including illegal payments to foreign government officials, and such fraud and deceit was conducted with the full knowledge of defendant KAVI N. CHANDER.

> 103. On or about the dates set forth below, while acknowledging responsibility for financial reporting, and representing, among other things, that the financial statements of ADG were fairly presented in accordance with generally accepted accounting principles, defendant KAVI N. CHANDER, knowingly and willfully made and caused to be made false statements to accountants of ADG in respect of litigation liability reserves established by Gerard Engineering and through fraudulent and deceptive devices engaged

in acts, practices and schemes to use such litigation liability reserves to manipulate earnings reported in such financial statements.

134. The allegations referred to herein had a direct impact upon the trading values associated with ADG securities registered pursuant to Section 12 of the Securities Exchange Act of 1934, including issued and outstanding common stock which traded on a split adjusted basis, during the above referenced periods, at values as high as $71 per share and as low as $22 per share, defrauding persons who invested in such securities in reliance upon the financial statements of ADG (with estimates of losses to such persons exceeding $10 billion).

After a while, the paragraphs all seemed to say the same thing. Bad things happened, people lost lots of money, and we blame Kavi, blah, blah, blah. It was too hard for him to continue reading, so he put the document aside and watched as Marc and Gil continued to read. They were so busy making notes on their copies, they looked like students taking a test rather than attorneys. They hadn't even reached the half way point, and since the document was so lengthy, Kavi knew it was going to be some time before the discussion started again. Getting a little antsy, he walked over to the window to join Henry, and watched as lightning periodically flashed in the distance. Henry told a story about getting caught in a storm on his way to the last day of some big trial, and how he'd made his closing arguments while soaking wet. After he'd won the case, one of the jurors told him his being so wet made him look more human and more believable.

The sound of the rain hitting the side of the building was soothing, and for a moment Kavi forgot where he was. Regaining his bearings, he looked at his watch and suggested they get started, but Marc asked for another ten minutes, which naturally meant twenty. Finally, they were ready to begin.

While walking to his seat, Kavi asked, "Is it significant that this document is so big?"

"I wouldn't read anything into that," Henry responded. "As you can see, there's plenty of boiler plate language in there."

Marc leaned forward and said, "They refer to the bribery, but unless I missed it, they're not saying Kavi violated the Foreign Corrupt Practices Act. Did you notice that?"

"You're right, but that makes sense," Henry explained. "Unfortunately, these guys know what they're doing. If they added those charges, it would put pressure on the government to demonstrate that Kavi not only knew about the bribes but was responsible for them in some way. If they failed to do that, it would leave doubt in the jurors' minds about the government's other charges. By limiting their case to securities fraud, all they need to prove is that Kavi was aware of the bribery and its impact on the financials."

"That's a very important point," Gil added, as he focused his attention on Kavi. "I take it you weren't aware of any bribes?"

Kavi was amused by Gil Robeson, and by his question. Looking at Gil, you'd never guess he was a good lawyer. He was just under 6 feet tall but was very heavy for his height, and had trouble keeping his shirt tucked into his pants. His tie wasn't tied well and one side of his collar stuck up—evidently the collar stay had broken. What little hair he had was a mess, partly because of the rain but partly because he didn't really care how he looked. What he lacked in grooming skills, he more than made up for with his knowledge of securities law. He had an encyclopedic mind and a photographic memory.

"I can tell you're not a criminal lawyer," Kavi said. "Henry didn't want me to proclaim my innocence. But for your information, not only did I not know about the bribery, but it was my follow-up that uncovered the whole mess. Maybe it would've been better if I'd have let sleeping dogs lie."

"So how do you think they'll go about proving you knew about it?" Gil asked.

Kavi rubbed his forehead with both hands, and took a moment before responding, "For one thing, they'll say I influenced our internal audit group as well as our external auditors, Larson & Kirsh, to reduce the scope of their work when it came to the business unit."

"Did you do that?" Gil asked.

"To be fair, the answer is yes, but not because I knew about any bribes. This was one of our best performing business units and it was a relatively straightforward one too. I believed there was a low risk of improprieties. Obviously, I was wrong."

"And you can imagine what L&K will say," Marc added. "They put the blame squarely with ADG management. That's what they did in their report and you can bet they'll do the same thing when they take the stand. They'll be more than willing to help the government make its case."

While struggling to push his shirt back into his pants, Gil asked, "Can they get any direct evidence that you knew about the bribes?"

Kavi took a deep breath, and then said, "They have a statement signed under penalties of perjury by the head of the business unit, Maurice Granville, that says I knew about the bribes."

Gil looked surprised and asked, "Any idea why he would say that?"

"Sure, he made a deal with the government and got rewarded for his handiwork. So now he's off the hook."

"But that doesn't make any sense. He should be their main target," Gil said.

"He's a French citizen, and he's rarely in the US," Marc said. "They knew they'd never get to him."

"And who knows what else they've got," Kavi said. "They also made a deal with Charles Goodman, our Chairman and CEO. He agreed to aid the government in their investigation, so for all I know, there'll be more so-called evidence against me."

Having abandoned his effort to tuck in his shirt, Gil shook his head and said, "That's all very troubling. Any one piece of evidence may not be enough, but when you put it all together, you never know."

"Last week I had to sit here and listen to Henry get me all depressed," Kavi admitted. "Now you're going to do the same thing?"

Gil looked over at Henry, then back at Kavi, and said, "I don't know what you discussed, but these are very serious charges. How can you *not* get depressed?"

For a moment nobody spoke, and then Kavi said to Gil, "When we met the other day, Henry was saying you never know what a jury might do. I'm sure he knows what he's talking about, but the fact of the matter is I really didn't know about the bribes. Even considering what the government has against me, I just don't think a jury can reasonably conclude that I knew."

"I hope you're right," Gil said. "Otherwise, you could be looking at up to twenty-five years in jail for each count of securities fraud. They've cited seven counts so that adds up to one hundred and seventy five years."

Kavi thought he might have heard wrong. "You're kidding, right?"

"I wouldn't joke about something like this."

Although Gil continued talking, Kavi couldn't hear a thing. He could see lightning in the distance but couldn't hear the thunder, and, looking across the table, he could see that Marc was saying something but he couldn't hear that either. There was just a loud and continuous ringing in his ears. Suddenly, the blood rushed to his head making him feel faint, and, thinking he was about to fall, he put both hands down on his chair to maintain his balance. He realized he should drink some water, but the bottle in front of him seemed to be moving from side to side, and, when he did get a hand on it, he spilled some out onto the table. Finally, after taking a drink, he slowly began to come to. Henry asked if he was ok, and he said he'd be fine.

"The government mentioned ten years," Marc said. "I thought that was the longest he could get?"

Gil shook his head and said, "They may have mentioned ten years as part of their plea offer. But for securities fraud, you can now get up to twenty-five years per count. Also, keep in mind that each year's financial statements stand alone, so even though it may be the same issue, if they prove their case for seven years of financials, its seven separate counts, and that would mean a life sentence, for all practical purposes." Gil paused while he opened his briefcase and took out four copies of a memorandum he'd prepared for the meeting. He handed them out and continued, "Look at the middle of the third page. It's got the section of the new law I'm talking about." He waited while the others read.

Whoever knowingly executes, or attempts to execute, a scheme or artifice-

1. to defraud any person in connection with any security of an issuer with a class of securities registered under section 12 of the Securities Exchange Act of 1934 (15 U.S.C. 78l) or that is required to file reports under section 15(d) of the Securities Exchange Act of 1934
(15 U.S.C. 78o(d)) ; or

2. to obtain, by means of false or fraudulent pretenses, representations, or promises, any money or property in connection with the purchase or sale of any security of an issuer with a class of securities registered under section 12 of the Securities Exchange Act of 1934 (15 U. S. C. 78l) or that is required to file reports under section 15(d) of the Securities Exchange Act of 1934 (15 U.S.C. 78o(d));

shall be fined under this title, or imprisoned not more than 25 years, or both.

"Just like I said, it's twenty-five years," Gil concluded.

Kavi still felt a little weak. He pointed to the memo and said, "There's no way they can say I did all this. Somebody tell me I'm not going nuts."

"Why do you say that?" Gil asked.

"For one thing, I didn't gain anything. When you look at all the other corporate executives being dragged into court, they're worth tens and hundreds of millions of dollars. You'd be shocked at how little I'm worth."

Gil got up and walked around the table so he could stand next to Kavi and point to his copy of the memorandum. "Look at what they need to prove. You say you didn't gain anything. Your compensation was partially tied to the stock price and the government may be able to assert that's how you stood to gain, but assuming your overall compensation wasn't excessive, it's a losing argument, so forget that. Ok, so you win on item number 2. But they need either 1 or 2, not both. Look at item number 1. That's a slam dunk for the government. They can easily demonstrate that an investor in ADG stock was defrauded. And ADG's stock is a security that meets these definitions. I'm telling you, the whole case will boil down to this word "knowingly' in the first sentence of the new section." As Gil walked back to his seat, he emphasized, "Can they prove you knew about the bribes and any problems in the financials? That's the sixty-four thousand dollar question."

Kavi looked around the room and was becoming more and more exasperated. His eyes seemed to be growing too big for their sockets and he was breathing much faster than normal. Finally, he sat back, stuck his arms out and said, "You guys are the lawyers here, but please tell me it isn't easy to send someone away for life. Isn't there some connection to the seriousness of the crime? I mean, even if the government proved that I knew about this, I didn't kill anyone. And this law takes up only half a page. Shouldn't there be more to it? Doesn't the Constitution say something about this? This is America, right? Somebody tell me I'm not going nuts."

"I certainly understand your frustration," Gil admitted. "And you raise some good points. Actually, there are some legal scholars who would agree with you. They think this provision is unconstitutional because it's too vague for a law with such serious penalties."

"And how about you?" Kavi asked.

"Let me put it this way. If I were making the determination, I'd say this provision *may* be unconstitutional, but don't rely on that. Even in the best case, the odds of winning a constitutional argument are less than twenty-five percent, and in today's environment of corporate fraud, I'd say with this particular provision, it's less than ten percent. For all practical purposes, this law is the law and we just have to live with it."

"He's right," Marc said. "It doesn't hurt to make the argument, but you can't rely on it."

Gil agreed, adding, "And even if you did win, it wouldn't mean securities fraud is legal. It would just mean this particular provision would be void. What if they added the specifics, and in your case only fifteen years of total jail time would apply? Under federal sentencing guidelines, I doubt you'd get twenty-five years per count anyway. Is any of this really helpful? The government's offering you a deal for no more than eight years in total, and that doesn't have any appeal."

"I understand what you're saying," Kavi said. "But please tell me the burden will still be on the government to prove that I knew. Putting all this stuff about the ineffectiveness of juries aside, it's still "innocent until proven guilty," right?"

"That's right," Henry said. "The burden will be on the government. Technically we don't have to prove a thing."

"So forget for the moment that I told you I'm innocent. Think about how I said the government will try to prove their case. Don't you think an independent person would conclude that I knew nothing about this?" Kavi asked.

Henry nodded for Gil to speak first. Looking uncomfortable, Gil replied, "I think that's an unfair question. To be perfectly frank, I don't know. But that letter from the business unit head certainly doesn't help matters, does it?" He paused and was apparently searching for the right thing to say. "No matter what we think, I'd say there's at least a twenty-five percent chance you could lose."

"That's an excellent way to put it," Henry interrupted. "Maybe from what's been said, you think I believe your case is a loser. On the contrary, if we take the right approach, I think we should win, but there's a serious risk that we can lose. Percentages give me heartburn, but twenty-five percent should give you a reasonable view."

"Perhaps we should stop talking about the odds of wining, and start focusing on our case strategy," Marc said.

"It's still premature to do that," Henry said. "What we should do is plan for tomorrow morning. It's going to be a media circus, and I'll have my first chance to address the public."

"So you couldn't get me out of that?" Kavi asked.

"No, the government wouldn't budge. There are some things we could have done but it wouldn't have been worth the effort. You were right about Bevins. He's a creep. And there's no question he wants publicity for both himself and the SEC. I'm surprised the Department of Justice guys are putting up with him. Back in my hockey days, I'd have rammed my stick down his throat."

"I know what you mean. So what happens to me tomorrow?"

Suddenly the group was startled by loud thunder and a bright flash. Evidently lightning had struck close by. Henry joked about the possibility of Gary Bevins getting hit, and added that a great many people would pay to watch it happen. Turning back to his notes, he said, "Meet me here at 7:30 in the morning. We need to leave by 8:00 to go to the FBI field office at 26 Federal Plaza. While there, you'll be fingerprinted and photographed, and then you'll be led in handcuffs across the street to the United States Court House at Foley Square where the charges were filed. The US Magistrate will unseal the Indictment and read some of it aloud, and when he's done, he'll set a tentative trial date. It won't really matter, because the date will likely be pushed back a number of times. Then we'll post a $50,000 bond and you'll be released. That's one thing I did get from Bevins. He wanted $2 million, but backed off. We could have easily managed to get it reduced and I think he didn't want to lose on any issue during the first day."

"But when we leave the courthouse, Gary gets to make speeches about me to the press?"

"Unfortunately, you can count on it," Henry said.

"And my kids get to read about it in the papers and see it on TV?"

"I'm sorry. You need to explain it to them."

"And just how do I do that?" Kavi asked. "Believe me, I've thought about it this past week, but I really don't know what to say." He looked down at the table, clenched his fist and grimaced.

Marc said, "One way or another we'll get through this Kavi. You have a lot of smart people on your side."

"Let's hope that's enough," Kavi said.

Henry hesitated a moment and then said, "So let's talk about what I'll say to the press. As soon as I walk out, we'll take the offensive. It seems to me we—"

Kavi interrupted, "I thought about that. And whatever you say, you know I'll just sound like everyone else. Can you tell me one time a defendant walked out of a courtroom and said they were guilty."

"What are you suggesting?" Henry asked. "I should tell the public that you *are* guilty?"

"Of course not." It was getting late and Kavi hadn't been getting much sleep. He turned his head and rubbed his eyes, and while refocusing noticed a small painting on the wall near the back of the room. It portrayed foxes on horses hunting an Englishman. "That's funny. I hadn't noticed that before. It's a great picture."

"One of my professors at the University of Chicago gave it to me as a graduation present," Henry said. "He told me I should always turn the tables on opposing counsel, like a fox going after an Englishman."

"So maybe that's what we should do tomorrow. Maybe we can turn the tables." Kavi massaged his chin and for a moment remained deep in thought. Then he shook his head and said, "Of course you'll say I'm innocent, but nobody will listen, so just say it once and then stop talking about me. Let's talk about Gary Bevins and the SEC. Let's talk about it as if they're the ones on trial. After all, what matters to me is what the jury will say, not what the public will think after listening to you on the news. What matters to Gary is publicity."

Marc looked at Kavi and smiled. Leaning forward he said, "I like it. We really shouldn't fight our case in public, so let's take advantage of the media exposure to make Gary and the SEC look bad. They can talk about Kavi. We can talk about them."

Becoming more animated, Gil laughed and said, "You may know plenty already but I can give you lots of ammunition against the SEC. Don't quote me on it though. They've been burned really bad, beaten to the punch on a number of public scandals. The enforcement division's been looking like a bunch of slow moving, ineffective bureaucrats with their army of agents. It's really amazing how they miss so much."

"That's been in the news, but we can still play it up," Henry said. "After all, the SEC won't like hearing it again and again, but that's what we'll do. Every time Gary gives a speech, I'll give one too. We'll make him pay for his airtime."

The group continued the discussion for another twenty minutes. They finished their plans for Friday, scheduled their next meeting and then broke up for the evening. When Marc and Kavi left the building, it had stopped raining, and the air had been partially cleansed. Needing to stretch their legs, they decided to walk to the garage where Kavi always parked his car, even though it was about a mile away. It was late, so there were very few people within view, and there wasn't much traffic. For the first two blocks they didn't say anything, so all they could hear was the sound of their footsteps as they walked. Kavi needed time to think and Marc wasn't sure what to say. At about the middle of the third block, Kavi asked, "What does it tell you when you're innocent but you still have a twenty-five percent chance of going to jail for years?"

"You'll get through this," Marc said. "Things have a way of working themselves out. I know it's easy for me to say, but I believe that."

"I was going to say it tells you there's no God. So you think things will work out. Why? Is it part of your religious beliefs?"

"Sure, good things happen to good people."

"Is that right? Keep in mind your God didn't do anything to stop millions of your people from getting killed during the Second World War. My God didn't stop England from taking over my country, killing thousands of people and treating the rest like shit. Cambodians couldn't be too pleased with their God. Rwandans have been slaughtered. African-Americans have their beef. I can go on and on. If there is a God, he or she or it doesn't seem to give a rat's ass about what's happening on Earth, and certainly doesn't care about me. I'm meaningless in the scheme of things."

Marc knew the saga was taking its toll, but things were even worse than he had thought. Kavi had always had a positive outlook on life and had never talked like that before. "You're a good person," Marc said. "Your family loves you. You have friends who will do anything for you. All things considered, you're far from meaningless."

"It's funny in a way, but I did consider myself a religious person. I believed in doing the right thing. But look at what happens. The real crooks can get off without a scratch. Sure, some get caught, and maybe they'll pay a big fine and serve a year or two in some country club that passes for a prison. But when they get out, they'll still have tens of millions stashed away from what they did. Now look at me. I never pushed for a big salary. I work for one of the largest companies in the world, but many CFO's make a lot more than I do. And you know about the Sisters of Jain. Aarti and I've given them so much through the years. Maybe in America crime *does* pay. Honesty certainly doesn't."

"Don't talk like that. What's happening to you is an aberration. You're a great example of the best thing this country has to offer. You came over here as a poor teenager, and you managed to become a top officer in one of the largest companies in the world."

"You mean I became a big target."

Marc stopped in his tracks, turned to confront Kavi, and started yelling so loud he could be heard a block away. "Stop feeling sorry for yourself and stop thinking about the bad things that might happen. Force that out of your mind. You've always been strong, but now you have to be even stronger. For your sake, for your family's sake, pull yourself together. Think about everything you can do to fight this thing and think about nothing else. You've got great lawyers representing you, and you've got Carl, Ken and me. We'll be with you every step of the way. So forget about what might happen. Just focus on what you can do."

Although Marc was right, Kavi wasn't in much of a mood for the pep talk, and he wanted to avoid a repeat performance, so he simply said, "What you say makes sense."

"You're damned right it does," Marc said. As they turned to continue walking he added, "We'll meet for dinner Sunday night. Both Ken and Carl have been pushing me to set it up and Ken said he's been wracking his brains trying to think of ideas for you to consider. Believe me, you'll feel much better after we all meet."

"Maybe you're right."

"You know I'm right."

Marc continued to talk all the way back to the car, and though he used different words, his message was always the same, "Keep your spirits up because things will work out in the end." Kavi wanted to believe that, but with everything that was happening, he had some very serious doubts.

Chapter 23

My car had started making strange noises and I was beginning to think the engine might fall apart at any moment. It was frustrating, because I'd just taken it in for a periodic service, and everything had been fine before that. The timing couldn't have been much worse because there was so much driving I had to do. It was Sunday, September 7, and my mother and I had planned on having an early breakfast together, followed by a drive to Long Island to visit Greenwood cemetery, where my father and older brother were buried. After that, we were going to visit her old neighborhood in Little Italy, and then the area around our old house in Brooklyn. When we were done with that, I needed to drive back to her apartment to drop her off, and then return to Manhattan in time for my dinner with the guys at the Iron Horse. It was going to be a long day and I couldn't afford to get stuck without a car.

I was sure I'd feel rushed with such a busy day ahead, but things slowed considerably when my mother and I arrived at the cemetery. It was hot and humid, and the weather ensured that there'd be very few people there, which was fine with us.

When my brother died, my father picked Greenwood because a group affiliated with our church had recently opened it, and there was plenty of available space. He didn't want my brother to be alone, so he bought five plots together, near a small hill. He figured there'd be enough room for the four of us, plus my wife, if I were ever to get married. There was a big oak tree there, and the way it was situated, they had the plots form a letter L wrapped around it, with four plots in a row and the fifth to the bottom right of the other four. My father had the arrangements all made. He would take the one at the top, followed by my brother, my mother and then me. And the someday dead love-of-my-life would presumably take up the fifth spot. I guess he didn't plan on my having kids. One particular aspect my father liked was having my mother lie between Joe Jr. and me. She took care of us during life, and he wanted to make sure she could do the same after death.

My mother was praying silently, and I stood back a few feet so she'd have some space to herself. We didn't talk much to each other when we were there. She stood alone with her thoughts and I stood alone with mine. At least we were able to be there at the same time. When my father was alive, it had been a much different story. My brother died 24 years before my father did. And whenever we'd visit, my mother and I had to stay in the car and let my father stand alone by the grave. Then, when he was done, he'd wave, and my mom and I would have our turn. My father wouldn't walk past us either; he'd make his way to the visitors center's men's room to wash his face and remove any evidence of tears before seeing us again. It didn't matter how many years had passed since my brother's death. My father insisted on visiting alone. Joe was his first born, a great athlete, a great student, and an all around great kid. My father had a very hard time accepting that he was gone.

My mother had a different view of the world. She was very religious, although she'd never throw it in your face, preferring instead to be the believing kind, not the preaching kind. According to her, my brother and my father were in a better place, and everything that had happened was meant to be. And she seemed so certain. I never did understand why her beliefs were so strong.

My car was holding up—the engine was still in one piece—and the strange noises had temporarily stopped. We finished with the remainder of our day's agenda and arrived safely back at my mom's apartment. I walked her to the front door, gave her a hug, and then tried to leave quickly in order to make it back to the city on time. But before I could turn away, she reached up and put both her hands around the back of my neck. She's not quite 5 feet tall, so she had to stretch. Looking quite serious, she said, "Tell Kavi he needs to have faith. This is all a part of God's plan."

"If it is, it doesn't seem like a very good one. Anyway, this is not a good time to talk about faith."

"But it's times like this when your faith matters most, not when things are going well."

"Fine. You pray for Kavi. But let me go, so I can try to help him."

* * * *

Despite doing my best to get to the Iron Horse on time, I was about thirty minutes late. The garage where I'd parked was only three blocks away, but it was so humid outside I was sweating heavily after having rushed over. The bar at the Iron Horse had cocktail napkins handy, so I grabbed a couple and made my way through the crowd to find the guys. The place was mobbed, so you could only see a few feet in front of you. Finally, I found them huddled around one of the tables at the back.

"We were about to give up on you," Ken said.

They pushed back the empty chair. I moved it in position with one hand and dried my face with the other. "The traffic was terrible and I was late leaving Brooklyn." The place was so loud they couldn't hear me so I sat down and repeated myself.

"You were with your mother?" Kavi asked.

"All day," I replied. "This morning, we left from her place to visit the cemetery in Long Island, then we drove to Manhattan and visited Little Italy, then we went back to Brooklyn, then I came back here. And now I'm ready to die."

"That makes two of us, kid." Kavi lifted his beer slowly. It was evident he'd been drinking for some time. He seemed lethargic and wasn't looking at me when he spoke. He reminded me of someone who'd just gotten back from a war and had that 'nine-mile stare.' Looking straight ahead, he asked, "Did you catch the show Friday?"

"You mean Gary Bevins? Yes, I watched it. He didn't look like anything I had expected."

"He looked like a jackass to me," Kavi said. "Isn't that what you expected?"

Ken passed me a beer, and while holding the cold bottle against my face, I said, "He looked much shorter than I had expected, and younger too."

"He is short," Marc said. "And young."

"And he's an asshole," Kavi added.

Ken nodded, and added, "He's got a big mouth too."

"But he actually sounded polished and very personable," I said. "It didn't seem to fit your description of him."

Kavi said, "He treats people like shit in private. But for the public he's a smooth talker."

I looked at Marc and began to ask, "If Kavi wins—"

Marc interrupted, "*When* Kavi wins."

"You're right," I said. "When Kavi wins, isn't there a way he can sue Bevins for slander?"

From Marc's facial expression I could tell the answer was no. "The government can come after Kavi and say whatever they want."

"It's our tax dollars at work," Ken said. "At least we can say Henry Jackson did a great job making the SEC look bad. He's a big guy, isn't he?"

"You'd like him," Marc said. "He's all muscle."

I leaned in to the table and asked, "So what did you guys cover before I got here?"

"Not much," Marc said. "We were waiting for you."

"Not that there's much for us to discuss," Kavi said, nursing his beer.

Marc shook his head, then spoke to Ken and me as if Kavi wasn't there. He'd do that at times if he wanted to make a point and didn't think you'd listen. "I told you about Henry Jackson and Gil Robeson. They weren't as encouraging as we'd hoped, and Kavi didn't take it very well. He needs to get his game face on real soon, and we need to help."

"It may not look like it, but I'm trying," Kavi responded. He took a deep breath and said, "But you don't know what it's like."

Marc basically ignored the comment and continued, "He's got to pull himself together. If this happened to me, I wouldn't waste my time feeling sorry for myself. I'd do nothing but focus on ways to support my case." He paused, then turned to Kavi and said, "I can imagine what you're going through, but—"

Ken forcibly interrupted, "How the hell can you do that?" The comment startled Marc, and his eyes widened, while Ken continued, "You say you wouldn't feel sorry for yourself. Tell me how you know that? How can any of us imagine what he's going through? Two months ago he didn't know anything about this, and now he's been marched into court in handcuffs like a common criminal. Has that ever happened to you?"

"No, but—"

"And his lawyers told him he has at least a 25 percent chance of going to jail for a good portion of the rest of his life."

"Can I just say—"

"And this idiot Bevins has been screaming at the top of his lungs that he should be congratulated for catching a criminal like Kavi. And the press has been eating it up."

"Ken, if you would just—"

"Come on. None of us knows what he's going through, and I hope we'll never know. So I suggest you stop acting as if you do."

Marc crossed his arms, sat back in his chair and glared at Ken, clearly pissed off by the admonition. Marc had been killing himself to help and apparently didn't think he deserved to be spoken to like that.

Trying to ease the tension, I looked at Marc and said, "You've been working real hard to help Kavi. We all know that. But maybe he needs more time to come to grips with the situation." Marc didn't respond, and I didn't want to push too hard, so I got up to get the waitress's attention, thinking some dinner might improve our mood. The place was so busy she wouldn't have noticed us had I not walked over to get her. After making it to our table, she took one look, rubbed a finger against her lips, then asked if anyone had died. Ignoring her comment, we just ordered the food.

For about twenty minutes we managed to talk about other things, but then Ken asked, "How's Aarti taking this?"

Kavi smiled and said, "She's strong, like a rock. I could use some of her strength."

"So she's holding up well?" Ken asked.

"Better than me, that's for sure."

Kavi said something else but I missed it, having been momentarily distracted by a couple making out in the corner. They were putting on a little show and it was hard to ignore, but they finally moved away. Not sure I was repeating anything, I asked, "Does Aarti have any great ideas?"

"She thinks we should kill Bevins. Then get the hell out of the country and go back to India."

"Is she serious?" Ken asked.

"About killing Gary?"

"No. About leaving the country."

Kavi shrugged his shoulders and said, "Maybe. I don't really know. Anyway, we couldn't do it." The waitress stopped by and Kavi ordered another round of beer. We were waiting for him to continue, but he'd apparently lost his train of thought. When it came back to him, he said, "Aarti always had mixed emotions about ADG. She was happy that I had my dream job, but she didn't like the way it consumed me. And she never thought we spent enough time in India. She always joked about my quitting so we could go back and spend some quality time with our extended families."

Ken leaned forward toward Kavi. "Are you sure she was joking?"

"Maybe not about the quitting part. She did want us to spend more time together."

"So why did you say you couldn't do it?" Ken asked.

"Do what?"

"Leave the country?"

"Ken, be serious," Marc interjected.

"I am being serious." Ken's eyes remained focused on Kavi. "Why can't you do it?"

Kavi smiled, leaned back in his chair, and looked away, apparently stalling for time. He turned to Ken and said, "For one thing, we don't have enough money. Vicki's got me putting a lot of what we have in a trust for the kids."

"But what if money wasn't an issue?" Ken asked.

"But it *is* an issue."

"Just assume you had enough. Would you go?"

Kavi, looking thoroughly confused, responded, "I hadn't given it much thought really. This is my home now. Would any of you leave?"

Without hesitating, I answered first. "I'd never go."

"It's a ridiculous question," Marc proclaimed. He looked at Ken and said, "What are you trying to say?"

Ken took a deep breath, looked down at the table and laughed. Then he looked over at Marc. "You're a good lawyer, damned good, and you're a good friend. But sometimes you're limited in the way you think, and you act as if you know everything, so you stifle other ideas. Sure, you bring in legal specialists like this Gil Robeson guy or Vicki Richards, and you'll listen to them, but they're like talking textbooks to you." He stopped, rubbed his forehead and continued, "I'm getting at something here. I don't know if I'd leave the country, but that's not important. What *is* important is that we identify options for Kavi to consider. We need some ideas that you and the other lawyers haven't been thinking about."

Marc sat back and glanced my way, apparently wanting support. When he didn't get any, he turned back to Ken and said, "But he doesn't have enough money."

"Just assume he could get more."

"How?" Marc asked.

"That's not important." Ken turned his eyes toward Kavi and continued, "Not unless you might really go."

"You're serious about this?" Kavi asked.

"I am. What if you had the money? Would you at least think about it?"

"This is his home," Marc said.

Nodding in agreement, I added, "Ken, think about what you're asking. Why would he ever leave?"

"Because he—"

Kavi interrupted, "Because I might lose. That's why." He chugged his beer and then studied the bottle closely, making sure every last drop was gone.

Ken hesitated and then finished his statement, "Because he might lose. Look at that low level finance guy in Texas who just got a 26-year jail sentence, without any chance of parole. And Kavi's charged with something far worse than what that guy was convicted of doing."

"Kavi's situation is different," Marc said. "And he should be focused on the best legal defense strategy, not how to leave the country."

"But Marc, I'm really worried about this," Kavi admitted. "Think about it. I might go to jail for years. It's a 25 percent chance, Marc. So go take four pieces of paper and put an X on one, then put them in a hat. How would it feel if *you* were the one who would get locked up if we picked the X?" He paused so his words could have their desired effect, and then said, "I don't know. Maybe I *would* leave the country."

Just as he finished, the waitress came over to bring us our food. She had a cute face and a great body, and under ordinary circumstances Ken would have been all over her. Actually, she looked so good, I might have been interested. But we all acted as if she wasn't there.

When she walked away, none of us touched our dinners. Marc pushed his dish aside and shrugged his shoulders. "So what did you prove? So he might have considered leaving if he had enough money. But he doesn't have enough, does he?"

"Not yet."

"What's that supposed to mean?"

"It means he doesn't have enough now, but I think he can get what he needs."

"How?" Marc asked.

Ken looked around at the crowd, and then leaned in over the table. And he motioned for us to do the same. "Maybe ADG can provide the funds."

"And why would they ever do that?"

"Well, what if they didn't know they were doing it?"

"You mean steal it?"

"I'd call it taking what's rightfully his."

We looked at each other and were amazed. It appeared that Ken had finally gone off the deep end. He was very aggressive and that was fine, but we never expected him to suggest anything illegal. I figured he was just mad at himself for not having come up with any great ideas, even though he'd spent the past week focusing on Kavi's predicament.

Marc shook his head, sat back and laughed. "You're insane Ken, you know that?"

"Why? Because I suggested that he consider taking money or because you think he might get caught?"

"It's the former. I never thought you were capable of suggesting something like this."

"Let me ask you something, Mr. Holier Than Thou." Ken grabbed the plate with his dinner, held it up in front of Marc and asked, "Would you ever steal this from me?"

"What kind of a question is that? Of course not."

"There are no circumstances under which you would steal this from me?"

"None whatsoever."

"What if you were poor, and your kids were starving. Would you steal it then?"

"So let's say, under the worst of circumstances, the answer would be yes. So what the hell would that prove?"

"It proves there's a time to steal, that there's a thief in all of us. It's just a matter of the circumstances we find ourselves in that determines what we're capable of doing. Now I say ADG had an obligation after all these years to stand by Kavi, but instead they were ready to sacrifice him to save their asses. And you know he could have earned a lot more from them over the years. Put it all together, and I think it's perfectly appropriate for him to take matters into his own hands to make things right."

Marc sat back, looking unconvinced. We were all quiet for a moment but then Kavi leaned in toward Ken and asked, "How do you think I could get money from ADG?"

"Come on," Marc protested. "You can't really be interested in this?"

Kavi immediately shot back, "Can I just hear what he has to say? Even if it's just a daydream, I could use a good one for a change." He turned back to Ken and was noticeably energized by the discussion.

"You're still the CFO, right?" Ken asked. "They haven't suspended you, have they?"

"Not yet, but there's a full board meeting coming up at the end of the month and I suspect they'll do something. They'll probably suspend me with pay, pending the outcome of the trial."

"How much money you guys pay in federal income taxes a year?"

Kavi looked startled. He smiled and asked, "What's that got to do with anything?"

"Just tell me, how much do you pay in federal income taxes?"

Kavi rubbed the back of his neck and took a deep breath. "Let's see now. We pay about $4 billion in total taxes a year, and most of that is for our foreign operations. I think we pay about $1 billion to the US."

"Ok. And you're required to pay that in estimated tax payments four times a year. One of the due dates is September 15, just over a week from now."

"That sounds about right."

"So you'll be paying about $250 million. That gives you plenty to work with."

"I can't believe you guys are listening to this," Marc said. He banged his hands on the table to get our attention. "You should stop right now. Don't forget my firm represents ADG and now you're talking about stealing from the company."

Ken ignored the comment and continued, "It's pretty simple really. You see, as the CFO, you'll be the one approving the wire transfer."

"That's right, but I can't change the payee. Our treasury department controls that, and there are three people involved for a payment this large. The money's going to the federal government and there's nothing I can do about it."

"I know you can't change the payee and I don't expect you to, but your tax staff will give you some paperwork to sign. That paperwork will include your internal ADG documents as well as an IRS form number 8109 that needs to be sent to the government."

"Ok, so why is that important?" Kavi asked.

"Form 8109 is the key. It tells the government how to apply the payment. When you make the wire transfer, all the government knows is that it got the money. It's the form that tells them the money should be applied as a payment of ADG's federal income taxes for the current year."

"I still don't see what you're getting at."

"It's the form that you can change. Let's assume you owned a company called Kavico. You could change the form to say some of the money should be applied as a payment of Kavico's federal income taxes. You include all the relevant information, including Kavico's federal taxpayer ID, and they'll do it."

"And then you try to get it refunded?" I asked.

"Exactly. The government applies it as a payment of Kavico's taxes and then you file a tax return showing the payment and request a refund."

"Wait a minute," Kavi said. "ADG's tax department will see that I changed the form."

"No they won't. Have them leave all the paperwork with you. When you're alone, sign what they give you and make a copy of the original form 8109 they prepared. Then shred the original and print a blank one off the IRS's site on the internet. Fill out the blank form with the information on the copy of the original but with the application of the payment changed. Keep in mind you're the one that sends the form to the government, so you send in the changed form. You give your tax staff all the internal ADG paperwork, plus the copy of the form 8109 they originally gave you, which they'll assume is a copy of what you sent in to the government."

Marc kept fidgeting and was clearly becoming agitated. I also recall feeling a little uncomfortable with the direction of the conversation. It was unlike any we'd ever had before, and just didn't seem real. It seemed like a good idea to make sure we couldn't be overheard, so I moved my chair back and tried to hear other people's conversations, but could only hear the steady noise of so many people talking at the same time. To hear us, you had to be sitting right at our table, and we were leaning in and almost talking in a whisper. I moved my chair back in and tried to refocus.

Kavi said "That can't work. Sure, our tax staff will think I sent in the original form, but they'll still know what we paid. At some point they'll see that the government shows a different amount, and they're sure to follow-up."

"But they won't know there's a difference until after they file ADG's federal income tax return. Think about it. They won't file this year's return until September 15 of next year. By that time you could have the money and be long gone."

He was going fast and I missed some of what he'd said. But Kavi was nodding and apparently was able to follow along. Though confused, I jumped right in. "But there have to be other problems," I said. "Let's assume he had $50 million applied to Kavico's taxes. If he filed a return asking for a $50 million refund, the government would get suspicious. Wouldn't they? There's got to be some sort of computer edit check or some other review before they pay out that kind of money."

"That's a very valid point, and I really don't know the answer, but it's not an issue. You see, you don't ask for the full $50 million. You file a return and make up some numbers to indicate you do owe some tax. Maybe you say you owe $30 million. You paid $50, so you ask for a refund of the extra $20 million. There's nothing unusual about a company making that kind of an overpayment. Happens all the time. I'm sure there'd be no problem getting the money."

Kavi and I kept searching for something that could go wrong, but Ken had an answer for everything. And for once, Marc wasn't the one asking questions, since there was nothing about the idea that he wanted to know. Since Kavi and I were intent on learning more, Marc tried to ignore us and eat his food, and at one point he went to the men's room and took so long we thought he might have gone home. When he got back he looked furious that we were still talking about it.

"But I don't own a company," Kavi said.

Ken responded, "It takes two days to set one up. It won't be a problem."

"But what about bank accounts and things like that?" Kavi asked. "You can't set everything up in two days."

"All you need before September 15 is the company and a federal taxpayer ID number," Ken said. "You'll have plenty of time to do everything else after that."

Finally Marc intervened. "Is the daydream over? Did you guys have fun talking about it? Now, let's discuss something more constructive. Something Kavi can actually do."

"Maybe you should go back to the bathroom," Ken said, only half joking.

"You have to admit, it's creative," Kavi said.

Marc reached over and patted Ken on the back. "I'll grant you that. This is the most creative guy I know. Now let's forget about this, and move on to something else."

"September 15. That's just a week from Monday," Kavi said.

"Hello, anyone home?" Marc asked sarcastically. "This is ridiculous. Nobody's listening to me."

Kavi focused on Ken's eyes, as if he was trying to look right into his head. "You don't really think I should do this, do you?"

"I can't tell you what you should or shouldn't do. I'm just giving you something to think about."

"Would *you* do it?" Kavi asked.

"That's an unfair question. Like I said before, none of us knows what you're going through, so none of us knows for sure what we'd do."

"Speak for yourself," Marc said. "I'd fight my case in court."

Ken was making me think, and he was making some very good points. So I said, "Maybe he's right. I mean, how can we really know what we'd do? My gut tells me I'd stay and fight, but who knows?"

Marc said "Look at all the corporate executives who've been indicted in recent years. You don't see any of them leaving the country, and they had plenty of money. I'll bet they never even thought about it."

Ken shook his head. "I'm not sure there's much to glean from what they did, and besides that, there's still time for some of them to act. Also, two of them have already committed suicide."

"That's true," I added.

"So what does that tell you?" Marc asked.

"I'm not sure. Maybe they weren't thinking clearly," Ken said.

Marc smirked and said, "I don't know about that. Those guys seemed pretty guilty to me. Maybe suicide was their best choice, and their minds may have been in perfect working order."

After a minute or two with nobody speaking, Ken said, "I'll speak for myself. I'm not sure, but it's entirely possible I'd take the money and run. I don't like the thought of spending time in jail. And taking the money is a way to say FU to the company. You never know. I might actually do it."

I put my hand on Kavi's shoulder and said, "It doesn't matter what we think. What's important is what you think."

Ken nodded. "That's right. So think about it, but don't take too long. You have to act by September 15. ADG won't make another federal tax payment until December 15, and it sounds like you'll be suspended by then."

Kavi closed his eyes and covered them with both hands, apparently deep in thought. Without moving his hands, he said, "So let's say I did it by September 15 to keep my options open, then if—"

"That's a problem," Ken interrupted. "You'd have to go through with it. Think about it. If you do everything I said, I'm convinced you'll get the money and be long gone before they find out, and they won't catch you once it's discovered. However, if you change the paperwork September 15 and don't do anything else, it'll take them a year or two, but they will find out and they'll know you did it." Ken picked up a fork and started playing with his food. He hadn't touched a bite. "Once you change the paperwork there's no turning back."

"So I have nine days to decide," Kavi said.

"You can set up the company and get a federal taxpayer ID next week. There's no harm in doing that."

"Can you help me with it?"

Ken sat back in his chair and looked out toward the bar. Then he leaned forward again. "I can't do any of this for you. It's one thing to give you the idea. But it's another thing to become an accomplice."

"Now we see what he really thinks of his idea," Marc gloated. "You said he wouldn't get caught. Suddenly you're not so sure."

"That's not fair. We're talking about two different things. Remember, he'd be long gone. I'd still be here."

"I understand," Kavi said. "It would be wrong to get you involved anyway."

We continued talking about it, but after a while there wasn't much more to say. Except for Marc, we hadn't touched our food and it was getting cold, so we finally took some time to eat. Marc took advantage of the lull in the conversation to get back to his original agenda. He needed Kavi to pull together some additional information for the legal team's next meeting. They were planning on getting together the following Tuesday, and Marc wanted to be prepared. It was interesting to listen to him talk, like he was back in control and intended to keep it that way. Ken just ate and let Marc have the floor.

When we were finished eating, the waitress cleared our table and said she'd get us another round of drinks on the house. The way we looked, I think she felt sorry for us. Just after she walked away, two women came up to our table to see if we'd buy them a drink. They were having trouble standing straight, so we knew they'd had enough and Marc stood up and told them we weren't interested. They were actually attractive but none of us were in the right mood. Suddenly some young punk who thought they were his dates came over and started giving Marc a hard time. Before we could say anything, Ken stood up and in one quick move, reached over the table, grabbed the guy's shoulders with both hands, lifted him up and over the table and threw him down on the floor. The guy must have weighed more than 200 pounds, but Ken handled him like a sack of potatoes. The guy was sprawled out on the floor. He was stunned and so were we. It was common knowledge that Ken was strong, but we'd never seen him do anything like that before. The guy tried to get up, but Ken leaned down, took hold of the guy's neck, and whispered something in his ear. I could see the guy meekly shaking his head back and forth. Finally Ken let go and the guy got up and sheepishly walked away. I turned to look for the two women, but they were long gone.

"Are you ok?" Marc asked.

"I'm fine," Ken said. "I just wasn't in the mood."

"I could tell."

"You never did that before," Kavi said.

"Don't forget, you didn't know me in college. What you just saw was nothing."

The whole episode only lasted two minutes, but the way Ken had backed up Marc reminded us how we stuck up for one another. The waitress came over with the beer, and when Ken tried to apologize she said there was no need. Apparently the guy had been causing trouble all night and she was glad to see him get what he deserved.

"Thanks for stepping in," Marc said.

"No problem," Ken said. "You would have given him much worse. I was really protecting the guy from you."

Marc raised his glass into the air toward Ken, and then said, "Sorry about what I said before. Your idea *is* completely nuts, but you're not insane."

Shaking his head, Ken grinned and said, "Sometimes you need to be a little crazy to come up with great ideas. You know, I have another idea for Kavi to consider."

Marc cringed. "Don't tell me. You want us to parachute into the Ivory Coast and kidnap Maurice Granville."

"That's a great idea," Kavi said. He was laughing and that was a good sign.

"No, I wasn't going to suggest that, but I like it," Ken said. "Actually, I was going to say we can help you get drunk."

"I'm almost there. It doesn't look like I need any help."

"We covered everything. There's nothing more you can do about it tonight. Let's just talk about something else so you can get your mind off this mess."

"I've got an idea," I said. "Let's talk about what we can do to Gary Bevins."

Ken didn't seem amused. "How is that changing the subject?"

"You wanted us to consider the great train robbery. I'd like to think about what we could do to Bevins."

"Carl, please tell me you're joking," Marc said. "I can only take so much of this shit."

"I'm not really serious. I just think it would be fun to think about. What would we do to Gary if we had unlimited resources and we knew we wouldn't get caught?"

"I can think of a few things," Kavi said.

We had to push Marc a little more, but finally he gave in. The episode with the two women and the guy probably convinced him to lighten up a little bit. Reluctantly, he said, "As long as you're not serious, I'll give it a try. Let's see, what could we do to the little twerp?" Rubbing his chin, you could tell all the wheels were turning inside his head. He took his time, and finally he said, "You get the feeling he wants to go into politics. That's why he's hogging the spotlight. So what do you do to hurt a future politician?"

"You get him involved with his own scandal," Ken said. "Something the people won't forget."

"Like an affair with another woman," Marc said.

Ken shook his head. "No, that's not enough, not if the politician handles it correctly. Look at the ex-President. It didn't stop him. No, to really get the guy you need something worse."

"Right," I said. "Like that congressman who allegedly had an affair with a woman who was found dead."

Kavi jumped in. "Look at Chappaquiddick. I wasn't even in this country and I knew about it. Being around a dead woman has a way of screwing up a guy's political ambitions."

"Ok, I agree," Marc said. "But you're not going to get a woman killed so you can set Gary up."

"No, but what if a woman had *already* been murdered?" Ken asked.

The place had emptied a bit, so I looked around again to check if we could be overheard. We were just fooling around, but discretion seemed the better part of valor.

Marc shook his head to indicate he thought there was a problem. "That's no good either. Let's assume you can pin it on him. Then what about the real killer? You don't want to do such a good job that the real killer stays free."

"You're missing the point," Ken said. "I'm not talking about *actually* pinning the murder on the guy, although that wouldn't be such a bad idea either. I'm talking about fabricating enough evidence so the public thinks he might have done it, but not so much as to get him convicted."

Marc again shook his head. "But what happens if the real guy gets caught? The people will know Gary didn't do it."

"How about an unsolved case?" I asked.

"That's it," Ken blurted.

"I'm sure there are plenty of murders each year that go unsolved," I added. "Let's say you picked a nice juicy one that occurred ten years ago. The odds are pretty good nobody's looking for the real killer anymore. What if you went back and fabricated enough evidence to implicate Gary? Remember, I did say we should assume we had unlimited resources. Just when his political career gains traction, you get the detectives to open up the case. Maybe they don't have enough to send him to jail, but they won't clear him either. He'd be killed politically."

"Why wouldn't you want him convicted?" Kavi asked.

"Because we'd know he's really innocent." Before I even finished with my sentence I knew what Kavi was going to say in response.

"But I'm innocent, and that's not stopping him."

"But he may not know that," I said.

"Are you sure?" Kavi asked.

"Why would he be doing this if he thought you were innocent?"

Before Kavi could reply, Ken jumped in. "Maybe he doesn't know, but I wouldn't put it past the guy." Ken continued, "This creep wants something, and he's using Kavi to get it. Who knows what he really thinks and what he's really capable of doing?"

Just then, the waitress brought us the bill, and remarked that we all seemed in much better spirits, in contrast to the way we'd looked before. We thought it best to keep our discussion topic under wraps, so we credited the beer and her pleasant demeanor. Unlike most places in the city, the Iron Horse only accepted cash, so we all chipped in. We added a rather large tip, and for some reason she thought that entitled me to a great big smile.

Ken waited for the waitress to leave, and when she was gone, he asked, "We talked about Gary, but what about Maurice?"

"I'm sure you can think of some ways to mess him up," Marc said. Then he leaned over to the middle of the table, as if the feds had planted a bug, and said, "But that would be wrong."

Kavi was in no shape to drive after we'd done our best to get him drunk, so we forced him to let me take him home. I really didn't mind, even though I'd already logged about 200 miles of driving that day, and was still afraid my engine could fall apart. His house was about 25 miles from my apartment, but most of it was highway driving, and my car did seem to be holding up. It looked like we might get a major storm, and when we crossed the George Washington Bridge we started getting a slight drizzle. My radio was on but you couldn't tell. It was so low that all we heard was the sound of the windshield wiper going back and forth and the periodic 'pings' from the front of my car. Neither one of us did anything, even though it would have taken all of two seconds to increase the volume. And we didn't say much either. I guess our minds were on other things. It didn't seem like we had been driving very long when we arrived at his house.

Making my way along the circular driveway, I pulled up by his front door. "Hope you enjoyed riding with Carl's limo service. Call again sir."

He began to open the door but hesitated, then stopped. "Say, Carl, what did you really think about Ken's idea?"

Actually, that's all I had been thinking about on the drive home. "I don't know. I'm a partner in an audit firm. I've never thought about doing something illegal."

"So you wouldn't do it?"

"It would have to be extraordinary circumstances for me to even think about it."

"These *are* extraordinary circumstances."

"You're right. I think you'll win in court, but I'm not a lawyer. So what if you lost? Can you imagine what it must be like in jail?"

"I'm trying not to."

He thanked me for the ride and got out of the car slowly. He looked like he wanted to say something else, but instead turned to leave. I watched as he headed for his front door, but before he could open it, I asked, "Are you going to do it?"

He walked back and leaned in the car window. "I can't answer that right now. I'm really exhausted and my mind needs a rest. I'll talk it over with Aarti tomorrow, so we'll see. She'll probably say it's a crazy idea."

"I'm sorry I can't give you any better advice."

"Nobody can give me advice. The ball's in my court."

I waited until he closed the front door before pulling away. As I made my way around the driveway, it occurred to me that I'd just asked my best friend if he was thinking about stealing money. Who would have thought things would ever come to that.

Chapter 24

It was Wednesday afternoon, September 10, and I still hadn't heard from Kavi. The temptation to call him was strong, but I figured my calling would do more harm than good. Things were in his hands, and he needed to be left alone. It was hard for me to imagine what he must have been going through, facing a decision that most of us would be afraid to face. All things considered, I wanted no part of it. On the other hand, I was sure Marc was taking full advantage of all the access he had. There'd been a meeting Tuesday with the full legal team, and he and Kavi had prepared for it most of the day on Monday. That would have given Marc plenty of time to convince Kavi to forget the whole thing. I wouldn't have been surprised if he'd succeeded. Marc could be very persuasive when he wanted to be. But Ken was more like me in that respect. He'd said all he could say, and was probably keeping a low profile.

As usual, things were busy for me at work, but they were manageable. There was nothing urgent, so I decided to call Vicki to see if we could meet for an early dinner. A Wednesday evening rendezvous fit within her concept of our relationship, so I expected her to say yes, and she didn't disappoint. It would be my next opportunity to expand the world's understanding of the life and times of Ms. Victoria Richards. Although we'd been together many times, she was still a mystery, but it was a mystery well worth exploring.

After getting off the phone with her, I had a good hour of high productivity and was on a roll when Ken called. I gave some thought to letting him leave a message, but figured he might have some news about Kavi, so I gave in. He asked me about my plans for the evening. When I replied, he suggested I cancel my dinner with Vicki. He said Kavi wanted to meet the two of us, and though he didn't know why, we both had a pretty good idea. Marc wasn't going to join us, so that was a meaningful clue. And with all things considered, it was good that he'd be out of the picture.

Calling Vicki to cancel was tough. I needed to take advantage of every opportunity I had to see her. Actually, if it had been up to me, we'd have seen each other every day, but she was especially good at keeping us on her desired pace, which included only three speeds: slow, slower and stop. It was like she had some date quota and we couldn't exceed it without becoming lovers and bursting into flames. Unfortunately, seeing the guys that night was more important, so I did have to cancel. But hearing her voice on the phone made me think there might be a chance I'd change my mind.

"Vicki, something's come up and I need to cancel for tonight."

"Are you playing with me?"

"No. Why?"

"You just asked me to dinner an hour ago. So tell me, what's her name?"

"Ken and Kavi."

"I see," she said. "You're really into men, aren't you?"

"If you give me the chance, I'll prove otherwise."

"That could be dangerous." She paused, and the silence got my blood flowing. "So what are you guys *really* up to?"

"We need to discuss Kavi's legal case."

"What's the rush? Nothing's happening tomorrow. So which strip joint are you guys going to?"

"Why, you know any good ones?"

"There's one in my apartment building," she teased.

"So now who's playing?"

"I'm sorry. I can't help it. It's just so easy to play with you."

"So let's really play. I'm free tomorrow night."

"But I'm not."

"So how about Saturday night? Even friends get together on a Saturday night once in a while."

"I'll let you know. In the meantime, have fun with the guys."

*   *   *   *

When I arrived, Kavi and Ken were going at it, and Kavi looked more like his old self. It was great to see him that way, smiling, gregarious, and using his hands as he spoke. The last time he seemed so animated was at the beginning of the anniversary dinner, just before the whole mess started.

When I got to the table he stood up and almost crushed my hand with his grip, and before I could sit down, he told me he was going to do it. He was going to implement the "Plan," which was his term for Ken's idea. Although Ken and I thought that's what Kavi would tell us, it was still strange to hear him confirm it. He seemed so comfortable with his decision, perhaps too comfortable. In typical Kavi fashion, he had everything all worked out. He said by the end of the week he'd have the corporation set up with its own Federal taxpayer ID. He also said that Monday would be his "D Day". That's when ADG would make the federal tax payment and the day Kavi would modify the paperwork as part of the Plan.

We spent some time talking about how there'd be no turning back. It was funny in a way, because it almost seemed as if Ken was trying to talk Kavi out of it. But what he was really trying to do was push Kavi to make sure he fully understood what he was about to do and was committed to going forward. And Kavi passed with flying colors. We asked what had made up his mind, and he said Aarti had a lot to do with it. That she jumped at the idea when she first heard about it. She really hadn't been joking about her desire to spend more time in India, and was very excited about spending time with their families and, most of all, spending more time alone with her husband.

Kavi did admit that if he could go back in time, and make it all go away, he would do so. However, recognizing that going back wasn't an option, he believed the Plan was the best alternative. He pointed out that working at ADG took up too much of his time, and that he was 46 years old and his kids were fully grown, so he didn't need all the aggravation any more. He said the whole mess had forced him to think about what he really wanted to do with the rest of his life. He told us he wasn't trying to rationalize his decision, and added that there were pluses and minuses associated with any decision he would make.

We asked if he'd miss the States and he said he would, but it was just a part of the overall bargain. He added that his kids both hoped to spend time overseas, so the Plan would make sense for them. Sanji wanted to live in England and Kris had always liked Europe. With the money they'd have in the Cook Islands trust, they'd get to live very comfortable lives and would see their parents often, perhaps even more often than they'd like.

Kavi told us he was planning on switching about $25 million of the tax payment to his company's account, which by his estimate would net about $10 million. We asked why he wouldn't try for more, but he said $10 million would be more than enough for him and Aarti, and the kids would be set with the money in their trust. He also agreed with some of the things Ken had said about ADG at dinner Sunday night. In Kavi's view, the company owed him about $10 million, and he could live with taking that amount without feeling guilty.

Finally, the discussion turned to our Iron Horse foursome and how we'd never be the same. Kavi did get a little emotional, but we said we might see each other from time to time. Ken joked that we could fly out of the country to meet Kavi every June 30, picking a place that doesn't have an extradition treaty with the US, so he'd be safe. We added that he'd have to pay for our travel expenses, since he'd have all that money.

There wasn't much more to say. Ken and I wished Kavi luck, and then the three of us split up. As it turned out, Vicki and I could have had dinner together, and I gave some thought to calling her, but decided it would look stupid to set up a dinner, cancel, and then try to set it up again. Aside from that, I had told her we were planning for Kavi's legal case, so it wouldn't look good if we were done so soon. I also thought about calling Marc, but decided against that too. It was pretty clear what he thought about the Plan and, if I knew him, he'd be calling me soon enough. In a way it was good that there'd be no turning back after D Day, as Kavi had called it. That way, Marc would have no reason to stay on our backs.

During the drive home it was hard to get the conversation out of my mind. In less than a week, Kavi would put into motion a plan to get $10 million. And there was nothing anyone could say to support it, like arguing that it relied on some creative interpretation of the law. No, it was stealing, pure and simple. Still, I agreed that ADG had given him a raw deal and he'd been underpaid during his tenure with them. Whichever way you looked at it, my best friend was about to become a criminal and, if successful, a fugitive from the US authorities. It was ironic that this could be done by a man with such talent and integrity that he'd made partner in a major accounting firm in less than 10 years, and had become the CFO of one of the world's largest conglomerates in his mid 30's.

Everything was happening so fast. We'd known each other since 1979, and the latest developments were difficult to accept after all the years. I was getting more and more fatigued just thinking about it, and my mind started to drift to some of our earlier days, when right and wrong were easier to distinguish.

* * * *

It was Saturday, July 7, 1982. Outside, it was a gorgeous day, but I was stuck in a windowless conference room with Kavi and Ken. We were at one of the downtown offices of Consolidated Trust Company, or CTC as they were known, one of New York's money center banks. It later merged with another large bank, then another and another, and, after about the fifth merger, I kind of lost track.

A few weeks earlier, auditors from the city had determined that certain securities being held by CTC on the city's behalf were missing. The bank was so large that it wasn't unusual for securities to be misplaced from time to time, but the city was making it a big to-do. Back in the mid 70's, it had faced a financial crisis and looked to its major money center banks for help, but all it got was the cold shoulder. Now the mayor had his chance for some payback and he planned to take full advantage of the situation. He made such a public fuss that CTC was forced to do a complete physical inventory of all of their securities, which was unheard of for a major bank. Any auditor would tell you such an exercise would likely do more harm than good. Nonetheless, it had to act to stop the bad publicity. Winston Knight & Co., as we were known at the time, was the audit firm for CTC, so we were hired to perform the work. The bank was so large it had securities in more than ten locations, and each one had more than one vault, and each vault was huge. It was a massive undertaking that involved hundreds of audit staff working nearly round the clock.

At the time, all four of us were still with the firm, but Marc had switched to the tax department the prior summer, so he wasn't involved. Ken wouldn't make the move to taxes for two more weeks, so he was still on the audit staff and had gotten drafted along with Kavi and me. And the three of us got assigned as one of six teams working on vault 13B at one of CTC's downtown locations. We sat at a conference table that was surrounded by hundreds of boxes filled with securities, and each of us had our own massive computer report that listed the securities we were supposed to examine. Aside from the three of us, two bank employees were asked to be in the room to observe us at all times. It was 4 pm, and though we'd started at 7 am, we still had about 4 more hours of work to do, plus a full day's work for Sunday. We were getting tired and needed a break.

"Look at this thing," Ken said, looking disgusted. He flipped through the pages of his assigned computer report that was so big it weighed about twenty pounds. "It goes on forever. I'll never get done by tomorrow night."

"So finish it Monday morning," Kavi said.

"I can't. I need to be at the Pan Am building. I've got seven more days of work on their pension plan audit and it has to be done by a week from Tuesday. You know Don Jansford. He's the supervisor, and I don't need him riding my ass."

"Word is he's an asshole," I said.

"That's what I think, but don't quote me." Ken slammed his computer report closed. "You know I was supposed to spend this weekend with Jennie."

"You've been seeing her for two months now," I said. "You planning on biting the bullet and getting married?"

Ken cringed and then said, "The words 'married' and 'Ken Tanner' are exact opposites and should never be used in the same sentence. There are just too many women out there for me to please. You think I could ever settle down?"

"I'm sorry I asked. Anyway, if you need me to take over for you after tomorrow, that's ok." While speaking, I finished with one box of securities, put it on the floor, grabbed another one and started unloading the contents in front of me on the table. "I'm in the middle of preliminary work for the audit of Ashford Securities. I should be there Monday, but I'll put in a call to my supervisor. He should be able to push it back a few days." I looked over at Kavi and smirked. "So some of us don't need to check with others, do we?" The normal track to supervisor was three and a half years. We had only been with the firm for three years but Kavi had already been promoted to supervisor three months before. They'd given him two large audit engagements and he was planning for that work, which would begin in full swing in August. He was busy, but unlike us, he had control over his schedule and didn't need someone's approval to spend Monday at CTC.

Ken walked over to a corner table that was a health nut's worst nightmare. It held typical weekend audit fare: donuts, coffee, sodas and pizza—we'd been told at the time that carbohydrates were good for you. He opened a soda, offered one to me, then walked over to Kavi, handed him a can and asked, "So big shot, how come you got stuck with peons like us counting securities?"

"Believe me, I tried to get out of it. Not that I mind counting securities. But spending my weekend in a conference room eating pizza with you guys? That sucks."

"You mean you'd rather spend a beautiful summer day at home with your pregnant wife and little girl?" Ken asked sarcastically.

I continued flipping through my computer report to match it up with the securities in front of me, but was getting sick of doing it. And my arms were starting to move on their own, with no help from me, which I thought was rather strange. So I just pushed it all aside, sat back in my chair, and tried to regain control of my limbs. While doing that, I looked over at Kavi and he seemed comfortable with what he was doing, so I asked, "How does it feel being a big-shot supervisor?"

Kavi smiled and said, "It's better than being staff, that's for sure. It's nice to have a title that doesn't sound like some sort of infection."

Ignoring the quip, I turned to Ken and asked, "So what's it like working for Jansford?"

"He's a pain in the ass. The other day he screamed at the top of his lungs, "Get me a staff guy for lunch." Someone who worked for the client overheard him and asked if he'd rather have a ham sandwich. None of us had the guts to joke like that."

"I could talk to him if you want," Kavi said. "Berris is the partner on the account and I've got a great relationship with him. He's the second partner on my two accounts. Don won't give me any shit."

"No, don't bother. I've got seven more days, and then I'm off to the tax department for good." Ken was thrilled that he was leaving the audit staff. He had tried to make the move to tax a year earlier when Marc did, but the firm wouldn't let him. They wanted one more audit season out of him so they could get their money's worth from all the firm's training.

"Now that Marc's there, you have to follow?" I asked.

One of the CTC guys watching us decided he also needed a break. He stood up, said something to the other guy, and then left the room.

"Marc has his own agenda," Ken said. "By the end of next year he'll be working with a law firm."

"So what's your story?" I asked.

"I'm tired of audit. Look at this. It's a beautiful day outside, but it could be raining heavily for all we'd know. We're stuck in a room with no windows counting securities. So this is why we went to college?"

Kavi laughed and walked over to get a slice of pizza. He asked the remaining CTC guy watching us if he wanted some. The guy declined and then said he was going to the bathroom and would be back soon. Kavi walked back and put his right hand on Ken's neck. "So you think it takes more brains to fill out tax returns?"

"That's just at the start. After I learn the ropes, I'll be doing tax planning work. That's where the action is."

Kavi walked back and shook his head. "I just don't see how you and Marc can be excited about tax planning. It seems pretty boring to me."

Just then it occurred to me that we weren't being watched, even though we were supposed to be observed by two guys at all times. I walked over to the door and looked outside. The two CTC "guards" were nowhere in sight. "Hey, did you realize we're alone?"

"So what?" Ken said. "You plan on doing something kinky?"

"Guys, look at some of these securities. They're bearer bonds." I picked up a bond from one of the boxes. It had a face amount of $12 million and was payable to bearer. That meant that whoever held the bond had the ability to get the money. Years later the laws were changed so that owners had to be registered, but back in 1982, bearer bonds were still prevalent.

Ken looked over to Kavi, smiled and then looked back at me. "But how would you collect? You don't think you can just waltz into some local bank and ask for $12 million, do you?"

"You laugh now, but wait until I'm rich." I put the bond back in the box and walked to the door to make sure we couldn't be overheard. "You set up some foreign bank account in a place like Bermuda where they'll keep your identity secret, then you collect through that account. And there are hundreds of bearer securities here. I'm not talking about just $12 million."

Ken laughed and said, "You haven't been out of the country and now you're an expert on Bermuda bank accounts? I'll bet you can't even find Bermuda on a map."

The two of them fired away with their questions and I had the answers. But we all knew I wasn't serious. None of us would have considered it, although we did conclude we could get the documents out of the building by putting them in our underwear. For some reason, CTC personnel never thought of the need to search the auditors because they didn't think we'd ever be left alone. Little did they know we were the only ones in our room for a good 20 minutes before one of the monitors returned. We didn't tell anyone, not wanting the two guys to get into trouble, but we weren't surprised by the episode, and figured what happened with us had probably happened to others. It just never occurred to anyone at CTC that an auditor could be a criminal. Sometimes I thought a great way for someone to make a big score was to join an audit firm and spend two or three years building up a good track record. After that, the vault would be open to him or her, with no guns or explosives needed.

Chapter 25

Fall was my favorite season, so I took the day off and was relaxing on the terrace of my apartment with a glass of kahlua & cream. It was probably the last chance I would have to do that before the year-end audit season started to heat up. It was Thursday, October 16, and the air was so clean and crisp, you could almost see into the individual apartments in the buildings directly across the river. Though Manhattan was only about a mile away, with my frame of mind that day, it seemed like another world.

While sitting with my drink at the ready, I wasn't thinking about anything in particular, and certainly wasn't musing about work. My Giants were playing poorly and looked destined for a losing season, so I did my best not to think about football. Of course Vicki was in the back of my mind. We were seeing a lot of each other and that was great, but she was still on her "let's stay friends" kick, and I was beginning to wonder if she'd ever be interested in something more. There were heavy barriers to be breached, and I had no idea how to do it. And it seemed the more that I learned about her, the less I knew. Vicki had no memory of her father, and she was an infant when her mother died. There were no brothers or sisters, and no extended family that she knew of. It seemed like a lonely existence to me, but she appeared to be genuinely happy with her life. Nonetheless, I thought she needed someone, and I figured that someone was me. My feelings for her were becoming more and more intense, and they seemed to emanate from deep within my gut. So much so, that it was becoming a real struggle to keep those feelings in check. I was sure that we were meant for each other, but could see no indication that she felt the same way.

Things were moving along with Kavi, although there really wasn't anything more for me to do, so I was pretty much out of the loop. The trial was set for January 15, but all sides appeared willing to delay it until April or even later. Every so often, there'd be a set of motions in front of the judge. Gary Bevins would make some public statements about the common good, and then Henry Jackson would blast the SEC, but I wasn't paying much attention. It didn't matter anymore. Kavi had set up his company and called it FHP Commodities Inc., a US corporation headquartered in Europe that acted as international traders in precious metals and industrial commodities. Of course, other than filing a tax return to get a refund, it wouldn't do much of anything. On September 15, with FHP already having been set up, Kavi did his 'paper caper' and officially became a criminal, so the trial would never really begin. We knew that, but nobody else did. Kavi was just going through the motions until he had the money and was ready to leave. Marc agreed to continue helping with the legal team from time to time, so the other lawyers wouldn't get suspicious. But he significantly cut down his involvement. He was ok doing his part, so long as he didn't know a thing about what Kavi was doing with the Plan. Marc was adamant that he be kept completely in the dark, so he would never be forced to choose between lying for a friend and telling the truth. He also counseled Ken and me to stay out of the picture and we all agreed. Although I did know that Ken was talking to Kavi about it every so often.

As had been expected, the ADG board suspended Kavi with pay, effective October 1. Little did they know it could cost them millions for not having acted about two weeks sooner. The corporate controller took over as acting CFO and, for some reason, Steve Halpern was given an expanded role. There was some good news though. Debra Jennings was promoted to controller and given a big raise in pay. Kavi was happy for her, although she was terribly upset at gaining from his misfortune. Initially, she considered refusing to take the job. But Kavi convinced her he was gone anyway, so it made no sense for her to decline the position. Her promotion confirmed the company's plans for Kavi. If he won in court and returned as CFO, the controller would presumably be out of a job, but that scenario would never be allowed to happen. Even if Kavi did win, we all knew he'd be terminated without cause. The sad thing is that he'd get paid more in severance than he'd have gotten by remaining in his position. Big companies had a fear of lawsuits from terminated executives and thought it was good practice to buy peace, so-to-speak.

There was no turning back, and Kavi wasn't the type to second guess his decisions anyway. But he did admit that he had his good days and his bad days. Some times he'd wonder if he'd made a mistake, but overall, it seemed he was becoming more comfortable that he'd made the right choice. As part of the normal pre-trial routine, his lawyers were gaining access to the government's evidence, and a very compelling case was being mounted against him. Maurice Granville had flown to New York and given a deposition where he repeated his assertion that Kavi had been aware of the illegal payments. He was so good at lying, if that's what it was, that even Kavi began to wonder if Maurice really did believe what he was saying. Charles Goodman had also given his deposition, and although he didn't lie, he did everything he could to make Kavi look bad. Aside from the two of them, other ADG executives, including Steve Halpern, were throwing in their two cents to keep in the government's good graces, and it was all adding up. You could say that Kavi was being screwed big time, and the odds of losing were probably much higher than the original 25 percent estimate. Fortunately, he didn't plan on sticking around long enough to hear the verdict. I was convinced he'd come to terms with his decision, but wondered if he'd had second thoughts about limiting the Plan to $10 million.

My mother was distressed with Kavi's situation, as she knew it, and I couldn't talk to her about the Plan. Other than Kavi's family, the four of us were the only ones who knew, and we had to keep it that way. I actually told my mother she was right about God's plan, but she knew I didn't mean it. It really disturbed her how Gary Bevins could be allowed to get on national TV and say such bad things about a good guy. What's worse, Gary sounded so honest she'd have believed him had she not known better, and was convinced others must have found him believable too. We all agreed that Gary had what it took to be a great politician, considering the way he had handled himself in front of the cameras. It was quite a learning experience for my mom. She'd always figured that people were guilty when the government accused them of some crime. But now she knew that wasn't always the case.

Everything at Winston Walker was going well. I had done such extensive work with the new Sarbanes-Oxley legislation that I became one of the firm's specialists on the new rules. It helped that I'd been known for my ability to develop effective audit techniques even before the new law was passed. Consistent with my being regarded as an expert, I was asked to participate on multi-partner panels during a three-day seminar in Lausanne, Switzerland. The firm wanted the European partners to understand the new rules, because they were involved in auditing foreign units of US companies and also had foreign clients that did business in the US. Seminars were always a nice break and I'd never shy away from a free trip to Europe. I'd asked Vicki if she would join me, but she didn't want to distract me from my work, even though I told her that wouldn't happen. She was right though. I'd likely be very distracted.

My mind continued to drift, and I watched as a replica of an 18th century mid-size sailboat made its way slowly down the river toward the New York harbor. It appeared to be incredibly authentic, although I didn't have a clue how they were really supposed to look. But with the help of a pair of binoculars, I could see that some of the guys on deck were watching a portable TV, and that image spoiled everything.

My cell phone was on the kitchen table and I thought I'd turned it off, but it started ringing. At first, it seemed like a good idea to just let it ring, but I changed my mind and rushed inside to see who had interrupted my day of relaxation.

"Where are you?" Ken asked.

It took me a moment to get my mind working again. Sounding a little groggy, I said, "I'm home. So what's up?"

"I've got some bad news. The judge ordered Kavi to give up his passport."

At first what he said didn't register. But after he repeated it, I asked, "You don't think he got wise to the Plan, do you?"

"No, he just wants to make sure Kavi doesn't skip town. And he'll also be required to check in with the court once a week. I didn't know it, but sometimes they do this in criminal cases. But apparently it's not typical for white collar crimes. You've got to admit that asshole Bevins thinks of everything."

"So you're telling me Kavi's stuck here?"

"No, he thinks he can still get out. He can get his hands on a plane and fly it across the border to Mexico. From there he can take a commercial flight to Europe. But once he leaves, he can't come back."

What Ken was saying seemed to make sense to me. The government had only limited resources, so you'd think they'd put more emphasis on stopping terrorists from getting into the country, rather than keeping people from getting out. "So shouldn't that be enough?" I asked. "After all, he doesn't need to come back."

"You don't understand. There's a lot of paperwork that has to be done offshore, and once that's done, it will take about two months or so before he can get the money."

"What takes two months?"

"That's the time it takes to open the offshore accounts, file the tax returns and get the refund. He was planning on leaving in December before the Christmas holidays. As soon as he left, he was going to set up the accounts, and then arrange to get the tax returns filed in early January. He planned on coming right back when he was done, and when the money was ready, about the end of February, he'd leave the States for good."

"So why can't he just stay out of the country after he leaves in December?"

"He can try, but now it's very dangerous. It's one thing to wait two months for the money when nobody knows there's a problem. Now, as soon as he leaves, the government will know something's up. Think about it. For two months he'd be a known fugitive without means. You don't know what the government would do during that time and you don't know what ADG might do. My biggest fear is that they'd somehow uncover the switch in tax payments before he got the money."

"But you said his tax department wouldn't know about it until after they filed their tax return, and that wouldn't be until September 15 of next year."

"That's right, if they weren't looking for it. But who knows what ADG would do if they knew Kavi skipped town."

It took a moment, but I was beginning to understand. "So now he shouldn't leave until late February when the money's ready. But he needs everything done offshore in late December and early January and now he can't do it himself."

"That's right."

"So why can't he just use a US bank account?"

"Because a US account won't work. You've got all kinds of due diligence required because of the Patriot Act. The government's trying to stop terrorists from moving funds, so there's all kinds of paperwork. And remember, he also needs someone to help with the tax return. And it has to look like a real one, with all the right bells and whistles. You don't want anyone at the IRS asking questions before the refund is paid. Kavi won't know what to do on his own, so he needs people to help. While he could get it done in the US, it's really best to do it offshore. For one thing, he'll want people who can work for clients without asking too many questions. Again, it comes down to tougher rules in the US, where financial professionals like accountants and lawyers have to know a lot about their customers before they do any work."

As Ken was speaking, I realized my door was open to the terrace so I closed it quickly to make sure no one in the neighboring apartments could hear my side of the conversation. "So can't he set everything up by phone?"

"No way, not with something like this."

I had to struggle to keep up with what he was saying, and my head was starting to spin. But it was very clear that he was worried and he was the expert. "So what's Kavi planning to do?"

"He doesn't know. I just got off the phone with him and he'd just heard from Henry Jackson. I'm sure that must have been some conversation. Henry probably didn't think much about it. After all, why would *he* think giving up a passport would be a problem? But you can bet that Kavi was upset, although he said he didn't let on."

Sitting down at the table in my small kitchen, I almost spilled my drink, but I kept my focus on what Ken was saying. Being partially inebriated, I wasn't in much of a state to solve Kavi's new problem. All I could think to say was, "There has to be something we can do."

"You mean something *he* can do. He's got a real problem but we can't help him. It would make us accomplices and that's not a risk any of us should take. That's a criminal offense and we'd be stuck here to face the music."

"Maybe he could hire someone to do it for him."

"Are you kidding me? You know what we're talking about. Someone who would do this could also be willing to set things up so they could take the money for themselves. Kavi would leave the country and find the money long gone, or maybe the guy would tip off the authorities so Kavi would get caught trying to leave. Who knows, but he can't take that chance."

"How about Aarti?"

"What about her?"

"Can't she set everything up?"

"They may take her passport too," Ken said. "Anyway, she wouldn't know what to do."

"So what does Marc say about all this?"

"I don't think he even knows. Anyway, I don't plan on asking him about it. He'll make me spell 'I told you so' five hundred times." Ken was silent but I could tell he was still on the line. Then he yelled into the air, not really talking to me, "This sucks."

"We'll think of something."

"Let me go, so I can think about this. I just wanted you to know."

It took me some time to think about what he'd said, but I basically got the picture. Certain things had to be done offshore before Kavi could get the money. He could do it himself but that would be dangerous because the authorities would know something was wrong as soon as he left the country, and he wouldn't get the money until about two months after he left. It would be much safer to have someone else do the advance preparation, and that had to be someone he could trust. The only candidates besides me were Ken and Marc, and they would never get involved, so it all boiled down to me, and it would be an easy thing to do. I had to be in Switzerland anyway, and that was the perfect offshore location. Their culture of secrecy was second to none. But that would make me an accomplice to a criminal act. I tried to think of other solutions but none came to mind. "To help or not to help," that was the question.

Although I wasn't sure it was such a good idea, I did call Marc, and he surprised me. He listened carefully, didn't preach and never once said 'I told you so.' In fact, he said he understood my desire to help. He told me it had taken him a few weeks to come to terms with Kavi's decision, but now he wanted nothing more than for Kavi to succeed, and was looking forward to the day when he had the money and was out of the country, free from the likes of Gary Bevins. Marc listened to what I had to say, and then told me I'd be risking everything if I chose to get involved, because an accomplice is penalized almost as much as the main perpetrator. What's more, I'd lose my license as a CPA and would never get a job as an accountant again. It all sounded very convincing, and just before he hung up, he told me—or maybe himself—that Kavi's future was not in our hands.

I wanted to call Vicki to get some advice, but couldn't tell her what was actually going on, and there was no way to come up with a good hypothetical scenario without her getting suspicious. It wouldn't be worth taking the chance, and, all things considered, I didn't know her well enough anyway.

Ken called back and said he'd just spoken with Marc and that I was crazy for even thinking about getting involved and should get the idea out of my head. I took the opportunity to ask him about the odds of getting caught, and he didn't want to respond, but I kept pushing until he did. In his view there'd be little chance of getting caught if everything was done carefully, but he couldn't be sure, and there was always the chance that he'd missed something, like the judge's decision to take possession of Kavi's passport, which appeared to come straight out of left field.

After thinking about it for about another hour, I decided to call my mom, but couldn't let her know any of the details and found it difficult to discuss in the abstract. It didn't surprise me when she said you can tell how close your friends are when times are tough. She said a true friend is willing to risk something for your benefit, while expecting nothing in return. In a way, I may have wanted her to say something else so I wouldn't feel guilty about not getting further involved.

Having done enough thinking about Kavi's problem for the day, I fixed myself another drink and was back out on the terrace trying to rest my mind. The Manhattan skyline was even more beautiful at night, but it wasn't quite dark enough to get the full effect. From my vantage point there was so much I could see. Straight ahead to the right was the Empire State Building, to the south, in the distance, was the Statue of Liberty and Ellis Island, and, to the north, I could see the George Washington bridge, and all the lights from the commuters making their way across it to New Jersey or back into the city. And there were all sorts of other great structures and buildings in between. The view had a calming effect, and it helped that my apartment was high enough above street level so everything was very quiet.

After dozing off, I thought I awoke but was still basically asleep, and quite disoriented. Still dreaming, I could see Kavi being hauled off by five small boys, who were escorting him to jail. It was strange because the skyline was sort of in view in the background, but the image of Kavi and the others seemed real. I was walking with them, but didn't try to get them to stop. I just kept walking. When Kavi was placed in his cell the bars were left unlocked, but I just stood there staring at them, and Kavi was yelling at me to get away. Then he began to shrink, and I felt nauseated and thought I might throw up. But then the images began to fade away, and I awoke and started feeling better. Still groggy, I walked back into my apartment, went into the bathroom and splashed some cold water on my face. While staring in the mirror, it suddenly became very clear what needed to be done. So I called Kavi and said I was coming over to his house to talk.

* * * *

Before he could finish opening the front door, I said, "I'll be in Switzerland anyway so I'll take care of everything."

Kavi shook his head and smiled. "That's why you wanted to see me?"

"I wanted you to know you'll be ok."

He shook his head and asked me to follow him toward the kitchen area where he had a midsized table in a breakfast room that seated six people. He took a seat and pushed another one out for me. Aarti popped her head in to say hello and then left us alone, but not before offering each of us a beer. I declined, having had more than my quota of alcohol for the day. As soon as she left, Kavi asked, "So you can help me when you're in Switzerland?"

"It's perfect. I need to be in Lausanne for a seminar."

"What's the topic?"

"It's all about the new legislation and related subjects. Believe it or not, I need to give a presentation on how auditors are required to beef up their efforts to identify criminal acts."

"So you'll give a presentation about catching criminals and then you'll go out and become one?"

"There's a certain symmetry to it, don't you think?"

"And you have it all planned?"

"I think it can work."

"I see." Kavi shook his head and laughed. "There's just one little problem."

"What's that?"

"I'm not letting you do it. Are you out of your mind? It's bad enough I'm in this mess, but there's no way I'm getting you or the other guys involved. Can you imagine what would happen if we got caught?"

"With my help you won't get caught, right?"

"Come on Carl. Think about what you're saying. You can't do this."

"I'm telling you I've thought about it and I know what I'm doing."

Kavi lifted his beer and said, "You're incredible, you know that? I'm going to call Vicki Richards right now and tell her if she doesn't grab you, I will."

"We need to talk about what I've got to do when I'm in Switzerland."

Kavi laughed again and almost spilled his beer. "You need to attend your seminar, see a few sights and that's it. We don't need to talk about anything else because you're not getting involved and that's final."

"You don't have a choice. I'm helping you whether you like it or not."

Kavi appeared to be surprised at my insistence. He stood up and walked over to the counter that separated the breakfast room from the kitchen. On one end was a grouping of six different family pictures, including one of him with his wife and kids. He picked up the photo, walked back and put it on the table in front of me. While pointing to his daughter, he said, "Sanji's beautiful, isn't she?"

"She looks just like Aarti."

He then pointed to his son, and said, "I sometimes forget Krishnamurthi is only twenty-one years old. He's way ahead of where I was at his age." He used his son's full name, but we always called him Kris.

"They're great kids. You have a wonderful family."

"That's right. I have a lovely wife and two super kids, and no matter what happens to me, no one can ever take that away. And that's what you should have. A family." He walked back to the counter and admired the family portrait before putting it back in place. "You think I could live with myself if you screwed up your life because you tried to help me? That's never going to happen."

"I told you I was helping, and there's nothing you can do about it."

"Enough Carl, forget it."

"I'm helping."

Suddenly Kavi slammed his right hand down on the counter, knocking over three of the pictures, and screamed at the top of his lungs, "I don't want your fucking help!"

Aarti was startled and came running over to see what was wrong. I told her she should let us be alone, and shouldn't be surprised if there was more screaming, that we were having a fight and would work it out without killing each other. She looked at me like I was crazy but took my advice and slowly walked away. As soon as she was gone, I looked back at Kavi, who had turned away from me and was hunched over the counter. "Do you care about me?" I asked. He didn't immediately respond, so I repeated the question.

"What kind of a question is that? Of course I do." He scratched the side of his head and looked down. "I don't want your help."

"But you're like a brother to me. And I once had another brother, you remember?" Although I had known the guys since 1979, I rarely mentioned Joe Jr., and they knew not to ask about him.

"I know, and he died of cancer before I met you."

"That's right, and I never really told you about him." I walked over so I could stand on the other side of the counter facing him, although he continued to look down and avoid eye contact with me. "My brother was a great athlete, did well in school and the girls loved him. On the other hand, I was mediocre at sports and was basically a "B" student. And the girls, well they never gave me the time of day. But you think my brother gloated? No way. I was his main man. All he ever tried to do was help, whether it was in school, with sports or anything. And I can't tell you how many guys he beat up because they picked on me. He was there whenever I needed him. So it was really important for me to someday be in a position to help him. Then, we learned he had brain cancer, and I'll never forget that day when I got home from school. He'd had some problems with his coordination while practicing with the basketball team, so the school physician referred him to a specialist. We didn't think anything of it, and then, when I got home, my father was upstairs crying, and he never cried. My mother tried to tell me what was wrong, but she couldn't talk. It was my brother who took me aside and told me about the cancer. Can you imagine that? He had just learned he was going to die, but he was more concerned about me. He said he felt like he was letting me down. He told me I should learn how to fight and should work hard in school. It just didn't seem real. It took only two months, but my brother's body just withered away and there was nothing anyone could do about it. When he needed me most, I couldn't do a thing."

When I was finished, Kavi didn't immediately respond. He looked very tense, and kept shaking his head back and forth and gritting his teeth. Finally, he took a couple of long and deep breaths, looked up at me and said, "You *did* do something for your brother. You made him very proud. Can you imagine what he'd say if he saw you today?"

It was clear I was doing a very poor job of getting my point across. I shook my head and said, "But you don't understand."

"Sure I do. You think you still owe something to your brother and me. But if you ever owed us anything, you've paid us back in spades." He took a moment before he continued. "Let it go Carl. There's nothing you need to do for either one of us."

"You see, you really don't understand." I walked back to the table, sat down, took off my shoes and put my feet up on another chair. "I'm not doing this for you. I'm doing it for me."

Kavi squinted and I could tell he was confused. He walked over to the other side of the table and sat down. He leaned forward and said, "I'm missing something here. Do you mind telling me how you're doing this for yourself?"

"There was nothing I could have done to help my brother and I've come to terms with that. But there *is* something I can do to help you. Now I remember what it was like to watch my brother die and how bad it felt. It wouldn't be the same, but watching you go to jail would be unbearable if there was something I could have done to prevent it. You don't know what that would do to me." I paused for a moment to collect my thoughts and to brace myself for a long fight. Whatever it would take, there was no way he was getting rid of me. "Get it through your head Kavi. This isn't for you, it's for me."

We sat quietly and Aarti stuck her head in to make sure we were still alive. We gave her a nod and assured her we wouldn't kill each other without telling her first. It took a while, but Kavi reluctantly accepted my decision. He did make me agree to stop if and when we determined there was any realistic chance of my getting caught. It seemed like a reasonable request and I really had no desire to get caught anyway. As we continued to discuss the details, it became more and more clear I'd made the right choice. The passport incident had scared him more than I'd realized, and he probably was planning on keeping that from us. I think it woke him up to the fact that things could go wrong, things none of us could anticipate. He wouldn't feel comfortable again until he was out of the country and had the money in hand. At least my getting involved gave him a great chance to succeed. But it would be some time before it was over and there was a lot to do. By our estimates, in a best case scenario, he'd have the money by the end of February and that was about four months away. It seemed more like an eternity.

Chapter 26

Things were starting to get very hectic for me. It was Saturday, October 25, and it looked like I'd be working seven days a week before leaving for my trip to Switzerland in mid-November. The end of October through Thanksgiving was usually a busy period for me. But aside from my typical client work, I also had to prepare for the presentation at the seminar as well as my activities in Switzerland to support Kavi's Plan. Needless to say, there'd be plenty of work until the holidays.

As fate would have it, the one time I didn't call Vicki for a Saturday night date was the one time she called to ask me. Although I'd be working all day, there was no way I was going to tell her no. Since I planned on doing my work at home, it made sense to meet her on my side of the Hudson River for a change. Within walking distance of my apartment building was a decent Italian restaurant, a casual place with good food and great views, so I suggested to Vicki that we eat there. It was nestled along the Palisades cliffs, about halfway up from sea level, almost directly below my building. The cliffs came down on an angle and there was a two lane road that wound its way from the top, past the restaurant, and down to what was called the River Road. I never understood why the owners had picked such an obscure site for their place.

Although Vicki said she'd get to my apartment at 6 pm, I was certain she'd be fashionably late, so I planned on working until about 6:30. But my grandfather clock had no sooner stopped chiming 6 times when the doorman buzzed, letting me know she'd arrived. We met by the elevator on my floor, and I bombarded her with apologies about the apartment being such a mess, before giving her a chance to see for herself. It was her first time there, and upon walking in, she made herself comfortable and immediately started to snoop. I had to admit, there was something special about giving her complete freedom to explore my personal space. It felt more revealing than getting naked in front of someone for the first time.

She made a quick comment about my ex-girlfriends, and added that I had great taste in women. I'd actually forgotten that some of their pictures were still on the credenza by the front door. Most were of Kim Darcy. She was incredibly photogenic and the particular photos she'd given me were quite good. But it was time to put them in their proper place—a file I maintained with the pictures of all my past loves—never wanting to throw them away. I told Vicki I'd need some pictures of her, but she said she despised having her picture taken so there were none to give. Before I could ask her about that, she disappeared down the hall. I took advantage of the time to organize the files that were sprawled out across my kitchen table. While I was doing that, Vicki must have been busy checking out my clothes, my bed and whatever else was in the other rooms. She was gone for nearly fifteen minutes, so there must have been something she'd found that was of interest.

With her snooping completed, we left my apartment and walked down the two lane road to the restaurant, taking some time to enjoy the view, since she'd never seen Manhattan from that particular perspective. We took a table next to a window and I let her have the chair with the view. And, as I'd hoped, the restaurant met with her approval. They never skimped on portions and the food was always great, although nothing compared favorably with my mom's cooking.

The dinner was going well, and, as usual, we had no trouble making conversation. We were rambling from one topic to another, and were in the middle of a discussion about politics when she abruptly changed the subject and almost made me choke on my food.

"So you're thinking about becoming a criminal?" she asked.

"What'd you say?"

"You heard me."

"Why would you ask that?"

She looked out the window into the distance long enough to make me squirm. Then she turned to me. "All those books in your bedroom about criminals."

"Oh those. It's nothing. I'm doing prep work for a presentation in Switzerland. One of my topics is a primer on how to catch corporate criminals. I'm supposed to tell our European partners how to develop better procedures as part of their audits to identify fraud and other illegal acts." That was the truth, but it wasn't the only reason for my interest in the subject. I thought it might make some sense to read about the criminal mind and perhaps glean something from the experiences of those who got caught.

"So why would the books be of any help?"

"It seems to me you need to think like a criminal in order to catch one. You know, you need to 'be the criminal,' so to speak."

She smiled and gave me one of those looks. Like she thought there was more to the story and needed to think of the right way to get at the information. While continuing to study my face for clues, she said, "You never cease to amaze me. I think you're getting a little dramatic though. Maybe you've been watching too many detective movies. You've got to start watching porn."

Ignoring her latter comment, I said, "What I'm saying makes sense. My firm's made up of a whole bunch of accountants. At least people in law enforcement have some idea about what they're dealing with. But we're like babes in the woods, and we're probably the last people you'd ever want looking for a criminal."

"But there are plenty of accountants who do commit crimes. Look at all the crooked CFO's. That's why Sarbanes-Oxley was passed in the first place, and that's why you're giving your presentation."

"Sure, but those guys were on the other side of the fence, inside corporate America. And something had to make them do what they did, and I'd like to know what it was."

"Duuhhhhh," she interjected. "It was money. Some of those guys stood to collect hundreds of millions of dollars."

"That's too simple to be the only answer. There are too many people who have access to money but don't steal."

"They're afraid of getting caught."

"So you think people will steal if they think they won't get caught?"

"Makes sense to me," she responded.

"That still doesn't explain the type of white-collar crime I'm talking about. These people were senior officers in very large corporations. They could have made big money legitimately, so I think money wasn't the primary motivation. And whether or not they were afraid of getting caught had nothing to do with it either. Maybe they wouldn't do anything if they were afraid of being caught, but that doesn't mean they'd do something simply because they thought they could get away with it. There has to be something else at work."

She was holding her glass up in front of her, and swirling the wine, seeing how close she could get it to the rim without spilling any. While doing that she said, "Maybe you're right. You wonder what really makes these guys tick."

"That's the question I've been asking myself. There may be some common thread that ties these people together. Something in their genes, or maybe the way they were raised, that makes them more likely to commit a crime. If we learn more about it, it could help us be on the alert in what we might call "high risk situations," and improve our audit procedures accordingly."

"Perhaps." While looking past me and out the window, she massaged her chin and, after a moment, started shaking her head back and forth, as if she'd found some major flaw in my reasoning. Turning to me, she said, "You're wasting your time with some of those books of yours. I'm no expert, but I'd have to think there's a big difference between some CFO who falsifies financial statements and someone who commits armed robbery. You should focus on books about white-collar crime."

"I couldn't find that many, and the books I did find weren't helpful."

"That just means you haven't looked hard enough."

"Three different bookstores and the internet should be enough."

"Did you only look at non-fiction?" she asked.

"Sure, why would I look at fiction?"

"Maybe it could give you some insight into what it's like to commit a white-collar crime."

Of course I couldn't tell her I was getting some pretty keen insight just by preparing to help Kavi. It was too bad, because she'd have been a big help if I'd been able to share it with her. Instead, I simply said, "I'll bet most of those books aren't very good."

"So you should write one after you're done with your research. I think the world could use a book about a Bonnie & Clyde who work for some large corporation. Maybe Bonnie is the CFO and Clyde is the Controller and they get together and commit some interesting crime."

"So the woman's on top?" I asked.

"It's always better that way."

Her continued interest in the subject caught me by surprise. She was getting really animated and it was amusing to watch her speak. In contrast, whenever I tried to ask about her, she became quiet and withdrawn. But her body language was noticeably different when discussing other topics, especially those she enjoyed. And this one really caught her fancy. I could see her mind was racing ahead, so I said, "Keep going with this. What would make them do it?"

"Maybe they never thought about it, and something happened where they had to stretch things just a little. Then, as things progressed, they needed to do more and more, until it was too late. They were in over their heads and had no choice but to go all the way."

"So it really depends on how they react to the initial problem, whatever it is."

"Right," she said. She turned to survey some of the other tables, turned back to me and smiled. "This is fascinating. Maybe I should help you with it."

"How?"

"I'll see if I can find some good books that you missed. We can both read them and compare notes."

I was about to ask if she'd reconsider joining me in Switzerland, but caught myself in time. Instead, I joked, "Just don't get any ideas and run off with all your clients' money."

Our 22 year-old waiter came over with the dessert menu and I actually tried to explain what the two of us had been talking about. He misunderstood what I was trying to say and told me it might be better if he didn't know. Then Vicki started telling him we were both modeling our lives after Bonnie and Clyde, but he had no idea who they were. After he left, I told Vicki she was more attractive than the young Faye Dunaway, although not by much, and pointed out that the Bonnie Parker character she played in the movie had sex with Clyde at least once. Vicki said if I could find a young actor who looked like Warren Beatty, she'd consider having sex with him too. Then, apparently out of nowhere, she said, "If I wanted their money, I wouldn't need to steal it."

"What?"

"You said I shouldn't run off with my clients' money. I'm telling you I wouldn't need to steal it. I'd just ask for it."

"And they'd just fork it over."

"You really don't believe me, do you?"

"I think you're playing with me again."

With a smile that was a little too suggestive, she said, "You'll *know* when I'm playing with you." She paused, then said, "I'm serious. They give me expensive gifts without my asking. Can you imagine what they'd do if I *were* to ask?"

"You *are* serious. So let's assume you're right. Why would they do that?"

"You're asking the wrong person. I know what they do, but I don't know why they do it."

The waiter returned and delivered about 2,000 calories to our table, but he assured us it was diet food. Vicki and I shared a number of things in common and one of them was our love for desserts. Although I never knew when to stop, she could be satisfied with just a small taste. Before I could continue with my line of questions, she stuffed my mouth with an oversized portion of her dessert. I had to wait until she was kind enough to remove her fork, and when she did, I said, "Maybe they think they can buy you. If you accept something from them, you'll feel obligated to go out with them."

"That's not it. I've already accepted whatever they've given, and they have to know I won't go out with them. But for some reason they just keep on giving."

"I'll bet they just don't give up easily."

"Perhaps, but I think it's something else."

"So leave the criminals to me. You spend your time researching married rich guys who give gifts to their unmarried female lawyers. Maybe check out unmarried guys too."

Suddenly a mischievous look came over her face, and she reached over and pushed our desserts aside. Then she leaned forward slowly so her face could be close to mine. I thought we were going to kiss, so I leaned in as well, but our lips never touched. She stopped when our faces were about an inch apart and closed her eyes, and it was hard to inhale anything other than her perfume. Speaking slowly, in a soft and sultry voice, she said, "If I wanted something from you, you'd give it to me, and you know it too." Then she quickly licked my lips and purred like a kitten.

My chest was pounding hard and I worried that someone would think I was having a heart attack and call an ambulance. It would have been so easy to say she was right, but I could hear a little Ken Tanner standing on my right shoulder screaming advice into my ear. So instead I said nothing, gave her a little kiss on the cheek and sat back in my chair.

She also leaned back and opened her eyes, which were immediately locked in on mine. There was no expression on her face, like we were playing a great game of poker and I couldn't tell if she was just bluffing. She was checking me out to see what effect her little experiment had had, and I was sure she could tell that I was breathing hard. Then her demeanor quickly changed back to what it had been before the episode. She turned her attention to her dessert and said, "This is delicious. I love this place."

She may have been acting, but something told me that's not what it was. It appeared as if another person had briefly invaded her body and then had left to pursue other things. That's when it became clear that she had a power over men. But maybe she didn't have it all the time, and maybe she didn't even know she had it. It was hard to tell and I wasn't ready to learn more. Actually, I was scared. It was like she had some internal mechanism deep inside her brain that would go off at just the right time. When it did, this other part of her would spring into gear, do its work, and then settle back in its place until the next time needed. It reminded me of when I was a kid spending the summer at camp. They got a guy to hypnotize some kids after dinner and one of them was my friend Jeff. The guy told him to stand up and yell 'kill the beast' at the top of his lungs every time someone mentioned eggs the next morning at breakfast. Then, the next day, everyone was just staring at him, and, sure enough, whenever we said "eggs," he'd jump up, his face would go blank, and he'd look straight ahead and scream at the top of his lungs, "kill the beast." After that he'd sit down quickly and get right back to his food, oblivious to what he'd done. In my mind there was no question that it was for real. I knew Jeff pretty well, and he wasn't that good an actor. After thinking about Jeff, I figured it would be safer to leave the subject for another day, so I took Vicki's lead and got back to my dessert.

Throughout the evening, I had entertained the fantasy that she would stay over at my apartment and leave the next morning. But when I mentioned it to her, she said she needed to get back to the city that night, and, in any case, didn't think it was such a good idea. Maybe another guy would have been more insistent, but not me. We walked back to her car and she opened the door to the passenger side first, asking me to sit with her until she was ready to go. One of my favorite Frank Sinatra CD's was in a CD case, so she started the car, I popped it in and set the volume at just the right level. Although I was disappointed she had to go, it was nice to spend some time with her in my arms while listening to the chairman of the board. But despite all the romantic lyrics, I knew full well there was a serious risk I was falling in love with a woman who could never love me.

Chapter 27

It was Wednesday evening, October 29. Kavi and I were relaxing in his living room and enjoying a glass of wine, while Aarti was in the kitchen putting the finishing touches on dinner. We had agreed to get together at his house, in order to determine exactly what I needed to do to help him during my brief stay in Switzerland. It was critically important that the detailed steps be well thought-out, so he could successfully get his money, and I could avoid getting caught. And we were prepared to attack the issues with the level of energy and intensity necessary to ensure a successful result.

If everything went according to plan, the tax refund would be paid to the offshore account, Kavi and Aarti would leave the country and get access to the money, and there'd be no way the authorities could trace anything back to me. Although the Plan had originally been Ken's idea, Kavi had been thinking about it for so long he'd become the expert. He told me he was convinced that once he and his wife had the money and were gone, the odds of their having a problem with the authorities were remote. For one thing, they were preparing to use new identities and would lead a low-key lifestyle. Aside from that, it would be very difficult for the US to get at him, even if they knew where he was. There are a number of countries with which the US has extradition treaties, but their use takes a significant amount of work. With all the terrorists running around that needed to be caught, Kavi would probably be low on any list of priorities. All in all, Gary Bevins would get to claim his big score, but after that the government would likely forget about Kavi and move on to bigger and better things.

On the other hand, I'd still be in the States. So my butt would be toast if we inadvertently left some shred of evidence that could be traced back to me. Of course, Kavi knew this, which is why he didn't want me getting involved in the first place. It's the reason I agreed to forego any involvement if my risk was considered to be more than remote. So that was the key. We had to come up with specific procedures where we could both step back and honestly say my risk was sufficiently low.

Aarti had been cooking all day, so her focus was on food. Naturally, she insisted that we eat first and leave our planning for later. The house smelled great from whatever was cooking, so she didn't get any argument from me. When she called us into the kitchen area, and I got to see for myself, I was glad she'd been so insistent. It was an authentic Indian meal. Not like the American style food you'd get in so-called Indian restaurants in the States. She had made two versions of the main course, one for herself and Kavi, and one for me. It was a chicken dish with a unique blend of spices, with their version made hot and spicy, and the other one mild, for wimps like me. Although Kavi warned me, I tried one small piece of the real thing and my mouth felt like it had burst into flames. I quickly made a mental note to forever avoid any Indian dish where the chicken had a reddish tint. Aarti had also made an assortment of chutneys, some with a fruit base that tasted more like a dessert, and others made with assorted vegetables. And it was all served with some of the best basmati rice I'd ever tasted. During the meal, she said there were certain herbs and spices you couldn't get in and around the city. She suggested that I visit the two of them in India where she could cook other authentic dishes I was sure to enjoy. India was actually one place I'd never been, and the idea of seeing some of the country and getting home cooked meals was very appealing.

When we were through with dinner, Kavi and I made our way back to the living room, stopping first in the study to get his notes. We pulled a small glass-top table close to the couch, and he took a moment to get his papers organized. There were two key things we needed to address before my trip: how to set up the necessary bank account or accounts, and how to make arrangements for preparation of the necessary tax return.

Kavi said he wanted to set up many accounts, but used 3 accounts for an illustration. Accounts 1 and 2 would be set up with two different Swiss banks. A third account would be set up outside Switzerland but in a country with similar bank secrecy laws. The tax refund would be wired to account 1, then he'd transfer the money to account 2 and finally to account 3, in order to significantly reduce the likelihood that anyone could trace the money flow through to his final location. Swiss banks are well known for their willingness to keep account information secret. Although the US authorities would know the tax refund was wired to account 1, they'd be unable to access any information about the account, including the destination of funds that were transferred out. Therefore, they would never learn of the existence of account 2, and the money trail would stop cold. However, there could be a situation where even a Swiss bank would be compelled to provide information. In that unlikely event, it would only lead to account 2 and the process would start over again, and, if pursued further, would possibly lead to account 3, but that would be in another country, with its own set of bank secrecy laws. The authorities would once again be starting at square one. Kavi planned on using a sufficient number of accounts, in different jurisdictions, to ensure that any effort to trace the funds would be abandoned along the way, well before learning of their final destination.

As I listened to Kavi describe that aspect of his plan, I could tell how much thought he'd given to the matter. It was consistent with the kind of effort he'd put forth on work-related problems throughout his successful 24-year career. And even though I wanted to give the matter more thought, it was pretty clear his plan made sense. He went on to say he'd probably use 10 accounts in 5 different jurisdictions, which, aside from Switzerland, would include Liechtenstein, Bermuda, the Cayman Islands, and the Isle of Mann.

The discussion turned to my exposure. With regard to Swiss account 1, we agreed the bank would likely not provide the US authorities with any information about me, but we wouldn't take any chances. Although we didn't think it would work, in order to explore all possibilities, we discussed ways that I could set up the account via a local phone call in Switzerland or through a middleman, but in each case decided it wouldn't be feasible. It had to be done in person. To be safe, we decided that I should use an assumed name and provide no information that would enable them to contact me. I would also wear dark glasses and loose clothing that I'd buy upon my arrival in Switzerland and would make sure to discard shortly thereafter. By doing that, even if they wanted to assist the US, they'd have no information about me to provide. And the authorities would have no reason to suspect my involvement so they wouldn't ask the bank about me, but even if they did, the bank would never know that I'd been involved.

As with any bank, I'd have to provide a signature in order to open the account. That worried Kavi, but I already had a solution. In junior high school, like most 7th graders, I had yet to develop my own signature. A kid named Brian Booker was in my class and he had a great one. And I thought it was so good that I tried to copy it, and after about four thousand tries, was able to match his handwriting almost to perfection. Then I played around with other names, and came up with fictional guys, like Arnold Archer, Steven Sawyer and Peter Packus. I'd doodle for hours by writing the signatures of these names, and it was always with handwriting that was very close to that of Brian Booker, although that was just a byproduct of my doodling. It never dawned on me that my junior high school exercise would one day prove to be useful. As we discussed it further, we decided that I'd use the name Peter Packus, and I'd say he was a Vice President of FHP Commodities Inc., an authorized signatory for the company and for the account. While at the bank, I'd also get the necessary paperwork to add additional signatories, and would have "Peter Packus" sign it and would give it to Kavi for his later use to access the account.

By using our approach, the odds were remote that anything would ever be tied back to me. However, whatever the level of exposure, it would be increased if I were to be involved in setting up additional accounts. So we agreed I should stick with account 1, since it was all that was needed to get the tax refund, and there'd be plenty of time for Kavi to set up the other accounts once he left the country.

Aarti had told us she wanted to serve coffee and dessert when we hit a breaking point, and it seemed as good a time as any to stop. She brought us assorted Indian pastries made with fruits and nuts that looked like a batch of rugelach on steroids. They appeared to be home made, but she admitted they came from an Indian bakery she'd found in Hoboken.

Kavi took one of the larger ones, and as he tried to take a bite, he dropped about half of it onto the couch. While struggling to clean up, he told Aarti it didn't matter, since they wouldn't be taking the furniture with them. He did his best, but gave up with the job about two thirds done. Looking at his notes on the table, he said, "I guess this is our last project together."

"You're right."

"And who would have thought it would involve disguises, Swiss accounts and changed identities?"

"If you had told me about this in June, I'd never have believed you." I looked over at Aarti, who had managed to squeeze in between Kavi and the end of the couch. She'd been in good spirits all evening, so I commented, "You seem to be doing ok with this."

"To tell the truth, until we go and he has the money, I won't feel good," she said, with her thick Indian accent. "But 'til then, I'll do my best."

"That makes sense to me," I said.

While massaging Kavi's back, she said, "But whatever happens, we've been blessed. Two beautiful children, great friends, a great job for Kavi, and plenty of money. And we set up a branch of Sisters of Jain and touched people's lives. We can't complain, and everything happens for a reason."

"You sound like my mother."

"That's because we share core beliefs. Catholic, Hindu, Jain, no matter. And your mother agrees." She took another large pastry, carefully split it in two, and put half directly in Kavi's mouth, so he had no opportunity to make a mess. Just before eating the other half, she said, "Everything that's happening was meant to be."

"So you think God wants us to set up a Swiss bank account?" I asked.

She looked away and tried to hide a smile. She turned back and said, "I'm sure you know what to do with that. But I'm talking of what comes later. Look what we can look forward to. Kavi will have time for me. That wouldn't happen if he stayed with the company. And we can put our time to good use. Some people in India need our help. We wouldn't be going if this didn't happen."

"You're right," Kavi said. "And we'll make the best of our time together."

I asked Kavi, "And you won't miss all the activity of being the CFO at ADG?"

"What do you think?" Kavi asked. "But that's gone for me. And now I can do other things I like to do. Like, fishing, reading, flying and......now I'll have the time to finish teaching Kris how to fly."

"No you won't," Aarti protested, as she hit Kavi softly on the back. "It's bad enough that you fly."

Kavi smiled and said, "And I won't miss Charles Goodman. I'll have Aarti to boss me around."

Aarti leaned back on the couch and focused on me. She sighed and said, "We'll be ok. But we worry about you."

"What's there to worry about? We'll make sure there's no way they can trace any of this back to me."

"Not that," she said. "Now who can help your mother look after you?"

"Have you been talking to her? Or should I ask, has she been talking to you?"

"She loves you, and we do too."

Kavi said, "Speak for yourself." He turned to me and said, "I just put up with you."

Aarti punched Kavi a little harder this time. Getting back to me, she said, "We all want you happy."

I asked, "You mean married, don't you?"

"Of course, with a home, a family. It's sad we won't go to your wedding."

"Maybe I'll never have one."

"That's why I worry for you," she said. "You have no faith in the future."

Kavi leaned forward and laughed. "No kidding Carl, she talks about you all the time, but I've done my best to protect you from her."

"Let me think about this." Focusing my attention on Aarti, I asked, "Kavi's getting ADG to involuntarily contribute money to the cause and the two of you are leaving the country for good, yet your big worry is what will happen to *me*?"

She nodded, smiled and said, "I'll bet God has something special planned for you. You do good things for others. One day, good things will happen for you. I'm sure."

"If that's right, it'll be fine with me."

After some further uncomfortable conversation about my status as an unmarried good guy with a bright future, Aarti finally left us alone to get back to our work. We still had to discuss arrangements for FHP's US tax return. We needed to find an overseas professional firm that could arrange to get it prepared and filed so the refund could be wired into account 1. We agreed it made most sense to work through a Swiss law firm. Although there were no circumstances we could think of whereby such a firm would reveal information about its clients, we again decided it would be best to play it safe. Therefore, we decided to have Peter Packus, glasses, loose clothing and all, be the one who meets with and hires them. As with the bank, I'd provide no information to enable the law firm to contact me. To add some apparent substance, they'd be told that, in time, FHP would ask for their assistance in connection with a number of interesting assignments, but the first order of business would be arrangements regarding taxes. I'd provide them with some basic information, and would say that I'd get them the full year's tax information sometime in early January, recognizing that you can't have final 2003 numbers in mid-November. Kavi would determine those final numbers and would get them to me by the end of December for submission to Switzerland. I'd request that they be prepared to arrange the filing of the return quickly, so the anticipated refund could be paid by the end of February.

Although I'd work through a Swiss law firm, and would give them a power of attorney so they could sign the tax return on behalf of FHP, I would instruct them to hire the local Swiss branch of one of the large US accounting firms to actually prepare the return. This somewhat complicated arrangement made the most sense considering the alternatives. The accounting firm would have all the necessary expertise to get the tax return filed properly, but they would have no contact with me. That was very important, since accounting firms do not have as much freedom protecting information about clients as do law firms.

We wrapped up our discussion and separated the notes so the final plan would be retained and all other paperwork shredded. All in all, it was a very productive, and interesting, session. While we were no experts on offshore accounts, for a couple of novices we had come up with a pretty decent plan. Based on our work, I understood exactly what I had to do in Switzerland.

Kavi said he could never thank me enough, and I told him he could pay for my periodic flights to India. As we walked out to my car, he asked for and I gave him an update on my relationship with Vicki. We both joked that Ken would have given up long ago. In fact, he'd had a rule when he was single that he'd dump any girl who didn't go to bed with him by the end of the second week of dating. We also talked about some meetings Kavi had to attend with his lawyers, and how he had to do his best to pretend it still meant something. Among other things, Henry Jackson had to escort Kavi to the court house at least once per week so he could check in with the judge. And Gary Bevins would be there and would typically think of something to make Kavi's day just a little more miserable.

It was almost midnight when I finally left. And on the way to my apartment I thought about our plan and couldn't find any flaw. Nonetheless, I was going to scrutinize it carefully before my trip to see if there was anything we might have missed. The consequences of a slip-up were just too severe.

Chapter 28

It was Saturday, November 8, and in one week I would leave for Switzerland. The advance planning for the Swiss bank account and law firm was done, and I had everything ready for my presentation at the seminar, although Vicki had some new ideas for me to consider. She was so intrigued with my research into criminal behavior that she began researching the subject herself. For Vicki, nothing could be done half way. Everyday she'd fax me more articles and references for books to read, and the other day she gave me the name of someone "we just had to meet." From what I understood, she had done work for a fellow named Andrew Greyson III. Like many of her clients, he was very well to do, worth more than $500 million by most estimates. One of the companies he controlled was Dureg Greyson, a firm whose main line of business was onshore and offshore oil field service work. Their people operated in very dangerous parts of the world like Iraq, Nigeria and Indonesia, so naturally they needed a strong internal security group. It just so happened that their top security officer was some ex-FBI guy by the name of John Huggins. Besides his government work, his resume included six years as a street cop with the Washington DC Metro Police, followed by college, then seven years as a detective in their homicide unit. Vicki had mentioned her new research topic to Mr. Greyson, and shortly thereafter, got a call from John, who said he had been instructed to offer any assistance he could provide. It seemed like her clients really did jump at the opportunity to show her their generosity. Vicki insisted that she and I meet with John before my trip to Lausanne, and I had no choice but to agree. It looked like I had created a monster by letting her know what I was doing. Still, I had to admit, I was interested in speaking with the guy, and it also gave Vicki and me something else we could do together.

I said I'd be available during the week but she had to promise not to talk to any more clients about her new found hobby. She seemed sincere when she assured me that her lips—the beautiful full ones, I might add—were sealed.

My mom had been bugging me all week to come to Brooklyn for dinner. I finally gave in, and was on my way to her place. It was remarkable how she always found a way of getting what she wanted from me. In this particular case, her strategy involved calling my office each day and telling my assistant exactly what to say, and the right way to say it, so as to make me feel really guilty. Of course my assistant gladly followed her instructions to a tee. My mom was upset that I had gone all of three weeks without seeing her. It didn't matter that I had been working late nights and weekends. To her there was never a good excuse for going too long without seeing each other. It made me wonder what she'd do if and when I ever got married.

As it turned out, my mom and I would not be eating our Saturday night dinner alone. She had invited over two of her friends from the old neighborhood, Esther Bernbaum and Rose Petrocelli, whom I hadn't seen in some time. They were both widows and close to my mother's age. Esther was Jewish and Rose was Italian, but you could never tell which one was which just by looking at them. They both used their hands to talk, loved to eat, spoke at the top of their lungs—even if you were sitting close by—and loved to argue, only to them it was called 'having a somewhat noisy discussion.' It really wasn't so bad eating with them, especially if you thought you were getting too fat. No matter how much weight you had gained between visits, they would invariably comment that you looked too thin. They were rather plump themselves, so in comparison, they were probably right.

Rose had a big family, but like my extended family, they were seeing each other less and less. At least most of them lived in and around New York City, so they hadn't completely lost touch. She had three sons and two daughters, and at any point in time one would be fighting with another, so they rarely got together as a full group.

For Esther, things were far worse. She had a son and two daughters and they had all moved to Phoenix years ago. From time to time she entertained the idea of moving to a retirement community out there so she could be close to them. But every time she brought it up, her kids said it would be best if she remained in Brooklyn. It was pretty clear they didn't want her around on any full time basis. Of course they'd fly her out to join them once or twice a year, and would call every now and then, but for all intents and purposes they had shut her out of their daily lives. Esther would tell us she had to reintroduce herself to her grandkids every time she visited Phoenix. She'd never let on, but you could easily tell how hurt she was. For me, it was hard to understand her kids. Although she could be a pain at times, I could never imagine shutting my mom out of my everyday life.

By the time I got to the apartment, I already knew Esther and Rose were there. They were busy with their favorite activities, eating and arguing, and you could hear them clear across Flatbush Avenue. When I walked through the front doorway, my mom jumped right in to give me the business, hiding a smile, and blurting, "Girls, call 911. There's a stranger at the door."

Esther was the first to get to me, almost pinching off half my face after I kissed her on the cheek. She announced, "And such a handsome stranger."

After that, Rose gave me a big hug, and then stepped back to examine me like she was examining a new dress. Speaking to my mom as if I weren't there, she said, "Anne, do you feed your son? He's losing too much weight."

Finally, I made my way to my mom, and she hugged me as if we hadn't seen each other in years. I think her friends made her really appreciate our relationship.

Everything was ready, so we sat down for dinner. It had been about six months since I'd last seen Rose and Esther, so we spent some time catching up. They didn't understand what I told them about Kavi's situation. Each of them seemed to think, like my mom had once thought, that anyone indicted must be a crook. They were impressed by my upcoming trip to Switzerland. Esther had never been out of the country, and Rose had only gone abroad once, on a one-week vacation to Italy. It was easy for me to take all my trips for granted, but talking to them reminded me of how fortunate I really was. We covered just about every subject except Vicki, but I knew that sooner or later her name would come up. Sure enough, we were in the middle of the main course when my mom asked, "So what's new with Ms. Mysterious?" But before I could say a word, she took about fifteen minutes to tell the girls everything she knew about her.

Having listened to enough of my mom's dissertation, I interrupted, "Since you know so much, how about *you* tell *me* what's new with Vicki?"

"See, my son doesn't like to tell me anything."

"Then how come you already know so much?" I asked.

"I have other sources," she replied.

Esther was very efficient, and had an amazing way of talking and eating at the same time. She had a decent-sized portion of manicotti in her mouth but still managed to say, "Sounds like this Vicki of yours doesn't know a good thing when she sees it."

Rose didn't have the same eating/talking skills, so she stopped eating, turned her head and gave me a big smile. "Tell me Carl, you really like this girl?"

"Of course he does," my mom said. "Why else would he spend all his time for three months with only one woman?"

"It's been three months?" Esther asked.

"Ladies, should I leave the room so you can have this conversation without me?" I thought if I hesitated a moment one of them would speak, but they actually wanted me to talk for a change. "It's been about three months since I met her, but I wouldn't say we've been dating that long. Actually, I wouldn't really say we've been dating."

"What kind of a thing is that to say?" Esther asked. "You should know if you've been dating. When I was a girl, you knew when you were on a date."

"Things are different these days," I said. "Women have more freedom, so they can socialize with men more often than they did in the past. Just because a man and a woman get together for dinner doesn't mean it's a date."

My mom took my plate to give me another large portion of manicotti. I didn't need it, I didn't ask for it, but I got it. While handing me back my plate, she asked, "So how come I haven't met her?"

"You haven't met her?" Esther asked.

"Not yet," my mom replied. "But he talks about her all time. I wonder if she even exists."

"It's a big step for a guy to introduce a girl to his mother," Rose said, once again speaking as if I wasn't in the room, even though she was staring right at me. "He's probably not ready for that."

"Actually, Vicki isn't ready for that," I said.

My mom looked surprised by my comment. "You already asked her and she said no?"

"No, I haven't asked her, but I know what she'd say. She just wants us to be friends, so I don't think she'd be comfortable meeting you. Is that so hard to understand?"

"Why are modern woman crazy?" my mom asked. "What's so tough about meeting a friend's mother?"

Rose looked at me and asked, "But you want to be more than friends?"

I looked over at my mom and was surprised she didn't answer for me. Taking advantage of the opportunity to speak for myself, I replied, "Sure I do, but that's really up to her."

"Does she see other men?" Esther asked.

"No. She really doesn't date much at all."

"Is that so?" Esther said. "And the two of you have been dating, or whatever you might call it, for three months now?"

"That's right."

Rose glanced at my mother and asked, "You said Vicki's mother's dead, and she has no memory of her father?"

This time I answered for my mother. "That's what Vicki told me."

"Did she say anything about her father?" Rose asked. "I mean, does she know where he went, or when he left, or whether he's dead or alive?"

"She said she doesn't know anything about him."

"How can you not know anything about your father?" Esther asked, pushing her plate away as if she'd suddenly lost her appetite. "It's not like she was an orphan. She knew her mother, right?"

"But her mother died when she was young," I said. "It makes sense to me that she wouldn't remember."

"Well it doesn't make any sense to me," Rose said. She stood up and began to clear the section of the table in front of her, and while doing that, continued, "You'd think she'd remember something."

They spent the next twenty minutes talking about it. The last time I checked, none of them had any degrees in psychology, and they hadn't actually graduated from college for that matter. Nonetheless, they had every intention of discerning the hidden meaning behind Vicki's inability to recall anything about her father. They didn't seem to need any help from me. In fact, most of the time they were talking, I wasn't even in the apartment. I said I needed some air and that was the truth, but I also needed a little break from them. They meant well, and were good people, but you could only take small doses at a time. Aside from that, Vicki was a sensitive subject, and it felt funny listening to them talking about her. It was nice to get away, but I knew they'd give me their theories when I returned, whether I liked it or not.

Sure enough, as soon as I stepped through the front door, Rose announced, "She must be hiding something."

For a moment, I thought about turning around and heading back out again, but realized it was too late for that. So I shot back, "She has no reason to hide anything from me. When I ask about something and she doesn't want to talk about it, she just tells me that."

"She's hiding it from herself, not from you," Esther said.

"And how do you hide something from yourself?" I asked, knowing that I would likely not get a clinically correct answer.

My mother gave me the layman's view. "You know people bury painful memories."

"Actually, I don't know anything about that," I said. "I've got my painful memories, and I have no idea how to bury them."

"Maybe her father was murdered," Esther surmised.

"Or he abused her," Rose suggested.

My mother got in the act and added her theory, "Or her father killed someone else."

"Or her mother killed her father," I said. They all nodded that I had hit on a realistic possibility. "Come on now. I was only joking. I'll bet the real reason is rather benign. For all we know, her father and mother split up before she was born, and maybe her mother didn't feel inclined to talk about the father, so Vicki never did know anything. Then, once her mother died, all information about him was lost. I think you're all reading way too much into this."

My mother started organizing dessert. There were only four of us, but she'd bought thirty full size pastries, enough so we could each take a bunch with us when we left. While serving, she continued the discussion. "So, if you're so smart, tell me this—does she know where she was born?"

"I think so."

"Has she gone back to check out the birth records to get information about her father?" she asked.

"I don't think so. At least she never said she did."

"Well don't you think if there was nothing wrong she'd try to find him?" Esther asked.

"That's what I'd do," Rose said.

It took me a while to think about it, but I had to admit they had a point. "I'll have to ask her." I started thinking that maybe they were onto something, but that didn't mean her father was a murderer or anything like that. But I wondered if her lack of knowledge about her father had anything to do with all the walls she had built around her.

"Be careful when you talk to her about it," Esther warned. "I'll bet she's very sensitive about it. You don't want to scare her off."

"And it sounds like she's a real keeper," Rose said, once again looking at me with a big grin on her face. "Just be patient with her."

"Be patient?" my mom asked. "My son's almost fifty years old and he's still not married. I think he's been too patient."

"I'm only forty-three."

"So see other women," Rose suggested.

My mother gave me the layman's view. "You know people bury painful memories."

"Actually, I don't know anything about that," I said. "I've got my painful memories, and I have no idea how to bury them."

"Maybe her father was murdered," Esther surmised.

"Or he abused her," Rose suggested.

My mother got in the act and added her theory, "Or her father killed someone else."

"Or her mother killed her father," I said. They all nodded that I had hit on a realistic possibility. "Come on now. I was only joking. I'll bet the real reason is rather benign. For all we know, her father and mother split up before she was born, and maybe her mother didn't feel inclined to talk about the father, so Vicki never did know anything. Then, once her mother died, all information about him was lost. I think you're all reading way too much into this."

My mother started organizing dessert. There were only four of us, but she'd bought thirty full size pastries, enough so we could each take a bunch with us when we left. While serving, she continued the discussion. "So, if you're so smart, tell me this—does she know where she was born?"

"I think so."

"Has she gone back to check out the birth records to get information about her father?" she asked.

"I don't think so. At least she never said she did."

"Well don't you think if there was nothing wrong she'd try to find him?" Esther asked.

"That's what I'd do," Rose said.

It took me a while to think about it, but I had to admit they had a point. "I'll have to ask her." I started thinking that maybe they were onto something, but that didn't mean her father was a murderer or anything like that. But I wondered if her lack of knowledge about her father had anything to do with all the walls she had built around her.

"Be careful when you talk to her about it," Esther warned. "I'll bet she's very sensitive about it. You don't want to scare her off."

"And it sounds like she's a real keeper," Rose said, once again looking at me with a big grin on her face. "Just be patient with her."

"Be patient?" my mom asked. "My son's almost fifty years old and he's still not married. I think he's been too patient."

"I'm only forty-three."

"So see other women," Rose suggested.

"Keep working on Vicki, but don't just wait for her to come around," Esther said. "Play the field, that's what I always say. When I was a girl, I never limited myself to just one guy." After saying that, she continued to go on and on about how good she looked when she was young, and how the boys would just line up to go out with her. Although I had to admit, she did look great when she was young. I had been shown photos once, and she looked a lot like Rita Hayworth in her prime. Except for her weight, she didn't look that bad now, not for someone in her late 60's.

"Aren't you all glad I came to dinner, so you could bombard me with advice?" I asked.

"Your mom just wants you to be happy," Rose said.

"She's lucky to have you," Esther added, as she put her arm on my mom's shoulder. "It's so nice the way you treat her. You try to hide it, but we know how it is with the two of you. As mothers, we can tell."

"Yes Anne, you're a lucky one," Rose said.

Esther got up to remove some dishes from the table, and when she returned, she reminded us, "I have to schlep to Phoenix to see my kids. They think they're doing me a favor when they call me every six weeks or so. And you think they listen to me? I'm a nut case as far as they're concerned."

"Did you ever think about moving to Phoenix?" I realized from her body language that I shouldn't have asked.

"Why would I want to live in the desert? Camels live in the desert, not people. And after all these years, you'd think they'd get some decent food. They took me to some place and said it was a Jewish deli. I told them I know a Jewish deli when I see one and that was no Jewish deli. Would you believe they had some Mexican guy serving sandwiches and he put mayonnaise with the corned beef? Can you believe it? And people were eating there like there was nothing wrong. Let me tell you, you want Jewish deli, you come to New York. And I'll tell you something else Anne, you can't get good Italian there either. One night they said we'd eat Italian, so they took me to a place called The Spaghetti Factory. It had more than one hundred kinds of spaghetti and that was it. What do I want with one hundred kinds of spaghetti? Maybe I'm in the mood for veal parmesan? You can't get it there, Anne. Believe me when I tell you."

We listened as Esther continued her tirade against Phoenix and its eating establishments. It was funny because nobody spoke when she finished. It wasn't often that the three of them remained silent for any extended period of time. But it was nice for a change.

Rose sighed, cut a cannoli in half, but didn't take a bite. She just played with it on her plate. Finally she said, "That's the way it is these days. It's easy for kids to grow up and move far away. And even if they live nearby, they don't get together, not like we used to do."

There were those words, 'Not like we used to do.' The phrase usually led them to a long discussion about the way things were when they were growing up. It usually lasted from a half hour to an hour, and this time was no different. They went at it for over thirty minutes. I know, because I caught a whole episode of the Andy Griffith show on cable while they were still talking. It amazed me how they could talk about it like they had never discussed the subject before, even though their past presumably never changed, and they probably talked about it three or four times a year. I figured it had been over three months, so they must have thought they were overdue. Though, in a way, it was nice to hear them talking about it in the background. It was their way of reliving their youth, and there was nothing wrong with that. The way I figured it, life was short, and there were only so many really good days in one's lifetime. So I didn't see any harm of reliving the good ones every now and then.

They finally finished their discussion and I decided it was safe to rejoin them at the table. Mom served coffee, after which the three of them took turns cleaning up the kitchen. Finally, when Esther and Rose were ready to leave, I offered to take them home, but Rose had driven her car, and they didn't have a long way to go. They both lived near our old house in Brooklyn, which wasn't far away. My mom gave them their full allotment of pastries, and we said our goodbyes.

I was sleeping over and would return to New Jersey in the morning, so after the others had gone, my mother and I sat on the couch for a little chat. I wouldn't see her again until after my Switzerland trip, and she wanted to take advantage of me while I was still there. We had a nice conversation. Of course, we never discussed Swiss bank accounts or anything like that. There were just some things a mother should never know.

Chapter 29

Despite the airline's having no record of my reservation that had been booked six weeks in advance, I managed to get a seat and left from Kennedy airport late afternoon on Saturday, arriving in Switzerland early on Sunday morning, November 16. The seminar was scheduled to start on Wednesday, but I wanted to get in early to overcome jet lag, and to take care of the miscellaneous tasks involved in the Plan.

There are some great cities in Switzerland, and Lausanne is certainly one of them. But in order to get there, I had to fly to Geneva first and take an hour's bus ride east along the northern shore of Lake Geneva. The ride did enable me to see more of the countryside, and I was impressed at how everything appeared to be so clean—even the dirt looked like it had been washed. The bus dropped me off in the heart of Lausanne's business district, and from there I took a taxi to the hotel. The city reminded me of a European version of San Francisco, albeit a greener version, with the business district at the highest point and a steep incline down to the lake, where the hotel was located. Riding the taxi to get there felt something like being on the down side of a roller coaster.

My firm had booked rooms in the Sage Francois Palace, a converted castle built on the shore overlooking the harbor. The rooms facing the water had wonderful views of France and the white-capped Savoy Alps on the southern side of the lake. As luck would have it, I was booked on the top floor facing the water. You could tell it wasn't an American hotel. The public areas were very large and well appointed, but the individual rooms were small. Not that I needed much space. The radio was on when I walked into the room, and when I turned the channels, I got French, German, Italian and then English, so it was clear I was in the heart of Europe.

The seminar would take up most of each day, Wednesday through Friday, so it made sense to take care of my little errands on Monday. That way, if there was any follow-up needed, I'd have Tuesday available to do it. In order to facilitate my efforts, I took some time on Sunday to get acquainted with the city. But first I asked someone at the hotel if it was safe to walk around, and the guy had to cover his face to keep from laughing.

Just about everything was closed, but I could at least determine where the offices were located and, in any case, it was good to get some exercise after the long flight. I found my way to 127 Avenue D'Ouchy and the branch office of Suisse Union, the bank we had decided to use for account number 1. We selected it through use of a highly sophisticated and statistically accurate method, making a list of the eight largest Swiss banks with offices in Lausanne, assigning each one a number, stuffing the numbers in a hat and picking one. It seemed as good a method as any. The selection of a law firm was more difficult. Kavi and I debated whether we should look to a larger or a smaller firm. Logistics made the choice a little easier. We did our research and only four firms had offices in Lausanne, and of those, we decided to use Lorenz, Gardner & Gaston, or the Lorenz firm as we called it. They seemed to be big enough to do what we needed, but not too big. The offices were about a mile from the bank, at 22 Rue de Condemine, and after passing by, I also made sure to check out the shopping district where I planned to buy some inconspicuous local clothes.

Back at the hotel, I relaxed and gave some thought to what I needed to do at the seminar. Actually, there were two presentations lined up for me. On Wednesday afternoon I had to discuss the requirements for auditors to review a company's internal controls under the new legislation. That was pretty easy since I'd been focusing on it all year. But Thursday afternoon would be the real show. That's when I'd get to join two other partners to discuss the firm's responsibilities regarding detection of corporate fraud. We each had our assigned piece, and I was curious about what the others had done to prepare. Whatever it was, I was sure they hadn't met with an ex-FBI guy. But then, they didn't have Vicki Richards helping them, and I did.

*　　*　　*　　*

Vicki and I had met John Huggins, her client's security guy, for dinner on Wednesday night of the previous week, and I learned more about criminal work talking to him for an hour than I had by reading the four books I had bought on the subject. He really knew what he was talking about too. When I mentioned that one of the books involved murder, he jumped right in, telling us all kinds of war stories from his stint as a detective in the homicide unit of the Washington DC Metro Police. After that, he segued into assault and battery and then to armed robbery.

After telling us about some 70-year-old grandfather who had robbed a bank, he said I should forget about trying to glean something about white-collar crime by reading books on the criminal mind. He said people had done all kinds of studies on the subject and were more confused than ever. In his view, it wasn't worth the effort to try to predict whether a particular financial executive would have a higher or lower likelihood of committing a crime, although he mentioned some organizations that were doing research in the area. His key was to focus on detection. I challenged that, because detection occurs after the fact, and the accounting profession would be better served by stopping fraud before it's committed. But John said if you use the right techniques and let everyone know about it up front, it *will* prevent crimes, because people will know that sooner or later they are likely to get caught.

He asked me how often we checked the personal tax returns and bank statements of our clients' top executives as part of our audits, and I was embarrassed to admit it was something we never did. He said we should follow the money, citing as an example a major fraud where three top executives had stolen over $300 million from the company. The audit firm never suspected a thing, even though its tax department prepared the personal tax returns for the client's top executives. Anyone with half a brain would have known the top guys had more money than they should have had based upon their legitimate sources of income. But the accountants never put two and two together, even though the evidence of fraud was staring them in the face. It wasn't until an ex-girlfriend of one of the three guys snitched, that the whole scheme unraveled. John said if we made sure a client's financial executives knew we'd check personal bank statements and tax returns, even on a test basis, we could significantly reduce the incidence of corporate fraud.

He started telling us about his other ideas, and I tried to listen, and, at the same time, think about what Kavi and I were doing together. We still seemed safe. If someone wanted to follow the money, by the time there was any to follow, Kavi would be gone, and the trail would never lead to me. And my tax returns and bank accounts would be clean. Interestingly enough, John did make mention of offshore accounts using an alias, but said the money would always find its way back home to be useful. I was tempted to say something about people who left the country for good, but decided against it.

Vicki made a point about an investment banker who'd been convicted after committing acts that netted him over $1 billion. All he had to do was pay a $600 million fine, and serve less than two years in a minimum security prison. John contrasted that with a 22-year-old man who was convicted of stealing $13,000. He had used a gun without any bullets, but he was sentenced to fifteen years in prison and had to repay the full $13,000. John said sometimes the moral is that crime doesn't pay, unless the crime is really big.

* * * *

Sunday night after dinner I tuned to a French-speaking station that was doing a two hour special on Piaf. What a treat—her music—a bottle of wine and assorted cheeses ordered from the hotel—and an armchair with a view across the lake to France and the Alps. To think the trip was free! The only thing missing was Ms. Richards. After the special was over, I flipped through the stations and settled on one being broadcast from somewhere in northern Italy. I couldn't tell what they were saying, although I was sure my mom would have understood. She had always pushed me to learn Italian, but it had never seemed important when I was young, and as I got older it became much too hard to do.

It was late, so I turned off the radio but had difficulty getting to sleep. Instead, I tossed and turned while thinking about my Monday agenda. Although I'd given the matter serious consideration, the time had finally arrived to go through with my plans, and that was much different than just thinking about it, and I questioned whether it was the right thing to do. While studying the ceiling carefully to see if it would ever move, I realized the next day would be a turning point in my life, my D Day, so to speak, after which there'd be no turning back. Not unless Kavi changed his mind, left the money untouched, and turned himself in. The possibility of getting caught entered my mind, and I wondered if we'd missed some important step.

I had almost fallen asleep, but then started thinking about what my father would think if he were still alive. For some reason, I hadn't let myself think about that before. I tried to explain it to him as if he were there, thinking of all the arguments in my favor. I wouldn't get any of the money, it was being done to help Kavi, he didn't have much choice, the company had hung him out to dry, etc, etc. But it was almost as if I could hear dad responding, like he always had, that he'd been exposed to crime his whole life, that he could have easily succumbed to temptation and rationalized his getting involved, but that he never did, even though he didn't have much money, and his accent was so thick that many people treated him like dirt, that he wanted a better life for his kids, and if you say yes to crime just once, for any reason, you start down a slippery slope and say yes again and again, until you are nothing but a common criminal, etc, etc. If my mother was right about life after death, then I'd get the chance to hear it all directly from him. But I figured there was still time before I died, so I'd think of more things to say in my favor. Until then, he would just have to come to terms with what I'd done.

Monday morning started off like any other day, although I woke up in a converted castle in Switzerland, with beautiful views of the Alps, and had breakfast with a staff of ten people going out of their way to address my every need. I asked for scrambled eggs and they were the best I'd ever tasted, although it was really scrambled butter with a little bit of eggs tossed in, but I wasn't complaining. The croissants were also something to write home about—they were mostly butter too.

After the artery clogging meal, I emptied my work case and left for the big mission. First stop was the main business district and a small shop on a side street to buy some loose fitting pants and a shirt that was one or two sizes too big. While standing in a private dressing area, I put my own pants and shirt into my work case and tried on my new outfit, leaving the shirt untucked to make it look like I'd added a few pounds, although I really didn't need the shirt to do that. About a block away I was able to buy sun glasses and a skipper's hat to complete my new look, knowing full well that had I been famous, I'd have certainly been named by People magazine as one of the ten worst dressed celebrities.

Sporting my new look, I made my way to the branch office of Suisse Union. But when I arrived, instead of walking through the front door, I gave one last thought to what I was about to do. Two women walked past me pushing strollers. A mailman walked in the opposite direction, carrying a bunch of packages. Across the street two old ladies were talking, while a nearby dog was having one heck of a good time with a worn out soccer ball. It seemed like a nice fall day in Switzerland, just the kind of day you'd want to open your first secret Swiss bank account. Gathering some courage, I turned and opened the door.

After telling the clerk that I needed to open a new account, he gestured toward a cute blond, blue-eyed woman, seated at a desk behind a three-foot partition, and I introduced myself as Peter Packus. She must have been in her mid-twenties, and not quite what I'd expected. I thought a Swiss banker would be some old sinister looking man, like Dracula in a suit. But she was just an ordinary person, and an attractive one at that, doing what for her was just an ordinary job. In English that sounded more like German, she asked me to follow her to a private office, which was down a small hallway toward the back of the building. When we got there, she unlocked the door and it struck me that the room had no windows and was very small. There was a rectangular table in the middle, with one chair on the left side and three chairs on the right. In the back were two large filing cabinets, separated by a small coffee table with a phone. She pointed for me to sit on the side with three chairs and didn't appear surprised when I kept my glasses on. In fact, without my asking, I was given a primer about how clients value secrecy and how all account information is kept strictly confidential. After that, she opened a lower drawer of the filing cabinet closest to me, and, in order to get the required forms, had to lean in such a way as to put her legs in full view. Although my eyes were hidden behind the dark glasses, she just had to know that I was looking. The forms were pretty easy to complete, and, after all the preparation, the whole process was rather anticlimactic. Peter Packus, the authorized officer of FHP Commodities, Inc., did his thing in less than thirty minutes, and the account was set up. Actually, if I hadn't been so worried about protecting my identity, I'd have asked Hilga, or whatever her name was, to join me for a night on the town.

The law firm was a different story, as the arrangements were quite complex, so I knew it would take some time. The Lorenz firm's main office was in Geneva, but they had a small crew in Lausanne and had rented the top two floors of a small office building on the northern side of Rue de Condemine. The building actually looked more like a three-story home. Stephen Marti was an associate with the firm and he met me, or should I say Peter Packus, at the reception area. I could tell from his welcoming smile that he must have thought I represented a decent-sized client, and, in a certain way, I really did. FHP Commodities was no ADG, but it was big enough to expect a $10 million tax refund. Marti explained that the office was relatively new and they were trying to build up their presence in Lausanne. He escorted me up the stairs to his corner office on the third floor, which in contrast to the room at the bank, had two walls that were pretty much all window. He did ask if I wanted to remove my glasses, but I mentioned some eye condition and kept them on.

As expected, it took a good two hours to discuss FHP and what we needed the Lorenz firm to do. While we were talking, it became clear that Kavi and I had made a good choice. For an associate, Marti was very bright, and he picked things up quickly. He also had a relationship with the local office of L&K which represented a large US cigarette manufacturer that had its main European headquarters in the city. He said it would be no problem working through L&K to get

FHP's US tax returns done, and I thought it was poetic justice that ADG's auditors, who had done their part to contribute to Kavi's predicament, would unwittingly help him get back at the company. It made me think it would be even better to figure out a way to pin the whole thing on them.

After finishing with the Lorenz firm, I headed back to the business district and found the entrance to public bathrooms off one of the main streets. Ducking into one of the stalls—which, by the way, were much cleaner than those in any public bathroom I'd ever seen back in the States—I removed the stupid hat, the dark glasses, and the oversized shirt and pants, and stuffed them into my case to be discarded in some dumpster back in the States. And when I walked back out onto the street wearing my own clothes, the day's deeds were done.

Walking in the direction of the hotel, I passed a small store with a mirror in the front, and stopped to examine myself to see if anything looked different, thinking you could tell the difference between a criminal and an honest guy. I looked the same. Nonetheless, I started feeling guilty. But when I thought of Kavi, and what it would be like for him in jail, I figured from then on that I'd be ok.

I spent most of the day Tuesday either relaxing or going over my notes. On Tuesday evening, the seminar participants started arriving at the hotel and it made it look like my firm was taking over the place. All in all, there were well over one hundred people who would attend from more than ten different countries. They didn't have anything planned for that evening, so a group of seven of us commandeered two taxis to take us to a fancy French restaurant recommended by the hotel. It was a great meal, but I was getting tired of eating fattening food, and wondered how some Europeans could eat that way and live past their thirties.

My Wednesday presentation went well and, surprisingly, everybody paid close attention. It was a pretty boring subject and I was speaking right after lunch, so I expected everybody to be half asleep. But that didn't turn out to be the case. The firm had done a great job making sure each office was aware of its new responsibilities, so everyone came prepared to learn. Although I didn't have Kavi's gift for storytelling, I decided I'd take a chance and open things up with a couple of canned jokes, and actually managed to avoid screwing up the delivery. One was about a rich guy with an inoperable brain tumor who wanted to prove he could take his money with him after death. He prepared three envelopes, each containing $30,000 in cash, and handed one to his doctor, his lawyer and his accountant, instructing them to throw the envelopes into his grave before it was covered up. After the funeral, the doctor confessed he'd taken $10,000 so his envelope only contained $20,000. Then the lawyer confessed that his envelope only contained $10,000. Upon hearing that, the accountant expressed his outrage, explaining that professional ethics would never allow him to betray his client's wishes, so the envelope that *he'd* thrown into the grave contained his personal check for the full $30,000.

The Thursday afternoon presentation started slowly but ended strong. My part came last, so I had to sit at the head table and listen to the two other presentations before getting a chance to speak. The first speaker reviewed case histories of all the corporate financial shenanigans of the recent past. We had heard it all before, and he didn't have anything new to add, but fortunately he didn't mention anything about ADG.

The second guy went through a lengthy slide presentation about recent changes in auditing standards involving corporate fraud. They'd been changed in 2002, and accountants were now required to do much more than they'd ever done before. In the past, we tried to avoid having any responsibility for catching fraud, because the main objective of an audit is to ensure a client's financial statements are proper, and the audit procedures would never be good enough in most cases to identify illegal acts. We were right, but that didn't stop the public from holding us partly responsible for the kinds of cases the first speaker had talked about. So from 2002 on we had to do more, and the second speaker was doing a good job discussing the new rules, although the audience of more than 100 people was struggling to stay awake.

When my turn came up, I did my best to shake up the crowd. The first thing I did was ask for a show of hands of who had stolen money. No one was stupid enough to admit to being a thief, but my question did get everyone's attention. I followed it by asking if anyone had ever *thought* about stealing. A few people who had a poor idea of what was good for their careers meekly raised their hands, and I followed through by providing statistics that John Huggins had been kind enough to provide, about the percentage of the population that has done one or both, and said we either had an unrepresentative group, or a bunch of liars. I threw some more Huggins at them, and they were slowly but surely moving towards the edge of their seats, and at that point I knew the crowd would be mine.

During the next thirty minutes, I instructed the group to assume we were top officers of a hypothetical client and needed to develop a scheme to successfully steal money. We had to make sure it would never be caught, either by the auditors, the company, or the authorities. Suddenly the group began to buzz with activity, and we started getting all sorts of ideas. The more people spoke, the more others felt comfortable chiming in. They did so much better than I had expected. For a boring group of professionals from a major accounting firm, they were coming up with things that would make the Godfather proud. Although I had some ideas of my own, like switching the paperwork for a client's federal tax payment, I thought it would be best not to share them with the group.

When we were finished with the exercise, I threw in the results of my research into the criminal mind and segued into the finale. I told them they could read the new audit requirements until they were blue in the face, but it wouldn't make much difference unless they spent some time thinking like a criminal, and they had demonstrated from the group discussion that they had every ability to do just that.

After my presentation, the group gave me a standing ovation, which was rare for one of my firm's seminars. It was ironic that what I was doing for Kavi had forced me to think in ways I had never thought before. It's certainly true that one's ability to focus is greatly enhanced when the consequences of screwing up include spending significant time behind bars. My contribution to the Plan had actually made me a more effective auditor and certainly a more colorful speaker. Perhaps I had done such a good job that some day people in that audience would actually uncover a client's fraud.

Getting back to my room, it was nice to know I had that evening and all of Friday to relax, and then I could head home. My work in Switzerland was finished.

Chapter 30

Thanksgiving week arrived quickly, and it passed by just as fast. It was Wednesday, December 10, the heart of the holiday season, although Kavi hadn't quite embraced the holiday spirit. The judge responsible for his case had issued an order mandating that both sides meet for a plea conference, and that meant that Kavi would have to put up with Gary Bevins again. Even though they weren't close to an agreement, the court still wanted them to give it the old college try. But the parties could never come to terms. Gary always had a hidden agenda, and now Kavi had one too.

At 9 am, Kavi arrived at the US Court House with Henry Jackson and Gil Robeson at his side. Henry wore an expensive overcoat that fit perfectly and added extra emphasis to his muscular frame. Gil wore a beat-up rain coat that had evidently been purchased before adding his last fifty pounds of girth. The buttons in the front could barely be closed, though he had long ago given up trying.

After signing in with the clerk, they were escorted to a small conference room on the second floor, and were told that the Department of Justice and SEC personnel were huddled in conference room 233, the room in which the full group would meet.

"We have about forty-five minutes," Henry noted. "I suggest we cover our objectives one last time."

"Getting through this without killing anyone," Kavi said. He waited to see if he had gotten a laugh—he didn't—and then he added, "Come on gents, you know this is a complete waste of time."

Henry rubbed his forehead, looked away and shook his head. He turned back and said, "I told you we need to do this in good faith. Do we have to go through this again?" For three months he had listened to Kavi tell him the parties could never settle. But Henry believed he could get the government to significantly improve its offer, and also knew the judge would not look favorably upon any party who didn't take the conference seriously.

"Ok, go ahead," Kavi said. "You know I've always loved agreements that could send me to jail."

"What if we got it down to one year or less?" Henry asked.

"Get it down to one day or less, and I'll think about it."

"You'd rather take your chances in court?" Gil asked.

"Come on guys, you're wasting your breath," Kavi said. "We all know Bevins won't budge."

"Forget Gary for a moment," Henry said. "You never know about the DOJ. If we can get a decent discussion going, we may find out where they're coming from."

"And I assume the judge can push Gary as well?" Gil asked.

While organizing his notes, Henry replied, "He can and he will, if we make some realistic progress." He turned to Kavi and added, "Let's change your point of view before we go into the other room. Just think of this as an exercise of coming up with the best deal the other side can give. And challenge yourself to get it. Even if it's not acceptable, we'll have accomplished a number of things."

"Like what?" Kavi asked.

"For one thing, the judge will know we acted in good faith. Believe me, in close calls at the trial we'll want him on our side, or at least not fighting against us."

Gil was actively nodding his head in agreement. He added, "You have to admit that makes sense."

Kavi didn't react, and Henry decided they had wasted enough time, so he proceeded to go over his notes, even if Kavi wasn't prepared to listen. Henry's objectives included a jail term of one year or less and a fine of no more than $100,000.

As it turned out, Kavi *did* listen, and he wondered if he could ever have accepted such a deal, thinking the odds were heavily against it.

Henry made a few comments about strategy and then the trio left for the main meeting room. As they walked up the hallway, they could see that the door to the room was closed, and Kavi joked that they should just stand there and eavesdrop on the government's conversation. Then he added that everybody had probably left, and suggested it might be best to turn around and go home. Ignoring the comments, Henry knocked on the door and was told to come in.

If there had been any doubt that they were in a government building, it vanished as soon as the door was opened. Room 233 was big, boxy, poorly decorated and in need of some tender loving care. It was dominated by a rectangular metal conference table that could easily handle twenty people, but had so many dings and scratches that you'd think it had spent years in a kindergarten class. It was actually the nicest piece of furniture in the room. The back wall was lined with an old fashioned radiator system which was running at full blast and making plenty of noise, but it must have been on its last legs, because the room was freezing. Needless to say, it didn't make for a cozy environment.

As Kavi entered the room, in addition to noting the lesser quality infrastructure, he realized his team was heavily outnumbered. Gary Bevins and Dennis Smith were there as expected, but they'd brought along ten others. They introduced themselves and the final tally was seven for the DOJ and five for the SEC. Henry and Gil made their way around the room to shake hands, but Kavi walked directly to a chair and sat down. The only way his hand would touch Gary was if it were thrown as a punch. The longer sides of the table could only handle ten people, so two of the DOJ folks had to sit on the small side, to Kavi's right. He wasn't sure, but he suspected there was a pecking order to the way the dirty dozen was seated, with Gary, Dennis and the other senior people sitting closer to the middle. They all had their little note pads and pencils out, and the meeting was ready to begin.

Henry started things off by reminding the group that these were plea discussions, and anything said at the meeting couldn't be used in court. Both Gary and Dennis agreed and allowed Henry to finish. With the discussion underway, he did the talking for the good guys and Gary did most of the talking for the government, although Dennis and a person sitting to his left would periodically chime in. The other government people remained quiet, but they were always busy taking notes.

At times Kavi would pay attention, and at other times he would think about something else. He could hear them talking about different pieces of evidence and going back and forth about their significance or meaning. It seemed to be going on for some time and at one point he looked at his watch and wondered what Debra Jennings was doing at that very moment. She was the one person at ADG he really missed, and he knew she missed him too. At least they had made a point of seeing each other every now and then since he'd been suspended. While daydreaming, he didn't realize he appeared to be staring at one of the government women, but she noticed him and was trying to hide a smile, apparently enjoying the attention, even if it was coming from the accused. But it didn't stop her from continuing to write in her pad. When he focused, he noticed her writing, and then he looked at the others who were busy writing as well. The discussion was meant to be confidential. There should have been no need for extensive notes and he was beginning to get suspicious. Gary was busy talking, so that also argued in favor of Kavi jumping in to interrupt.

"Excuse me," Kavi said. "Nothing we say at this meeting can be used in court, right?"

Gary looked at the ceiling and took a long deep breath. He then looked down, and as if he was talking to the table, said, "Mr. Chander, as your counsel mentioned at the start, these discussions can not be used by either side as part of the criminal proceedings. Now may I continue?"

"So let me ask a stupid question," Kavi said. "If it can't be used in court, why are so many of you taking notes?"

Gary didn't immediately respond, so Dennis jumped in and said, "It's standard procedure. When we finish the meeting, we'll prepare a draft memorandum summarizing what was discussed. Each person will get an opportunity to review it and make any comments based upon their notes, before it's issued in final form."

What Dennis said was basically true, but it wasn't the only reason for the government's interest in taking notes, and it didn't explain why they had so many people doing it. As it turned out, the guy to Dennis's left was some big shot litigator who was assigned to help with the case, and he wasn't taking notes, but the other nine people were. They had been split into groups of threes with one group asked to watch Henry, one to watch Kavi and one to watch Gil. They were to write down what their 'target' said, as well as other things like their body language or their reaction to specific questions or discussion points. Gary intended to milk the conference for all it was worth, and he and Dennis had arranged to mention certain aspects of their evidence at different points in the discussion. They would key the others so they could match reactions and comments with specific points. The verbal and, more importantly, the non-verbal reactions they would get could provide insight into the strength of individual pieces of evidence and might also provide clues as to other avenues that might be beneficial to exploit.

There was another reason for all the notes, and a more sinister one at that. Gary had said the discussion could not be used in court, but he'd said nothing about using it with the press. It bothered him that every time he discussed the case in public it was followed by one of Henry's tirades against the government and, in particular, the SEC. And Henry's assaults were taking their toll. Gary needed ammunition and he looked to the plea conference as one way to get it. He knew if Henry or Kavi said something that sounded like a lie or sounded inconsistent with earlier statements, it could be put to good use. And it was just that sort of thing he was looking for. Of course he couldn't tell his people to make them up, but he knew that any three people would likely have a different version of what had been said. So even though their meeting notes were taken in good faith, there would be differences to exploit. Gary intended to review each person's notes and pick and choose the version of events he liked best. In the end, he could honestly say the final memorandum was prepared by government people based upon what had been said at the meeting, even though quotes reflected therein would likely bear little or no resemblance to what had actually been said. It would be the word of someone indicted for a crime and his counsel, versus the word of government personnel. In the war over public opinion, that was a battle Gary would win every time.

"So you need twelve people to attend a meeting so they can tell you what happened at the meeting?" Kavi asked. "Maybe we should have done something like that at ADG. We could have tripled our employment levels."

"You may joke about *our* procedures. But I'd say there were a number of things *you* should have done differently," Gary said

"Yeah, I shouldn't have returned your first phone call," Kavi quipped.

"Need I say more?" Gary asked.

Henry leaned over to Kavi and in a very low voice said, "Let it go. This isn't the time or the place." Then he turned his attention back to Gary. "We should get the discussion back on track." Henry was successful and Gary returned to what he'd been discussing prior to the interruption.

Kavi tried to tune out of the conversation again but was finding it harder and harder to do. Gary's voice was beginning to sound like someone scratching their fingernails against a blackboard, and it was making Kavi cringe every time he heard it. It didn't take long for him to conclude that jail time couldn't be so bad in comparison. Although Gary wasn't using his "public persona," he was saying many of the same things he had said about Kavi in public. He had done such a good job that people were beginning to mention Kavi and ADG interchangeably with the names of the other individuals and companies involved with scandals in the recent past. It was bad enough getting it via the media, but it was much worse in person. Despite his best efforts, Kavi just couldn't ignore it, so he gave in and started to pay attention, and managed to catch the end of Henry's question.

"So it's still eight years?" Henry asked.

"That's correct," Gary responded.

"And you think that's fair?"

Gary looked at Kavi and smirked. "Mr. Jackson, please keep in mind that your client hasn't shown any sign of remorse for what he's done."

Kavi blurted, "You little piece of—"

Henry quickly put his hand on Kavi's shoulder to stop him from continuing. Then Henry leaned forward and said, "We both have an obligation to discuss this in good faith."

Gary shook his head, "And that's what the government is doing Mr. Jackson."

"So you can look me in the face and say a prison term of not more than eight years is fair? And you can say you're talking in good faith when the deal you're offering now is not much different than the one you offered when we first met?"

Gary started to laugh but quickly caught himself and said, "Let's get something straight." Then he focused his eyes on Kavi and said what sounded like "nah, nah, nah, nah, nah," but actually he said, "I'm not the one who bribed foreign officials. Your client should have thought about this before he violated the law."

"That's unfair," Gil blurted. He too was trying to remain quiet and let Henry take the lead, but just couldn't help himself. "You haven't even charged him with being responsible for the bribes. You're just arguing that he knew about it."

Gary looked at Dennis and smiled. Then he turned back to Gil. "And your client should be thankful for that."

Kavi leaned in toward Henry, but spoke loud enough to be overheard. "This is good faith?"

"You see what I mean, Mr. Jackson," Gary said, looking satisfied with the way things were going. "Your client does not take these matters seriously. But with what he's done, that's understandable."

"Is this some kind of a game to you?" Kavi asked.

"Perhaps that's what it is to you," Gary replied.

At this point Kavi was ignoring Henry, who was imploring him to keep quiet. Kavi remarked, "It's amazing how you can play with people's lives and get away with it. You're like Joseph McCarthy. You make up all this crap that you tell the press, and your targets are never there to defend themselves."

"I'm not the one on trial, Mr. Chander. I comply with the law."

"Oh you do? How about your little deal with Maurice Granville?" Kavi looked at both Gary and Dennis and said, "I wouldn't mind getting a transcript of the conversation you guys had with him before he resigned. You can't tell me you really believed him."

"You're in no position to tell us what we believe," Gary said.

Kavi sat back in his chair and took a deep breath. "I should stop wasting my time. You're just too good at lying."

Gary half-heartedly tried to get up, like he was ready for some sort of physical fight, but Dennis held him down, which was comical since Kavi would have killed him. Gary glared at Kavi and said, "It's not appropriate for you to make accusations against anyone."

"Oh come off your little bullshit act," Kavi insisted. "You don't believe any of this, but that doesn't matter to you, does it? You have an agenda, and nothing's going to stand in your way."

Dennis interrupted, "I think we should move on."

Kavi ignored Dennis and kept his eyes on Gary. "You knew what you were planning to do when you first showed up at our offices, didn't you? And I wondered why you never went after Steve Halpern. I guess you only needed one target and it was easier to frame the CFO."

Gary blurted out, "What is it with you people? You come to this country and think you can bring your contempt for the law with you." He stopped and realized he had made a mistake. He waited for someone else to speak, but the room was silent as everyone tried to make some sense of the comment.

After more than a moment's hesitation, Henry looked at the others and then leaned forward toward Gary and slowly asked, "Who exactly are you referring to when you say 'you people?'"

Gary sat back in his chair and was breathing heavily. He took a moment to look down at the floor and catch his breath. Then he replied, "You know what I mean."

"No, I assure you I don't," Henry said. "As an African-American I've heard the term 'you people' more times than I care to remember. But in this particular instance, I'd like to know exactly what you mean."

Gary looked at Kavi and said, "You are from India, are you not?"

"I'm a United States citizen. You should know that, since you had the court take away my passport. I came here from India more than twenty-five years ago." Kavi squinted and scratched his chin. "So is my being Indian what this is all about?"

It seemed clear that Gary had temporarily lost control of the conversation, so he took some time to regain his composure. Had he not done that, he might have provided an accurate response, by saying he would have graduated number one in his class in law school, had it not been for an even smarter guy, who just happened to be from India. Instead, after swallowing hard a couple of times and taking a deep breath, he replied, "You gentlemen can try to make this personal, but I can assure you the government is color blind when it comes to application of the law. What matters here is that you broke the law, not the color of your skin or your country of origin. I am simply stating as part of these plea discussions that your contempt for the law may have been something you learned before you came to this country."

"Nice try at a recovery, but I think we know where you're really coming from." Kavi laughed and shook his head. "So tell me something about *your* origins. Where does the name Bevins come from?"

Gary was becoming visibly upset, and announced, "You're wasting our time. I can't see how my background is pertinent to this discussion."

"It's not pertinent, but neither is the fact that I came here from India."

Henry realized the conference was turning out to be a complete bust from his perspective, but he wanted the record to reflect that he had given it his best effort. As soon as Kavi finished speaking, Henry said, "It seems we have little hope of bridging the gaps between us, but we should stick to the subject matter of this plea conference." He nodded at Kavi to keep quiet and looked back at Gary, who seemed eager to move on to something else. Henry continued, "Now Gary, please tell me what is so magical about eight years. Not to say we'd find it acceptable, but couldn't you offer something like six or seven years?"

Gary appeared to be stalling for time so he could completely regain his composure before responding. He looked around the room, checked his watch again and sighed. Finally he said, "These are very serious charges. Now I think we may have been too generous when you and I first spoke. We should have proposed fifteen years, so now eight years would seem like a major move on our part."

"Come on Gary, your whole case is weak," Gil said. "You know this isn't your typical securities fraud case. You're not saying Kavi manipulated the financials; just that he knew about the bribes and didn't make the proper adjustments on the books. Even if those allegations were true, eight years would be rather harsh, don't you think?"

"The allegations are true," Gary said, his eyes almost bulging out, as if Gil's comment had insulted him. The person to Gary's right leaned in to whisper something in Gary's ear, and then he relaxed a bit and continued, "And don't forget about the litigation reserves. That was a blatant misstatement of the company's books and records."

Kavi leaned over to Henry. "Let's put an end to this, ok? We're getting nowhere with this asshole."

"At this point I have to agree with my client. This has been a complete waste of time." Henry paused for a moment and then glanced Gary's way. "But perhaps it has been an eye opener."

Gary pointed at Kavi and exclaimed, "Let the record reflect that you had your opportunity to discuss a plea. This meeting is now over."

Dennis stood up and said, "That means what you say from this point forward is not part of the plea discussions, and can be used against you in court."

"You mean if I tell Gary to fuck off it will be used against me?" Kavi asked.

Gary turned his head, looked up at Dennis and said, "Now you see what we're dealing with here."

"I think it's best that you leave," Dennis said, looking over at Kavi and his team.

Henry grabbed Kavi's shoulder and looked at Gil. "Let's go, gentlemen."

The government team remained in the room as Kavi and his lawyers got up to walk out. Kavi was last, and when he got to the door he overheard Gary say something about people from India. Kavi quickly turned and asked, "What'd you say?"

"I don't see how that's any of your business," Gary replied.

Henry stepped back in the room to grab Kavi. "Come on, let's go."

"No, I want to know what this little twerp said." Kavi tried to make his way to Gary, but before he could get to him, three DOJ guys including Dennis Smith reluctantly moved to cut him off.

"Please leave," Dennis implored. "It's really for your own good."

Kavi knew he could easily force his way through, but thought better of it. After coming to his senses he blurted out the word "asshole," turned, and walked out the door.

After leaving the courthouse and taking some time to calm down, Kavi and Henry shared a taxi uptown. Gil needed to stay behind to meet with another client who had an office nearby. On the ride back, Henry said he wasn't really expecting much progress, but he was nonetheless surprised at how badly the meeting had gone, and was concerned that the heated discussion could make Gary more determined to make his case. Although he did add that Gary's comments may have alienated him from some of the other government people. While Henry continued to analyze the day's results, Kavi wondered why he had been so foolish as to say anything at all. He realized, with all things considered, it would have been better if he had just kept his big mouth shut.

Chapter 31

With cost cutting efforts in vogue, big corporate Christmas parties were becoming a thing of the past. But that wasn't the case with ADG and its big holiday extravaganza. Each year its "organizing committee" would book the entire Rainbow Terrace, the five star restaurant on the 50th and top floor of a building in the Rockefeller Center complex. They'd book the place for themselves from noon through midnight, and would add all sorts of bells and whistles, like exotic imported foods and top musical performers. Needless to say, it was never a very productive day for the New York office. The committee typically picked the Friday before Christmas week and, for 2003, that was December 19, which just happened to be my birthday.

Party day arrived, and by 2 pm the festivities were in full swing, but if you looked closely, you'd see that certain 'corporate' people weren't there. Debra Jennings and many of her colleagues had another gathering they needed to attend. She had wanted to throw a surprise party for Kavi, and figured the best day to do it would be Friday the 19th, so her ADG compatriots would be able to get away from the office without their absence being noticed. At first she thought it might be difficult to get people to attend, but the favorable response was overwhelming. The 'grunts,' as they were sometimes known, were still loyal to Kavi. Of course, none of the ADG big shots were invited, but they wouldn't have attended anyway.

Debra got Marc involved with the advanced planning, and he had arranged to have a late lunch with Kavi. The plan called for the two of them to meet at Marc's office, and from there walk over to the restaurant, with an ETA of about

1:30 pm. By that time most of the invitees would be ready for the big surprise, including Kavi's wife Aarti, their daughter Sanji, and their son Kris.

Marc suggested it be held at the Bombay Bunker, which bore absolutely no resemblance to the Rainbow Terrace. The Bunker was located below ground, in an area that had been used as a civil defense shelter back in the late fifties and sixties—so if the Soviets dropped a nuclear bomb on New York, you'd be safe, or so you were told. It served great Indian food, but the owners didn't have a liquor license, so you needed to bring your own booze, which was a little tricky because you had to navigate a tight circular staircase from street level to get in. When push came to shove, the place could handle about fifty people and maybe a few more. Debra was expecting just under that number, so she'd asked Marc to reserve the whole place for the party.

Upon arriving, Kavi almost fell off the stairs when he heard everyone scream 'surprise.' I stood against a side wall in the rear and watched as he got mobbed. Kavi knew the ADG gala was being held that day, and from the look on his face you could tell it meant a lot that so many people had chosen instead to be with him. They spent some time giving him gag gifts, including a doll with a removable head upon which a photo of Gary Bevins had been pasted. Kavi immediately decapitated the doll and threw the head against the wall to a rousing round of applause. The last gift was the front page of a newspaper that looked like the Wall Street Journal with the headline 'ADG Executive Wins Big Case—Expects to Sue Government for Damages.'

The refrigerator at the restaurant wasn't big enough, so as the party progressed, it wasn't long before we had to send out a group to get more beer, and Ken and I volunteered to go. The liquor store was three blocks away, and we bought three cases and headed back. Of course I was struggling with one case, but Ken had no trouble carrying two. We hadn't seen each other in a few weeks, so the walk gave us a chance to catch up.

"So you have any more *special* trips planned?" Ken asked.

I was pretty good at keeping developments regarding the Plan to myself, but since he brought it up, I replied, "I'll be back in Lausanne the second week in January."

"And everything's in place?"

"We think so."

"So what happens in Lausanne?"

"You sure you want to know? We don't need your help at this point."

"I'm not Marc," Ken said. "Give me the basics and make it quick."

"I'll be visiting the Swiss law firm we picked. They'll arrange the filing of the 2003 tax return, and we want them to do it as fast as possible after the end of the year. At this point, all we need to do is to get them the information to put on the return, and of course we can't do that until January."

"Makes sense that you do that in person."

"We tried to think of alternatives, but you're right, I've got to go. The trip will be a real pain though. I don't want any evidence that I was back in Lausanne, so I'm flying to Paris and staying there. I'll take a train to Lausanne, do what I need to do, stay overnight at some dive hotel, and then I'll take a train back to Paris. I'll use cash and an assumed name for the Lausanne leg, just to be safe."

"You sound like an experienced criminal," Ken noted, after which he quickly added, "No offense."

"Thanks for the compliment, if that's what it was."

"You must have given it a lot of thought."

"We both have, and we're looking forward to the day when it's all done and he has the money. From what you told us about tax refunds, he should get it near the end of February."

"Is he still looking to net $10 million?"

After taking some time to rearrange the way I was holding my case of beer, I replied, "Probably. Kavi prepared the numbers and I haven't seen them yet."

"The way he's being treated by ADG, he should try for more."

"You know money's not that important to him. But I'll tell you, he'd love to speed things up if he could. It's difficult for him to just sit around and wait. The end of February can't come soon enough."

"So how's he planning to leave the country?"

"It's basically the same as what he had told you a few months back. He and Aarti will take a commercial flight to Houston, and from there he can get his hands on a small plane that he can fly over the border to Monterey, Mexico. No passports needed. There are some guys that make the trip back and forth between Mexico and the US, and for cash they'd take him, but he didn't want to get involved with any shipment of contraband. So they agreed to rent him the plane for a one way trip, and he'll fly it himself. From Monterey, they'll take a commercial airline to Mexico City and meet up with one of Aarti's relatives from India, who'll have two Indian passports for them and they'll all fly back to India together."

"How can they get their hands on passports?"

"I don't know, but apparently Aarti has some well connected relatives."

We arrived back at the Bombay Bunker, and after lugging the beer for three blocks—and managing to get it down the circular staircase without killing myself—I needed to stand in a corner and stretch. And, while confirming for the crowd just how inflexible my body had become, I got another chance to watch Kavi interact with his former-staff. I remembered how he had said they were always intimidated by him, but that didn't appear to be the case at the party. With all the noise, beer and Indian food, everybody seemed to be comfortable and having a great time. I could tell from the people's faces that they really cared about him, so I half-jokingly suggested to Marc that they be called as character witnesses at his trial, although Mark just gave me a funny look, presumably in reference to the fact that there'd be no trial.

After a few minutes of crowd watching, I walked over to chat with Sanji, who appeared to be in great spirits. That was good to see, because I did wonder how the Plan was affecting her. She was such a terrific kid. Smart, good natured, and a stunning beauty, with exotic dark eyes that seemed capable of hypnotizing any man, including me. She was only 22, and I thought of her as somewhat akin to my niece, but if I were twenty years younger and had never met Kavi, I would certainly have asked her out. We talked about the actual man in her life, an English guy who worked with her company. He was based in the head office in London, and spent a good portion of his time in New York, making sure he saw her every time he flew in from England. She told me there was a transfer in the works and she'd likely be moving to the London office by the end of May. We were in the middle of talking about that when a couple of guys squeezed in on both sides of her to flirt, so I let her go.

Making my way to the back was a challenge. The place was mobbed and it was hard to walk even a few feet. Aarti was busy talking to some guy, and while passing I caught her eye and she grabbed my arm, pulled me toward her, and gave me a big hug and kiss. It was a real kiss too, not one of those little pecks on the cheek, and I was actually a little embarrassed and told her to be careful not to make Kavi jealous. She knew all the risks involved with what I was doing and was becoming more and more appreciative with each passing week. We talked for a few minutes and she asked about Vicki. I told her the latest scoop. Vicki had some big shot client in town, so she couldn't make it to Kavi's party. We had arranged to get together for dinner Saturday night, but she might have to cancel if her client stayed in town over the weekend. She said it was strictly business and I believed her, although it was getting to the point where I wasn't sure if it mattered. We hadn't taken our relationship to the next level, and my patience was running out. I could actually hear the voice of my mother's friend, Esther Bernbaum, telling me to "play the field," and it was getting louder every day. Aarti was supportive and said some nice things, but she also appeared to be hiding a smile, and I had no idea why.

After leaving Aarti, I managed to get to the back where Marc was talking to Kris. He was 21, and, like his sister, was also good looking and smart—near the top of his class as a senior in college. I had just joined the conversation when Sanji climbed onto a chair on the other side of the restaurant and called for Kris. He smiled, shrugged his shoulders and left to join her.

Marc and I hadn't talked much all evening, so we grabbed two chairs in the corner to be alone, although the wall of people was still just three feet away.

"Kris seems depressed," Marc said.

"What makes you say that?"

"Some of the things he said. I don't think he likes what's going on."

"Well neither does anybody else."

Marc gave me a look like he wanted to say something but couldn't. "So you're doing ok with everything?"

"Yes Marc." I knocked on the wooden chair for good luck. "It looks like everything's under control."

"So tell me what's happening with Vicki."

"We're getting together for dinner tomorrow night."

"The Saturday night before Christmas. You must have big plans."

"I'm not sure we'll even get together. She may have to cancel because one of her big clients is in town." I shook my head and turned away, trying to hide my disappointment. Turning back I said, "If we *do* get together, I think we'll probably break up. Not that we were really together in the first place."

"What are you talking about?" Marc asked. "You two seem like such good friends."

"That's the problem. That's all we are, and I want more. It's been four months now, and if she isn't willing to go further, then we should call it quits. I plan to tell her that and I know exactly what she'll say. She wants to remain good friends and, if that's not enough and I want to break up, she'd be disappointed, but it's my choice. I've heard it about thirty times before."

Marc nursed his beer while continuing to study the crowd. "It seems to me you're making a perfectly reasonable request."

"It doesn't matter. There's no right or wrong to it. If she doesn't want more, there's nothing I can do about it. You know the customer is always right, and she's the customer."

"Good luck with her."

"How old were you when you got married?"

"Let's see, it was 1987, so I was thirty-three," Marc replied.

"And Kavi was 23 and Ken was in his late twenties. I turned 44 today, and I'm still single. What's wrong with me?"

Marc advised, "Try not to think about her. Just enjoy the party."

It looked like he was trying to hide a smile, just like Aarti had been doing, and I was just about to say something when I heard some big commotion in the crowd. The next thing I knew, Ken was making his way over with a big birthday cake, and right next to him was none other than Vicki. And everybody immediately began singing a rousing rendition of Happy Birthday.

We both stood up, and Marc had to scream in my ear so I could hear what he was saying. "I'm sorry I couldn't say happy birthday. We wanted it to be a surprise. I called Vicki and she said she'd be late but would make sure to get here. We didn't want to celebrate your birthday without her."

When they were finished singing, Vicki came over, offered me her cheek, and then took hold of my right arm and wrapped it around her.

"So what happened with your client?" I asked.

"I ran over to get here as soon as we finished meeting."

"But I thought you'd be meeting all day and possibly tomorrow?"

"I just made that up," she admitted. "I'm sorry. I just wanted to really surprise you."

"Well that you did. So I take it we're on for tomorrow night?"

"Not if I meet someone here. I noticed some good looking guys on the way in."

"There are some attractive gals too."

"I told you I wasn't into women."

"I'm glad I heard the commotion. Marc and I were talking about you just before you walked in."

"Don't you have better things to discuss? So, was it something good or bad?"

"How can I say anything bad about you?"

"Maybe you don't know me well enough."

Kavi walked over and tried to squeeze all the air from my lungs. When he was through, and before I could fully recover, he stood between me and Vicki and started telling her what a great guy I was, and how she would never find anyone better. The crowd seemed to be getting noisier by the minute, and Vicki was saying something to Kavi but I couldn't hear a word. Ken leaned in and said she looked great. Then Debra and some guy started handing out pieces of my birthday cake. It didn't really mix with the beer and Indian food but nobody cared. It turned out that Marc had bought it and arranged to have it stored with the restaurant ahead of time. It meant more to me than I thought it would. Admittedly, I had been disappointed when none of the guys had said anything about my birthday.

All things considered, Debra's party was a big success. Kavi got his surprise and I got mine. After most of the others had left, I walked Vicki about a mile back to her place, making sure not to say a word about my agenda for Saturday night. It was a rare occasion when I actually chose to be patient, since there was no reason to get to it a day early. She may have been a little surprised when I kissed her at the entrance to her building and quickly said goodbye, but we'd have our chance for a lengthy and serious discussion soon enough.

While driving home, I thought how great it was to see Kavi so happy. He hadn't looked that way since the beginning of our anniversary dinner at the Iron Horse back in June, and that seemed like ages ago. Time appeared to be moving much more slowly than usual. But late February would arrive soon enough, and by that time Kavi and Aarti would be gone.

Chapter 32

▼

There comes a time in any relationship when you know which way things will go. And for Vicki and me, that time was only hours away. It was Saturday, December 20, a date that would mark a turning point in our relationship, for better or for worse. Upon leaving my apartment to head into the city, I was prepared to confront her, having given the matter extensive thought for the previous two weeks. But when I parked my car in Manhattan, I had lost all confidence and was beginning to second guess everything. And the weather didn't help matters any. Although her apartment was only a few blocks from where I had parked my car, the walk over was treacherous. It had been a very cold day but it had just started to rain, and the winds had picked up and were whipping through the streets. Despite the weather, there were still plenty of people out and they were all struggling. I couldn't help but notice that the ones who were in couples seemed happy and the single people seemed disgusted, or maybe it was just my imagination. At least my raincoat held up well, and my new umbrella was big enough to cover a car, so it was able to withstand the heavy winds.

I knew what Vicki and I were going to discuss, although as far as she knew, we were getting together for a casual meal and easy conversation. But the time for "casual" was over, and I had had enough easy conversation for four months. So one of us needed to do something. Otherwise we were destined to be perpetually stuck in neutral. I tried to think positive, but while planning for the evening, I pegged the odds of a successful outcome at something less than even money.

Her building was in an upscale area of Manhattan on the Upper East Side. It faced Second Avenue and was located between 66th Street and 67th, wedged in between an open-around-the-clock grocery store and an Italian restaurant. The weather had caught the grocer by surprise, and wet fruit and vegetables were scattered along the sidewalk. After navigating the organic minefield, I walked through the main entrance and pushed the button for Jacob Astor in apartment 3 L. He was an imaginary friend Vicki had when she was a kid. And the listed ID was just her way of maintaining a low profile. I heard the inner lobby door buzz, and it wasn't opened more than an inch when a small cat pushed it open even further and darted through the front door, which had yet to completely close, and out into the rain. As I closed the inner door behind me, I looked around for the cat's owner, but no one was there, so I gave up and made my way up the stairs to her third floor apartment, trying to shake off water from my umbrella along the way.

When you walked through her front door, you'd think you had walked into an annex to one of New York's museums. There was exotic stuff everywhere and I was afraid to move for fear of breaking something expensive. Some of the things she had bought on her overseas trips and others had been given to her as gifts. I didn't know which was which. The apartment had five rooms, including two bedrooms, and over 1,000 square feet. Someone had told me a nearby studio rented for over $3,000 per month, so I knew her place had to be expensive.

After gingerly walking through the living room, I made myself comfortable on a burgundy leather couch near the window. It was flanked by three marble tables from Italy with an emerald color that was a perfect complement to the couch. There were magazines on one end of the largest table, so I flipped through the most recent copy of National Geographic to pretend that I was reading, while she finished getting herself ready in another room. Suddenly I was jolted by a loud bang coupled with a bright flash. Within seconds all the lights went out in her apartment and all along the street. We didn't know it at the time, but lightning had struck a nearby transformer and power was off throughout an eight block area. After we got organized and lit some candles, she struggled to finish getting ready in the semi-darkness.

It's usually relaxing to sit by candlelight, but relaxed was no way to describe my condition at the time. I was nervous and the lightning strike didn't help. While waiting, I was trying to build up the courage to begin what would undoubtedly be a very tough conversation. Although I didn't think I was ready, when she walked into the room I started saying what needed to be said.

"Vicki, it's time we had a little talk. You know we've been seeing each other for over four months."

Walking toward me, she hesitated, and then asked, "You want to know which of this stuff was given as gifts?"

"That's not what I had in mind."

She sighed and said, "No, I didn't think so." Squeezing onto the couch next to me, she put her hand on my thigh and asked, "Do we have to do this now?"

"I think it's as good a time as any."

She looked away, down at the floor, and didn't say anything in response. All I could hear was the rain being blown against the window, and the periodic crackling of thunder. Her hand was sliding off of me when she said, "Let's not make things more complicated than they need to be."

I couldn't sit still, so I got up and carefully followed a path to the window, pausing along the way to catch an expensive vase before I completely knocked it over. The rain was coming down so hard you could almost feel the moisture, and it was actually seeping through the bottom and side edges of the windows. They were more than 30 years old and had been poorly maintained, even though she paid a fortune in rent. While standing there, I regained some courage and decided since we had begun "the conversation," we might as well continue. So I said, "I'm not trying to make things complicated. I just want to know what we are and, what's more, what we can be."

"We're very good friends," she said.

"And that's all?"

"I think that's enough, don't you?"

It was uncanny how the conversation was going just as I had expected. And that wasn't a good thing. Retracing my path back to the couch, I kneeled down in front of her on the floor and took hold of her hand, and for some reason she started crying. Looking up, I asked, "How can you sit here and say it's enough? Don't you want more? What good is it to go through life and all it has to offer without someone who can share it with you?"

She pulled her hand back and turned away. "I don't know what to tell you."

"Well, you need to think of something. I've been very patient up until now, but I'm through with that. One way or another we're making progress tonight."

"Why can't we just remain friends?"

"Because that's not good enough for me. Not anymore." I waited for her to say something, but all I could hear was the low murmur of her sobs. So I continued, "Think about it. We've been seeing each other for over four months, and we haven't even slept together."

"Is that what this is about, sex?"

"Of course not. It's about love. And unless you're blind, you can tell that I'm *deeply* in love with you."

"You don't know that. Carl, you hardly know me."

"Don't tell me what I know. I've been around long enough and there's no doubt about my love for you." After pausing, I asked the question I was most afraid to ask. "Don't you have strong feelings for me?"

One of the candles on a marble end table started to flicker, so she got up to replace it with another, apparently stalling for time. Upon returning, she had to know my question couldn't be dodged forever, so she meekly said, "I care about you, if that's what you mean."

Her place was still dimly lit, but the way the conversation was going, I preferred it that way. It was almost like a confessional at a church, where you couldn't completely see the other person and as a consequence felt more comfortable talking about a difficult subject. The atmosphere enabled me to say, "I'm glad you care about me, but I'd like to know if you *love* me."

Again there was no immediate answer. Instead, she followed a different, and apparently safer, path to the window and I could see her silhouette looking out. I did my best to retrace her steps and stood behind her. My hands were gently massaging her shoulder while we both stood quietly and watched the rain. After a little prodding, she finally said, "I think that's an unfair question."

"Why is it unfair? You either love me or you don't."

"But we've only known each other four months," she said. "I don't think that's nearly enough time."

"If we were teenagers, I'd say you were right. But I just turned 44, and you're 34. I think four months should be plenty of time."

The rain seemed to be coming down even harder and I could barely hear her when she softly said, "You won't like the answer I have to give you."

I removed my hands and stepped back into the room. There was a four foot tall Buddha on the floor and the flicker of the candles made it look like he was alive and was sympathetic to my cause. Whether I liked it or not, she had given me her reply. Not in so many words, but it didn't take a genius to know she didn't feel the same way about me that I did toward her. And at that point my insides felt like they were caving in, and I'd have thrown up if I had had anything to eat. It was such a sick feeling, and I'd had that feeling too many times before. When I was crazy about someone and I first learned that they didn't feel the same way about me. Someone once said it was the price for happiness. That you had to be in the lowest valley to appreciate what it was like to be on the highest mountain. Well, I had spent enough time in the valley, and I was damned tired of it. I wanted some time at the top of that mountain, but was beginning to wonder if it really existed. Maybe none of us were destined for true happiness, and the smart ones learned their lesson early on in life and settled for something less than perfect, but the idiots like me kept struggling along.

For about five minutes neither one of us spoke, and I had no idea what she was thinking. I was hoping beyond hope that she'd suddenly turn around and announce that she really did love me and was just afraid of her feelings, but that never happened. I wasn't really sure what to say next. The thought of never seeing her again frightened me, so I considered just changing the subject so we could have that casual dinner we'd been planning—plus the easy conversation. But I had promised myself not to settle for the status quo, so I couldn't back off. My agenda had thrust me onto a horse named reality and I had to ride it wherever it went. Coming around the stretch, I asked, "Do you think you could *ever* love me?"

Standing quietly at the window, her silhouette was briefly lit up by lightning in the distance. She turned toward me, and I could tell she was wiping tears from her eyes, although I couldn't make out the expression on her face. In a melancholy tone she said, "I'm sorry Carl. I never meant to hurt you."

And I knew that was it. To push any further would be like trying to lift a car with a string. So I crouched down on the floor while saying, "Believe me, I'm sorry too."

"I don't think we should go to dinner tonight, do you?"

"Who cares about dinner? I don't think we should see each other again."

She slowly turned to look back out the window. "I'm sure you know what's best."

It was difficult to do in the dark but I found my way to the entrance of her apartment. I was about to walk out the door when I heard myself say, "I'll bet you can't love *anyone*."

"Don't make this any harder than it is Carl," she instructed. "We'll both regret it."

My heart had been smashed, so there wasn't much chance of making things any harder on me. And once I started down that destructive road I figured I might as well continue. "So that's what it is, isn't it? You can't love anyone, can you?" She didn't reply, and without thinking about what I was doing, I found my way back to where she was standing, grabbed her shoulders from behind and spun her around so she faced me. "There something about your past that's holding you back."

"That's not true. You just can't accept the fact that I don't love you."

"You said your mother died when you were young, and you have no memory of your father, right?"

She grimaced, pushed my hands aside, and said, "You're stretching Carl." She marched over to the couch, threw herself down, and thrust her feet atop one of the marble tables so hard that I heard something fall off. Sounding pissed, she said, "I know you're hurt, but you'll hurt even more if you keep this up."

"Vicki, you never tried to get in touch with your dad, did you?"

She laughed and said, "So what does that have to do with anything?"

"Tell me, why didn't you try to locate him?"

"Jacob Astor doesn't exist."

"What? What's your imaginary friend got to do with this?"

"Just let me be alone!" she demanded.

"Vicki, please tell me, why didn't you try to find your dad?"

"That's none of your damned business."

"I'll bet you don't even know why."

She started tugging at her hair and asked, "What is it with all you guys? You think you're so smart, don't you? You take a few facts and you twist them any way you want, because you can't believe some girl might not be interested in you. Stop looking for reasons that aren't there."

"But Vicki, I'm just trying to understand."

She got up, ran over to where I was standing, grabbed my face with both hands and started shaking my head. "I just don't love you, Carl. Can you get that through your thick head?" After releasing me from her grip, she pointed at herself, then at me, while saying, "Jane no love Tarzan. Got it? Now get the *fuck* out of here."

I was startled, shocked, distraught and thoroughly beaten. While standing there, I could see her silhouette slowly fade away into the darkness of another room. My first reaction was to follow her and apologize, but it made more sense to leave. As I got down to the front entrance I noticed the stupid cat was waiting on the other side of the door so I held both the exterior and inner doors open to let it in. It was soaking wet and looked more like a wet sponge that needed to be squeezed. Just then I realized my umbrella was still in Vicki's apartment, but I was in no mood to go back up. My legs just started moving and I found myself walking along Second Avenue in the wrong direction. I wasn't ready to just head home. It was funny in a way, but the evening couldn't have gone much worse. I'd never heard her curse before, and it was very hard to take. Certainly a moment that I'd never forget. Perhaps I had struck a nerve, but who cared? Regardless of the reasons for it, the girl didn't love me, she never would, and it was stupid of me to try to find out why. Maybe *she* was right. Maybe she just didn't like me, and there was nothing more to it. Anyway, it wasn't the best way to start my forty-fifth year.

Chapter 33

Kavi took advantage of the Christmas week and New Year's holiday to spend time with his family and friends. It would be his last December in the States, and a chance to achieve some closure with respect to this phase of his life. Aarti was a tremendous influence, and helped him maintain a positive attitude. In her mind, he'd been blessed with a charmed life, and the ordeal was just an obstacle he needed to overcome. She helped keep his focus on their future together and what they had to do to make things turn out right. Her efforts paid off, and Kavi entered the New Year with a renewed sense of purpose and the strength to finish the Plan and leave his troubles behind.

It was Tuesday, January 6, and the first order of business was Kavi's weekly trip to the US Court House, with Henry Jackson at his side. Gil Robeson generally didn't attend the weekly sessions and, in any case, was out of town on a skiing trip, and wouldn't be back until the end of the week. Neither Henry nor Kavi could imagine what it would be like to see the portly securities lawyer out on the slopes. But they both agreed that if they were there, they'd make sure to stay out of his way.

There wasn't much to do, and they expected to take up less than fifteen minutes of the court's time. Aside from just checking in, the only matter on the agenda was the delay of the trial date beyond January 15. Both sides had discussed the matter at some length, and although different start dates were discussed, a day in mid-April seemed to make the most sense. The time in front of the judge was expected to be brief, but Kavi nonetheless had to be patient and wait until called. As it turned out, it was a busy day for the court, and after two hours, he was still waiting. Henry spent most of that time using his Blackberry or his cell phone in the hall, but Kavi didn't have any work to do, so he stayed in the courtroom and watched the other proceedings. It kept his interest for a while, but soon enough he became bored, and started getting restless.

Gary Bevins and Dennis Smith finally arrived, and Kavi caught a glimpse of them out of the corner of his eye. They were joined by two of their colleagues and made their way to a row of seats near the front. Shortly thereafter, Henry returned to his seat, and said it wouldn't be long before they were called. When their time finally came, they both walked to the front and were joined by the government personnel. The judge spent a few minutes with some procedural matters, and was about to address the trial date when Dennis asked for permission to address the court.

"Your honor, the government requests that the trial date not be delayed. We will be fully prepared to make our case if the trial begins as scheduled on Thursday, January 15."

This caught Henry completely by surprise, and Kavi didn't know quite what to think. He wasn't planning on leaving the country until the end of February and had no idea how long his trial would last. For all he knew, if they kept the original date, it could be over before he had a chance to leave. He whispered to Henry, asking what it all meant. But Henry didn't know, so he put his arm on Kavi's shoulder and asked him to wait.

"Your honor, may I speak?" Henry asked. He was about to continue, but stopped when the judge held up his hand.

The judge was also confused and carefully studied Dennis before asking, "What's going on? I've understood you were amenable to a three month delay. What's behind the government's sudden change of heart?"

Dennis swallowed hard and said, "Your honor, it is true we have discussed deferring the initial trial date beyond January 15. However, it has always been the government's intention that any such delay be used to facilitate the possibility of reaching a plea agreement." Dennis stopped and quickly glanced at Kavi, then back at the judge. "But as the government has informed the court, we believe the defendant has no intention of discussing a plea in good faith, and furthermore—"

Henry interrupted, "Your honor, if I may, at no time has the government made us aware of any connection of the trial date to progress with plea discussions. In fact, it was the government that suggested an April date in the first place. They're saying that we're not acting in good faith. But this is the first I've heard of their desire to stick with January 15, and if that's not a sign of bad faith I don't know what is."

"But your honor, it should be noted that—" Dennis stopped speaking as soon as the judge raised his hands again.

"Gentlemen, I'm sure everybody's dealing in good faith." The judge took a moment to look up at the clock and sighed. He looked down at Henry and asked, "I take it you won't be ready January 15?"

"No your honor, we will not," Henry admitted.

Dennis asked, "Your honor, may I continue?" The judge nodded with a less than enthusiastic approval. "Contrary to Mr. Jackson's assertion, the government has on many occasions stressed its sincere desire to arrive at a fair and equitable plea agreement. Unfortunately, as evidenced by the complete lack of progress at the December conference, it has become clear to the government, and we have concluded, that a plea in this matter will likely not be achieved."

The judge wasn't amused and didn't hesitate before jumping in. "So you don't think you can conclude a mutually acceptable agreement. That may be the case, but it sounds more like a self-fulfilling prophecy to me." The judge held up his hand to keep Dennis from interrupting. "But Mr. Smith, as you may know, today is Tuesday, January 6, and it's past noon for that matter. Why is it suddenly so important to start this trial in nine days?"

"There are a number of reasons, your honor." Dennis took a deep breath, and then continued, "Any delay in the trial date will prejudice the government's interests. As you know, our resources have been severely strained and we're handling an unusually large number of cases at this time. Yesterday we added two more cases in front of this court and have two more to add later in the week. We're ready to move forward with this case and would appreciate the opportunity to do so in order to expedite the release of our personnel to address other matters. In these very difficult times, it is—"

The judge was making a habit of holding up his hand, and he did it again. "Mr. Smith, I'm aware of all the fine efforts being put forth by the Department of Justice. All I need to do is read the papers to know that. But please leave the speeches for the press." He looked at Gary Bevins, and then he winked at Henry. "Now you say you have other reasons? Can you give them to me in four words or less?" Gary leaned over and whispered in Dennis's ear. Then Dennis whispered something back. After a moment, the judge intervened. "Gentlemen, you can use five words, if that makes it any easier for you."

"It will also be in the accused's best interests," Dennis responded.

"That's nine words, but not bad," the judge deadpanned.

"Your honor, may I ask how a January 15 trial date can possibly be in our best interests?" Henry asked.

The judge laughed, and looked at Dennis. "I think that's a very fair question. We're all ears, counselor."

Dennis tapped Gary on the shoulder to prod him to reply. "Your honor, may I speak?" The judge nodded, and Gary continued, "We also wish to request that the accused be held in pre-trial confinement as of and after today. Although the court has taken possession of his passport, we nonetheless believe there is a serious risk that he will attempt to leave the country before commencement of the trial. If you grant the government's request, it will be in the interest of the accused to begin the trial as soon as possible, in order to minimize the period of incarceration, should he be found innocent of the charges."

Kavi couldn't believe what was being said. He had never heard the term pre-trial confinement before, but he knew it meant going to jail until the trial was finished. Henry said something to the judge and Gary responded, but Kavi lost track of the discussion. All sorts of things were racing through his mind and he couldn't concentrate on what was being said. What happened to make the government conclude he might leave the country? Was there some flaw in the Plan? Did something go wrong in Switzerland? He started to feel faint but realized it was critical that he pull himself together, not wanting to provide any clues as to his true intentions. He started thinking about the football playoffs to clear his mind and calm his nerves, and after a few minutes he more or less succeeded. The judge was talking, and Kavi was able to focus on what he was saying.

"So some other guy skips town, and now you think you'll lose *him*?" the judge asked, pointing to Kavi.

Gary responded, "Your honor, may I remind you that the accused is Indian."

"Is that so?" the judge asked. "I have his passport, and it says he's a US citizen."

"With all due respect, your honor, we've done our research, and he and his wife have a great many relatives in India." Gary looked over at Kavi, then back at the judge. "If he leaves, we'll never get him back, and justice will not be served."

Before Henry could respond, he was asked to hold his comments. The judge wanted both sides to remain quiet until he had a chance to collect his thoughts. He rubbed his eyes, scribbled a note to himself then looked down at Henry. "Mr. Jackson, I'm sure the government's request must come as a complete surprise to you. I can't say it's anything that I had expected, and it's quite unusual in a case like this. Nonetheless, this court does have an obligation to give their request serious consideration. Now, on the one hand, I know your client has complied with all orders of this court and has shown no indication that he won't be here to stand trial. But on the other hand, the government may have valid reasons to keep him in custody. In any case, I would agree with their contention that, should pre-trial confinement be granted, we can't wait for April to start. Can you be ready with a three-week delay?"

In the three seconds it took Henry to respond, Kavi thought about what the judge had just said, and realized there was a chance he wouldn't be going home for the evening, or leaving the country for that matter. Why else would the judge ask about a three-week delay? Kavi looked around the room, and wondered if there was some way he'd be able to escape. He wasn't seriously thinking about it, but even if he was, there was such heavy security as a consequence of September 11th that he'd never stand a chance.

Henry said, "Your honor, I don't think I can respond at this time."

The judge looked down at Kavi, studying him closely. He glanced quickly at Gary, and then looked up at the clock and took a deep breath. "Gentlemen, let's reconvene at 3 pm. This will be the first matter on the afternoon docket. And, Mr. Jackson, please understand I would like you to remain with your client until that time. I'm sure you can find a nice place to eat nearby."

* * * *

Henry knew a decent restaurant two blocks away. Although the service could be very slow, the food was good, and they did have over two hours to kill before they had to be back in court. On the walk over, Henry was complaining about the government's bad faith, but Kavi had too much on his mind to talk. He didn't even know how he should act. If he appeared to be overly worried, Henry might get suspicious, but if he looked too calm, that might look suspicious too.

As he thought about his predicament, he realized if the judge went ahead and granted the government's motion, he could wind up with the worst of both worlds. He would be forced to stand trial, and if he lost his case he'd remain in jail, maybe for the rest of his life. But even if he were to win, he'd be forced to leave the country and take the money, otherwise the work he had done with the Plan would catch up with him. In the latter case he'd be a fugitive, with the knowledge that he had never needed to implement the Plan after all. And what an irony *that* would be, to have a jury conclude he's innocent of all the charges, have Henry stand next to him in front of the media with a very public victory, and then to leave the country shortly thereafter as nothing more than a crook. It was such a crazy story, he imagined it could be made into one hell of a movie.

At the restaurant, Henry did most of the talking while Kavi played with his food and pretended to pay attention. Whatever Henry said didn't mean a thing.

All that mattered was what the judge would do, and he would do it at 3 pm, which was shaping up to be the most important moment in Kavi's life. He kept checking his watch every few minutes because he wanted the moment to hurry up and arrive so he could learn his fate and move on, but time seemed to be moving in slow motion. So he kept hitting his watch to speed it up. That didn't work, so he slipped into the bathroom to call Marc and update him about the morning's developments. Of course he couldn't get into any details, but Marc understood. He said he was really surprised, and wanted Kavi to call as soon as he knew where he stood.

They finished lunch, and on their way back Henry's cell phone rang, so he stopped to take the call. Kavi walked a few feet ahead to a vendor selling papers on the corner. Looking back, he could see that Henry was concentrating on the call and wondered if this was his last chance to escape. He looked across the street and figured he could get away, call his wife, and meet her somewhere but they'd need to make their way to Houston. He wasn't prepared for it, and it would be risky. Henry would be required to alert the court and there'd be a good chance they'd be caught. He nixed the idea just as Henry finished his call.

* * * *

Although the judge said they'd reconvene at 3, it was 3:30 and they were still waiting around. Kavi didn't know if he could take it any more when the judge finally walked in and they were ready to begin. When the judge started speaking, Kavi felt his whole body become numb.

"The government has requested pre-trial confinement and, assuming the request is granted, has asked that we retain the January 15 trial date. This court does not have sufficient information with which to make a decision on the matter at this time. Therefore, I order a pre-trial hearing to be held on Friday, January 9, to further explore the merits of the government's request. I anticipate a decision can be made at or shortly after the hearing. Of course, this leads us to the question of what to do with the accused until then." The judge paused and looked down at Kavi, who was holding his breath and about to pass out. Then the judge continued, "It is the judgment of this court that the accused be released to the custody of his counsel, pending the Friday hearing."

* * * *

Right after Kavi called, I cut things off at work and headed straight for his house. He told me what had happened in court during the day and it was one heck of a development. As a consequence, it would be his last chance to say goodbye, and he and Aarti wanted me to get to their place as soon as possible. They'd also asked Ken and Marc to come. Once Kavi told me what had happened, I knew he had to leave, since he couldn't take a chance by sticking around to see how the judge would rule. And, as it turned out, he was very fortunate to have been given a couple of days to get away.

On my way over, I realized there'd be no reason for me to go to Switzerland again. Since Kavi had to leave anyway, he might as well make it to the Lorenz firm's office and take care of things himself. Although the latest developments were forcing him to leave about six weeks sooner than he had planned, my efforts had still given him a big head start.

Pulling up in his driveway, I could see that Marc and Ken had already arrived. They must have done the same thing I had done, and dropped everything to leave as soon as they got the news. Kavi had spotted me, and stood waiting at his front door, apparently in a great mood.

As we shook hands, I asked, "Why the big smile?"

"I faced death today and survived." He replied, while grabbing my shoulder to escort me into his living room to join the others. "Come on in and grab a beer. We might as well use whatever we've got. After all, we can't take any of it with us."

"Did I miss much?"

"Just a little of Aarti's crying and hugging," Ken said, while relaxing in a reclining chair in the living room. He pointed his apparently empty beer can toward the kitchen area. "Sanji and Kris are with Aarti in the kitchen. You should say hello."

I made my way down the hall, and gave Aarti a big hug and could see that Ken was right. She'd been crying and couldn't hide it. Sanji wasn't as emotional. She walked over to greet me and, while kissing her on the cheek, I could see Kris out of the corner of my eye. He had remained seated at the table in the breakfast room and was staring out the window with sort of a blank expression on his face. When I said hello, he didn't acknowledge me, and Aarti quickly apologized, but I told her not to make a big fuss. We all knew that Kris was having a difficult time dealing with the situation, and with what had happened during the day it couldn't have gotten any easier for him. I thought about giving him some helpful advice, but didn't have any to give, and figured he was old enough and smart enough to understand what was happening and it was perfectly appropriate for him to be upset. So I said nothing and headed off to the living room to join the guys. It was funny, but when I got there, as usual Marc was busy asking questions.

"So you're sure about this? You know the judge may not grant the government's motion."

"I just can't take that chance," Kavi said. He was leaning against the armrest of his couch and I recalled that many times Aarti had warned him against doing that, for fear it would break. I guess he didn't care about his furniture any more. He continued, "There's no way I'm setting foot in that courtroom again."

"You're making the right move," Ken said. "At this point you have to leave, and thank heavens you're getting the chance to go. From what you said, it sounds like you had a close call today."

"You just can't imagine what it was like at lunch. It was the longest two hours of my life. Then, when we got back to court, the son of a bitch judge was over thirty minutes late. I was so scared, and it was all building up inside of me. When he said I'd be free until Friday, I was so relieved I had to think about football so they couldn't tell anything from my body language. The first thing I thought about after splitting up with Henry was to call you guys to see if you could come over. It would have been terrible if we didn't get a chance to say goodbye."

"So how'd you leave it with Henry?" Marc asked.

Kavi laughed and replied, "We scheduled a meeting for Thursday afternoon at his office. That gives him some time to prepare, and we can both go over his proposed strategy before our Friday date with the court. Of course, I'll be in Mexico Thursday."

"So what's the full itinerary?" Ken asked.

"Aarti and I will drive to Philadelphia early tomorrow morning and from there we'll fly to Houston."

"Why Philadelphia?" I asked.

"I had to book the flight using our real names and I thought the government might have alerted the New York airports."

"I doubt they'd do that," Marc said. "Not for a domestic flight anyway."

"I'm not taking any chances. I feel much safer leaving from Philadelphia. After that, I've made arrangements to get a plane I can fly from Houston to Monterrey in northern Mexico. Believe me, you don't want to know any of those details. Then, early Thursday morning, we have a flight to Mexico City, where we'll stay until Saturday when Aarti's uncle can meet us. He'll have Indian passports for us and we'll leave Mexico together on Sunday."

"You arranged all of that since you got home today?" Marc asked.

"Keep in mind it's the way we were planning on leaving in late February. Except for the Philadelphia part. I just had to speed up the trip."

I added, "But if the government starts looking Thursday, they may find your Houston flight and know you went on to Mexico while you'd still be there."

"He'll be gone by then," Marc said, talking like he had suddenly become an expert on the subject. "Henry may try to alert the court late Thursday when you don't show up for the meeting, but it's more likely he'll do that Friday morning. I think he'll first spend some time trying to reach you, and he probably won't even think your leaving is a possibility. On Friday, the government will move as fast as they can, but the first thing they'll do is check international flights. I'll bet they don't find out about your Houston flight until Monday at the earliest, but even if they found out before you left Mexico, there's not much they can do about it. Once you get to Mexico you're in the clear."

We spent some more time talking about the arrangements. Kavi said they'd make their way to Europe first. I asked Marc and Ken to leave the room so Kavi and I could talk about some details with respect to the Plan. Ken remained, but Marc went to the kitchen to talk to Aarti and the kids. Kavi said he had all the tax information ready and would deliver it to the Lorenz firm in Lausanne sometime next week, so I should just cancel my Paris trip. That was fine by me. January was a very busy month anyway, and I wasn't looking forward to flying to Paris just so I could take an overnight train trip to Switzerland and then back. The Plan was now completely in Kavi's hands and my days as his sidekick were over. I was comfortable that what I'd done had given him just the edge he needed to ensure success.

When we finished the discussion, we joined the others in the kitchen area. Aarti wound up cooking pot luck with everything she had, so there was a wonderful buffet laid out on the kitchen counter. We made some jokes about how much food she still had in the house, but we knew she didn't expect to be leaving so soon. We talked about what it would be like cooking in India, and then discussed what they'd miss most about the States. The latter topic appeared to depress Aarti and she wanted to change the subject. Unfortunately, she did so by asking if I had heard from Vicki.

"The way we left things, I think it's safe to say she won't be contacting me again." While pouring a glass of a soon-to-be-needed beer, I continued, "I'm glad all the arrangements for your trusts have been finished because I wouldn't be comfortable working with her again."

"Kavi told me. I'm sorry," Aarti said, looking as if it disappointed her more than it did me. "And I'm surprised."

"I was too," Ken said. "You two looked so good together at the party. I thought you'd finally found the one."

Marc was busy preparing his plate when he chimed in. "You basically predicted it. Remember, just before she arrived at the party, you told me what you thought she would say, and you were right."

"Yeah," I said. "It seems that I'm a regular Nostradamus."

Aarti carefully studied my face and remarked, "You look ok."

"It took a week or so, but now I'm fine. I have experience with this you know." Truth be told, I really wasn't fine. My insides still felt like they'd been ripped out. Although I was proud of myself for handling it as well as I could, doing my best each day to force her out of my mind. But it didn't help that they had brought up the subject, so I tried to get them to move on to something else. I asked, "So what happens with the house?"

"Who knows?" Kavi replied. "Of course the kids will have the keys, but at some point I expect ADG will get it. You know, after they find out about the switch in the tax payment."

"It's a shame," Aarti said. "After all the years. The kids should keep it. That would be best."

"I don't want it," Kris announced. "And after tomorrow, I'll never come back here again."

Sanji started saying something about her taking care of the place, but while she was speaking, I heard Kris say under his breath that by the end of the summer there wouldn't be any Chanders left in the US.

"So this is it then?" Marc asked.

Kavi sighed and replied, "It is."

Marc studied him carefully and asked, "And you'll be ok?"

"We'll be fine."

"So let me propose a toast," Marc said, as we all raised our glasses. "To Kavi, Aarti, Sanji and Kris, may they find happiness, peace and prosperity in the old world."

Kavi looked at his kids and pointed at Ken, Marc and me. "I hope you find friends like these, friends who would do anything for you, and would stay by your side through thick and thin."

Ken asked us to raise our glasses again. "And here's to the Iron Horse Club. It's been twenty five-years and we're still together. And no ocean can split us up. This isn't the end, gentlemen. It's not even the beginning of the end."

He continued with his impersonation of Winston Churchill after the Battle of Britain. We shared a few more toasts, relived some old stories, and made the best of Kavi's last day. None of us wanted the evening to end but it was getting late and he and Aarti had to get up early to begin their rather long journey, and they hadn't even packed. Finally the time came, and we said our goodbyes to Aarti and the kids.

The four of us found our way to the driveway in front of the house. I watched as Kavi said goodbye to Marc and gave him a big hug. They just held each other with their eyes closed without saying a word. Then Marc got into his car, shook his head and drove off.

Ken was next to leave. He also gave Kavi a hug, and I could have sworn there were tears in Ken's eyes. He managed to maintain his manly composure. Keeping a stiff upper lip, he got into his car, gave Kavi the thumbs up and drove away.

Then it was my turn to go.

"We'll never forget what you did for us," Kavi said.

"I'm just glad I could help. And you know you're going to get the money. I don't think there's any way they can figure this all out by the end of February."

"I know," Kavi said. "And I can never repay you."

"Sure you can. Make sure you two get the hell out of the country tomorrow."

"We will. And we'll be thinking of you guys every step of the way."

"And don't worry about your kids. While they're still here, they've got Ken, Marc and me. So don't you worry, ok?"

"We'll worry about you," Kavi admitted.

"I'll be fine."

We hugged, and it was hard to let go. We were sure to see each other again, but we didn't know when or where. Stepping back, there wasn't much more to say. After getting into the car, I gave him one last look, and then made my way down his driveway and out onto the street. As I drove off, I took one more glance back in the rear view mirror and could see that he still hadn't moved. But then I turned the corner, and for all intents and purposes he was gone.

Chapter 34

It was 3 pm, and if the firm knew just how unproductive I had become, I'd have probably been fired. My office was full of paperwork, but all I could think about was Kavi, and his multinational trek to the promised land. It was Friday, January 9, so that placed him somewhere in Mexico City. I figured he was at his hotel, sitting by the pool with a margarita in hand, and enjoying the weather and his new found freedom. I envied him, since I was stuck in the middle of my firm's busy season and had to deal with New York City and its freezing temperatures.

Undoubtedly the feds were already on the alert, since Kavi never did make an appearance at the morning's hearing. I wondered what it must have been like when Henry Jackson told the judge he had come alone. I'd have given anything to have seen the look on Gary Bevins' face when he first got the news.

My radio was on low, and was tuned to a round-the-clock news channel. I was hoping to catch something about Kavi becoming a fugitive from the law, but there was still no word. I wondered if Gary might have been too embarrassed to stand in public and admit that he'd lost his man, or maybe he was keeping it quiet until he could make up some sort of pro-government, and pro-Gary, spin. Regardless of what he was doing, he must have been having a very bad day.

Actually, I wasn't doing that well myself. Everything had happened so quickly during the week, and I didn't have much time to think about what it would all mean to me. But now that it was over, it hit me that my best friend was gone for good. Sure, he would be ok, and maybe we'd see each other every couple of years, but he was out of my daily life forever. Ken and Marc were still around, but somehow things wouldn't be the same, not without Kavi.

At least the other guys had their families, but other than my mother, there was no one for me. While feeling sorry for myself, I got the urge to call Kim Darcy to see if we could get together, but I hadn't spoken to her in over five months, so I passed on that idea. Then I thought about Vicki, but that made me feel like an alcoholic who had been sober for three weeks and was about to take a drink, so I took some time to force her out of my mind. I was actually somewhat relieved when Ken called to interrupt my brooding.

"Heard any news?" he asked.

"No, and I've had the radio on all day. I thought we'd hear something by now."

"It seems strange doesn't it? Now that he's gone."

"I miss him already."

"We all do," Ken admitted.

"I have this feeling that if I walk over to ADG's offices right now, he'll be there."

"It's the end of an era pal."

"So we'll start a new one."

After he hung up, I stared at the paperwork on my desk—and it stared right back—although I did my best to at least pretend to be an accounting firm partner at work. Fortunately, I did have all of the following week available, since there was no need to fly to Paris. If I had made the trip, I had planned to take work with me, but I'd never been good at doing anything but read or sleep on planes, and Paris was too beautiful a city in which to work, so I would probably have accomplished little or nothing. In a way, Mr. Bevins had done me a favor.

I figured I had done enough procrastinating for the afternoon, so I turned off the radio, forced everything else out of my mind, and got myself busy. Work was actually getting done, and it wasn't until 8 pm that I hit a breaking point and looked up. I'd be back in the office over the weekend, so it was as good a time as any to leave.

While walking out, I decided to take a quick detour. Instead of heading straight for the elevator, I turned to walk toward Kavi's old office—the one he'd had when he was a partner in the firm. The door was unlocked, so I walked in and took a look around. Partners are the only ones in the firm who don't share their offices with someone else, so he was the first in our group to get his private space, and we envied his ability to close the door and be alone. His old furniture was still there, including a leather couch on the side that was pretty worn now, but it had been brand new when he first moved in. It wasn't unusual for the two of us to be working late on a Friday night, and I would stop by his office and relax on that couch before going home, and we'd talk about anything and everything. Oftentimes while I was there, Aarti would call and blame me for keeping him at the office too long. It seemed like a good idea to sit on the couch one more time, just for old time's sake. As I made myself comfortable, I looked over and really thought I could see him sitting there with shirt sleeves rolled up and his feet up on the desk, and he was telling me to relax, that he was in a good place, and I should take the ball he left behind and run with it. Just then, someone from the janitorial department walked in to clean the office, and as I walked out, it seemed prudent to stop thinking about the past.

On my way home, I was listening to some oldies-but-goodies station and not really thinking about anything in particular, when I decided to switch to the news station once again to check for any word about Kavi. This particular news station said if you give them twenty-two minutes they would give you the world, so I figured I'd listen for that amount of time and, if I didn't hear anything, I'd switch back to music. I was crossing the George Washington Bridge about five minutes later when I heard.

"In late breaking news, federal authorities have indicated that the wreckage of a plane which crashed late Wednesday evening in Kingsville, Texas, contained the body of Kavi Chander, a senior officer of American Dynamics Group, who was scheduled to stand trial in New York later this month on charges of securities fraud. Chander, who was accompanied by another passenger, believed to be his wife, apparently attempted to make an emergency landing at a small airfield in Kingsville during a severe storm. Authorities do not know why Chander was in Texas, or where he was going at the time of the crash."

I crossed the bridge, took the first exit, pulled over at the side of the road and just sat in my car staring at the radio. I'm not sure how long I was sitting there, but at some point I picked up my cell phone and hit the number for Marc Abrams.

"Did you hear the news?" I asked.

"What news?"

"You didn't hear? Kavi and Aarti are dead." The line was silent and I thought he'd hung up, so I repeated myself.

In a very soft voice he said, "That can't be."

"I heard it on the news. Their plane crashed in some small town in Texas."

"He's in Mexico City. If they'd crashed in Texas, we'd have heard something yesterday."

"Let me go. I need to call Ken."

Before calling, I thought about why it might have taken so long for the news to come out. The plane crashed Wednesday night, so they must have been examining the wreckage by Thursday morning. But they'd have to do some work to identify Kavi's body, and once they knew it was him they would probably try to reach his next of kin. That's when it hit me. What was happening with his kids? I figured I'd call Ken and then would call Sanji and Kris.

"Did you hear?" Ken asked.

"Yeah, that's why I called. Marc thinks it's not true."

"Forget Marc. As soon as I heard, I called Sanji's New York apartment, and some government social worker answered the phone. Kris was there too. The social worker said they told the kids about two hours ago, before releasing it to the press."

"So they're both really gone?"

"That's right," Ken replied.

"It's unbelievable."

"Right now we have to think about the kids."

"Maybe I'll turn around and head back there."

"No. Just head home. Jennie and I will get them and bring them to our place. They shouldn't be on their own tonight."

When I got back to the apartment, it was non-stop use of the phone. I tried calling Marc back about six different times before finally getting through. I spoke with my mother twice. When I first told her, she was so shook up we couldn't talk. It was over an hour before she called back. Ken called me really late and said Sanji and Kris were at his place. Sanji was still shook up but Kris was handling it rather well. We agreed he was probably in shock.

I was in shock too, and when the phone calls were finished, I turned off the light and collapsed on my living room couch. Lying there, my eyes adjusted to the darkness, and I could see faces of people in one of the paintings on the wall. It was as if they were staring at me, but they'd look away whenever I looked back. Finally, I started to doze off, but I didn't sleep for long. The chiming of my grandfather clock woke me up, although I was usually able to sleep through it. I was still half asleep, and when I looked across the room, I was startled to see Kavi talking to my brother Joe. But I knew it couldn't be them, so I tried to wave them away, but my arm wouldn't move. The images became clearer, and they both stood up and walked toward me. I tried to get up to greet them, but my whole body wouldn't move. They were no more than two feet away when suddenly I heard someone who sounded like Vicki laughing in one of the other rooms. Kavi and Joe pointed to my bedroom and motioned for me to follow them as they walked back. I struggled to get up but just couldn't do it. They got to the end of the hallway when Vicki, or whoever it was, called out. They looked at me one last time, then walked toward her voice and out of sight. Although I remembered trying to get my legs to move, I suddenly found myself staring at my hand and managed to get it to move. It took me a moment but I was finally able to stand up and made my way to the bedroom. No one was there.

Saturday morning arrived to find me lying on my couch, which was rather peculiar, because I didn't recall coming back to the living room the night before. I was still a little spooked, so to be on the safe side, I walked around my apartment and checked every room carefully to confirm that I was, indeed, alone.

Later in the day, I got word that the funeral would take place on Sunday. The two bodies were being flown back to New Jersey, and would be held in a mortuary not far from their home. I was told that the normal practice in Kavi's tradition was to have the funeral within twenty-four hours of the time of death, but these were exceptional circumstances. They hadn't even identified the bodies until Friday morning.

My mother and I discussed the possibility of my making it back to Brooklyn to take her to the funeral, but she was coming down with a terrible cold, and we agreed she might as well stay behind. We were sure that Kavi and Aarti would understand.

Throughout the day there were some further news reports about the crash, but not nearly as much as I had expected. Although I did get to see Gary Bevins speaking about it on one of the cable news channels, and playing it up as evidence of Kavi's guilt. Unfortunately, he had his big public victory after all. It just didn't seem right that he should be given a forum to bad mouth Kavi, while he and his wife were stuck in a casket somewhere awaiting their funeral.

I needed some fresh air so I braved the freezing cold weather and walked along Boulevard East, the route that ran past my building. The air was so crisp and clean that when you faced the city it looked like you could just reach out and touch Manhattan. A bunch of kids were playing games in a small park and I sat down at one of the nearby benches to watch. It was interesting that two of the kids looked like they were Indian. They were all having a great time, but I felt empty inside. First I lost Vicki, and then Kavi. There was nothing left inside of me to lose. I must have been deep in thought, because I suddenly noticed it was getting dark and the kids had already gone, but I didn't recall having seen them leave.

The funeral was to be held early in the morning, so I needed to at least try to get some rest. My appetite was completely gone, so I skipped dinner, curled up in my bed and immediately fell asleep. In the middle of the night I awoke to some noises that appeared to be coming from my living room. After confirming that there was nothing there, I fell back asleep but about an hour later heard the noises again. And trying to ignore it didn't make it go away. It sounded like voices and I thought I was going nuts. Once again I checked all the rooms with the same result. The lack of sleep was getting to me, and my nerves were completely frayed, so I kept the lights on like a kid who was afraid of the dark. It worked though, and the next thing I knew my alarm was going off and it was time to wake up.

I was one of the first ones to arrive at the cemetery. After parking my car, I walked to the main building where the religious ceremony would be held, and waited for others outside. Then Ken pulled up with his family, along with Sanji and Kris. When they got to where I was standing, Sanji looked at me and I didn't know what to say. She put her hand on my shoulder, reached up and kissed my cheek. I gave her a hug and watched as Kris came walking up. Without saying anything he reached out his hand and shook mine with a very firm grip. As the two of them walked inside, I thought that I was the relative and they had both consoled me.

Ken remained with me, while his wife and kids followed Sanji and Kris inside. Ken and I were both leaning against the wall just to the right of the entrance, and he was kind enough to tell me that I looked like shit. I mentioned my bout of sleep deprivation, but neglected to say anything about voices and ghosts. It wasn't very long before Marc and his family pulled up. We greeted his clan and Marc asked the two of us to take a walk while his family went inside to join the others. He commented that I looked lousy and I mentioned that I'd already heard.

When the three of us stopped at a remote section of the parking area, Marc checked in every direction as if he wanted to make sure nobody was near, and then he looked at me and said, "I have to ask you something. If Kavi hadn't died, were you still planning on helping him with the money?"

I was a little punchy and it took me a moment to realize what he'd asked. Finally I replied, "No, once he was forced to leave the country, he didn't need me anymore."

"Ok, but what happens with it now?"

"To tell you the truth, it's the last thing on my mind. So why do you suddenly care about the money after all this time?"

"Because nobody anticipated Kavi's death, and I'd like to think about how it can screw up your plans. I don't want you to get caught."

"He won't get caught," Ken said. "If he doesn't do anything else, they can't trace the money to him."

"I'd like to make sure," Marc said. "So what was Kavi going to do?"

"He was meeting with a law firm in Switzerland next week so they'd arrange to file the tax return. By the end of February the refund would be deposited in a Swiss bank account I had set up, and then he'd transfer it out and he'd be done."

"Are you sure no one in Switzerland can identify you?" Marc asked.

"Absolutely. I was very careful when I was there."

Ken put his hand on Marc's shoulder and said, "Stop worrying. Believe me, he'll be fine."

"But the company will one day follow up," Marc said. "And now, Kavi can't finish with his plans."

"So who cares?" Ken asked. "No tax return will have been filed, so the money will still be with the government and ADG will get it back. They'll think Kavi was trying to steal it, and they'll be right, but that's it. No one will learn about the Swiss account or the Swiss law firm. And the Swiss know nothing about ADG." Turning his attention to me, he added, "But just to be safe, you should contact that law firm to make sure they don't file anything, and do it before March 15, which is the original due date for the tax return."

Marc looked around again, commented on how cold it was, and then asked, "How much was it?"

"How much was what?" I asked.

"The tax refund he was going to get."

For some reason it took me a moment to recall the amount. As soon as it came back to me, I replied, "He had told me $10 million."

"It's a shame to waste it," Ken noted. He looked like he wanted someone to agree with him. When we didn't, he shrugged his shoulders and added, "Well that's what I think."

"It's the company's money," I said. "And obviously Kavi doesn't need it any more."

Marc nodded in agreement, after which he rubbed his chin and carefully studied my face. Then he quickly shook his head and said, "Ok. It seems as if you're as safe as you can be. So let's not talk about it ever again. And I'm sorry I had to bring it up."

"So let's go," Ken said. "It's freezing, and we have a funeral to attend."

After walking back, we entered the main building and followed some people through the reception area, down a long hall and into a room which looked like the inside of a small church. There were three sections of seating, each with about fifteen rows of benches. I estimated at full capacity it could probably handle slightly over two hundred people, with about half in the middle section and the rest in the two outer sections. The floor sloped down sharply until you reached the third row where it leveled off. In front of the room were two closed caskets. They were covered with flower petals and raised about four feet off the ground by what looked like funeral pyres made of reddish brown wood.

Ken joined his wife and kids who were sitting in the front row with Sanji and Kris. Marc's wife and kids were sitting behind them in the second row and Marc waved for me to follow as he walked down the aisle to join his family. I motioned him ahead and stood aside near the back, so I could watch as other people walked down the aisles and found their seats. There were a lot of Indian people who came in, as well as a bunch of people from ADG whom I recognized from Kavi's surprise party. At one point I noticed Debra Jennings walk in, accompanied only by her young son. She was wearing dark glasses, but you could still tell that she had been crying.

The ceremony was about to start so I couldn't keep standing in the back. But for some reason, I didn't feel comfortable leaving my spot. Watching Marc and Ken interact with their families, I didn't think I belonged with them. For a brief moment, I gave some thought to finding a seat in the last row, but that would have been a mistake. I had such an empty feeling inside, and it was a struggle to pull myself together and focus my thoughts on Kavi, Aarti and their kids.

Marc turned around and gestured again for me to join him, but then a strange look came over his face, and he slowly turned his head back to the front of the room. Suddenly, a warm hand took hold of mine, and I turned to see that it belonged to a teary eyed Vicki Richards. I felt a little light headed, and it took a moment for me to remember where I was. When I did, without saying a word, Vicki and I walked hand in hand to the second row and sat down next to Marc and his family.

The priest recognized that many of us had not been to a Hindu funeral before, and he began by explaining the process. He said if the ceremony had been held in India, they would have started at Kavi and Aarti's home. He would have read the Mantras and when he was through, the procession would walk through the streets to a cremation site, with the eldest son in the lead, carrying a clay pot filled with burning coal embers. The bodies would be carried by the group, on stretchers covered with flowers. Upon arrival at the cremation site, the stretchers would be placed on two separate funeral pyres made of sandalwood and other scented woods. The eldest son would then use the burning embers to set the pyres ablaze. The priest said it would take just over five hours to completely consume the bodies, but most people would leave about an hour after the fire was lit. When the process was complete, the ashes would be given to the eldest son who would typically disperse them in a holy river.

Since this wasn't India, the priest said he would read the Mantras, and then other people would be given a chance to say a few words. After that, the group would be asked to make its way to the crematorium on the premises, where the caskets would be placed in the ovens. Kris would push the button, symbolizing his lighting of the funeral pyre, after which people would be free to leave.

When the last speech was finished, Ken and I helped carry Kavi's casket to the crematorium, while Marc joined the group that carried Aarti's. Kris led the procession with Sanji walking two steps behind, and when we arrived at the crematorium we placed the caskets on a gurney which was then raised to the level of the opening of the furnace. The caskets were slid into place, and the furnace window was closed and sealed. Kris turned to embrace his sister, said a brief prayer, and then turned back and reluctantly pushed the button to start the ovens.

After about two hours, most of the people had left. The priest said they would keep the furnace going for another four hours and said the kids didn't need to wait around. When the process was finished they would collect the ashes and hold them on behalf of the family until Kris and Sanji decided what to do. Kris said he might make arrangements to have them taken to India and dispersed in the Ganges River.

We all walked out to the parking lot and said goodbye. Vicki and I watched as the others drove away, and I looked at her and had absolutely no idea what to say.

"You look so tired," she said, while gently running her fingers along my brow.

"Yeah, Ken told me that I look like shit."

"I wouldn't put it that way."

"I know. You're more diplomatic." Our bodies seemed to be walking in the direction of her car, which was about fifty feet away. While walking, I continued, "I've been having trouble getting to sleep. I keep seeing visions and hearing things."

"That doesn't sound surprising," she said. "After all, you two were very close."

"That we were. You know, with my brother I had some time to prepare, but with Kavi......well, his death came out of nowhere."

"When I first heard the news, I thought they'd made some big mistake. I mean, why would he be in a small plane in Texas?"

"It's a long story Vicki, and it's not what you're thinking. Well, maybe it is what you're thinking, but believe me, there's a lot to it."

"You don't need to explain," she said. "I know he was a good person."

We stopped near the driver's side of her car, turned to face each other, and simultaneously took deep breaths. I took hold of her hand and said, "It means a lot that you came here today. I was feeling so alone. Having you with me really helped."

"I'm glad."

"So what made you decide to come?"

"I wanted to pay my respects." After a brief pause she continued, "But I also wanted to see you." It looked like she wanted to say something more, but instead she reached into her purse to get the keys, and then unlocked the door. She opened it about half way and stopped. With her eyes still focused on the door, she said, "Carl, I really don't want to go right home."

"Actually, I was hoping you wouldn't go."

We were both relieved, and we agreed to go to dinner at a restaurant near my apartment. She followed me, and on the drive over, I realized I didn't know why she wanted to see me or where dinner could possibly lead. But I was too exhausted to really think about it, and figured it was out of my hands anyway.

We got to the restaurant and took a booth with a window, near the entrance. There was a radiator nearby running at full blast and Vicki had to remove her sweater so she didn't suffocate from the heat. She just pulled it over her head in such a way that her shirt was disheveled and her hair was a mess. She didn't seem to care and I had never seen her look that way before. But from what everyone had been telling me that day, I didn't look too good myself.

"So you wanted to see me?" I asked.

"Sure. Are you surprised?"

"Actually, I was sure I'd never see you again."

"I'm really very sorry," she said.

"Don't be. You had every right to do what you did. I was the one that was pushing. You know, that last time we were together seems like it was a lifetime ago."

"It was."

Reaching out to hold her hand, I said, "And now you're here."

"Yes, I'm here."

"So you'll head back to Manhattan after dinner?"

"I don't know." She sighed, looked out the window and said, "The feeling to stay with you is very strong." As she said that, she squeezed my hand.

We ordered our dinner, and while she ate I recalled some stories about Kavi and his past. I did tell her about his desire to leave the country, but didn't say anything about the financial aspects of the Plan, and shared nothing about my involvement. She sat patiently and listened while I reminisced. It was a much needed release of some of the tension that had been building since getting word of Kavi's death. Then I realized I was doing most of the talking and wanted to hear something from her.

"You're so quiet," I said.

"It's nice to hear you talk."

"I must admit it feels great to get some of this off my chest. It's helping me deal with it."

"And you're helping me too," she said.

"I am?"

"You are. The holidays were very tough. I gave a lot of thought to what you had said, about my father and about me. I don't want to talk about it now. But I will tell you it feels much better being here with you than sitting alone in my apartment."

"So you didn't have some big date for New Year's Eve?"

"No, I just spent a quiet evening at home."

After paying the check, we decided to walk back to my apartment so we could continue to talk. It was interesting, but I wasn't really thinking about the idea of the two of us being alone at my place. I was just too tired, and from the looks of it, so was she.

She sat down on my couch and I explained how I had slept on it the night Kavi's crash was reported and how I had visions of him and my brother. I also told her about the voices coming from one of the other rooms and how I had thought it was her. She said she'd spent that night thinking about me.

I turned on some soft music and sat down next to her. She put her head on my shoulder and started to slowly caress my hair. With each stroke of her hand, the demons that had been with me for two days were being brushed further and further away. Then my body became partially numb when I felt her lips gently kissing the back of my neck. We held each other and listened to the music for what seemed like hours, and when my grandfather clock chimed at 2 am I knew it was too late for her to leave.

We walked into my bedroom hand in hand and when we reached my bed she turned and began to slowly remove my clothes. As she was undoing my shirt I leaned in to smell her hair and inhale her perfume. When she was through, I began to undress her, like a boy who was seeing a woman for the first time, and as she stood in front of me I kneeled down and ran my hand gently up and down her body while she caressed the side of my face. She sat down on my bed with her hands by her hips, while keeping her eyes focused on mine, and without turning her head she pushed her way back to the middle of the bed and I followed so I could lie down beside her. She slowly ran her hand down my body and gently massaged me while I felt the desire building up inside. She leaned back and put her hand on my face and I touched it to make sure it was real, and when I did, all of the feelings that I had for her, that had been forced to the back of my mind since we had last been together, were suddenly released and flowed toward her like a fast moving river, and I was caught in the current and found myself on top of her as the two of us became one.

Sometime later, before the sun came up, I awoke and watched her as she lay sleeping. And as I watched, it felt as if she had become a part of me, and I had become a part of her. If there had been any doubt about my feelings, it was long gone, and at that moment I knew she loved me too. Looking toward the door in the darkness, I wondered if I would have been able to spend another night in my apartment alone, but with her next to me, there were no visions to be seen, and the only noise was the sound of her breathing, which was soothing, and I soon fell back asleep.

Chapter 35

It was Thursday, March 4, and I was getting myself organized to meet Vicki after work for dinner. Our getting together was becoming pretty much routine. Somehow my clothes were finding their way to her apartment—I was spending most of my weekday evenings there—and I kept finding her lying next to me on weekend mornings at my place. It was a wonderful arrangement, although I was still grieving for Kavi and Aarti and would be for some time.

Vicki and I had become a couple, and the walls around her were gone. Actually, they weren't gone, but we'd apparently managed to punch a hole through one of them, and there was just enough room for me to squeeze through. We both discovered that she could love a man, and as luck would have it, that man was me. That revelation, combined with the trauma of our December breakup and Kavi's death, had prodded her to finally confront her demons. Shortly after the funeral, she agreed to seek professional help, and she began seeing a therapist in late January. I didn't know much about the progress to date—the therapist encouraged her to keep details of the sessions to herself, at least for the time being—but I understood there was some evidence she'd been abused by her father at a very young age. We did consider the possibility of trying to research information about her dad, but decided it would be best to let the therapy take its course. There would always be time to find him later, if that proved to be desirable.

On the lighter side of things, although it had only been about six weeks since I'd brought Vicki to meet my mother, she was already welcomed as a possible future part of our family. My mom was treating her like the daughter she'd never had, and Vicki ate up all the attention. Aside from that, they both agreed they could coordinate their efforts to keep close tabs on me.

After leaving work, I headed for our favorite Mexican restaurant, and met Vicki just inside the front entrance. It was too cold to eat outside, so we did the next best thing and grabbed a table along the front with a decent view. After getting settled, we started what had become our little routine. She would briefly tell me about her day, and I'd proceed to bore her to death with way too much information about mine. She was so sweet though, and she'd sit patiently and listen, or at least pretend to listen.

We'd been sharing so much with each other, but I never did give her any details about the Plan. Somehow I now felt an obligation to tell her, like it was some meaningful information about me and she had a right to know. It had been on my mind lately because I'd been thinking about Ken's suggestion that I contact the Swiss law firm and tell them to stop all work. I had to call soon, because the due date for the corporate tax return was ten days away, and there was a chance they'd file a form to request more time.

"Earth to Carl, are you here?" Vicki asked.

"I'm sorry. My mind had drifted."

"So you're bored with me already?"

"I'll never be bored with you. So what did I miss?"

"Well, I was just saying it might be time for us to leave the country."

It was music to my ears to hear her say that. I leaned in, took hold of her hand and asked, "So what did you have in mind?"

"I was thinking about going back to Istanbul, and it could be our first trip together."

"You figure I could keep up with you if we limit the trip to one city?"

"You won't keep up. Not with what I have planned."

Suddenly her energy and enthusiasm came pouring out onto the table. So much so that I had to let go of her hand. It was fun to watch, and for the next fifteen minutes she was the one doing the talking, telling me about her first trip to Turkey, her one day in Istanbul, her research into the city—I never knew it had once been the capital of the Roman Empire—her prioritization of all the key sights she wanted to see, and her ideas as to how to squeeze it all in. She was right. Not only would I not keep up with her, but I was exhausted just listening to her telling me about it. My suggestion was that I stay back in the hotel and guard our stuff. After Turkey, we started talking about other possible trips, and when we got to India, I realized it was time to come clean.

"So Vicki, you never asked if I knew about Kavi's plans to leave the country."

I must have caught her by surprise. She sat back in her chair and looked out the window, and for a moment I thought she hadn't heard what I'd said. But then she turned to me and responded, "Maybe it's better to leave certain things in the past."

"Perhaps, but I think I need to share this with you." While drinking more than half my glass of water, I wondered if I was making a mistake. I was afraid of what she might think of me after learning the truth. But I gathered my courage, put down the glass and said, "There is something I'd like to tell you about Kavi's plans, and it involves me, and in ways you can't imagine."

"You sure you want to share this with me?"

I nodded, and proceeded to tell her everything about the Plan, from the first time we discussed it back in September, through my involvement in Switzerland, and up through the time of the crash. While I was speaking, her body language provided no clues as to what she was thinking, and when my confession was through, I waited for her absolution.

She looked out the window again, and had to quickly cover her mouth after letting out a brief but rather loud laugh. Smiling, she turned to me and said, "You guys are incredible."

"You're not upset?"

"Why would I be? You were willing to take big risks to help a friend, and that says a lot about you." She leaned in across the table to give me a kiss, and her lips confirmed that my telling her was the right thing to do. It felt as if a weight had been lifted from my shoulder.

As she sat back in her chair, I could tell the wheels were spinning inside her head. She smiled and asked, "Why wouldn't he take more?"

"All he wanted was $10 million. I told you money didn't mean much to him."

"But with all that effort, and being a fugitive," she leaned in toward me and continued in a whisper, "The way I would do it, I'd need much more."

"You've given the matter some thought?" I asked.

"Oh, I've dreamed about it, what it would be like if I hooked up with one of my rich clients and left the country. For my money, it would be Australia."

"Australia? I would have thought you'd say some exotic island."

"I'd live just outside Brisbane, in a house on the Gold Coast. The beaches there are the best in the world. And I'd also have an apartment in Sydney. It's like a smaller and cleaner version of New York."

"And you can't live there with $10 million?"

"Sure you can, but there could be risks if you're a fugitive. To make absolutely sure you're safe, you'd need plenty of money to grease the skids, so to speak."

"How much?"

"I'd say $50, maybe $60 million."

"And if you had that kind of money, would you leave?"

"The money's not enough. If it were, I'd have already left with one of my clients. I'd need the right guy." She paused, then admitted, "I'd need you."

"You'd run away with me?"

She leaned forward, took hold of my hand and said, "I'd go anywhere with you."

After taking some time to savor the moment, I said, "We'll, if that's true, we'd need to spend a lot of time together, planning trips, taking trips, talking about them afterwards, and, if that's true, it must mean you think I'm the right guy for you, long term that is."

"Was that a proposal, Carl? Because if it was, it sucked!" She laughed and continued, "I remember when you first asked me to dinner. Did you know the Gettysburg Address took less time? We'll need to work on your communication skills."

She continued ribbing me while I caressed her hand. We both knew what I had asked, and we both knew her answer. But there'd be another time for a more formal reenactment to get it right.

$$* \quad * \quad * \quad *$$

The following morning, the alarm went off just before 7 am in Vicki's apartment. We had both taken the day off and were planning on heading down to Broadway later in the day to see a show. I told her there was one small errand to take care of first. I had to buy a temporary calling card, and use it to call the Lorenz firm in Switzerland. I planned on using an old fashioned pay phone—the kind with the door you can close—in the era of cell phones the size of a peanut, a real phone booth was a rare commodity, but you could still find a few in the city. Taking into account the time difference, I had to call early in the morning eastern time to make sure they'd be there. It would be my final act in regard to the Plan. The money would remain with the US government, with no tie to Switzerland whatsoever, and at some point ADG would follow the paper trail and would get that money back.

Vicki came with me so we could get some breakfast after I was through. She was standing outside the phone booth when Peter Packus was put through to Stephen Marti.

"Hello, Mr. Packus. I'm very pleased that you called. I assume you can clear up all the confusion."

"What's wrong?"

"It seems we had a little bit of a mix-up, and we had no way to contact you."

"I don't understand."

"We made arrangements for the tax filings with the local office of Larson & Kirsh. They were given all the information about FHP Commodities that we had, and were told that $25 million had been paid and that you expected the final tax liability to approximate $15 million."

"Yes, I understand all that. It's what we discussed when we met."

"That's true. But they also contacted their people in the US and were told FHP could file a form requesting a refund, even before filing the tax return. So, since we didn't hear from you in January, and since we had signature authority for FHP, we told them to do it."

"Do what?"

"L&K prepared the form to request the refund, and we filed it in early January. It was a rather simple form really."

"You requested the $10 million refund?"

"That's right."

"So what's the mix-up?"

"Well, I'm embarrassed to say we didn't get the $10 million that we requested. You see—"

Needing some time to think, I quickly interrupted Marti, telling him to hold the line while I put the phone against my chest. With Kavi's death, I wanted the money to remain with the IRS, so it was a good thing that they didn't pay the refund. On the other hand, it was somewhat scary to think that, had he lived, he would have been overseas without the money. It would have been a nightmare, and he'd probably have been forced to come back to face the music. Somehow, someway, despite all of our thoughtful planning, we had overlooked a fatal flaw, or flaws. We were a bunch of good, hard working businessmen. But taking money from others wasn't our thing. And somehow we'd screwed it up. But fortunately—or unfortunately—the matter was moot. So I raised the phone and said, "Don't worry about it, I was calling to tell you—"

"Mr. Packus, please let me finish. We got $210 million."

"What?" I screamed so loud Vicki could hear me through the glass.

"The IRS said that FHP paid $225 million in taxes, and since the estimated tax was $15 million, they wired over $210 million. It's sitting in the account at Suisse Union."

Out of the corner of my eye, I could see Vicki mouthing the words "what happened." I turned so I could concentrate on the call. "Let me get this straight. You're telling me there is $210 million sitting in that account right now?"

"That's exactly what I'm telling you."

"When did you get it?"

"It was wired just last week. So, Mr. Packus, what would you like us to do?"

It took me a moment and I decided it was best to punt on the matter. "I wanted to tell you there was no rush to do anything."

"In that case, Larson & Kirsh would suggest that we file to extend the tax return due date, but we must do so before March 15th. I understand you can get an additional six months. Shall I go ahead and arrange for them to do that?"

I figured they had already filed something, so another form didn't make any difference. "Sure, go ahead. And I'll be in touch."

After the call, I felt light headed and had to brace myself against the side of the booth. Vicki pushed the door open and asked, "Did something go wrong?"

"What?"

"Are you ok?" she asked. "You look pale."

"I just need a moment to catch my breath. It just makes no sense."

"Tell me what happened."

"There's $210 million in the Swiss account."

"What! How can that be? You said they didn't file anything, so how could they get *any* money?"

"They did file something. Apparently there's some form a company can file to get a refund, even before they file their tax return. And guess what? They filed that form."

"So why wasn't the refund $10 million?"

I walked a few feet to the nearest building and sat down on the sidewalk, bracing myself against the wall, and motioned for her to sit next to me. Thinking out loud, I said, "Kavi told me he had switched $25 million of the tax payment, so if we said FHP owed $15 million, it would get a $10 million refund. He also said ADG had to pay about $250 million in total. So the IRS was supposed to apply $225 million to ADG and $25 million to FHP, but maybe they got the numbers mixed up. Somehow $225 million was paid on behalf of FHP, so when they filed the form saying $15 million was due, the government wired over $210 million. Boy, Ken was right when he said a corporation asking for a big refund would have no problem."

"You don't think Kavi could have intentionally switched $225 million, do you?"

"If he had, at some point he would have had to tell me. I was the one who was planning to deliver the tax information to the law firm, although that wasn't the original plan. He was supposed to do it until I had to get involved, and he was holding onto the final 2003 numbers until the last minute." I hesitated then continued, "No, that wouldn't be like Kavi. He couldn't have done it intentionally. Not him."

"So what will you do now?"

"I guess the same thing I was planning to do, nothing."

"Wow. Carl. Think of it. You guys were just a bunch of accountants and yet you were able to take about a quarter of a billion dollars from one of the largest companies in the world."

"You seem impressed with it."

"I am. It's one of the biggest heists ever."

"It wasn't meant to be a heist. We were just trying for some sort of involuntary restitution. But I guess I'd be excited if Kavi's plane hadn't crashed, and he was calling me from India to say he had that kind of money."

We walked into a nearby restaurant for breakfast and sat away from everyone else, near the back. I had a view of the counter at the front, and could see people rushing on their way in and out, as they ordered their coffee, bagels or eggs to go, as part of their daily routine. It seemed so unreal to be watching them ordering breakfast while Vicki and I were discussing the fact that somewhere in Switzerland there was $210 million, and I was a signatory to the account. The more we talked about it, the more we realized without saying it, that we were contemplating whether we should take the money. It was interesting, but I'd never given any thought to taking it when the amount was $10 million. But now we were talking about something in a different league, and if we took it and left the country, as a character in some movie once said, we'd be fugitives with means. Vicki's estimate of $50 to $60 million aside, we both knew that $210 million was more than enough to do the trick.

Naturally, we skipped the idea of going to Broadway and spent the day walking through Manhattan and talking about the money. We actually passed the offices of ADG and as I watched people walk in and out of the building, I couldn't imagine letting the company get the money back. Then, in the late afternoon, we got into my car and left for Brooklyn, so we could discuss the situation with my mom. It would be a rather difficult conversation, since she hadn't been told a thing, and I was very worried about what she would say.

I had to repeat certain aspects of the story more than once before my mom understood. When she realized it wasn't a joke, she looked at Vicki, smiled, and in a loud voice that might have been heard throughout New York asked, "So when are we leaving?"

"You're joking, right?" Vicki asked.

"Hey honey, do I look like I'm joking?"

"We've been going back and forth about this all day," I admitted.

My mother shrugged her shoulders and said, "So do what you think is right. But in my book, Kavi and his wife were killed by this legal crap, and it's the company's fault. They have enough money, so let them lose a little. And just think what you could do with it. You can help those two beautiful kids of theirs, and that charity Aarti always spoke about. What was that?"

"The Sisters of Jain," I said.

"So you could use some of the money for them." She paused, put her hand on mine and continued, "Ask yourself what Kavi would have wanted you to do. I doubt he'd want the company to get the money back, not after everything that happened."

"But what do you think dad would have said?"

"Don't worry about your father. You didn't go looking for this, right? Didn't it fall into your lap because you were looking out for a friend?"

"Ma, you never cease to amaze me."

"I'm an amazing woman. Now go away and plan our trip, while I fix dinner."

Chapter 36

It was early evening on Wednesday, June 30, and I was relaxing in Vicki's apartment with a glass of red wine. She was still working and wouldn't be home for another hour or so, and I was taking advantage of my solitude to sit back and reflect. It had seemed like any other summer day in and around New York City. The Yankees were fighting for first place—the Mets weren't—the kids were out of school—the sun wouldn't set until late in the day—and the temperature was in the 90's. But something was different for me. For the first time since 1979, I had no anniversary dinner at the Iron Horse to attend. Actually, Ken had suggested that the three of us continue the tradition, but Marc and I weren't up to it. Not without Kavi.

Unfortunately, I was learning the hard way that it takes a long time to get over the death of a close friend. Although I should have realized that I'd continue to grieve. After all, I had *never* gotten over the loss of my brother. At least the kids were doing ok. Sanji was starting to come around after months in a deep depression. She was pulling her life together, and making arrangements to move to London sometime in August. As for Kris, he had been doing well all along, although we were waiting for a sudden breakdown, but it hadn't happened. Not yet, anyway. He managed to keep himself composed, and graduated from college on time, with his sights set on beginning a career in Europe. But not before seeing some of the world, and spending some time in India.

Things at work were going well for me. I'd been given some new administrative responsibilities, which meant a higher profile within the firm, but that also meant less time with clients, and that was one aspect I didn't like. Marc had received some great news. He'd been asked to head the New York State Bar Association Tax Section beginning in the fall, and he said it was a very prestigious position. As for Ken, NV Industries gave him a fat new three-year contract, with a big raise in pay and other expensive perks. He'd earned it, having saved them so much in taxes over the years.

The best news was that Vicki and I became formally engaged in May. I did the full routine, getting down on one knee in the middle of a crowded restaurant. Although she knew I would propose one day, it was still a big surprise. I had carefully prepared for the special moment, and, unlike my past queries, kept the words to a minimum. I simply said, "Please spend your life with me." Our relationship was the only good thing that had come out of the ADG fiasco. After all, if it hadn't happened, she and I would never have met. I was convinced she was the one that I'd been searching for my whole life. Even my mom had to admit that I'd made the right move taking so long to find "the woman." It was funny though. Shortly after Vicki and I became engaged, Kim Darcy called to say that she really missed me and wanted to get together. Maybe Ken was right about some things.

The therapy was still in progress, but Vicki had come a long way. It was becoming reasonably clear that she'd been abused by her father at a very young age. So we finally accepted John Huggins' offer to do some research. John learned that her father had used the alias Jacob Astor, and had managed to get himself killed in a car crash back when Vicki was in high school and living with friends.

Regarding the Plan, I had to give Ken credit for getting it right. It had been more than nine months since Kavi switched the tax payments, but ADG still didn't have a clue. We were sure they'd be forced to make it public once they learned, and we'd heard nothing. Of course, it was just a matter of time before they would discover what had happened, but they would never get that money back, thanks to me and Vicki. We followed Kavi's plan and moved it through ten accounts in five different countries, so the money was long gone. For a while, we gave some thought to taking it for ourselves and skipping town. That's to be expected. Anyone would consider it, if they had $210 million suddenly dropped into their lap. But we couldn't do it. We loved our work, loved living in the States, and had and would have plenty of money. It was startling, but pleasing, to learn just how profitable Vicki's boutique practice really was. She was making more than five times as much as I was, and I made a lot, or at least I thought I did. Having said that, we did consider the $210 million as a retirement fund—a really big one—to potentially be exploited some day, if and when we decided the Australian Gold Coast was the place to be.

It wasn't as if the money was going to sit untouched. We were committed to taking care of Sanji and Kris. Though, with their trusts and additional life insurance proceeds, they already had plenty of financial security. The Sisters of Jain were also pleased to learn of an anonymous overseas donor who would contribute funds every now and then. Aside from that, there were two other matters which, if pursued, would require sufficient funding.

At a party, I had mentioned to John Huggins how we had joked about having Gary Bevins framed for a cold-case murder. John became intrigued with the idea and did some follow-up work on his own, determining that there were quite a few unsolved murders of young women in and around the DC area during the years that Gary had attended nearby Georgetown Law School. John also said that Gary's fingerprints, strands of his hair and other personal material could find their way into the files for one of those cases. All it would take is the right amount of money and John's old contacts. We also learned that the cold-case files are reviewed every few years for new leads or for the possible application of new techniques to evaluate evidence. Vicki and I were surprised by John's initiative, and put the information in our pocket for possible future use. In any case, we liked what Gary was doing at the moment. In April, he decided to go after L&K, and he was giving them all they could handle, so the prognosis for multi-million dollar penalties looked good.

We also had the matter of Maurice Granville to address, and we knew exactly what we could do. He was spending most of his time in the Ivory Coast, and was making regular trips to other countries in Sub-Saharan Africa. Most of those jurisdictions had onerous penalties, like life in prison, for possession of illegal drugs. It would be relatively easy to ensure that sufficient quantities turn up in his hotel room during a surprisingly well timed government raid.

We didn't know if we would *actually* move against Gary and Maurice, but with $210 million at our disposal, we knew that if we chose to, we could do it and succeed.

*   *   *   *

It had been exactly one year since Kavi received his fateful call from Debra Jennings. I'd have to say, it was one of my worst years, but it was also one of my best, and I could never imagine having another one like it.

About the Author

After graduating from Arizona State, Ron spent nine years with two public accounting firms, which later merged to become PricewaterhouseCoopers. Later he joined MAXXAM, a diversified multinational, where he spent fifteen years as a senior corporate officer with significant finance related responsibilities. He left MAXXAM to return to the New York City area, where he lives with his wife and two daughters.

978-0-595-67344-5
0-595-67344-9

Printed in the United States
35047LVS00005BA/1-42